The Moondust Sonatas

MOVEMENT Nº 1: A HUNTER'S MOON

ALAN OSI

SMOKE & SHADOW BOOKS

Smoke & Shadow Books
Cleveland Writers Press Inc.
31501 Roberta Dr.
Bay Village, OH 44140

www.clevelandwriterspress.com

Printed in the United States of America
Paperback ISBN-13: 978-1-943052-02-8
eBook ISBN-13: 978-1-943052-05-9

First Edition: December 2015
10 9 8 7 6 5 4 3 2 1
Smoke & Shadow Books is an imprint and trademark
of Cleveland Writers Press Inc.

The publisher is not responsible for websites (or their content) that are not owned by the publisher. Library of Congress Cataloging-in-Publication Data on file with the publisher.

Cover Design by Monkey C Media
Cover Photo by Peeter Viisimaa
Edited by Tim Staveteig; www.myliterarycoach.com

To fiction itself, the dream-eater.

CONTENTS

33. PERCIVAL
34. MAXWELL
35. PERCIVAL
36. MAXWELL
37. PERCIVAL
38. HAILEY
39. MAXWELL
40. PERCIVAL
41. MAXWELL
42. JUSTINE
43. HAILEY
44. WILLIAM
45. PERCIVAL
46. MAXWELL
47. PERCIVAL
48. MAXWELL

SUNDAY, OCTOBER 1, 2006

49. PETER
50. CHESTER
51. MAXWELL
52. WINSTON
53. MARK
54. HAILEY
55. JUSTINE
56. MAXWELL
57. JUSTINE
58. WILLIAM
59. SALLY
60. VIOLET
61. ROB
62. WILLIAM
63. CLYDE
64. MAXWELL
65. CLYDE
66. WALLY
67. MAXWELL
68. PERCIVAL

MONDAY, OCTOBER 2, 2006

69. YVONETTE
70. PETER
71. CHESTER
72. BARRY
73. CLYDE
74. HAILEY
75. MAXWELL
76. NAOMI
77. HAILEY

TUESDAY, OCTOBER 3, 2006

78. GREGORY
79. WINSTON
80. HAROLD

THURSDAY, OCTOBER 5, 2006

81. PETER
82. CHESTER
83. HAROLD
84. MAXWELL
85. HAILEY
86. MAXWELL
87. HAILEY
88. MAXWELL
89. PERCIVAL
90. WALLY
91. HAILEY
92. MARK

FRIDAY, OCTOBER 6, 2006

93. MAXWELL
94. LEONARD
95. MAXWELL
96. LEONARD
97. ANNIE
98. STEVEN
99. SIENNA
100. ROB
101. YVONETTE

SATURDAY, OCTOBER 7, 2006

102. JUSTINE
103. PETER
104. MAXWELL
105. LEONARD
106. HAROLD

SUNDAY, OCTOBER 8, 2006

107. PERCIVAL
108. JUNE
109. HAILEY
110. LEONARD
111. PERCIVAL
112. MAXWELL
113. MARK
114. ANNIE
115. WINSTON
116. YVONETTE
117. ELBA
118. HAILEY
119. PERCIVAL
120. JUNE
121. HAILEY
122. MAXWELL
123. ANNIE
124. LEONARD
125. PERCIVAL
126. YVONETTE
127. WALLY
128. PERCIVAL
129. MAXWELL
130. LEONARD
131. HAILEY
132. JUNE
133. HAILEY
134. LEONARD
135. PERCIVAL
136. HAILEY
137. MARK
138. HAILEY
139. LEONARD

Monday, September 25, 2006

....

1. LEONARD

Okay, listen. I was underground, right? In New York, where I lived. This girl from my building named Vonnie rode the subway with me, screaming metal and blinking lights flowed outside plastic windows. Each block was its own universe, galaxies flew by like graffiti stars.

When our station finally roared in, the doors pinged open, and we went up: out of the dark, humid underground into the city swirling colors. We went to get moondust from this kid named Clyde.

He lived in SoHo somehow, in a second story apartment. The sun still shone. But, time was flying. I was 26 and aimlessly flowing around town. I hustled for the cash I needed, I did anything and everything, but mostly stayed small time: scrapping, small scams, grabbing stuff, selling stuff—things like that. The money sucked, though.

I'd never tried moondust before. It was something new, and new drugs could be real bad. But, I'd known Clyde for years. We ran together, and you can only really know someone when you hustle. So I figured moondust was safe 'cause he wouldn't give me anything heavy. And I figured it was good shit because I texted him, but didn't hear from the dude in three weeks; when he finally got up with me, this morning, he sounded different, and all he'd say was, "You have to try this shit." So I called up Vonnie and told her we were going for a ride. She asked to which stop, I answered the one in her cerebellum. I said get ready and hung up, and got her, and we rode metal underground.

Now, on the streets again, kicking our toes at the sky, Vonnie kept bugging me because she wanted to know what to expect.

"What's this called again?"

"The name ain't gonna change no matter how many times you ask."

We got to his house, rang the buzzer, and clicked up the stairs. When I knocked on the door, it opened, because it was dead bolted ajar. Inside Clyde sat on his couch in boxers and a wife beater, holding a vial of gray powder, with his eyes closed and banging around under the lids. But, he was grinning and crying, and his hand kept going up, moving like he tried to feel something.

We watched him do that for a while, not speaking. Wasn't any need to talk, seeing what we saw.

I swear my pupils dilated out of sheer expectation.

Eventually, his eyes slowed. He breathed suddenly, real deep, and opened his eyes. He dried some tears, then looked up at Vonnie and me.

And all he said was, "You guys got to try this shit."

....

2. Clyde

I saw God.

God is alien to us, completely. Not at all like they say. They always said God made us in His image, I always pictured Him something like us. God is nothing like us, more like a living sun. But, also so far beyond that. We can't imagine, we can't get anywhere close.

I saw the truth. That's what this drug did, and you can't tell me different. Ain't no language for the feeling. Best high ever.

The first time I took moondust, I was up on Bedford, at some rooftop party. All these arty kids lived in the building. Anyway, I stood by the ledge checking out the scene and spotted some kids nearby doing what I thought was coke. My product was pure, I was looking to expand my business, and these fools had enough money to pay whatever I asked. Once I realized that I could get top dollar from rich hipsters, I never went back. So I walked over to them, and I pulled out my bag, and I said, "Hey."

"What?" One of them said, with the hard edge of someone who'd just been interrupted doing drugs.

"Can I join? First lines are free, and my shit is bomb."

I'm bold so I did this kind of thing, even though it wasn't really done. You didn't roll up on people in the city. But, I wasn't much for following rules, none of these kids were thugs, and I was a hell of a salesman.

First step: Set their minds at ease, make them feel in control. But, these kids' eyes had none of the fear or distrust I expected.

"You got the bomb, huh?" One dude said, mocking. "You think we need you?"

I answered, "I'll put a hundred on mine being better than whatever you got."

They all laughed. That never happened before.

"I'll take that bet," another said.

So I opened my bag to start cutting small lines. But, the guy who'd spoken last, a black kid with a neck tattoo, held up his hand saying, "Wait. We aren't looking to do coke, I just want your money. So you're going to try mine, and then you're going to give me a hundred dollars."

That threw me off. "Coke?"

"No. Moondust."

"What the hell is moondust?"

"You've never heard of it. But, it's safe. You'll have some and pay me for the privilege, because we made a bet. Right?"

I nodded. He took out his baggie, and said, "Sit down and hold one eye open." And when I did, he dropped powder into my eyes, and my back arched, and I disconnected from my body.

Another world, made of solid light.

When I came out of it, I gave him a hundred dollars and three hundred more for a good amount of moondust. He wouldn't give me his phone-number or name.

Before moondust, I never thought much about religion one way or another. This, however, was G-O-D. But, I didn't want to philosophize, I just wanted to go back. Only there was no going back. When I took moondust again, I went somewhere else, into another person's life: a beggar in Madras.

The third time I took it, I saw the world through the eyes of a Scotsman.

After that, I was a farmer in some hot, sun-dark nation. Next, a shopkeeper in Asia. After that, a homemaker.

I never felt anything like it. Not quite a high, just a wild, fully realized experience. Like, absolutely, 100 percent realistic, I was truly inside other people. But, I couldn't control nothing, I was along for the ride.

So when my boy William called me up, yammering about how I'd been MIA for weeks, I told him to come here, because we had business to attend. The guy who gave it to me was right, his stuff was better than mine. I planned on fixing that.

....

3. Yvonette

My name is Vonnie and
I'm an actress and I
Tried moondust 'cause this guy I knew, William,
He called my house and then came to my door. I was asleep when the phone rang,
And he didn't notice.
He said we were going on an adventure and
I like adventure so I agreed
And we went into Manhattan.
SoHo is so electric. I was wearing:
Rainbow colored wool gloves, a light white jacket over a red blouse, a green un-slit denim miniskirt, black tights, and black Pumas with red trim.
William, wearing a yellow T-shirt, old jeans, and filthy sneakers.
Took me to this guy's apartment, Clyde. Near Broadway. I don't remember which street. But, it was a real dirty apartment.
I would have told this Clyde guy so,
But when we arrived he was so-o f'ed up!

We just stood there, watching him for a while,
He was talking to himself and making noises like an animal.
Then he came out of it.

"You gotta try this stuff" is what he said then.
Do you want to know about me?

My name is Yvonette. It's a silly name.

I tell people that my friends call me Vonnie.
Viola! Instant friends.
Not that I need them, but I like it when people are kind to each
other.
I'm a dancer and actress, but I've never gotten paid to act or
dance and
I really wait tables and
I stopped auditioning.
Just-can't-do-it-right-now.

I didn't like my parents.
They were uptight.
Okay people, but horrible parents, maybe. I didn't worry about it
too much.
Except—and this was important—
I always thought, "Fuck God."
Because most of the reason they were bad parents was their
heads were up Jesus' ass all day.
They treated me so badly, kept me prisoner,
Because, "I ignored the Lord's will." Told to me by whom?
Them? And how did they know?
And why did the Lord care so much if my room was clean?

I ran away from home. When they found me, they dragged me
home, and things were worse.
I just waited until I was 18, too old to be stopped, and left for
good.
"Fuck God" was what I'd think if you asked me if I believed.
I'd say something more polite,
But not really. And I'd do it with relish.

I was so over it. Because God wasn't even real. The thing that fucked my childhood up was my parents' imaginary friend.

I believed that until this guy Clyde shoved powder into my eye.

Afterward, all I could say was, "No way" and leave. I just knew I'd never do moondust again.

....

4. WILLIAM

It went like this: we sat down on the couch, and he smiled like the serpent. "Ladies first," he said. Then he started talking to Vonnie, softy, to reassure her.

"Open your eye. Hold it open. Yeah, like that. Okay, don't blink now."

He dropped some powder into her eye. Her eyes closed.

Her mouth opened.

She gasped, writhed, and tears came down her face. Her expression read somewhere between ecstasy, horror, and fury.

"Whoa," I said. "Where is she?"

"Oh man, she's in Heaven," Clyde said.

I didn't take him seriously. Meanwhile, her face kept flowing between joy and rage.

"So, what've you been up to?" I asked, to make conversation.

"Pretty much, this," Clyde answered.

"What's it like?"

"So far, it's different every time."

"Oh."

We watched Vonnie in silence, for about three more minutes, until she came out of it. When she did, she went insane. Like, horns sprouted from her head. She started swearing and throwing things across the room. Whatever she could grab: a pen, a plastic cup, a bag of potato chips, a dirty plate. Clyde didn't do nothing, he just stood there. He let her tire herself out. When she did, she started yelling.

"What the fuck was that? You asshole, you couldn't have warned me?"

Clyde asked, "What could I have said?"

"Fuck you. This is bullshit."

She grabbed her purse, stormed out, and slammed the door.

In the silence she left, Clyde and I looked at each other. Through the walls, we heard the click of her heels stop, and the sound of Vonnie retching somewhere in the hallway. We studied the door, imagining.

"What's in this shit?" I said, impressed.

"I... actually don't know. But, it's safe though."

"If you don't know what's in it, what makes you sure it's safe?"

"Trust me."

"Okay."

I took a deep breath, and I put my hands to my eye and held back the lids. The lids fought me for control, trying to close. Clyde stood above me and moved gigantic, fuzzy zeppelin fingers right above my eyeball.

Some dust fell into my eye, and it stung like hell. But, only for a split second.

Then I couldn't feel anymore.

I went down a tunnel, but my body stayed behind.

All of my body's sensations, like my heart, my pulse, and my skin, felt so far away I quickly forgot them. I was only spirit or soul or energy. Our physical realm was out there, somewhere, but it meant jack to me.

Listen, no way you can imagine that unless you've experienced it. My soul swam in light. In joy.

Not that the word joy cuts it. That word is tied to worldly pleasure or happiness, both of which are thin, flimsy tricks, mockeries of what's up there.

Afterward, you can't even remember, not really. It's impossible for your brain to recall a place so far beyond you, something far too big for your mind to hold. You'd felt things you couldn't dream.

Eventually something changed, and my soul-body connection reset, surged, and drew me back.

I could feel my spine again. My back arched, hard, my eyes opened. I gasped for air.

The joy faded.

"Holy shit," I panted. Tears dotted my face; later I would learn tears washed away the powder, which is why I'd returned.

"I just saw God."

"I know," Clyde said. "You're welcome."

Thursday, September 28, 2006

....

5. JUSTINE

By the brownstones of the wealthy on Sutton Street, in one of the few quiet places to be found in Manhattan, a little so-called park comprised only of benches bolted to concrete over the water, and one word written in wild-style fluorescent on a concrete wall opposite the river—I held his hand. The wind whipped through my jacket, and I shivered.

He, Maxwell, worked in the editorial department of The New York Globe, moving up the ladder through determined hard work, and we had something, I hoped.

I, Justine, worked for Action, Now! a non-profit organization. At the moment, we fund-raised to aid a humanitarian crisis in South-East Asia.

Maxwell and I lived in New York: I in Harlem and he in Hell's Kitchen. I loved my neighborhood, its speed and ceaselessness, the children playing on sidewalks and in gutters. I loved Manhattan, its abrasive humanity.

We'd eaten dinner up the street, at March. Now, river-side, we spoke sweet words, told jokes, whispered nothing in particular.

And then he asked, "You never said. Do you want kids one day?"

I answered, "I don't know. It's complicated."

"Complicated by what?"

"Everything," I said. "You want to explain my future in a soundbite."

"The kids' part. Is that complicated?"

"Isn't it early for this conversation?" I asked, because it was. Very, way.

"Well," he said, "I like the idea of getting the big stuff out of the way."

Fair enough. But, still, I decided to answer in generalities. "I think I like the idea of having children, but I don't think I like the world I'd be raising them in."

"People have been saying that since the dawn of time."

"Not true. People have been saying that since the dawn of industrialization."

"Like everyone was happy before the steam engine. You forgot to ask me if I want kids. Don't you want to know?"

"To be honest, not yet, not by a long shot."

"Ask me anyway."

Sigh. "Max, do you want kids?"

"I don't know," he said, grinning. "It's complicated."

I play-punched his midsection.

He grabbed me and held me to him, rocking me, and in my ear he whispered, "One day, a long time from now, I'm going to own a little house right by some deep, dark, scary-wild woods. And I'm going to have a wife there, and we're going to raise three children, who will play in the woods, go to school, and grow up to rule the world."

"Are you serious?" I asked because I had no idea what to do with this.

"More or less."

"You're domestic."

He didn't answer, but smiled a bemused smile. In my heart, a whisper of doubt appeared. I would need to mull this later.

Behind us, we heard steps on the stairway leading up to the street above this recessed park. We turned, and saw a man in an outdated, disheveled, gray suit. Gray-shot hair bunched in odd patches on his head, and disquiet filled his eyes. Thin lips, crooked nose. But, still, in spite of everything, he had magnetism, intrigue.

"Can I ask you a question?" he said. "Have you ever wished you could directly experience God?"

The question seemed so ridiculous I didn't know what to say. Maxwell answered instead.

"Look, pal, we don't want your Jehovah's Witness, eight-fold Hari-Krishna stuff or whatever, so go away please."

"I come from no false religion. What I offer is truth, the real and true experience of God. But, if you want me to leave, I will."

Maxwell worked for the newspaper, and if a new religious movement stumbled across his path, he had to pursue it. He was waiting for his "big break," after all. So I understood when his eyes lit up.

"What do you mean by 'the experience of God'? What church are you from?"

"I am with no religious organization of any kind—they're all false—which is part of the reason I'm standing before you tonight."

Oh, and what is the other part? But, I didn't say anything.

"So what's this 'experience of God' stuff about?"

"This," he said, and slowly, calmly reached into a shallow coat pocket to produce two small plastic bags, each with a miniscule amount of gray powder inside.

Max snorted. "A drug? Get the fuck outta here. ... No, wait. Is, is that like some new drug?"

"This isn't a drug. It's from the angels." He handed Maxwell the bags. "If you wish to see God, put a small bit of this in your eye, and you will, until you cry the powder out. Do not contact me, you will never see me again. I'm simply a messenger."

With that, he turned and left.

We sat in slightly shocked silence, listening to his footfalls recede. I said, "May I see?" And I reached for one of the bags.

It contained fine gray powder, and when I held it up to examine it, the baggie weighed nothing at all. It comforted me. I couldn't explain why.

"This could be huge," Max said. "We have to get these analyzed right away." He held his bag up also, studying it.

"You can run off and get yours analyzed if you want. But, this bag is mine."

Max, shocked, said, "Huh?"

"He gave us two. One for you and one for me."

"You're not planning on taking that, are you?"

"No."

"So why do you want it?"

"Because this has never happened to me before."

"Okay, but just don't take it. I have no idea what's in there."

"Of course not." I said, standing up. "You should go. You have a story to chase."

"Wait," he said. "Whatever I did or said, I'm sorry."

Had I overreacted? Whatever emotional truth I reacted to had not distilled yet into a clear grievance, and if I didn't know why I was irked, maybe I shouldn't be. So, instead of walking away, I paused.

Max stood up, and put his arms around me. "Don't leave."

We went back to my place, and slept there.

In the morning I woke up to find him dressing, rushing off to work. Distracted, he barely even said goodbye.

After he left, I showered and dressed, ate some corn flakes, then got on the computer and read the news. It was an important ritual; in my line of work, current events mattered.

But thinking about news made my head turn to where my purse lay, innocently, on a chair. And inside of it, a small bag of gray powder.

I wanted to hold it again. And so I opened the purse and reached inside. I couldn't find the baggie at first, and a small panic arose. When my hand eventually stumbled across it, I felt that same inexplicable comfort.

Friday, September 29, 2006

....

6. MAXWELL

I left Justine's apartment first thing in the morning. I was onto something, something that might put my career on an exponential curve.

I'd been working for The New York Globe for about two years, building my resume and waiting for a break. Breaks were hard to come by. I thought maybe I'd found my chance when some weirdo in a suit threw a drug in my lap and told me it showed people God. The guy might have been nuts, of course.

I needed to get this stuff analyzed ASAP. I also needed to find users for potential interview subjects. From there, I would play it by ear, investigating based on the leads I would find. When it was all said and done, I'd go to the paper to give them an article—waiting to go to press—that would make me famous and them rich.

I considered it a great pleasure and joy to be engaging in pure journalism. Things had pushed so far out of whack in our industry, every office of every newspaper and cable-news channel was permeated with an atmosphere of fear and frustration, often closing down. Newspapers shilled for the corporations and parties. Everyone knew readership was down, but no one knew what to do about it. Owners everywhere sold to conglomerates and shady billionaires. Lay-offs left and right. Hard-hitting, truth-telling journalism, daring investigative reporting, and general onion-peeling—these were actively discouraged. As a novelist once wrote, we slid down the surface of things.

Well, here was a chance to do something that mattered. I would crack the right way a story demanding national attention. A story without pussy-flashing alcoholic celebrity bimbos or disgruntled sociopathic football stars. No bullshit, just the shocking, dark, twisted truth. God was now being sold as a drug, and I would get to the bottom of it.

Even though he told me not to, I needed to go after the man who gave us the substance. He would likely be resistant to inquiry, but this is what professionals do. I would start small, only asking the name of the stuff I had. Because even after getting its chemical composition and ascribing a pharmaceutical label, I was writing blind if I couldn't access the drug's street identity. Without that, I had no way in with the users.

But first things first. Go to the laboratory the paper used as a source in an ongoing investigation. They'd made me play courier, which turned out to be a boon, strangely enough. I knew one of the chemists now. When I'd called to see if any staff were working, he answered. That was a big stroke of luck for me, because he said he could squeeze in my job, today. It would cost, he'd said. But, the newspaper would pay, so I didn't care too much.

I decided to take the subway instead of a cab. Despite the cool day, the train car roasted us, and I found myself dabbing perspiration and contemplating removing my sweater.

Right before this became a problem, I was back on the street and down the block toward the building at the corner of 93rd and Amsterdam.

The chemist, Peter, greeted me when I found him in his lab's break area, reading the newspaper, sipping coffee. "Oh, Max," he said. "Hey."

He was a tallish man with a big belly, and a hairline receding into non-existence. Peter waved a few fingers at me, and I could see on his hands the deep grooves and rough patches of a working man. Now in story mode, locked on to that detail, I needed to know why a chemist had a laborer's callouses.

So I said, "I'm curious. How does someone in your line of work develop rough hands like yours?"

"I have hobbies."

"Like what?"

He only smiled. The silence thickened, and Peter sat drinking coffee, reading away.

I sighed. "Okay, never mind. I have something real interesting for you today."

"Do you?"

I put the baggie of substance on the table in front of him. "I don't know what it's called. But, I've been told if you put it on your eyeball, you see God. It's some new kind of drug."

"You put it on your eyeball, and you see God?"

Something in his tone gave pause. "Have you heard of this stuff? What can you tell me about it?"

"It's nothing."

"What?"

"Just some stupid joke about a scientist who got a sample in his eye."

"And?"

"He goes to hell."

"Well, that's not really this, is it?"

"Which is exactly why I didn't volunteer. You want the works on this?"

"Is it possible to rush?"

"I'll add an extra 20 percent for that. But, sure. Come back in three hours."

I hailed a cab rather than take the subway back to the office. Once inside the cab's smooth interior, I engaged to gather intel.

"Sir," I said to the driver, "can I ask you a question?"

"Sure, sure."

"Do you ever overhear customers talking about weird drugs? Psychedelics? Something new?"

He seemed hesitant.

"Trust me," I said, "I'm curious, that's all. I'll make it worth your while."

"I hear the usual. Cocaine, Marijuana, E... They're sick, these children. Sick."

"But nothing new?"

"I hear nothing unusual."

"Do any of them ever mention God?"

"What would they know of God? God does not come in a powder," he said, waving his free arm. I smiled at the irony.

The ride was quiet, only the squawk of his radio and the ever-present blast of car horns disturbing me. I thumbed the business card of Harold G. Westgate, impatient.

When we got to The New York Globe, I paid the driver, then rode the elevator up to my floor. On Fridays like this, the place was relatively empty. When I got to my desk, I dialed the number Westgate gave me, but his office's switchboard denied his extension and kicked me to a receptionist. I asked for Harold Westgate. They employed no one with that name. A dead end.

I couldn't write this story without the drug's street identity.

I set about the task of finding Harold's personal information online. I wanted telephone numbers and addresses, anything to help me track him down. After a few more dead-ends, I found an address, using a sneaky and somewhat shady web service. He lived in Brooklyn, on Flushing in the Bushwick neighborhood. No telephones listed.

So I called a car and told dispatch to book a round trip.

On the way to Brooklyn, on the bridge, I acted on a sudden urge to call Justine. When she picked up she sounded distant somehow, as if, while speaking to me, she attempted to smile.

....

7. HAROLD

In my new life as the messenger, I needed to be well-spoken, always. I would dress neatly, in professional attire only.

I rode the train, making a list of the things to do in my new life. I had just taken more steps toward becoming pure—freeing myself of the burden of owning an apartment and having a job. I still gave out my old business card when I spread my love of the Lord throughout this city, however. The card served as an ice-breaker, nothing more, and it did not affect my transition to my new life.

I believed God would be happy with my progress, but it hadn't been enough to be allowed to see God again. I hoped I was working hard enough to please Him. But, I would never know until He allowed me to return.

After I finished my list, I looked around—a mostly-empty train—and dropped moondust in order to pursue my Lord.

When my soul first left my body, I could, as usual, feel the barest whisper of the Angel's song, a beautiful, lingering, holy joy. Then I was a farmer's wife.

This small failure only strengthened my resolve. I only needed to grab a few things from the apartment I was vacating; the remainder were trappings, unnecessary. I would live without possessions, the way the prophets of old did.

How else could I continue, having been confronted with the majesty of God? The stranger who gave me this powder must have been an angel in disguise—claiming to be just a man dying—and the last of a long line who carried this secret through generations. I did not believe him. He was an angel giving me a mission, to teach the world. I would do so by living simply, and spreading God's vision as far as I could.

It sometimes seemed such a far cry from the life I lived before, so strange. But, as always when this happened, I remembered I was building a better world.

When the Morgan Avenue stop came, I got off the train and walked until I reached Flushing, where I rented an apartment over a small diner.

Realizing I would miss both the diner owner and her food, I craned my neck to try to get a glance of her through the window, as I walked toward my door. So I didn't notice the man waiting for me by the doorway until he spoke.

"Mr... Messenger?" he said, after clearing his throat. "You may remember me, you gave me some white powder yesterday, and I need its name."

I turned on him quickly. I remembered him as an initiate I enlightened uptown.

"I told you never to attempt to contact me," I said, quietly, and probably with menace, for he shrank back.

"Easy, guy. All I want is the name. That's not a lot to ask. I'll even buy you lunch."

I looked into his eyes. "It's called moondust. Now disappear."

As he turned to leave, I said, "Never try to find me again."

"I won't," he called over his shoulder. I made a mental note to find an alternative to the business card, which showed my real name. He tracked me that way.

Inside of my old apartment, I gathered the necessary things and placed them in a large duffel bag. I saw God here, and because this site was holy, I resented the necessity of abandoning it.

As I left, I paused at the door, and let my eyes return to the spot of my awakening. I could almost see my former self there, lying on his back, experiencing the nexus of existence.

Then I stepped out of the door, into my new life, becoming an instrument of the Lord.

....

8. MAXWELL

My brief meeting with the messenger left me with an intense disquiet. He struck me as a madman.

The good news: now I knew the name, moondust. The bad news: I had nothing else.

Because enough time elapsed, I went back to my chemist; this story demanded hustle. With that maniac giving drugs to anyone, I couldn't even be sure I was the only one after this.

Since the car left while I waited for Westgate, I took the L-train back into the city. I got a seat as soon as I got in the car, making notes to myself via pen and notepad and trying to determine next steps. I made little progress. Lacking the underworld contacts I needed for this story, I hoped the chemist could give me something to chase after.

If the chemist wanted more for a big lead, it was possible. I needed to try to score some moondust myself, on the streets. Buying drugs was never something I did, leaving me dangerously ignorant of the lingo and procedure. Perhaps I could find an apparent drug-den, walk in, and tell of my strange encounter with the messenger, pretending I'd taken moondust and wanted more.

But first things first. I reached my stop and walked to the lab. This time, when I entered, Peter was leaning over a computer, somehow managing to type furiously and wolf down what appeared to be a roast beef sandwich at the same time.

"Peter, hello," I said. "How'd it go?"

He finished a bite of his sandwich, chewing slowly, not looking at me. After he swallowed, without looking at me, he said, "Interesting stuff you gave me."

"Yeah?"

"Yeah. What you got here, this stuff defies principles."

"Please elaborate. What kind?"

"Well, the subatomic kind. Actually, every kind—what'd you say it was called again?"

"Moondust," I said. "What kind of subatomic principles does it violate?"

"All of them."

"Meaning?"

"None of my tests work on this stuff. All I can tell you is it's a complete unknown. It'll probably end up challenging everything we know about science."

"Wow," I said. "That sounds big."

"Yeah."

"Can you explain what's happening?"

"Well, the first step in analyzing something is weighing out a small amount of it. When I went to do that with this stuff, the scale said it weighted 7.68 grams, which surprised me; that's an extremely high weight for the volume I measured. So I tried it again with the exact same sample, and the second time the scale said 0.42 grams. Third time it said 14.93. So I figured the scale was busted, and I tried a different one. But, those readings were all over the map, too.

I went to a third scale, same thing. It wasn't the equipment.

"I tried quite a few different types of tests. The results were either inconclusive or varied unbelievably every time. Moondust seems to be an impossible substance."

I said, in a measured voice, "What do you think that means?"

"I have no idea. Beyond that, this substance defies science as I know it."

"If you had to guess why it defies science?"

"Scientists don't guess," Peter said.

"Indulge me."

"It reminds me of Heisenberg's uncertainty principle, if that principle governed not only velocity and location of subatomic particles, but somehow magnified itself in relation to a specific substance, affecting atomic makeup, weight, everything."

"Was that English?"

Silence followed this.

"Please tell me more?"

"The basic idea of the uncertainty principle is that it is impossible to know both the location and velocity of very, very small particles. For some, the basic takeaway is that the observer changes the observed." He scratched his beard. "It's an abstract principle that's acted out on the subatomic level in multiple ways. It has even been shown to violate our understanding of the laws of cause and effect, as well as space-time. It just supersedes them.

"The uncertainty principle raises a tricky theoretical question: If the act of observing a thing changes it on a subatomic level, is consciousness interacting directly with reality? If so, how far does that go? That's the kind of philosophical leap we scientists rail against. I never took the idea seriously. But, now, having seen moondust..."

"Okay, let's pause for a second," I said. I took out my minidisk recorder, the kind used for interviews, and turned it on. "Peter, I've followed everything you've said, and it's been helpful. But, I was wondering if you could boil it down? Give me something I can put in an article. We can use your name, or not. It's your choice."

"The substance you brought me cannot be studied, at least by my equipment. The results of all the tests I tried to run fluctuated wildly and for no particular reason I can determine. No set of data was ever duplicated, and I mean, not a single datum. It's almost like I created each datum merely by looking for it, and it generated itself randomly. You've found something that perhaps illustrates either hitherto unknown subatomic or atomic forces. I can guess about how that is, like saying maybe science needs to rethink the uncertainty principle, what consciousness is, and how it interacts with matter. Or whether we're living in a dream world. All I really know is my life just changed."

"Sounds like we'll be famous."

"Famous? Sure, if that's what you want. Does this really do what you said it does?"

"I sure hope so," I said. "Do every test and analysis you can. Please."

"Sure."

"Good. If there's anything I can do to help, call."

"I could use more of the substance."

"You need more?"

"As much as you can get, yeah. Study requires samples and independent verification. Also, if you can find out how to make it. That's important."

"That's a big ask. But, I'll do what I can. I'll be in touch."

"Good luck," he said.

Outside, I felt like singing for joy. I was about to break the story that a new drug—some kind of religious, farcical experience—was on the streets of Manhattan, that this drug violated subatomic principles—or stretched them or something—and that it would spark a scientific revolution, proving... what? I wasn't sure.

I felt a wave of doubt. I stood there, in the street, watching people walk by, looking up at the skyline. I pulled out my phone, and I called Justine.

Justine told me she was lying on the sofa, watching a movie. Something in the manner of her voice made me able to imagine, vividly, her heavy eyes as we spoke. I shrugged it off, and tried not to think about the fabric of reality.

....

9. JUSTINE

When Maxwell called, my instincts told me to lie, and I acted on them without thought. Almost without my permission, my mouth said the words, "Oh, I'm sitting on the sofa, watching a movie."

An innocent fib on the surface. But, since I'd been staring at this small packet of powder all day long and remembering my faith, it seemed rather significant.

The reason I lied—that I didn't want him to know how I once believed—became clear to me as soon as I finished saying the words. The implications made me queasy.

I didn't want to think about it, so finally I put the stuff away, in a box under my bed.

During the phone call, Max had said he wanted to have dinner. I wasn't interested like I should have been.

I remembered the church I'd gone to as a child with my father, before his accidental death.

The tall, pointed, stained-glass windows, filtering sunlight into holy pictures. The altar, the priests, the rhythmic, comforting drone of Latin prayers.

Today I dressed simply in jeans, a beige T-shirt and flats, my hair

pulled back in a pony-tail. I read a magazine. But I barely even saw
the words.

It'd been thirteen years since I'd gone to confession.

Thirteen years since my father died.

I don't think I ever resented God. But, without my father, I
couldn't go back to church. I just couldn't. I needed to be distant
from faith: I needed the promise of holy happiness to fade. Without
my father, I could not reconcile it.

And now perhaps God was in powder form under my bed. As
ridiculous as it seemed, I knew, intuitively, that this was so, and I
wondered what I'd say in the presence of God. Would I feel contrite
for having forsaken His church? Or angry at of the loss of my
father? Would I ask about all the suffering in the world, and indeed
the pedophilic actions of some of priests, which strengthened my
resolve to be alienated from the flock? Would I dare?

I was reminded of the book of Job. I went to my bookshelf to
where I'd buried a copy of the Bible, and I took it out, and read
the story. As always, the cruelty with which God and the Devil
conspired to ruin Job's life, and more importantly, the callous
disregard for the lives of his wife and children, disturbed me.

It'd been so long since I read that. I came into the world a Catholic,
and there were questions one was not supposed to ask. So I did what I
always did: I closed the Bible and put it away. Max would be coming
to get me in two hours. He left our destination a surprise, and we'd
take a cab there.

He was an avowed atheist. I respected this in him at first, his
resolute conscription to the laws of logic. But, now I wished... that
he was more spiritual. At least, in a tiny part of me.

I remembered Daddy singing hymns, his expression calm,
reverent.

Religion wasn't defined by that anymore, as it had been when I
was a girl. Now it had nothing to do with me staring up at the

person closest to me in the world, as he sung sacred hymns. Now, religion was scandals on the news. Suicide bombers and doomsday policies.

I badly needed to think about something else, so I picked up another magazine. But, nothing caught my interest. I turned on the television on which a model interviewed Little People. I turned off the television, showered, and got dressed.

When Max arrived, he embraced me hurriedly. He wore the same blue collared shirt and kakis as this morning, when he left. He hadn't gone home. Mania tinted his eyes. But, that might have been my imagination.

"Are you ready?" he asked, as if he couldn't see. I checked my outfit, now doubting it. I felt that distance again.

"Where are we going?"

"To celebrate," he said, and kissed me. I let him, but barely returned it, disentangled myself.

"Celebrate what?"

"This story is going to make me. I got that stuff analyzed by the lab. You know, the powder that guy gave us? It's going to rewrite the laws of science. It'll change everything."

My heart quickened. "Tell me all about it," I said. And he did.

Of course, he only cared about his story. But, for me, this meant about something else entirely. He described a substance beyond science, an impossibility—or a miracle. The man who gave it to us called it a portal to God. I'd held out a crazy hope it was real, and science proved it.

We went to dinner, with me in a daze. Max didn't notice until some time after our food arrived; he was too busy yammering away about his opportunity.

"You seem quiet," he finally said. "Everything all right?"

I almost wanted to laugh.

....

10. Maxwell

Justine stayed quiet after I asked about her day, which bothered me. I wanted her to be happy with me.

"Can I ask you a question?" she finally said.

"Of course."

"The... moondust. You said it doesn't respond to scientific inquiry?"

"Yeah." I took a bite so I wouldn't have to say more. I'd been explaining so much I barely touched my food, and I was hungry. The chicken was a classic coq au vin.

"Do you think it's possible it's holy, like we were told?"

That froze me. "You can't be serious."

"Why can't I be serious?"

"Because you aren't religious. Are you?"

Was she? Justine never spoke about God, so I assumed she left God in the realm of superstition where He belonged. But, the look on her face made me doubt.

"What if I was?" she said.

"I thought you were smarter than that."

Justine's face grew harder and colder. I said, "I didn't mean to offend you. But, God is a fantasy, you know that. Should I have been more PC?"

"That's your truth," she said. "Not the truth. There's a difference."

"So... shit, you are religious? Since when?"

She responded, "I want to try it."

"Try what?"

"Moondust."

"That's the stupidest thing I've ever heard. What's wrong with you?"

She threw her napkin on the table, grabbed her stuff, and left. I couldn't believe it.

....
11. William

I swear the whole world changed shape. Everything I believed, I now questioned. The good news is I never believed in much of anything, so I could stand it. I'd first taken moondust five days ago.

At the moment, I was sitting on a roof in Benson Hurst, Clyde's friend Rob's building. Clyde had introduced me to moondust, and he was explaining it to this Rob guy now, but taking his time. It certainly wouldn't hurt Rob to have another second to get used to the idea that his world was about to change shape, for good.

I was thinking about existence. Not directly about God, but about what my vision of God had showed to me. I'd gained an appreciation of beauty. The sunset floored me.

The lecture finally ended. "All right," Clyde said, "Let's do this. Rob, tilt your head back and hold your eye open."

"How do you mean?" said Rob.

"I'll show you," I said. Clyde started to protest, so I added, "You don't have to wait for me to come back. We can be gone together."

I sat down on the roof-tar, and I held my eye open. Clyde dropped moondust in, and I felt that terrible sting. And again, my soul was ripped from my body.

And this time I became a file clerk in a jail in Tucson.

I had big, calloused hands. I had wrapped these hands around my girlfriend's neck and squeezed until she had no breath in her. Some days, like today, I could still see the look in her eyes as her light went out. It wasn't the only bad thing I'd done, but maybe the worst. I told people I was innocent, just for the hell of it.

They said I killed her out of anger because she cheated. But, I hadn't loved her and never really felt betrayed.

Prison made sense to me. Everything inside was right on the surface, immediate. No ambiguity, but I missed women, and at first it was agony and that made me hurt people. But, after a while I barely noticed anymore.

On this particular day, while filing mail, I was thinking about the afterlife. Did they consider your circumstances when they decided where you go?

Probably not, I figured.

All the sudden, a shout sounded down the hallway, then two more, then the thumps, bangs, and grunting you hear when the guards beat someone compliant. I expected the usual lockdown noises after that, but instead came the sound of people running and more shouts. It didn't have nothing to do with me. I just kept on doing the mail.

I thought about the outside. Like I'd done a million times, I imagined myself in a car. Any car, as long as I was free. Just driving.

The shouts got louder, and I realized I smelled smoke; distant teargas scratched my lungs. I put the mail down and snuck over to the door to peek out. I didn't see anything so I walked down the hall a little, toward block A.

A-block was pandemonium. Some inmate ran by holding a shotgun. A guard in the distance fired at people I couldn't see, until he was hit by a flying chair and went down. I went back into the mailroom.

A riot.

Going out there gave no win for me. Not yet, at least. I decided to wait it out in the mail room, knowing anyone who came in and saw me, sitting in my chair smoking cigarettes, would view me as a non-combatant.

The guards would probably take the ward back soon. If not, then things would definitely get interesting.

I sat down, put my feet up on the desk, and lit up, listening to the sound of rioters outside. First riot I'd seen or even heard of. The sirens finally came on, and after a moment, I thought I heard the distant sound of helicopters. Automatic gunfire couldn't be far off.

I wondered what had taken the sirens so long. Either some inmate was real smart or some guard was real dumb.

I had a flask hidden under a desk, which I'd gotten from a crooked screw I did stuff for sometimes, just like the cigarettes. I pulled it out and took a deep swig—the beautiful burn of whiskey. I killed my cigarette and lit up another, content to wait. Outside, the gunfire picked up again.

And then I came rushing back to myself, William. Clyde was looking down at me; that guy Rob sat next to me, his wide eyes darting back and forth, an overjoyed grin plastered on his face.

"How was it?" Clyde asked, and I shrugged, and reached into my coat to pull out some weed and papers. The remains of the stranger I'd been echoed all through me. It was difficult to say anything.

I'd found moondust was like that, maybe the only thing that still shook me. This was my fourteenth ride. So I'd been hitting it pretty hard, but it was just so wicked. It had no side-effects, nothing to come down from, at least aside from deep thoughts about life. It was the cleanest...drug. It barely even felt like a drug.

"You want me to put in on the joint?" Clyde said, offering to add his own weed to mine. I didn't need more. But, I appreciated the offer, so I nodded.

I always thought crazy violent dudes, like the guy I'd just been, weren't that cold or that calm or calculating. But, he was capable of anything, all the time. For him, hurting people was easy.

I was never going to be like that. I never realized it until then. But, when it came to the life of crime, I was a tourist. Just another kind of fucking hipster, playing a role because I thought it was fun. I was a little disgusted in myself, but quite a bit disgusted in having seen inside the kind of person who really did have what it took. That kind of person would break me, no question. I wouldn't stand a chance.

Luckily we had a new plan. It was going to make us lots of

money, and I would never have to tangle with his type. It was perfect. The big score. If you hustle, then you dream of this kind of thing, to corner a market, make tons of bank, and get out before enough heat comes down to burn you. We would move from city to city, setting up shop, flooding the market, and moving on before competitors had a chance to track us down. Was it a dangerous plan? Sure. But, how could we not try? This would make us. We would be legends, kings of the underworld. Everything I ever wanted.

I tried to focus on rolling the joint. The papers were Bambi, and I glued two together. It was a difficult operation to do on a roof, with wind and without a table or even chairs.

I was free.

I wasn't in jail, I wasn't that guy who I had been in jail. And, thanks to moondust, I would soon be very rich, and live the life I always wanted.

I was freer than most, because now I understood what it was like not to be. I felt really, really happy about that.

....
12. ROB

So my guy Clyde and this dude Will came by my house; we went up to the roof, and they gave me this new drug.

Son.

I can't even tell you about this hit.

I can't even begin to describe it. Sickest feeling ever.

I traveled. I... fucking... traveled. I'm not even going to tell you where I went. And when I came back, I opened my eyes and this weirdo Will went, "Whoopeee!"

Usually a dude doing something that lame would make me want to slap him. But, instead I laughed right, and I went "Hell-fuck-yeah!" And stood up and jumped all around, all geeked on the raw joy moondust showed me.

Clyde and I hugged, and I was crying, I guess, because the moondust was still in my eye. But, it was more than that too, because I could see the whole city from my roof, gleaming, and I thought it was beautiful. I'd never thought that before.

Will lit up a joint and passed it, grinning like a fool, and I grinned right back at him.

I saw Heaven, son.

There. I said it. Moondust took me to Heaven. You don't believe me? Get a pinch yourself. I dare you.

As Will told it, you don't see Heaven every time. He'd just been in jail, in an inmate. That's how he said it, and when I didn't understand, he said, "Well asshole, I guess you'll have to take moondust again," and he lit a cig and strangely, I didn't even think of kicking him in the nuts or shooting his kneecap off because he didn't know me like that.

But then he was like "No, seriously," and Clyde smiled and threw me the pouch.

I said, "No way am I ready to do that again."

"You won't go back... there. You'll go somewhere different."

"I said no."

"You'll go into a different person," Will said.

"Could be now or the past," Clyde added.

"Or the future?" asked Will.

Clyde shrugged, and passed the joint.

I wanted to know what they were talking about.

....

13. Clyde

It was a crazy moment, all of us jumping around, celebrating being alive, because of moondust. I bet everyone who took it had that kind of moment sooner or later. After enough trips, you feel thrilled to be you.

And it was good, because I needed these dudes with me. I needed a crew because in order to distribute it, we needed to find out how to make it, which would be tricky. It made sense to form a crew for this, anyway I thought about it. And I'd thought it through a lot.

Will had been my friend for a while, he'd have my back. Rob was a fighter, hardest guy I knew well enough to bring in, street smart and hungry.

There was tons of money to be made on this stuff, plenty to go around. We'd be rich.

I turned to Rob. "Take your second trip," I said. "I hate to rush you. But, it's different the second time, and you need to know what you're getting into."

He looked up at me, face blank. "Since when are you bossy?"

"I'm asking with courtesy."

He glared at me before giving a predator's smile. He held open his eye, and I took a pinch from my vial and sent him off again.

He slumped down, his eyes closed, in REM—his face strangely blank.

"What are we going to talk about?" said Will, as we finished the joint.

"Business," I said. Will nodded.

We watched the skyline for a while or Rob's face. Will said my name.

I responded, "Yeah?"

"What now?"

"That's what we're going to talk about. Trust me."

Neither of us said nothing until Rob came back. But, after a while, I decided I misunderstood Will's question. He'd meant something bigger.

....

14. Rob

Captain Wilkins finishes up with "end of story any questions" like he always does, and we shake our heads.

Well, I'll have my Garand rifle until the end, and the end will leave me on the field in bloody pieces or sitting on some troop carrier going home with dead friends behind my eyes, but only if this Garand bucks so pretty that Krauts fall to embrace flowers with their teeth and lady luck fucks me as I sleep. It's just another pretty day in France, hot and my hands shaking because my blood fills with pillows and thunder. We start walking hunched over moving east out of a field that once had things in it like sheep. But, now we are nearly dead, only stepping on flowers and wild grass growing out of the dirt that had been shit from sheep who were dead now because sheep die first in war to feed the killers or to rot in piles on dead grass. Our regulation boots making no noise, olive colored and painful.

We crouch lower because in the distance buildings appear over the hill, farmhouses and barns full of soldiers, which you can tell, because they are silent and curdled like death, and everything seems wrong the way it always does. Parts of me scream to return to anywhere where the windows are safe and no one, quietly behind one where you can't see, breaks the silence by pulling a trigger so that with a zipping sound Hudson from San Diego's head opens up causing the sergeant to scream "sniper" and me to dive for cover finding none close. But, the hill itself offers some protection so I roll and drag myself down. I go deaf, can't hear the explosions, I only feel the ground quaking.

Sergeant shouts commands. I can't hear the slams of igniting bombs, which fills the whole world, but I can't hear. I get on my knees into a crouch. Here I can't be spotted by rifles throwing bullets screaming for limbs, lung, hip, or brain that will leave me here to become grass uncolored. I slowly nudge up the horizon the sky line slides.

Boom. Boom.

Boom.

Screaming of soldiers and the word medic means it's real and happening like it does every time, and I turn my head to see our medics running low, hoping it won't be their turn to catch metal bees screaming. I turn my head back and limp up the hill, the horizon un-spills the roofs so I breathe, pull the rifle up to my eye, my eagle's blood is silent death in my fingers. I spy a window with a pane of angry broken glass, and I crouch and wait until a metal flash of light illuminates the soldier behind it, and I aim to create murder of my own. When my trigger finger pulls, there's a beat, then an arm falls through the window, breaks the glass, and does not move, which is copasetic. But, I duck anyway because I gave my position away and lie on my back for a second, staring up at the pretty blue French sky before home flashes behind my eyes, just for a second, then it's gone. Sergeants scream, and a burst booming shock happens and reignites fear; I swore I felt something brush my helmet, and suddenly I can listen. But, sergeants only say, "Forward, goddamn it, move forward, cover fire; go, go, go," and up ahead wait Yama Anubis the Reaper Ahpuch Hel Mictlantecuhtliand Thanatos Morrigan, and everyday German soldiers with angry rifles, firing pain and death under pretty skies. But, I go forward anyway because death is everywhere, inside and out. I see how they fall with knees buckling—my brothers and friends and enemies—

falling like dolls or dead men.

I run to a tree close enough to make it. I dart and zag and crouch and zip and zip, and slower for a split second, then even faster, I run and dive hearing the sweet horrible bright sound of bullets hitting bark. Fear, fear, fear is the emotion of the day, served up on hot plates by murderous Germans who love their madman shooting at me with vicious intent. But, the tree between them and me takes their punishment, gets pulpy and aerated with metal smoking holes. If I could unlink my frozen bones, then I could fire back. I could survive the day if only I could stop screaming.

Then I manage, but my legs are wet. Somewhere sergeants shout, "Forward return fire, covering fire, forward grenade." Explosions happen, which is a good time to lean from behind my tree to see German raised barrels pointing at my blood, and they're southeast of us in the wrong place, which means we're flanked and fucked. I fire twice and then again. I duck back hoping I hit someone. They hold the trench and another position behind a fence, and it's a good time to throw a grenade because I'm trapped, but I won't panic. Instead, I'll rain fire—yank it off my belt, pull the pin, cook it, and throw blind. But, I know it lands right because, even blind, I throw like an angel, and I pop out from behind my cover when the explosion happens, perfectly timed to do damage.

Feel impact and burn in my side, shock-tinged pain legs buckling, cough blood, then I fall and struggle to breathe for seconds or years until someone pulls me into cover behind the tree. Too late, shock falling darkness, they scream medic. But, the medic won't come in time, and I hope I wake up somewhere.

....

15. WILLIAM

And then Rob came out of it. We'd been waiting in silence, me staring at the skyline. The words echoed, What now? But, there was no answer, and I didn't need one.

When Rob's eyes opened, he looked around, then up at us.

"Holy shit," he said.

"Where'd you go?" asked Clyde.

"World War II."

"You survive?"

"Doubt it."

"I went to France once, World War I," Clyde said. I'd never seen war, myself.

"You survive?" Rob asked.

Clyde shrugged and said, "It was hell."

"Is it anything like Slaughterhouse Five?" I asked. "You know, in real life."

Rob said, "What?"

"Slaughterhouse Five. It's a book about World War II. I read it in juvie."

They looked at me like I was crazy. I figured they either hadn't gone to juvie or hadn't read Slaughterhouse Five there.

....

16. ROB

What the fuck was this kid talking about?

17. CLYDE

Anyway, it was time to talk business. Verdun, France, was the last place I wanted to think about.

"Okay. Rob, here's the deal. Moondust is new. Right? It ain't any controlled substance we've heard of. It sure as hell ain't no medication. The government don't know about it yet. So—"

Rob cut me off. "Police can't touch us."

"Right. If we don't attract attention, then we can make tons before cops notice. We make enough, when they finally catch on, we retire and move to Hawaii or somewhere, find some big titty women, and live out our days in paradise."

Rob asked, "You got a plan?"

"Yeah. Follow the trail back to where this stuff came from and figure out how to make it. Next we set up bank accounts, sell this shit like mad until the government makes it illegal or we're so rich we don't care anymore. You in?"

"Hell, yeah."

"Good," I said. "I got it on a rooftop in Williamsburg. We're going to that building. The guy who sold it to me was a black kid with a tat on his neck, some kind of chalice, real recognizable. We're going to find him. So get your asses up."

18. PERCIVAL

The bad buzz wouldn't go away. So now stairs, down to my apartment from the roof. The banging of the bass diminished, but not enough. An ocean of vodka inside of me, unquiet.

I stumbled through the hallway, unlocked and opened the door to my place and fell onto the mattress. My arm hit someone; a girl was in my bed somehow—Ramona. I didn't invite her. But, she knew I kept my window open, and we shared the fire escape. Her fingernails caressed my shoulder with a question. But, I flopped over and closed my eyes. I wanted vacancy. In the morning, maybe, but now I just wanted her to turn the light out. I wanted the noise on the roof to be over. I wanted a cigarette without having to smoke. I wanted nonexistence.

Sleep pulled me into a dream where there would be no more moondust in the world, anywhere, ever. In the dream, we couldn't make it anymore, the technique no longer worked. Hailey cursed a storm as we all stood over a moon-drenched crop that wouldn't turn, realizing sadly that it was over. Mark kept throwing his hands through piles of dust, desperately hoping to coax it into spreading. He wore a linen suit and mumbled nonsense to himself. I looked up at the sky, thinking nothing lasts forever.

I woke up thirsty. I went and got some water and sat on the bed, thinking of how everything changes. I lay back down and woke Ramona, made wordless love, and fell back asleep; thankfully I didn't dream.

When I woke up the second time and stretched, I noticed Ramona wasn't in the bed. I heard her in the kitchen, and I yawned and got up. I put on a robe, went to my bathroom, and brushed my teeth.

When I finished, I played music by Beirut. It flowed through the apartment, and I came out dancing a little.

She was cooking something on the stove. "What's for breakfast?" I said.

She gave me an odd look before responding, "It's three o'clock," she said. "This is a late lunch."

"Okay, what's for lunch?"

"Omelet."

"You're having an omelet for lunch, and you expect me not to be confused?"

She laughed, sharply. Her laugh always grated on me, I never believed it. I kept smiling. But, something cold came over me, and suddenly all I wanted was to be alone. She was here uninvited, and I'd asked her not to do so before. Now that I was fully sober, this was a problem.

"So... can I ask you a question?" I said. "I don't mean to be rude, I really don't. But, why are you here? Didn't we talk about this?"

Hurt, anger, weariness, defensiveness, and resignation all shuddered through her face. The anger stayed. She left the omelet on the pan, went into the bedroom, grabbed her shit, pulled on her shoes, and left without a word.

Had I been cruel? Absolutely, but Pat Benetar was right about love. I'd made no promises, no demands. I hadn't even invited her over.

I finished cooking her omelet, and let it cool as I rolled a joint. I smoked the joint and ate the omelet at the same time, which was kind of a tricky thing to do, and ultimately not worth it. After I finished eating, I rolled another joint, watching the reality show about grandiose conflict, the mixed martial arts league.

On this Friday afternoon, I had nothing particular to do but mix music on my laptop, the thing I loved most of all. My social calendar was pleasantly empty, and I was making plenty of money with Mark and Hailey selling moondust, so I had no financial worries to attend.

How did this happen? After a surreal night on acid, we three had woken up with this powder and hand-written instructions. I think they came from this dude we spoke to at some point, at the time I thought his skin oozed, which really freaked me out. Mark remembered receiving something from him, and thinking it was a package of light.

The instructions detailed how to take it, and how to replicate it.

We instantly went into selling. Artists only; any and all types, as long as they were good. A good artist would never betray the dealer of something as inspiring as moondust; it was like we bottled the muses. So when we said, 'No contacts other than yourself, this number goes to no one,' our clients listened because competition was fierce in the art world.

The quality of this stuff meant clients would pay quite a bit, and it was fast and easy to make. But, because you could only get thirteen crops a year, supply was naturally limited, and this also increased worth. It was beautiful. We got paid, and we were safe.

After an hour or so, someone rang my doorbell. I wore only boxer shorts, no shirt, but I didn't care. I opened the door. It was this guy Quincy. He lived in the building, and we weren't quite friends.

"What's up?" I said.

"Um... there are some guys on the roof asking about you."

Anybody could get into this building.

"What? What do you mean?"

"They're looking for the apartment number of a black dude with a grail tattoo on his neck, and they claim it's about a business deal, and they're in 'creative.' But, they won't say what industry or what company or anything. They just say 'you don't need to know.' It seems shady."

I was alarmed.

"Right, thanks," I said, and closed the door. It was time to leave. Fire escape.

I put my pants on, grabbed my keys, my wallet, my phone, my cigarettes. I put a shirt on, grabbed my shoes.

Opened the window, glanced up to see if anyone on the roof was watching, then I looked down at the street. My blood pumped. My hands shook—no one was looking, so I squirmed out of the window onto the fire escape, closed the window, and started to make my way down.

They saw me when I was about halfway.

I knew because I got this intense version of that feeling you get when someone is looking at you. I looked up, and there was a dude on the roof staring down at me. When he knew I saw him, he turned, shouted something, and ran.

I booked like hell down that fire escape.

It was a pretty long way, but I was so quick that when I hit bottom, I just knew there wasn't anyone coming after me. But, sure enough, the building's door banged open, and as soon as I saw the tip of a sneaker coming out of the door, I was off. They'd had someone waiting in the lobby, probably, like I'd figured.

But I ran like Hermes.

I flew down alleys, I zigged and I zagged, then I slipped into a diner after a few minutes when I was seriously winded and sure I had lost them. I'd run fifteen, twenty blocks.

There was no telling how my next few days would go; so because I could, I ordered pancakes, bacon, coffee, and grabbed a copy of The New York Globe. The headlines were so sensationalized, the articles crafted with such simplicity, it felt like dispatches from a dream world. I put off coming up with a plan until after I'd read and eaten. I ignored the fear, because fear was useless. The coffee tasted better.

....

19. MAXWELL

After Justine left me at the restaurant, I sat alone at our table, considering next steps and finishing my meal. After I told her what my scientist learned about moondust, she told me she wanted to try it, and I told her that was crazy. Taking drugs was stupid, and taking new, experimental street drugs was especially idiotic, lethally so. I was not wrong, and I should not have done anything different, even though she stormed off.

Why on earth would she want to try it? When the guy who broke 'heroin use high among Vietnam vets' told his girlfriend about it, did she run out to score out of curiosity?

I figured I needed to go after Justine, so I flagged down the waitress while devouring the last of my chicken, handed her cash, said keep the change, and left.

Outside, I tried Justine, but her phone went to voicemail. "I'm sorry," I said after the beep. "I said the wrong thing. Call me anyway, okay? We need to talk this through... you can't take that stuff. You just can't. Call me back, alright?"

I walked to the subway, holding the phone, hoping and expecting she would call me back before I got to the entrance. When she didn't, I called again. But, I went straight to voicemail, just like before.

Well if she was going to be like that, I needed to do what I should be doing: chasing the story. I boarded the train, heading south, toward Chelsea.

....

20. JUSTINE

I took a cab home. Max called me twice during my ride, and I ignored both calls. I had absolutely no desire to speak to him. I'd never seen that pompous, narrow-minded side of him before, although I suppose I should have noticed the signs. It was far from attractive, and his belittling of my parents' faith was completely unacceptable. If I wanted to do something risky, perhaps he had the right to raise concerns. But, he did not have the right to call me or my desires stupid.

When I got home, I didn't even change out of my clothes. I left my shoes and purse by the door, and sat down on the couch, staring off at nothing. Soon I cried a few stray tears, but not because of Max. I thought of my father, who comforted me as a child.

His gigantic, kite-sized hands on my back.

It was true, moondust tempted me. I missed the quiet assurance of God. Religion gives you comfort, a grid over the world, a way of explaining everyone and everything. Questions had answers. When my father lived, there was a quieter version of me, young and innocent, believing the world was just, safe, reasonable and fair; because my father believed so, and our religion told us the love of God would protect us from the darkness. I do not know if it protected my father on the way toward whatever greeted him in infinity. I know it did not protect me from the pain of being left behind.

And now Maxwell's tests proved moondust was something outside of the secular. As unbelievable as the whole situation was, there was a chance I held the answers in my hands. I could be reconciled.

Was I brave enough to take it? I'd only tried marijuana once in college, an unpleasant experiment resulting in disdain for all those who claimed they enjoyed such activities. And yet, here I was. If moondust were a miracle, and if it fell into my lap, then didn't I, once a child in His flock, need to experience it?

I still wasn't sure. These weren't questions I ever pondered before. And the memories of church, of the songs and holy water, had mostly faded, buried beneath a million other, more pertinent ones. Photographs in the bottom of a shoebox, under the bed.

Desire made my mind for me in the end, not logic. The ache I hadn't known I felt. With shaking hands, I put the powder up to my eye.

....

21. MAXWELL

In terms of next steps, my plan was simple. A new designer drug like moondust had to be all over the fast and fleeting elite club scene, and so that was where I was headed. I called my co-worker Alexis, who owed me a favor, to get me in the hottest place she could. She gave me an address in Williamsburg. If I told them that I was her friend and that I worked for the paper, then I could get in.

I couldn't stop thinking about it—what Justine planned to do was inexplicable and dangerous. I hoped she hadn't, she could be hurt.

I went home, and changed into an appropriate outfit for the task at hand. Then I called a cab, because I wanted to make an entrance. The driver arrived in one of those shiny black cars and drove me over the bridge. My destination was an unremarkable steel door with a bouncer standing in front of it, from which poured the subsonic tremble of bass. I paid the cabbie. I gave the bouncer Alexis' name, paid an exorbitant amount, and entered.

The club was so damn hip it broke my heart. Its design was, of course, stylish: Asian influenced, minimal, based on a foundation of industrial chic, but more fleshed out. The vibe recalled a colder, much cooler version of someone's living room. The bar was rosewood, shaped in an undulating curve, with candles in built-in niches giving warmth.

Beautiful people were everywhere, so I was sure Alexis steered me to the right place. I smiled and thought about whom to ask for moondust.

My eyes fell onto the DJ and stayed. I simply knew he'd have come across this stuff. Those guys were always smacked out of their heads: How else could anyone stand being a DJ? He was my target. But, he was in the middle of a set, so I decided to go Hunter S. on the whole situation and get drunk. I felt like it and also figured it would help my credibility.

I went with the work-horse of drinks, the gin and tonic. I finished the first, then ordered a double. I talked to some girls, full of confidence, having nothing to gain or lose.

I was pretty drunk by the time the DJ took a break. He came out onto the floor for a moment, and chatted with the bartender. I chugged the liquor left in my glass, burning inside, and walked up to them.

"Barkeep," I said, "Tonic me."

I smiled and dropped some money on the bar. Then I turned to the DJ.

"So, what do you call that?" I asked.

"Uh, what?" He said.

"DJs always have such specific titles about their genre, and when I tell all my friends how fantastic you are, I want to get it right."

He laughed. "Well, if that isn't the best bunch of bullshit I ever heard."

"What? I can't be a fan of your ludicrous genius?"

"Okay," he said, "What do you want?"

I decided this was my moment. "Moondust. Ever heard of it?"

His faced changed so dramatically, I had what I needed before he even said a word. "Moondust? ... No. Who are you?"

"You have heard of it. I know that look. My name is Max. This guy calling himself the messenger gave me some, and I need more. How 'bout it?"

He said nothing, only stared.

"Look, man," I said, faking what I thought withdrawal might look like, "I need it."

"You look," he said. "I've never heard of it. But, if I had, talking to you about it could get me cut off, so go away."

"I'll level with you, friend. I know you're lying and I'm not going away. Even if you never speak to me, I'll be following you, so I'll eventually learn where you get it. Because you will be going for more, right? Why not save us both the trouble?"

He glared at me. Then he took out his cell phone, and made a call.

"Hey. Yeah. No. No, that's not it—there's this dude here, and he says he's after some imaginary drug called moondust, and I told him I'd never heard of such thing. But, he won't listen, and he says he's going to follow me. I'll be coming by soon to pick up my... stuff, so I figured you should know that. If there's some guy behind me, looking suspicious, he's not a cop so I recommend you shoot him. See ya."

He hung up the phone.

He turned back to me as if to tell me off. But, the phone rang before he spoke. He looked at the number, then picked up. "Yeah? Okay. Uh, what? Seriously? Alright, alright. Fine. I will. I will. Will you relax?" He hung up the phone. "Jesus Christ!"

He stared at me, dully, and said, "I'm to 'kick your motherfucking sorry ass until it hemorrhages,' and while I do so I'm to tell you it's not okay to follow people or show up at their buildings and chase them, and we do not forget shit so don't fuck with us."

"What are you talking about?" I said.

"I don't know, if you don't, dude," he said, and sighed. "I'm going over there." And he left.

I faked resignation, knowing I'd won. Anyone who told this kid to kick some ass must be a lightweight, not someone to fear. Since the DJ accidentally confirmed he would pick up more drugs soon, trailing him was my next move, and the risk was low.

Faking glumness, I finished my gin and tonic, and went on my way. I even walked around the block, for effect, until I reached the alley leading to the club's back entrance. A van parked by the back door was probably the DJ's, so I found a good vantage point and waited.

22. YVONETTE

It'd been only days since
My friend William
Took me to this guy's apartment,
And they gave me

This drug and
I saw
I didn't want it to be.
I spent the first two days trying to convince myself it'd just
Been another hallucination.
I'd had plenty of those, and that was nothing new.

I could have used
More hallucinations. But, I did not need
Whatever moondust had been.
The problem with
Lying to myself
Was that I always knew the truth.

I was working at a place called Venice. It was
Italian food,
Obviously,
And I'd worked Italian fine dining before.
It was nothing new,
And without the ridiculous strict difficulty of the French
system.
Which was too much of a bitch.
Really.

It was fine, but

Everyone was always staring at my butt,
And none of those bastards in the kitchen or even
management
Were above an ass-grab,
If I were the kind
Not to report
That sort of behavior.
Fuck them.
They were gross,
Worst examples of a mediocre kind.
Un-sublime.

I needed a tryst.
Something to get my mind off
Everything I didn't want to think about
None of these pigs would do, of course.
Meaning my coworkers.
Even if I believed in workplace romance,
They were irrelevant, boys masquerading
Playing
Not paying attention.

Well, when I got off, I went out looking.
I went home first, so I'd be
Smoking,
Hotter than Hoboken.

Had to find me a
token man to fill some hours.

Just a fling.
Because I know

Life is life. I am me, alone, with no judge.

And perhaps he'd be the type to stay...

It could happen.
Into the shower. I scrubbed
And I rubbed.

Out of the shower.
Out with the hair-care supplies, perfectly applied. On
With the makeup.
This would be a night.
And when I was primped, pressed,
Dressed,
I left.
I, neon in a purple dress.

Called a car, which
Took me to a guarded door
The club.

Wally Beaver was the DJ,
I'd seen him at Kush,
And Whale Belly.
He was good, he would do
Provided music to shake, to grind
If the moment happens that way.
And my earrings were flashing, and the golden brooch
Hanging into the dip of flesh
That begins my chest.
Passing the bouncer, not paying. Had it like that.
Going up to the bar to get a Jack,

Mixed with Diet Coke to aid ingestion.
Sitting back. Checking out the bar,
Lay of the land. It had nice
Décor, all metal and glass,
Red and marine accents so the room stayed warm.
And the boys were handsome, sophisticated, hot.
Talked to one, a reporter, working for a newspaper. He was
all smiles and disrobing eyes.
Not my type,
But speaking to him worked, it passed the time.
Let the boys see me being seen.
Talked to another, 'in the market' or something, and then
the DJ.
Wally Beaver, I never noticed his eyes.

Oh, the drama, a DJ for me, me standing there almost
outclassed,
For the place was full of fantastic specimens. Professional
hotties.
But when I saw those eyes, I knew. So I screwed up my
courage,
To wait for the moment,
And to stand near his space,
Glance-into-his-pupils-and-say-nothing,
And offer.

(Wanna?
Wally Beaver, let's dance the dance.
Drink some drinks
Let nighttime enfold us.)

23. WALLY

Oh man, it was a cool scene, but such a drag, like spam out of a can. My new suede shoes and skinny jeans, aviators, and posh sweater made me feel too cool, because everyone else manufactured their cool, unlike my original awesomeness.

Moondust showed me I was the coolest boy in history.

My guy Percival, a pretty good DJ, slid this drug my way. He said he got it from a hallucination or something, and when I took it, it let me embrace my awesome. The first time I went to like Heaven, and after that, I got to view people's lives, all through history and stuff.

I could tell you that my life was the coolest life in the history of lives. I always knew it, but now I had proof. The music I played could only be described as sublime.

Tonight, I played this place down in Manhattan. I preferred Brooklyn, which felt more indie. But, Manhattan gigs paid better money, and this place had a great rep.

I was still cooler than it, though.

I slid on this track by Grim Avenger to end my set, then I wanted a break so I went over to the bar for a drink. I wanted to take it outside, whiskey and cigarettes went together awesome.

But this drunk dude slid up to me, and he went, "You're like the coolest, bestest DJ in history."

True. But, what the fuck? I laughed at him and said "What? Geek."

"I can't appreciate your genius?"

I laughed again because he could if he wanted to. "What do you want?" I said.

His eyes got all hungry, and he said, "Moondust. Ever heard of it?"

I figured him for an autograph hound or something ridiculous like that. But, this was different.

"No," I said. "Who are you?"

"Please," he said, withdrawal—that I didn't know you could have!—bleeding from his eyes. "I need it."

I had to be intimating, I'd been taking these acting classes so I put on my Crime and Punishment audition face, viciously.

"Look, I've never heard of it. But, let's say I had, dude. Anything as far out as moondust would be kept under severe wraps and talking to you about it would get me cut off, so go away."

"What, you think I can't just follow you?"

This was out of control. I figured after all this time Percival must have bought himself some protection, he always hinted about it. A gun, I mean. So I called him.

"Sup, Wal?"

"Hey."

"So what," he said, "you coming by?"

"No. See, there's this loser here after some imaginary drug, and I told him I never heard of it. He won't listen, and he says he's going to follow me. But, I'll be coming soon to pick up my... stuff, so if there's a guy behind me, looking shady, shoot him. Alright? See ya." I hung up the phone, sure my performance had been convincing. I stared at the dude, waiting for him to vanish. But, Percival called me back.

"Yeah?" I said.

"You fucking idiot, some dude shows up asking about drugs, and you call me? Kick his fucking ass! You do not come to see me unless you are alone because his legs are broken, understand me? So kick his sorry ass until it hemorrhages!"

"Um, like, seriously?"

"Kick his motherfucking ass! It is not okay to follow people,"

"Alright, alright," I interjected, but he kept going, way jazzed up.

"And it is not okay to show up at their buildings and chase them,"

"Fine! I'll tell him!"

"And we do not forget shit like that so kick his fucking ass!"

"Will you relax already? Jesus Christ!" I hung up on him.

This sort of thing did not happen to the coolest boy in history. So I just looked at the dude, bored with the whole situation. "I'm to kick your motherfucking ass until it hemorrhages, yadda yadda, blah blah, do not fuck with us. We will bury you or whatever. Seriously, dude, drop it. For your own sake. I'm going to go over there now."

Convinced I handled the situation as well as could be expected, I went back to my booth for set 2 and did what I did with excellence. The whole night looked like it would be a drag, then I saw this girl sitting by the bar in a purple dress. She was lava. Just the thing for tonight. Pick it up a little.

So I went back to the spinning table jam, and I noticed that jerk finally got up and left, so I relaxed a bit, perfectly focused.

I would probably sleep with her later. But, for now I had a vibe to attend to.

....

24. MAXWELL

I waited behind that dumpster forever, with my phone primed to call a car service, which always arrived within five minutes. I figured I had at least that long between when the DJ first started loading his truck to when he left.

Relaxing behind a dumpster proved difficult, with theoretical cockroaches all around. I kept canvassing the environment for another spot, anyplace, where I could hide and not be seen, without luck. This was it.

I crouched for hours, trying to avoid being crawled on, keeping sentry against a rat invasion. At some point I texted Justine, a long message asking her to respond, to say anything. She didn't answer.

By the time the DJ came out, I'd been fighting leg cramping and a serious loss of circulation. It'd become a losing battle, and when he came out, I was half-standing in order to get my right leg to wake up. When the door opened, I ducked back and saw the DJ carrying a load of cables, opening the van, and getting in to put the cables somewhere. I took out my phone and pulled up the car service's number; when he went back into the club, I moved. I walked as quickly as my one-and-a-half legs could carry me, and while I did so, called a car to come to the corner.

I must have looked pretty strange, standing at a street corner banging my leg. But, the DJ wouldn't be able to see me, so I didn't worry too much. When the car came, as fast as promised, I slid in the back seat and told the driver the score.

"We're going to sit here and wait," I said, "until a van drives out of that alley. When it does, we're going to follow it."

"I don't do that."

"How much?"

"I said I don't do that."

"And I asked how much. I'm trying to make it worth your while."

I hated dipping into the trust fund for this ruffian. But, moondust was my break.

He sighed, "Two hundred."

"Oh, Come on! One hundred."

"Get out."

"Two hundred, okay."

The driver nodded and turned on music, something like reggaeton, which was annoying. Sitting in the car—my legs aching like hammer blows—the incessant beat wasn't helping my mood at all.

"Hey. If I gotta pay you two hundred dollars for this, you mind turning off the tunes?" I said.

He glanced back at me, and turned it up.

After the images of me beating him into bloody sea-foam faded, a headache rooted in my brain. I was not happy about this. But, the driver had me over a barrel, and the music wasn't as bad as sitting behind a roach-infested dumpster. I'd be thrilled when the DJ's van finally pulled away. I wondered what his name was. Probably DJ Delicious or something stupid like that.

....

25. YVONETTE

DJ Wally
Beaver
Pushed me up against a wall
Intermixed our signals.
I kissed back,
And my hand went,
With delicacy,
To his waist.
This was the magnetic hour.
With a laugh, he tried to pull away,
Begging that his gear remained unpacked. But, I would not relent,
Grabbing his flapping lips with my teeth. Ridiculous boy.

We were starlight under a shining city,
Glowing crimson and clover, and I grabbed him again.
He kissed back. A hand went
To my breast. I moaned.

But the gear had to be packed, and so he slipped

Eel-like from my embrace,
Coming back, and saying nothing. But, 'get in the van,'
Galaxies of bedsheets burning in his irises.

This was the magic hour.
He went off to pack his gear,
Speedy. I went and sat in the van,
Checked my hair,
Prepared. I was drunk and saw beauty
In clouds and concrete.

And when he came back,
Climbing into the van with a smile,
I felt my lower lip crawl between my teeth.

We reached his place,
Floating up to his apartment on the fourth floor,
Swelling out of our clothes,
Clasping each other,
Smothering our differences.
Once again, I felt Free.

....

26. MAXWELL

I followed the DJ's truck to an apartment building in Brooklyn.
My driver whined incessantly. But, I ignored him. When the
DJ parked, a girl got out of the passenger side; I recognized
her. I spoke to her earlier, in the club. She'd been too flirtatious,
generally not my type.
But apparently the DJ dug her; they were all over each other. He

wasn't leaving his apartment until morning, so I wrote down the building's address, and I told the driver to take me home.

"I take you home. But, I turn on the meter."

"No deal, pal. I just handed you two hundred dollars for an hour-and-a-half's work, so quit bitching and take me home."

I'd invested quite a lot of money to get only an address, and my poor rate of return caused a dark spirit on the ride back. Still, I would stay in. You can't win, if you don't buy.

I thought about heading back to Justine's—telling the driver to take me there, dealing with the requisite whining while the cab rolled until the city became her neighborhood. I thought of ringing all the bells, but hers, knocking on the door once I got in. I thought of enfolding her in my arms.

Just fantasies.

I texted her because I wanted her to write something back, anything. Chances are she'd be asleep. But, I needed to know she wasn't dead because of a drug I should've taken away from her.

I wrote, "r u ok?"

The city rolled by, flowing toward my home, not hers. No answer for a while, until, surprisingly, my pocket vibrated. I took the phone out and flipped it open, saw one word on the screen, "NO."

I may have felt hopeless in that moment, maybe even furious. And I did tell the driver to turn go to her house.

"Fuck you," he said, "You wanna give me another address now?"

"My girlfriend's sick. Do it."

"You're the one who's sick—yo, sick in the head. Chasing people around, making up lies... you know what? Fuck this. Get the hell out."

"Oh don't even—"

"OUT. You know I have a gun up here, and I know you don't. So get out the back seat, and I hope you get mugged, stupid ass."

After I watched his car pull away, I flipped open my phone and called Justine. She didn't answer. But, after I lowered the phone, I started walking, trying to figure out what to do, and she sent me a text, two words, "not now."

I wrote back "when?" And waited. No answer.

I needed to find the nearest subway station; I had to go home.

What happened to her? She took the moondust—I knew it. For a second, the alcohol in my stomach bucked. What kind of world was this? My girlfriend was on drugs and refused to see me... I was stranded in the middle of Brooklyn... everything was wrong. Some goober accosts us with a weird powder, and now everything had gone belly up.

I walked in a random direction, hoping I could stumble upon a subway station before being mugged. Tomorrow, I'd wake up, shower, and either go to Justine or to the corner of Hubert and Welsh, to an unnamed building where I'd pick up and tail a DJ wherever he went. It was a huge decision, one I couldn't yet contemplate. Too drunk, too tired—making my way through inky Brooklyn took all my focus.

....

27. JUSTINE

What an understatement to call moondust unexpected.

As my eyes opened, echoes of crushing joy reverberated through me. It'd been so powerful I felt sick—as if someone extracted every nice feeling from my whole life, combined and multiplied them by one billion, and shoved the result right into my belly.

I couldn't handle it. That was not the God I'd known, nor the Heaven I'd been taught; instead something alien, strange, and inside of it, I had been alien and strange, too. It put a fracture in my brain, something I could never reconcile.

I threw the packet holding the powder across the room, I started drinking. I had three quarters of an open bottle of red wine remaining, and so I went into the kitchen and grabbed it, no glass.

In my stomach were still the fading knots of ecstasy I couldn't understand. I started praying to Jesus, as I did when my distress got this unbearably high, as my father had taught me. But, suddenly and irrevocably, I knew that there was no Jesus to hear me.

There'd been nothing like his calm, comforting presence with moondust. Nothing at all.

Yet, in that light, I'd felt... whole, and a sense of joy I'd never known. My head hurt. I drank more.

At some point my phone beeped, it was a text message from Max, asking if I was okay.

I told the truth, which was no. He wanted to come to me. I told him no again.

After dawn seeped through the window, when I finally felt sleep taking me, I felt enormous gratitude.

Saturday, September 30, 2006

....

28. Yvonette

And in the morning,
Deflated.
Merely human again.
All the thoughts sex sends off-line, returning.
And I, next to
This strange man. In his strange bed.
Strange smells all over my skin.
But I was an expert at the after-shock,
Love's remainder.

No, I did not hope
That Wally Beaver would have built magic
From the space our skin collided.

I got dressed.
I yawned and stretched.

As was sometimes preferable, I tried not to think
about the sex.
It'd been okay. He was drunk and
Showed it. C'est la vie.
I checked my reflection in a mirror. Saw the usual.
But as I made to leave, something unexpected:
He awoke and spoke.

Not that unusual, I guess. Not at all. I just figured
Wally Beaver wasn't that type.
In the daylight,
Something in his whole vibe lacked depth.
One of those with no hope of intimacy left. Not that I'm
judging.
I could even be the same.
It's possible.
"Leaving already?" he said.

So I turned 'round.
"The shoes on my feet would suggest it,"
Was my riposte.
Admittedly, a great line to leave on,
But instead of walking
I crossed my arms.
"Don't be a butterfly, baby,"
He said, with a stretch, "Stay. I'll show you things."

My arms did not uncross.
"You'll show me things?"
"Oh yeah." said he. "But first, come here."
He was better in the morning. He kissed like he meant it.
And I was

Unaccountably distracted. But, still,
I found a groove and fell into. C'est la vie.

And when I released my brain fuzz, a flower grew between
our skins,
Bloomed,
And died.
Not the biggest,
But worth the time.
I thought maybe we'd be something for a while.
It could happen.
Still, when we lay side by side, breathing,
Coming down,

It seemed time to let time carry me
Elsewhere.
So I got up, and made to get dressed.
But he said, "Wait.
I said I have something to show you."
"Oh?" I replied. Wiggling into my bra. "Here I was
thinking that you just showed it."

And he laughed.
"Trick, that's something. But, it ain't nothing."
Arms crossed again. Trick, he calls me?
The nerve.
And nerve's a funny thing,
Some is to be punished. Some makes the blood flow.
Which this was, I hadn't decided.
He didn't notice my glare. "Come here," he said.
"No. I'm trying to decide whether to slap you."
"Decide after you try this." And he reached into a drawer.

Pulled out white powder.

And I thought, Oh, God, no.

"It's called moondust," he said,

"It's the ride of your life,"

Oh, God, no.

I could not help the tears that fell. Don't ask me why.

It seemed so unfair,

It made me so angry

To see that again.

The last thing I needed.

I made an exit of it.

I shouted.

Threw something. He shouted back.

C'est la vie. In the hallway,

I lit a cig with shaky hands. It was illegal,

But law be damned.

I was usually a very calm and rational human being.

But now forever in my brain was

Echoes of joy—unearthly music,

And I could not abide it.

....

29. PERCIVAL

The rain kept coming, it rained all morning. I sat in a nondescript diner in the Bronx, because I never hung out in the Bronx.

Figuring out what to do.

The situation: I—your hero DJ, lover, and all around quality type—was on the run from some sort of bad element because some time ago, I'd gotten my hands on an unusual drug called moondust, and my caring nature led me to share with friends, neighbors, and associates. Yesterday, some goons came to my building, looking for me, and moondust was the only possible reason why. I ran, and they chased me. I'd been on the bounce all night.

Where was the justice?

There was no telling what that idiot Wally Beaver had spilled when they got to him. He'd called me! Someone was with him, trying to get moondust, some dude he didn't know, who was asking questions, and the dumb shit called me! My circle had been infiltrated at the weakest link.

But if they could track me through Wally, I could back-track them the same way. If they could ask him about me, I could ask him about them.

Right now, I needed information more than anything.

Plans help when paranoia threatens. Everyone had been looking like a threat. Old ladies, children, cops... well, always cops. But now I suspected a whole new level of crookedness and malice. I'd be much better off, if I knew what I was dealing with.

I felt in my pocket, reflexively, for five packets of powder. All the moondust I had left, although Mark and Hailey, my compatriots in the moondust adventure, had plenty and could make more.

I hadn't ever been worried about arrest: Moondust was an unknown compound, not yet illegal. Now I was worried about everything, which brought me back to Wally Beaver.

I was an artist's artist: I believed completely in who we are as a tribe, and what we do. But, I also believed some kids were just along for the ride, the scene. Wally Beaver was a classic case. And with half-a-brain, to boot. I couldn't believe how dumb he'd been.

I called Hailey, to check in. While the phone rang, a pretty girl with pink hair caught my eye, and we locked gazes.

Hailey's phone picked up. "Hablame," she said.

"You okay?"

"Laying low. We figured that was the move. Fucking Wally."

"Yeah. You and Mark have any problems?"

"Not one with those assholes," she said. "We just want to get back to business as usual. I have a group show in Astoria tonight, I don't need this. We have moondust for adventure."

I laughed. "Yeah. Go anywhere interesting recently?"

"Dark side of the moon, just the usual," she said. "Hey, did you know Shamans could really do magic?"

I didn't really believe it. "For real?"

"I don't know, I guess. I mean, whose reality are we talking about?"

"Listen Hales, I'm going to talk to Wally. I wanna face this head on."

"Are you sure that's wise?

"No. But, I'm doing it anyway."

"Then we're with you," she said. "Hey, I'm hanging up now. I'm on the J-train and people are wigging out for some reason. I need my wits about me. Later." She hung up.

So now, at least in the short-term, my path was clear. To Brooklyn and Wally Beaver. Once more, the breach.

....

30. MAXWELL

I'd been scoping out the DJ's house for hours. A cold rain sapped my strength. But, I, Maxwell Smith, intrepid reporter and soon to be national name, was on the track of a story. And the story went right through a dumb shit DJ in Brooklyn.

Around one o'clock, the girl he took upstairs last night came stomping out of his building, clearly enraged, maybe crying. Which didn't say much for my mark, but I was okay with that. No guilt.

The waiting was cold, wet, and super boring. I had my iPod, and this cut through the drudgery. But, stake-outs required greater patience than I could muster.

I spent the time in two ways: first, dreaming about my article, the prestige, international fame, world domination, and so forth; and second, worrying about Justine.

There was nothing I could do about her right now, and I hated that.

Things heated up around three o'clock. I wasn't the only one hanging out around the building. A ruffian with a green hat pulled low and a black coat watched me from a distance, while failing to be inconspicuous. He seemed ill-at-ease. This was getting interesting.

So, I had a few options.

The first concerned my general health and well-being. I was dealing with a stranger, and I didn't know his motives. Logic suggested a strategic withdrawal. Leave the scene, absorb the new information, come up with a new plan, and execute it.

The second option maintained status quo. I would follow the plan, tailing the DJ at a safe distance.

The third option was to go over and talk to the guy in the green hat. Holding the ideal of the press, and what we do, ahead of me like a shield. Maybe we could help each other.

These options rested on a continuum of nerve. The nerviest choice isn't always the best, and in a situation like this, how do you know with what you're choosing? Head, gut, testicles, or cowardice? A safe action—regrouping—was also running away. A bold action—direct confrontation—was also bullish, dangerous.

As I thusly considered my options, Justine's image, her pretty face, flitted through my mind.

To hell with caution. I walked right up to him.

....

31. Percival

When I got to Wally's place, I did a couple of walk-byes for reconnaissance. I put my hood up to make detection harder and went by the place like I was going somewhere down the street.

Someone stood in front of Wally's building, not doing anything, trying to be inconspicuous.

He wore a three-quarter length cashmere coat, chinos, and brown shiny shoes. A total college boy, the type who can't wait to tell you he's Ivy League. At least, that's how he looked.

It was pretty weird. I wasn't sure what to make of it. He could have been waiting for someone else, meaning I had nothing to worry about. He definitely didn't look like the hustler type. Maybe he was in disguise?

I decided to pick a spot down the street from him and stake him out. I wanted to watch him, and I wanted him to see me doing it. I figured if he made a move toward me, I could always run. If Wally came out or in, I'd also be able to observe what happened.

After about an hour, he walked right up to me.

I was unarmed. Still, I decided to let the situation play itself out, because, looking at him, I was sure I could take him. Of course, he could have been armed. But, he just didn't look the part.

"Who are you?" I said.

"Maxwell Smith. You?"

He smiled, which really didn't fit the situation. Definitely not a hustler.

"Don't worry about who I am. Why are you here?"

"Nice day, isn't it?"

"It's raining, fool."

He laughed. "Yeah, it is. Look, I think the question for us right now is: 'Why are we both here?'"

"I'm about three seconds from kicking your ass. Who are you?"

He held up his hands, in a gesture of peace. Adrenaline made my blood vicious.

"I'm a reporter," he said.

"Reporter?"

"Reporter. I'm looking for information. Moondust. You heard of it?"

I believed him. I was almost speechless.

....

32. WINSTON

Doing God's work tended to bring moments full of His peace and well-being to one. Brief sections of time in which the perfection of His plan, and all He wrought, came clearer and more beautiful than the most uplifting hymn.

Today, before my duties in the confessional, I had such a moment. The church, in all its majesty, seemed surreally calm, in such a way the very spires seemed to whisper His name.

Some of the older priests chalked my vigor up to my youth and would say things like, "Faith is a truth which ages like wine." They tended to think me erratic. I simply believed things could be better. Often we disagreed.

Then again, a few in the priesthood thought that perhaps I was especially touched. For me, better to put such ideas out of my head—I was what I was, for better or worse, and I lived in the service of Christ.

And so, I set it in my heart to do my duty, solemnly and joyfully. My time at confessional began usual enough: I confessed a woman who had lustful thoughts about a neighbor, then a man who took money from his place of work. I spread the forgiveness, love, and light of our Lord. I confessed a little boy who'd been stealing candy, and a young woman who made love to her boyfriend out of wedlock.

This work, this spiritual work, was beautiful to me. In this small way, I helped ease the burden of humanity, helped save souls, and helped people find their way to our Lord Christ's restorative forgiveness.

The next woman I confessed, however, was an extremely special case, and one that, afterward, left me quite troubled.

"Bless me, Father, for I have sinned," she began, and I noticed immediately how small her voice sounded, and how it quivered.

"How long has it been since your last confession, child?"

"It's been... years, Father. Many years since my last confession."

"Very well. Tell me your sins."

"I... I wouldn't know where to begin. I lived with a man three years ago... I, um, had carnal relations, I..." She trailed off.

"Is this why you have come?"

"I'm ashamed."

I could barely hear her. "You are loved by our Lord in spite of your sins, child. What is it you wish to tell me? What brought you here? Perhaps we should start there."

"I... I took a drug."

"A drug?"

"Yes. It was... blasphemous."

"All drugs are sins in the eyes of God. Which drug did you take?"

"It was called moondust."

"Is this something you do regularly?"

"No, Father. I... my boyfriend Max and I were out and... a man gave it to us. He asked us if we wanted to experience God."

I sat up a little bit in my seat. "Please say that again."

"He told us that if we took it, we could experience God."

"But, of course, he was misleading you."

"Father?"

"Yes?"

"What do you think God looks like? What do you think it would be like to be in His presence?"

"The Holy Bible tells us that one cannot experience His presence without leaving this world. To believe otherwise is blasphemy."

"I know, but... what if you could? What do... you...?"

"We cannot know. Christ alone could answer that question, child."

"I'm afraid," she said, after silence.

"What do you fear?"

"What if—it wasn't a hallucination?"

I sighed. "This substance will lead you down the path of temptation and damnation. You must recite ten Hail Mary's, repent in your heart, and never ever again stray onto the path of illicit drug use. Am I clear?"

"Father?"

"Yes?"

"It felt like joy."

....

33. PERCIVAL

"Moondust?" I worked out, through my shock. "What, dude?"

Said the preppie journalist, "You know what it is. You take it."

I just stared at him.

"Oh come on. You and I both know the stuff is unknown and therefore the government hasn't formed an opinion on whether it's legal. So I'm not police or FBI. I mean, look at me. Do cops dress this well? You have nothing to worry about.

When I didn't respond, he continued. "In fact, you have no idea how safe from criminalization moondust is, and by extension, how much you have to gain by being open, and talking to me. To build the cliental, so to speak. I can tell you just how safe you are, and then you can adjust your plans. Would you like to know? If so, we should talk."

"I don't know you."

"Here's how it'll go. We'll dip into a coffee shop, and I'll tell you what I've found out, and then you answer some general questions about moondust. Nothing about yourself. I just want to know who, what, when, where, and why.

"What?" I said, because I needed to keep him talking while I decided.

"Who? Which segment of the population is into this stuff? I don't need names, I need demographics. What? As much as you can tell me about what it's like. When? How long it's been on the scene. Why? How this new drug is hooking whoever it's hooking. What's the draw, and how far can we expect the trend to go."

"Why would I tell you all that?"

"Look, if you knew what I know, no matter what your deal is with this stuff, you'll want this article to happen. But, you don't have to believe me yet, just come and listen to what I have to say. As a matter of fact, once you do, you may want to tell me your name. Your face being on the cover of Time Magazine might sound possible, and like the best thing that ever happened to you in your life. I might make you rich. Just listen."

The man had an argument.

"But you already know who I am," I said.

He chuckled. "No, how do you figure? I'm not that good of a reporter."

I stepped closer to him—chest to chest.

"Because you sent three fucking goons to my place to find me, that's why. Or, you're a goon yourself, sent by your boss."

"Whoa," he said. "You have people following you? That's a story I want to hear. Off the record, of course."

I looked into his eyes for a while. He didn't flinch; he was believable—except for the so-called off-the-record part; that part was bullshit. He planned to scam my story out of me. But, I could deal with that. So I exhaled.

"Alright, fuck it," I said. "But I pick the place, and you pay."

"Done."

....

34. Maxwell

It may have been the best performance of my life-to-date. Of course, a lot was at stake. During my pitch, the sting of rejection was not my biggest concern, which helped. A no would have come with broken legs. So, victory or death.

I really amazed myself when I told him he may even choose to become the face of a movement. It just came to me.

I could do a gritty investigative journalism piece. I could go to the edge and nearly become the people I observed.

I followed him now, a little behind and to the left, out of reach, because he kept looking behind as though he expected me to attack. He was skittish.

I realized I needed a name to call him, for the article.

"Hey," I called up the street to him. "I need to be able to call you something. A fake name if you prefer."

"Call me Childe," he said. "With an E."

"Childe? Alright."

We kept going only a little bit farther. We dipped into a neighborhood place, a restaurant and bar, dark, small, and quiet—a good choice, I had to admit. I ordered coffees, sat down at our table, rolled up my sleeves, and got down to business.

"Do you want a muffin?" I said, joshing with him a little. "Corn dog?"

He glanced my way as if bored. "Do you want broken teeth?"

"Not particularly. Biscotti?"

That earned me a chuckle. "Get talking, Fredrick," he said.

"Fredrick?"

"That's your name, isn't it? Or... was it Mandrake? Pennington?"

"You're mocking me; I get it. Here's the story. A man calling himself the messenger stopped my girlfriend and me on the Upper West Side, and he offered us moondust. I had a sample from my bag analyzed."

"Wait," Childe said. "Some dude's giving moondust away on the island?"

"Yeah. An odd sort, too," I said. "He walks around in a business suit, gray, asking people if they want to experience God. I tracked him down. But, he was not open to conversation. I could tell you where he lives, maybe, if it's worth my while." I smiled a bit.

"As I was saying, I had moondust analyzed. Testing it turned out to be useless, and that's what you need to know: Moondust cannot be studied or categorized by conventional methods. When you do routine analytical tests, the results come with a different data sets every time. The stuff appears to be shape-shifting."

I scanned his face for his reaction as he leaned back in his chair, getting as close to horizontal as possible. His eyes betrayed his affected breeziness.

I continued, "In other words, moondust is immune from governance. Even if the government wanted to, it could only ban the results of one test of one sample; a meaningless, useless gesture. As far as moondust goes, we're in the wild West."

I stopped talking; neither of us said anything for a moment. He reclined in his chair, staring off into the distance, most likely trying to gauge how much he believed me.

"And another thing," I said, "'Childe' is a stupid name. I'm going to turn this into an article, and I need a name that could be real. Not something out of a children's tale about maze gardens."

"My name's Wally Beaver," he said. "I'm a DJ. What do you want to know?"

"Everything. Like I said before. Who. what, where, why, and when?"

And he started telling me his story.

....

35. PERCIVAL

Things had gotten interesting.

It was looking like moondust could become a whole different vehicle for me altogether. If what the man said was true, I could write my own ticket. We all could: Hailey, Mark, and I, mystic narcotic discoverers.

All we'd have to do is give the reporter what he wanted: the story of moondust, an underground movement taking off in New York, soon to take over the world.

At the same time, we would start throwing parties and arranging nights at clubs, and we would replicate a ton of moondust to give it out for free. I'd create and spin music just for the occasion, psychedelic, deep and throbbing, a shadow of moondust itself.

In short, we'd blow their fucking minds.

Then, as the buzz about us rose to a crescendo—and it would— the article would come out.

Boom. Instant fame. This would make our careers. We might even get rich.

The idea of riches! I gave up that dream a while ago. I liked slugging it out on the front lines—spinning, turning around reality, creating the sounds that later, failed models would become famous for when their fourth-generation recycled and whitewashed 'indie-doorstep' bullshit hits the ignorant public's eardrum. But, we true artists didn't care; we'd already be on to the next thing.

But this...if there were ever a vehicle worth breaking into the public scene, moondust was it. Moondust could change the world. The implications were staggering. The reporter dude barely even had to say two words about it; the puzzle was so perfect, it fell into place by itself.

Could you imagine me, living in Manhattan? The idea was laughable. I was Brooklyn all the way. If I got posh, then I'd move to Grand Street.

But to keep this going, I needed to feed the reporter some buyable bullshit. I did some quick thinking, while taking a long sip of coffee. I figured my best bet was to keep the story as real as possible, including locations. But, change all names, and include nothing traceable back to the three of us. So I started talking: I threw in this story and that story, mostly idle bullshit I heard from people while out on the town. I used this as a backstory for the drug community, "You have to understand who I, Wally Beaver, am," I said. (He had a digital-recorder running, I'd given permission.)

And then I went into all this stuff about what I'd done. "But moondust is different," I said, and about that, I told the truth.

He asked questions, mostly along his who-what-when-where line, and some insightful ones like, "What do you think moondust has cost you?"

My answer, "The illusion of control."

He asked me to elaborate. But, I declined. Still, I liked these questions the best. They were the most fun. Such as, "What do you think moondust has given you?"

"Perspective."

"What would you say to someone who wanted to ban moondust or stop you from using it?"

"I'd say, 'Your whole life, you've only been yourself. What do you know?'"

"And what would you say to someone thinking about trying moondust?"

"You'll never be the same."

So the interview went.

....

36. MAXWELL

The kid coughed up beautifully. The worst I could say was that his performance was on the pretentious side. There was even a bit about "the illusion of control," for goodness' sake. Hardly what you want to hear from your article's poster-boy, herald of a terrifying and degenerate new trend.

But it was a start.

To continue, I needed a sample ASAP to give to my chemist, Peter. I figured this DJ could help me with that.

I also needed him to let me shadow him. I needed descriptions of everything. I needed gonzo journalism. I needed to see kids tripping—or whatever—on moondust and to interview them when they came down. In sum, I needed access.

Then, I needed to go into the bleeding heart of the thing, to scrape its arteries and tattoo its blood across the front of America's newspapers.

"Well, I think that's all for today," I said. "How can I get in touch with you?"

"Text me at (718) 555-2315. No phone calls."

Whatever. "Sure, fine," I said. "Hey, you know what would be excellent? I want to observe you—or someone—take the stuff. What do you call it, when you take it? Hitting? Scoring?"

"No."

"Then what?"

"Dropping, I guess, if we call it anything."

"Why's that? The word dropping, I mean."

He gave me a smile that clearly called me a moron. "Because it involves the force of gravity."

"Ah." Undaunted, I pushed on. "So, how about it? Can I watch sometime?"

"Is that important?"

"It can be the difference between a mediocre article and a great one, I think."

He gave a long pause, studying me, thinking. "I don't know. I don't want to introduce you to my friends, Pennington. You're not really our type."

I sighed. "I thought we discussed what was at stake here? How it'd benefit you?"

He sipped his coffee, buying time again. "Alright. But, you watch me. And me alone. If I like your answers; we've reached the point where you need to fess up."

"To what?"

"How did you get to the apartment you were staking out? Why were you there? Your story doesn't add up, dude."

"Oh—yeah. Well, I figured happening young people such as yourself would be my best bet at finding moondust, and so I went to a club, asked a DJ about it, and I got lucky. Then I tailed him to the apartment where you saw me. I saw you outside and figured I'd take a shot."

His eyes lit up. "Skinny kid in skinnier jeans? Dyed-black hair, green eyes, about five-foot, seven-inches?"

"Yeah, that sounds like him. ...What's his name, anyway?"

"Him? Don't worry about it. Give me your business card."

I did as he asked. He took the card and scrutinized it. Then he took out his phone and dialed a number.

"New York," he said. "The New York Globe." He gestured to me for a pen, and wrote the paper's number down. I realized he had called information,

On his next phone call, to my paper, he asked for me by name. Satisfied with the result (my voice on a voicemail recording) he hung up. He made another call, to a car service, asking for a pick-up at this address.

When he hung up he said, "We're going to your place. You're paying." He stood up, went outside, and lit a cigarette. I guess that meant I was paying for the coffee, too.

....

37. PERCIVAL

I'd given him Wally's name for two reasons: first, because Wally was a shit, and therefore a great person to use as a fall guy; and second, because I wanted to see what 'Maxwell's' response would be. As an information gathering technique, it worked brilliantly.

The bad news was that I'd been wrong: The people who showed up at my apartment had nothing to do with Wally Beaver or this reporter. So we still had a problem.

The good news was that I now had a place to hide out—the reporter's couch, ready-made—that would also advance my career.

He didn't know I'd be crashing on his couch, yet. But, that wasn't an issue at all.

We didn't talk much on the ride to his Manhattan apartment, which was surprising. I'd figured he'd throw a thousand insipid questions my way, so the silence was welcome. I used it to ponder who was trailing me.

According to what my neighbor told me, when they came to my

apartment building whoever-it-was had known I lived there and had seen my tattoo. But, they didn't have my name. So I figured I'd met them directly. But, briefly, probably on the roof of the building. Maybe they saw me there and were looking for me. But, they didn't know anything about me—where I lived in the building, who I ran with, my name, and so forth. If they knew any more information, they would have used it.

Which, when I combed my memory, lead me to the inescapable conclusion that this was all my fault.

According to my admittedly hole-filled recall, I'd only slipped up on my no-strangers rule once. I'd been drunk during a rooftop party, and some cocky coke-dealer showed up, being an ass. I'd so wanted to scramble his brains, so I let him have some moondust, and it seemed to have been one of the dumber things I'd ever done, because now, obviously, he wanted more.

And he had friends.

I needed to find out who they were, which meant finding out who knew of the guy. Someone had either invited him as a friend or had ordered some coke. We needed to know who.

Because I had to stay removed from the situation, clandestine, the obvious choice was to have Hailey and Mark, my associates, ask around. I sent Hailey a long double-text to that effect, shortly before we arrived at Lord Maxwell's apartment.

I had to admit, when I stepped out of the cab, I was impressed. It was a building with style. "I say!" I quipped to reporter-man. "Lovely building, old man."

"Yeah, yeah," he said. "Follow me."

And I did.

....

38. Hailey

Things suddenly became interesting, forcing me up off the couch. I'd been hanging out with my latest boy, a kid named Cameron—a sometime installation artist, tall, lanky redhead, who tended to be pretty good in bed.

My man Perce, on the run, just texted me that we—Mark and I—needed to figure out who hunted him. Who were we, spies? Was I Joan Bond?

"Where do you think you're going?" Cameron said.

"Um, nowhere? I think better standing up. Blood-flow."

"Did you know your synapses fire 12 percent better when you're stoned?" As he said this, he pulled out a bag of weed and dumped it on the table. He absolutely had to be bullshitting about 12 percent. But, the kid rolled the tightest, most beautiful spiffs I ever saw. Far be it from me to tell an artist not to practice art. But, he took his sweet time about it, every time.

I was cool with the wait, though, I had thinking to do.

First, I tried to remember details, if any, from the party Perce mentioned. I didn't have much to go on. There'd been quite a few affairs over at Percival's place, and they all ran together. We lived in Brooklyn—the prospect of remembering one guy at a long-ago party seemed an impossible task. Perce said his antagonist sold cocaine. But, that wasn't quite enough to go by.

As soon as I started to write off the possibility of figuring out who the guy was, however, a course of action presented itself to me. I could ask our close friends if they had ever done moondust with their coke dealers and go from there.

So embarrassing! No one likes this kind of question. Whose business is that sort of thing anyway?

Fuck you, Perce, I thought, for putting me in this position. But, Cam finished the spiff so I didn't stay annoyed for long.

After lighting and taking the first toke, Cameron looked at me, long and slow, and said, "You going to tell me what's going on?"

I weighed sharing against being secretive, and in the end, after I exhaled beautiful blue smoke, I told him the deal.

"So what, you're going to interrogate your friends? You suck."

"You suck. And it's either that or... what, let Perce down in his hour of need?"

"Isn't there another way?"

"Like what?"

"The guys chasing him don't know what you look like, right? They sure as fuck don't know what I look like, and I ain't scared of those shitheads. I'll cut their asses."

The look in his eye spoke to more than simple bravado, although maybe only a little more.

"So... what?"

"Well, your friend's scared they're at his place. Let's go check it out. If anything looks suspicious..."

"What if nothing does?"

"Then your guy's having a bad trip or something." He exhaled, blowing smoke. "Either way, you're good."

"Yeah, maybe. But, what do we do if they're there? Burn their faces into our memory? We're the types to have short-term memory issues."

"Good point. This is why I'm not Sherlock Holmes."

"I know, right?"

"We could take a cell-phone picture of them. Send it to your close friends. See if we get a hit."

"That just might work," I said, glad that we had a working plan, glad that, in this, we were a we. Luckily, my camera took high-res pictures. As long as we did it in the daytime, I could get a reasonable likeness.

39. MAXWELL

I was about to witness something incredible, something the journalism community hadn't yet broken. I would define history.

This guy behind me, this "Wally Beaver," sauntered up the stairs on the way to my apartment, as if he was bored of the whole situation. Coolness was 90 percent manufactured boredom—looking immediately tired of any situation in which one may find oneself. Sure, he'd taken moondust before. But, not like this. Not when it mattered, not when the world was watching.

I opened the front door, and let us both in. "Make yourself comfortable," I said. "I'm going to review my notes before we begin."

"Sure, guy, you got any cola?"

"Help yourself to anything in the fridge. If you touch my whiskey, then I'll kill you."

I went into the bedroom, took off my shoes and coat, grabbed my notebook and pad, and walked back out. Strictly speaking, I didn't actually need to bone up on any information. I was acting, mostly, maintaining control of the situation, keeping the all-important upper hand.

When I sat down and flipped my notebook open, staring at the notes I'd taken at Peter's chemistry lab, I thought of Justine.

Should I call?

Maybe later. I shook her out of my mind and threw myself into my work.

The main thing I needed, after watching him, was to obtain a sample—assuming he had access to a stash.

I figured I may have to pay out of pocket for it. But, I didn't foresee difficulty. It seemed like everything would be smooth sailing.

"Okay," I said, "ready when you are."

Beaver—and calling him that, in my head, made me smile, I'll admit—Beaver, beer in hand, sat on my sofa. He used his other hand to aimlessly flip through channels on my television, never staying long enough to ascertain content. "It's time" I said, and he nodded. He turned the television off and dug in his pocket.

He pulled out a rather large vial of moondust; there was a ton in there. It wouldn't be hard to get Peter a sample at all.

"I got to say, dude," said Beaver, "This ride really isn't a good spectator sport. Not much to see from the outside."

"Really."

"Yeah. If you want to know about some things, you experience them yourself. This is one of those things."

"Can I quote you?"

"Sure." He took a pinch of the powder between his right thumb and forefinger, leaned back into the couch, and held the hand over his head, and dropped the powder into his eye.

....

40. PERCIVAL

I was awoken at dawn, by the sound of the camels screaming. Nasty, ill-tempered creatures, camels. I had been closer to them on this trip than I had for any extended period in my life, and it was not an enjoyable experience.

The desert was freezing this early in the morning. One could see one's breath. Our Berber guides had been up for some time, judging by their voices and the noise, breaking camp and trying to get the uncooperative beasts to their feet. The camels' unwillingness to be used so early caused a ruckus that always awoke me.

The cold seeped into my bedroll, so I didn't look forward to letting the morning air greet my skin. But, we needed to get going. The desert waits for no one.

This was my first caravan, and it was, indeed, my caravan, so I needed to set a good example. Despite the cold and my general discomfort—not to mention the raging pain of my backside where I'd been riding a stone-hard beast of burden—I forced myself up and took a minimal drink of water from my sack. Shivering, I left the tent, facing the dawning day.

With pleasure, I noted the guards, rough looking fellows all, were also up and about, and acting as one would expect them to act, given the circumstance.

I couldn't help staring balefully at the camels while breaking down my tent. They wouldn't be quiet. Despite the ministrations of the Berbers, only a few had gotten to their feet. The rest had my Berbers cursing and tugging with full strength at their reigns, while the camels, quite literally, bellowed and spat in the poor men's faces. They had to be the most uncivilized creatures that Allah, in His infinite wisdom and mercy, had ever seen fit to create.

Not that I would ever doubt the most high. But, at moments like these, I had to wonder at His infinite plan, and my own inability to understand why certain things, like the nasty temper of animals, were necessary. If it were up to me, then I'd have them all rounded up and lashed. For there seemed to be an intelligence to their disrespect.

God grant me strength and wisdom!

I tried to spit sand out of my mouth. But, it never worked. I could only hope and trust that my cargo of carpets—the finest in Istanbul that money could buy—would make it to the market without taking any damage. We were so close.

My hand, almost unconsciously, found and tightened around the sword hilt at my waist. Strange, how the late stage of our journey increased all my apprehension. I found my eyes scanning the horizon for raiders almost all the time now, without my thought or consent—even though they most often struck in or around oases, and we'd past the last of those two days ago. In theory, we were home free, and yet, I was more anxious than ever. Allah protect us.

By the time I'd finished Morning Prayer and broken fast, it was time to go. A Berber brought me the camel I'd be riding for the day, and I shuddered as I straddled its back and, with its terribly awkward rocking motion, the animal got to its feet. Cursing its ancestry, I flicked the reins, and we were on our way. The horizon seemed clear of danger, and the sun rose fast.

And then the vertigo rushing feeling of a soul returning to a body. And I was me again. Percival, me. Today, Saturday. Here.

....

41. MAXWELL

His eyes rolled back into his head, darting as if in REM sleep. On his lips were half-formed words from another tongue. His hands twitched, drool spilled from his slackened lips. This was not a seizure. This was moondust, the latest and most dangerous designer drug that is now taking New York by storm.

That's how my article would start. It would land me in the hallowed halls of canonized journalism. I had scrawled it out on my pad by the time Beaver regained consciousness, wiping tears and rubbing his reddened eyes.

"Was it good for you?" he said, and took another sip of his beer. As if nothing interesting had happened.

I disliked the guy. It didn't help that his next move was to try to light a cigarette.

"No way," I said, and grabbed it before he lit up.

"Temper," he smirked and put his feet up on the coffee table. "So, you got questions?"

I restrained myself. I placed my digital recorder on the coffee table, and pressed record. "Describe, from your perspective, the hallucination you just had."

"It wasn't a hallucination."

"What would you call it?"

Pause. "A fully realized consciousness experience."

"And how does a 'fully realized consciousness experience' differ from a hallucination?"

"When you hallucinate, you are still yourself. When you take moondust, you're not."

"Who were you this time?"

"Can I smoke my cigarette, now?"

"No. Answer the question."

"I was a merchant taking a shipment of rugs through the desert to Marrakech."

"Describe the experience in detail."

"I'm having trouble with recall at the moment. You know what always helps? Cigarettes!"

"Smoke your goddamn cigarette."

He lit up, and I hoped his story would be worth the stench filling my apartment.

"I woke up in another man's body, with another man's thoughts. I was concerned with getting my cargo safely to the markets, nervous about bandits. Dawn had just begun. I slept until the camel screams woke me up."

"Why were the camels screaming?"

"I guess they just do that in the morning."

"What happened next?"

"I got up, left my tent, prayed, ate, and helped break camp."

"And then?"

"That was it."

His story was not worth the tobacco stink.

"Come on," I said. "There must have been more."

"No, not really."

"So you got up, prayed, and ate, while camels screamed. That's it?"

"Only the surface of it. But, yes. I told you, it's something you have to do to understand."

"I'm not taking that stuff. So why don't you try explaining a little bit better?"

A pause ensued, I could tell he struggled to capture a concept in words. He said, "I saw this television show once. An anthropologist called the meaning of life an unanswerable question. We think we want the answer when we actually crave the experience of being alive. We get, like, numb to ourselves. We grow to miss our own lives, even as we're living them.

He stared into my eyes and gave it a second go. "When you take moondust, you're someone else. When you're someone else, you experience the feeling of being alive, of being a person, more vividly than anything since when you were a child, not yet numb to life. And when you come back from moondust—now you again—it's like coming home. You end up reinventing your whole idea of what your life is. You examine your thoughts and beliefs in a whole new way. You experience living again, instead of going through the motions."

"I see," I said, my heart sinking.

This information wouldn't translate to an article at all. Not even a usable soundbite.

The obvious and unethical fallback now appealed. If the actual account of the drug was metaphysical, existential bullshit, and only a few people knew the truth of it, I could jazz it up however much I needed to. Strictly speaking, I wasn't limited by the reality of what my source told me. I could manufacture soundbites.

"So," I said, "let's talk addiction."

"Addiction? No, it's not that kind of thing."

"But, surely people are compelled to take the stuff again and again, right?"

"You could say that about anything people enjoy, that's not necessarily addiction. People go back to moondust because it's an enlightening experience. Walking in another person's shoes, you know?"

"How often do you take it?"

"I don't know, once or twice a day, depending."

"And your friends, who take it also, they take it about the same?"

"I don't know, dude. I guess so."

"Do you ever take a few days off?"

"I never really thought about it. So I guess not."

"Is it expensive to make?"

"Not at all."

"But you sell it at a pretty penny."

He grinned. "We do have our expenses."

"So what keeps your customers coming back?"

"Like I said, the experience of being alive."

"Elaborate."

Pause. "It's the wildest ride I've ever been on, it's pure genius. Nothing else in the world can give you an experience like this. If it's an experience you want to have, you go back. Simple."

"But it's different every time, right?"

"Bingo."

"So can you ever really go back?"

"If you went into the same person twice, it wouldn't be the same. So the answer's yes. Hey, what's for dinner? I'm going to be hungry soon. Being interviewed really takes it out of you."

"Tell you what. If this interview works out of me, I'll order you a pizza. You have anything to add? Something good?"

"Define good."

I took a deep breath. "When I get this article published, it's going to be read by people all across the country, the world. People who've never heard of moondust, people who have less experience, in general, with drug culture than you do. You've maybe had a moondust experience of someone like that?"

"Of course," he said.

"Okay. They're the people who're going to be reading this article, and they're the people we need to reach. Speak to them. What would you say to them? What should they know about it?"

"They should know their lives are all a dream."

More existential hogwash. But, I decided to run with it. "Elaborate, if you will."

"Surely you've heard the life-as-a-dream idea before."

"Of course. But, I want what you meant, not what I've heard before."

"Everyone is living from a narrow bandwidth. People believe that everything they believe is true, and everything they don't believe is false. Which is understandable. But, it limits them.

"Me, I've experienced feeling things I don't believe being true. You sneered when you said drug culture. Do you understand that my experience with hallucinogens is the only thing that kept me sane after moondust?"

"How so?"

A long pause. "Flexibility. Having taken moondust, I believe—I know—that everything, every possible belief or experience, is true. Even when they contradict each other. There is nothing false."

I'd never heard such sophistry in all my life. "So... moondust is some kind of super-hallucinogen, is that what you're saying?"

He sighed. "Like I said, it's not a hallucinogen at all."

"So, you say that we should know our lives are all dreams. Do you intend to wake us up?"

"What I intend doesn't matter a bit. Moondust is the truth, if you take it, you understand."

And with that, we were back where we started. I needed some

time to reassess. "I think we should take a break," I said. "Will you stick around for a while?"

To my surprise, he grinned, wolfishly. "Yeah, sure. You going to order that pizza?"

I laughed. It's funny how the people you're using think they're using you.

I went into the next room, presumably to order a pizza. But, instead, I called Justine.

She didn't answer. I left no message. If she wouldn't talk to me, then I had nothing to say.

....

42. JUSTINE

I left the confessional, the church, my faith. Lacking aim or direction, I drifted, something like a ghost, ending up in Union Square. I wandered into a theatre, I saw a movie.

A comedy.

It's an empty feeling you're left with, when you lose the things you take for granted.

Where are you, when everything you struggle to believe in is challenged—so completely—you don't know sunshine from rain?

....

43. HAILEY

My adrenaline kicked in three blocks or so away from Percival's apartment. My hands wouldn't stay still. For a minute, I felt like a little girl, putting herself in serious danger, in over her head.

I hoped take a photo of some dangerous people, with only

Cameron watching my back, because they were after Percival, one of my partners in moondust.

Luckily for me, I now had a wealth of experiences to draw on. Moondust rides. Of intrigues, war, dangerous situations: seen through eyes of victors and victims.

So, like I learned in India, I controlled my breathing. And like I learned in Africa, I emptied my mind, by focusing on the sensory input around me. The brisk fall wind on my face. My sneakers hitting the concrete, denim rubbing the skin of my legs. The rushing, layered sounds of New York: ten thousand stories happening all at once.

Unexpectedly, my fingers twitched in the pattern of a Welsh thief, whose fingers would jerk before "it was off," and he broke in someplace. Was I taking a piece of these people with me every time I came back from a moondust trip?

How could I not do so? It probably happened automatically.

Cameron stood next to me, looking stoic, cracking his knuckles. I made my thoughts stay steady. Even if the people chasing Perce were still outside his place, I had no reason for us to expect confrontation. They didn't even know who we were.

"Hey," I said, "It's going to be all right."

He smiled. "I know."

"So, did you have any specific game-plan ideas? Anything I need to know?"

"I say we walk around the block once. Look for anything out of the ordinary, like people hanging out in a parked car or something. Maybe we should go up to his floor and see if anyone's around."

"Sounds good."

I redoubled my efforts to quiet the butterflies in my stomach when we reached Percival's street. Not many people were around. We walked, casually scanning everything. A few people walked a brisk New York pace.

One person, however, stayed still. A ratty looking dude. Definitely something shifty about him, which made me think he could be our guy.

Still, I ran through other possibilities. Maybe he was waiting for someone. Maybe he sold drugs.

I said to Cam, on the sly, "Let's cross the street now and turn around."

"What's the plan?" he asked.

"We're going to sit here and watch that guy. Wait, I changed my mind about turning around. We're going to sit on this stoop like we live here, and kick it. Can I bum a cigarette?"

He got the picture without me having to draw it out for him and pulled out two Camels. I took one and sat down on the steps. We played the part of the smoking couple, hanging out on their stoop for a while. It was a little cold for it. But, it didn't matter. We sat far enough away from the guy that he couldn't see us in any detail, even if he did notice us, which he wouldn't. One of the laws of New York: our city was filled with so many stimuli, people hardly noticed anything.

We stayed for twenty minutes or so. He didn't move, he didn't make any calls—he wasn't waiting for anyone. That eliminated one option. Cameron and I discussed and decided on the direct approach to eliminate the other. We screwed up our courage and went for it.

I gave him my phone, because it had a great camera. He took it out, set the camera, and primed the flash. Then he started faking a conversation. Finally, we started walking toward our mark.

"Hey," I said to the prospective hooligan, when we reached him, "What are you selling, dude? I'm buying ludes, coke, e, and smack. The works."

"Beat it." He didn't even look at me. Good sign.

"Come on," I said. "Do we look like cops to you? Since when do they hire five-foot two-inch high white girls?"

"Scram. I ain't selling shit."

"My mistake, bruddah."

At that, the code word, bruddah, I started running, and Cameron snapped the guy's picture.

"Art project," Cam yelled over his shoulder. "Thanks for the help!"

....

44. WILLIAM

This stake-out bullshit really got on my nerves. There were some real dumb-asses in this city, I tell you. "Art project." Snap a picture and run. Fucking bohemians.

The saddest part, it was the most eventful thing that had happened since we started watching this place.

While it seemed like the thing to do after we'd lost the guy, I wasn't feeling very hopeful about our mark ever coming back. I figured he was long gone. Only a dummy would come back.

Still, a job was a job. I should have been a dentist or something.

....

45. PERCIVAL

When my phone beeped to tell me I had a text, I got the most intense déjà vu. It lasted for like ten seconds, and I seemed to know, before I picked up, that it was Hailey. Her text said, "bon appetite," which I felt like I'd read before. And the picture seemed familiar even though I'd never seen the person in it. White, tallish, lanky type of guy, darkish hair, some kind of scraggly beard. The photo itself was blurry. You couldn't see his face all that well; just well enough to identify a stranger.

Searching his picture for detail, I kept having this weird feeling I'd done it all before. The sensation didn't pass as it usually did. Instead, it lingered. I wondered why.

But that question had no answer, and so I put my mind on things that mattered. Like, what to do now? I still didn't have a clue who was messing with my life. But, just because I didn't recognize the guy in the picture, didn't mean he was unknown to my friends. Since my working theory was that I met the dude at a party on my roof, there was a good chance one of my friends might know who he was.

So I pushed some buttons until I forwarded the message to everyone on my global distribution list. Usually I used that list for notifications about batches of moondust. But, today's message read, "Have you seen this boy?" It included the picture Hailey had taken, and stressed how important it was to get back to me with intel.

Moondust tended to be a powerful incentive, and my people tended to trust me. So I figured I would hear from someone, if there was something to hear.

I put my phone back in my pocket and kicked my feet up on the arm of the couch. In this stranger's apartment, the television mutely blared a movie, Devil in a Blue Dress, I think. It was an averaged size Manhattan apartment, which is to say small and cramped, probably the ancient parlor of a long-dead Dutchman's brownstone. The walls sagged and leaned with age, never once meeting at right angles. It was a bachelor's kind of apartment, messy and sparsely decorated; but, like the man himself, it was preppy, and the few decorative touches tried to keep up appearances. Still the attempt at décor would not pass anything but the most casual inspection. A rug that seemed Persian. But, was probably made in Jersey. Some of those mass-produced retro art-deco posters featuring French words, chic drawings of cocktail beverages and tasteful silhouettes of women. A wet bar stood under one such poster, featuring whisky, vodka, and fancy little used alcohols and ingredients for martinis, bitters, and the like. The bitters collected dust. But, the bottle of Maker's Mark sparkled like new.

I found myself getting thirsty.

While my host hadn't exactly used the words, "Make yourself comfortable," I figured the invitation was out there anyway. I went to his kitchen and found a high-ball glass, grabbed some ice from the freezer, and poured myself a few fingers.

Déjà vu. It was a fascinating and strange thing. Science types said it wasn't real, just some specific pattern of random brain activity. Still, every once in a while, with a strong one, it went beyond that. At least it felt that way.

And in these troubled times, I took it as a good sign. I needed positive omens, because I was in the middle of trouble escalating quickly, now beyond my control. I supposed something like this happening was only a matter of time. We had tried to keep our operation as small as possible so we could keep the lid on everything. Assuming the small theatre we'd created could last forever—that was our folly.

If I'd learned anything from life, both mine and other people's, it was this: When the currents begin raging, you couldn't fight them. So I took a drink of whiskey and began to analyze the situation.

Here's how the ground lay: My friends and I were the only people we knew of who had the recipe to produce moondust. While there was, in theory, at least one other person who knew it— while we were on acid, someone had given us the powder and the instructions—we didn't know who that person was and whether he or she had told anyone else. Logic dictated that, if not the only outfit, we were one of a small number of people involved in making and selling moondust.

And we weren't hurting on profits by any means. Only our desire to stay small-time and focus on our artistic endeavors had kept us living humbly. This drug was a new front, and it was highly lucrative.

And so we tried to avoid attention, because any criminal, organized or otherwise, would kill for a gravy train like this. When it came to customers we stuck to people we knew and told them to keep our existence under the most severe wraps, on punishment of being dropped from our clientele. And for the most part, we selected our customers very carefully. And in this way, for a while, we were successful and invisible at the same time.

Our first mistake had been Wally Beaver. It'd been Hailey's call. They'd had a thing, and she let him ride the moon. Mark and I thought he was an idiot, and would never have included him on our list. But, by the time we'd met him, the damage was done.

But, all things considered, it seemed that damage was minimal, the reporter was the only person outside our circle who'd had contact with Wally.

The second mistake was the issue. Somehow, someone who wanted the moondust business for themselves figured out who I was and where I lived. They'd used my tattoo to describe me, which suggested they'd seen me. So that mistake was likely mine.

For the sake of covering all bases, I considered that maybe one of my client-friends had let my identity slip. It also might have been one of my friends chasing me, betraying me with some group of thugs.

But if one of my friends was directly involved somehow, the guys would know my name, and they would know Mark and Hailey, who hadn't run into any problems. The only logical assumption was that my antagonists had seen me with moondust. And because they knew only that I lived where I lived and had moondust and this tattoo, it was also logical to assume it'd been at my building that they'd seen me. Therefore, this was all my fault.

But, as the wise man said, "Where you stumble, so too is your treasure." If I hadn't messed up, then they never would have chased me out of my place. And, if they hadn't chased me out of my place, then I never would have met the reporter. The opportunity was here to turn this into a boon.

And so, using Wally Beaver's name, I was going public with moondust. Check that: I wasn't going public with it, Max was going public with moondust, and I would help him. It would let me manipulate the flow of information and be ahead of the events this would cause. Because I couldn't stop it even if I wanted to, advanced knowledge might be everything.

In the process, I learned something invaluable: Moondust was not illegal and could never be.

A flash of inspiration said, we needed to incorporate. If it couldn't be illegal, then we could use all legal business protections—for example, getting our manufacturing process patented—and business techniques to our advantage.

But that wouldn't stop underworld types from using illegal methods to get into the moondust business. This danger would increase if the article came out, and if they chased down Wally to get to me. (I made a mental note to tell the reporter not to use my real name, which he thought was Wally Beaver, so we'd be under a double-blind.)

I continued sipping my bourbon and ruminating. After ninety minutes or so, I texted Hailey and Mark to tell them no one   had responded to my text looking for a name for our enemies, and to set up a meeting tomorrow. I suggested Mark's place.

....

46. MAXWELL

Looking over what Beaver gave me, writing my article as previously envisioned seemed less than realistic. The simple story I'd imagined, hallucinogen ravages New York, would stand little scrutiny. When lesser journalists went into a moondust feeding frenzy, I would be exposed.

The true story was confusing, boundless, and hopelessly existential. Not exactly the lead on local news affiliates.

The themes were broad. There was the science of it. There was a hint at religious implications, there was a social psychology angle, and there was something else I couldn't quite name. I went through the audio and reread my notes one more time, this time with an eye for the themes, the threads, the load-bearing walls. I found some common threads in both Peter's and Beaver's statements.

Beaver, "They should know that their lives are all a dream."

Peter, "Or science should consider whether we're living in a dream-world."

Beaver, summarizing): Every time one's mind interfaces with moondust, one's mind experiences the life of a different conscious entity.

Peter (summarizing): Every time one's equipment interfaces with moondust, one's equipment measures the composition of a different chemical or element.

I made a note that I needed to make a strong theme of the ramifications on society of such an ungovernable, variable substance: a scientific revolution in a powder, and in terms of so-called right and wrong, a watershed for anyone who experienced it. Thus, any agency with a stake in morality or belief systems, such as churches or governments, would likely be threatened.

The takeaway was that the moondust phenomenon was disturbing on multiple levels. So disturbing, I realized, that if I played this right, I could write multiple nationally syndicated articles, Newsweek pieces, and appear in CNN segments as a talking head.

I needed to start churning out articles. I could probably write three articles before anyone else had one out. The trick was going to be appealing to different types of media outlets.

This was a good time for brain-lubricant, aka whiskey. When I went out to the living room, I saw a glass already on the coffee table. But, no Beaver drinking it. Instead, a mute television played to an empty room. I caught a whiff and saw him sitting outside on the fire escape, smoking. Guess he'd climbed out the window.

Whiskey in hand, I went back to my task.

Looking at my options, I decided my best was to start with two articles. One for my own paper, The New York Globe, and the other a higher-end piece, for a marque outfit such as the New Yorker, The Economist, or Newsweek.

I needed to establish the themes and basic outlines for my articles. While the outlines could change, I needed them to map what information to gather. I finished off the whiskey and set about my business.

....

47. PERCIVAL

I was beginning to think the guy wasn't going to order pizza after all, which would make me a lot less cooperative. But, eventually the doorbell rang and Maxwell, prep school wonder boy, pulled in a large half-cheese, half-pepperoni pie with a large Coke. I had to appreciate his classic taste. The pizza was typically New York, cheesy and delicious.

"Pie to your liking?" he asked.

"Sure," I said. "You can never go wrong with the half-and-half."

"Indubitably," he said. He actually said that. I don't think I've heard that word since I was a kid, watching Gilligan's Island reruns. I'd met the real-life Thurston Howell. I could only shake my head in wonder.

We ate our pizza in silence for a time. I greatly enjoyed my Coke as well, all the more because I'd poured whiskey into it when the guy went to the bathroom to wash up for dinner. Somehow, the deception made the flavor sweeter. I really didn't like Max. He was judgmental. Being an anything-goes type myself, the only prejudice I tolerated was against people who believed they peed ambrosia, and everyone else was always wrong.

"Beaver," he suddenly said.

"Excuse me?"

"Um, would you prefer Wally?"

Oh yeah. I kept forgetting I'd given him a fake name. "Whatever dude. Continue."

"Wally, we need to talk. I need to meet your friends. How can I make that happen?"

"I thought we discussed this," I said.

"We did. We're discussing it again."

"Did you ever hear that quote about insanity being expecting different results from the same old shit?"

He leaned forward, rested his elbows on his knees. He pressed his fingers into a power triangle. I didn't know people actually did that outside of 1980s movies about stock-brokers. Then, he said, "I'll level with you. I can turn this into something huge for me. But, only if I have your full cooperation. That includes letting me meet your people and letting me observe people using moondust in their natural setting."

As if we were fucking rhinos or something.

He continued, "I need to make that happen. I've heard you say you're not willing to help me. But, what I'm doing now is entering into a negotiation. Would you like to negotiate with me? You name your terms, we start talking."

Both reporter Max and I let silence linger, tense, like tectonic plates pushing together.

Then I lit up a cigarette. To me lighting it was like throwing a stack of chips onto the poker table, raising the stakes. He visibly tightened. I think I saw a neck tendon pop out.

"Did I tell you about the guys outside of my apartment?" I said.

He answered like he spoke through a clenched jaw. "No. Do I need to get my recorder?"

"Nah. Long story short, some dudes are staking me out. Not cops, someone else. I don't know who. I need a place to stay for a while—until it blows over or I can figure out who they are."

If we weren't in such a serious moment, the expression of horror he failed to hide might have made me laugh. "For how long?"

"If—and it's a big if—I take you to my people, I'd have to start our negotiations at three days on your couch. But, it won't be enough."

Silence.

I said, "Maxwell, old boy, try to understand what you're asking of me."

"What am I asking of you?"

"You're asking me for everything. I have people, friends, I work with on this, and it's been great for us because we've kept our operation low-key. If we have one rule, it is do not bring random people into each other's space and do moondust with them."

He scoffed, said, "Whoa. I'm a reporter, I don't plan on—"

"Oh. But, you will do moondust with us, if you're there with us. That's how these things work. Do you think I'm going to show up at my friends' place and say, 'Hey, this guy is going to stand around watching and taking notes while we do our thing?' Get real."

"Surely there must be another way."

I spread my hands, took a drag, and blew it out slow. "I'm all ears."

Silence.

Max said, "I can't do moondust."

"Your call. But, I can't take you with me if you don't. If you want into the inner world, then you have to pay admission. Didn't you ever read, Among the Thugs?"

Shock registered on his face; he must have figured I didn't read. "Yeah. But, Bryson didn't throw bricks through any windows."

"I'm not asking you to. The point is, he respected the rules of the people he observed. Right?"

"Listen—"

"No, you listen. You're trying to write about something you don't understand. And you're trying to leech off of me to do it. You want to meet my friends, you want to watch us do our thing, and you want to turn us into caricatures in order to make your journalistic bones and get rich. You expect me not to notice that everything I tell you, you get to twist however you like?"

I paused to glare at him.

Then I continued, "You expect me to believe I'll get fair treatment? I never bought that. But, it's one thing exposing myself. Now you want me to bring my best friends in this world in, so you can shit all over their good names? Make us out to be junkies? So I'll get to turn on the news one day and hear you telling the world that I'm dealing and using the worst drug since crack?"

Again, I paused so my words could sink in.

Then I continued, "Because that's what you're trying to do, isn't it? That'll get you a premium position as one of Rupert's principle ball washers, right? Asking me if it's addictive. Trying to get me to say stuff about how dangerous moondust is. Fuck that. You don't get it, and while you don't get it, you're going to be the one introducing it to the world. And when you do that, who's face is going to be on it? Whose name is going to be in that article?"

I took a puff of tobacco. He didn't say anything.

I could tell Max was trying to think up something, so I kept going. "What's worse is you don't even want to get it. You want to know what you are? You're not a journalist. Milton Bradley was a journalist. You're a vulture. You're not after the truth, you're after a reputation."

"Milton Burrows," he said. "Milton Bradley made board games. If you're going to insult me, get the facts straight."

It was a pretty weak attempt at a rebuttal, especially because I didn't give a damn. In fact, his correction made me laugh.

"Here are the facts. Something I've learned is—if you want the truth of something, you have to live it. Truth isn't a concept, it isn't words on a page, and it isn't a blurb in the evening post about what the experts believe. Truth is an experience lived. Moondust taught me that, and if you want to tell the world about it, you're going to know what I mean. Or, we're going to part ways, and you get to run with what you have now. So what'll it be, old boy?"

....

48. MAXWELL

It was out of the question. He sat there, smugly sneering at me, thinking he had me checkmated. If I did it—despite the fact that I would have become a thing I admittedly hated—I'd be giving in. My journalistic integrity—and my impartiality—would be shot.

So it was something to be avoided, to say the least. I also needed to refrain from slapping this jerk around like a piñata full of bearer bonds for even suggesting it. The nerve.

I started with a deep breath. And, I stalled by dealing with other problems first.

"Okay," I said. "Those are your demands. Now we'll negotiate. For example: You want to stay here because you can't go home. But, what if I take care of the people staking out your house?"

I had an idea. It was far short of brilliant. But, after the mistake happened, pressing on was the only thing.

His body language suggested he was as skeptical too. "How are you going to do that, Mandrake?"

"That's my problem. But, I think it would go a long way toward showing good faith. No?"

"I don't think showing up in an ascot bearing martinis is going to do any good. And if they go away, it only does me good if they don't come back."

"If I can deliver, I don't do moondust, and I get in with your friends. If I fail, then I shoot, or ride, or whatever you call taking the stuff. Deal?"

"If you can convince me the situation is handled, I'll ask my friends. I'm not the boss of them. If they don't want anything to do with you, then that's not my problem."

"Not good enough. You give me an introduction. We ask them together."

"Deal," he said.

"Great. It's a deal. I'll have them gone soon. We'll start with you telling me what you know about these guys and anything you suspect. Next, I'll need more moondust for study by the scientific community."

He showed me the picture his friend took and gave me what information he could about the people chasing him. Which was almost nothing. He said he couldn't remember much about when the breach of security, so to speak, happened.

This problem defined working with druggies: If, best case scenario, they were present enough to understand the world around them, then their recall sucked.

So I had more problems than solutions, and all I had to lose was my mind, health, and, if things went far enough sideways, my life. In a perfect world, I'd have come up with a better alternative than dealing with a crew of anonymous thugs. But, not here. Still, international fame and fortune trended tough to come by, so danger was par for the course. Didn't reporters in warzones deal with death every day? Mine is not a profession for the faint of heart.

After a good hour or two of heavy brainstorming, a workable idea finally came to me. Trouble was, someone would need to put himself in harm's way, and no way could I convince someone else to jump on this particular sword.

As long as they didn't see through the ruse, everything would be fine. They get what they wanted, we get what we wanted. Easy-peasy. At least, that's what I told myself.

As much as I wasn't happy about having to confront Beaver's thugs, I dreaded one task more—Justine.

The clock read 1:38 a.m. I needed sleep. So much to do tomorrow.

I brushed my teeth, washed my face, undressed, jumped in bed. As I waited to fall asleep, I tried not to think. Thinking wasn't doing any good. She was not my girlfriend now, and if there was doubt, there wouldn't be tomorrow.

Try not to think about pink elephants. Fill your brain with other things. Sublimate.

Sunday, October 1, 2006

49. PETER

Nothing had been right.

I was a chemist, my life built on the foundation of science.

This guy Max, a reporter I know, brought me a substance to analyze. A drug. But, it refused to be categorized by any means available to me.

I tried to get access to specialized equipment. But, all the people in control of or using the equipment weren't giving out favors. I was urged to "file grants."

Fuck grants. The bag of substance Max lent me burned a hole in my desk.

I just kept staring at it, and it just kept sitting there violating everything I knew to be true. And I lacked access to the tools needed to understand.

Could anything be worse for a scientist? I devoted my whole life to understanding. Now moondust sat staring at me, violating my understanding utterly.

I devoted every test I could to this stuff given the limited resources at my disposal. My findings remained consistently inconsistent. Variable weight. Variable conductive properties. It varied in everything, impossibly. Every test was like a calculator telling you one plus one equaled one or a million or seven or nineteen. But, never two.

I've heard that in lucid dreaming, you know you are asleep because words or numbers are not static, they change as you look at them. The brain-function on which reading depends is not accessible because you're asleep and in the dream-world. Moondust felt exactly like that. Was I in the dream-world then as well? A nightmare?

My watch read 10:32 a.m., Sunday morning, I sat in a coffee shop drinking a particularly bitter cup of the house brew. The coffee really stank. But the shop was close to me and cheap. I usually brought the coffee back to the office. But, it was Sunday, and besides, I couldn't stand to be in there right now. Maybe later, I would check to see if Maxwell got me a new sample.

So instead, I drank it there, splitting my time between reading and staring out the window at the city. I read a copy of The New York Globe, Sunday edition. The headline was usually New York's latest sports catastrophe and today a hockey brawl splayed across the headlines that, atypically, was bad enough the hockey players all got suspended. Inside, the paper held the usual junk-food news stories. It was just what I needed on a day like today, not to think.

As dedicated as I was to non-thought, it didn't work. The same things kept running through my head.

If all the basic meat-and-potato tests came back with impossible results, wasn't it foolish to expect more cutting edge technology to show any different? Take for example quantum sequencing. While quantum sequencing was a fancier kind of testing, I had no reason to believe, given the relationship between moondust and scientific inquiry, there would be any difference in the result. The best I had any right to expect was further verification, which scared me.

The cornerstone of my world was that scientific inquiry was the best and only way to approach any equation, question, or mystery and that cornerstone was gone. Blown to smithereens.

My phone buzzed; it was Max. "Hey there, superstar," he said, "How's my favorite scientist doing? Have you earned that Nobel, yet?"

I had a choice between laughing or taking the spoon in front of me and jabbing the handle into my eye socket. "If I can pose a counter question: What's the likelihood that the Vatican would reward a priest who proved that God did not exist?"

"Um, slim to none?"

"So we agree: I'm not likely to get the Nobel Prize any time soon. Glad to hear it."

There was a moment's silence on the other line. "Where's the sunny optimism I know and love?"

"I lost it when you ruined my fucking life."

"Okay, I'm sensing some hostility. Care to tell me what's going on?"

I sighed. "I can't tell you what's going on. That's entirely the problem. You've handed me an unsolvable riddle. The only thing that can be proven about moondust is that there can be no proof. You son of a bitch."

He cleared his throat. "Peter, I'd say I've handed you the scientific riddle of the twenty-first century. And you get a crack at it before anyone else. So you haven't solved it in a weekend. Boo-hoo. Now, are you going to suck it up, or should I terminate our working relationship?"

"Okay," I said, after a few deep breaths. "But I got to tell you, I don't think this has an answer. I think our names will live in infamy."

"Then, you have to decide, do you want it to be your name or someone else's name? It's your call. Make it now, because I have a lot to do. I need you with me."

"Yeah."

"Than tell me what you need."

I have become Yama, destroyer of science. "I need... more sample. And I need to know how it's made. Maybe that will tell me something about it."

"Sample I can do. I had my source give me some more last night. The second thing might be tough. But, I'll work on it. Keep your head up, Peter. This is where careers are made."

"Sure."

"I'll come by the lab by tomorrow afternoon, latest. In the meantime, call me if you have a breakthrough. Bye now." And then he hung up.

Science failed. But, there was still one avenue open to me.

I kept thinking back to how the guy who discovered LSD didn't know what he had until he put it on his tongue. He even submitted his experience-based journal to the reviews. Was it scientific? Absolutely not. But, perhaps there was a part of knowing that existed beyond tests and theories.

What if we had gravity wrong?

What if electromagnetism was something else entirely?

Proof vanished before my eyes...

It opened a fissure in me that just kept spreading.

A dead end, an unpardonable sin, an unanswerable question.

It started to rain.

....

50. CHESTER

Office hours had to be one of the cruelest, most searing indignities of the academic world. Which was telling because this world never wanted for indignities. Waiting for some student to come to your office any day, let alone Sunday, sniveling and angling for special treatment—better grades, a leg up on the upcoming exam or paper, extra credit to boost a limp GPA—made me wonder how dentists had the highest suicide rate of any profession.

This thought brought the echo of Betsy's latest dig into my brain: Ches, get over yourself. You're the most melodramatic jerk I ever met.

But she didn't have office hours. No surer proof existed that the educational system failed western society than spending five minutes alone with a college freshman.

Betsy was going to leave me, I just knew it. I'd never been good with women. I never had the secret decoder ring necessary to figure out what they really meant, or what to say. My only real skill with the fairer sex was the uncanny ability to recognize the slow slide into irreconcilable differences, which ended of all my relationships. The swirling vortex, my paper love-boat going down another drain. Davey Jones shouting: Release the Kraken.

I buried my head in my hands. I felt like being drunk. I wondered if any of my students would even notice if I were terribly soused while they gave me their bullshit excuses. As long as I gave them what they wanted? They'd probably think me cool for once.

The problem with being tenure-track at this particular university, however, was no matter how much I didn't actually want the job, somehow I couldn't do anything to jeopardize it. The promise of tenure: a prison without walls or guards.

God, I am a melodramatic bastard. She was right.

But she was cruel, always on her high horse—a figment of her imagination. A fucking optometrist at fucking U.S.A. Lens Makers. "Get your eye exam and new glasses in one hour or your money back!" What a joke. The daughter of closet alcoholics, to boot. What gave her the right to criticize me all the time?

It didn't matter, though. Realistically, I couldn't do better. Didn't have money. No one would ever confuse me with George Clooney. No one ever called me suave, and 95 percent of my attempts to make strangers laugh—whenever the nerve or insanity to do so caught me—ended in silence, which to call it awkward would be flattering. Time made me neither younger, thinner, nor more capable with the fairer sex.

The idea of being single again terrified me. I'd rather be Luke facing the Rancor without use of his light-saber. I'd rather be Nicolas Cage.

I was saved from this line of thought and corresponding queasy feeling by my first student visit of the day, a young man named Thad, about as intelligent as his name made him sound. In order to get that which he wanted, he carried the pretext of actually caring about chemistry and needing help to understand it. He neither cared nor had the capacity to understand, it seemed, because he asked nonsensical questions and my answers may as well have been in Mandarin.

Still, I admired his tenacity. As thin as his subterfuge, as blatantly obvious that he'd neither read the material nor cared, he didn't give up. No signals I threw at him would divert him from his chosen path. Which meant our conversation, if you could call it that, went on and on.

When I neared tears, he finally went for the jugular. "Well shoot, Professor Bradford, I still don't really get it. I just don't know how I'm going to get the assignment due tomorrow in on time. Do you think maybe I could get an extension?"

"Sure. You have an extra week. See you in class." He lacked the savvy to hide his eyes lighting up. But, it was worth it to get him out of my office. Especially since I didn't care, either.

Tragically, as soon as he happily bounced out of the door, someone else came in. I groaned inwardly, and then took a look at him, and some mild curiosity peeked. He didn't seem to be a student.

He seemed to be in his late twenties or early thirties, and he wore smart, well-fitting slacks, woolen pea coat that looked like it cost about half my salary, and Italian leather shoes. Given that your average student seemed allergic to clothing under the business-casual umbrella, and would melt in the sun if not for the requisite baseball cap, he must have been something else than another nameless collegiate widget.

"Can I help you?" I said.

"Am I to understand you are a chemistry professor?" As he asked me this, he took a seat in the chair in front of me. Something about the way he did it annoyed me, like how his body language seemed to show he assumed control of the situation. This was my office, damn it.

"Are you a student here?"

"I'm a reporter. I'm here with a unique opportunity, given your access to a lab and ability to analyze a substance." He pulled out a small bag from his pocket, the type that had a tendency to hold small quantities of Marijuana. "This powder is called moondust, and I'm doing an article on it. The first chemist I engaged to study it said it had heretofore unknown chemical properties, and I need someone to verify his findings."

"What kind of chemical properties?"

"If I told you that, it might influence your results. It suffices to say that we're anticipating its study could have major scientific repercussions and result in serious accolades for a chosen few." He tossed the stuff onto my desk. "Take a look, why don't you? The most basic tests should give you an idea of what you're dealing with. If you're not impressed, throw it away. All I need you to do in return for this scoop is, when I call, tell me what you've found."

"Just that?"

"That's it. Here's my info." He handed me a standard issue business card: it said Maxwell Smith, The New York Globe, and gave a land-line and a cell number. "Use the cell if you need to reach me. If I call you tomorrow, would Monday be too early?"

"If I agree, you should know that I'll only have time for a few basic measures. Nothing very intricate—"

"That's all we'll need, I promise. You'll be hearing from me. Believe me when I say this will be worth your while."

Oddly enough, I did believe him. In the silence he left in his wake, I considered his offer, and an urgent kind of curiosity grabbed hold of me. It wasn't forbidden, I decided, to take office hours in the lab. As long as I put a note on the door, students (at least those intelligent enough to follow simple directions) could find me. Having a task to amuse myself felt something like a stroke of luck, perhaps even a godsend; if I believed in God that was.

....

51. MAXWELL

So far so good. The office didn't question when I called in sick for Monday; no one could know what kind of story I had until I wrote it. And after reviewing my progress, I liked my ideas and my heading. The winds were with me.

My chemist's morale was the only negative development. I wasn't sure of his problem—sitting, as he did, on the opportunity of a lifetime—but whatever bee was in his proverbial bonnet, I could handle it. He was expendable as a source, and since I needed two scientists anyway to verify authenticity, it would be easy to switch out my quoted expert.

Everything so far was merely a prelude to today's major action.

I decided I would stop by Peter's office to leave him the sample he requested. Beaver gave me a decent amount, and I didn't want to keep it a second longer than necessary.

My next task was more important. I needed to talk to clergy about moondust, its religious implications, the effect on the faithful—issues like these. I had a church in mind, low-key enough for my purposes. I knew it because it was near to Justine's house. It was memorable because in our brief time together, we'd passed it a number of times, and she'd cross herself each time. When I asked, she called it a reflex.

Talking to Justine was the worst thing I needed to do. A reporter—no matter at what personal cost—investigated in order to bring the news to the people without bias, pulling no punches. A reporter had to be leather and steel. My path was set. Justine was religious and therefore committed to a position on this question. Yet, I wanted to know that she was safe.

And after that, conning a few street toughs would be easy. Self-loathing could only help me play my part.

Still. I wanted to call her one more time, to give us another chance. I took my phone out of my pocket, pulled up her number from my contacts list, and stared at her name on the screen.

I was on the train, and I must have sat, frozen, for five minutes before I put the phone back in my pocket, the number un-dialed.

....
52. WINSTON

I sat in my office. I should have been preparing my remarks for my homily for next Sunday. The church had a tradition of using the same Bible passage from Monday through the following Sunday evening. Every funeral or other ministerial act (except on a feast day) used the same text. Being ready with my studies fulfilled my priestly duties.

Instead, I reread a favorite novel, Franny and Zooey. While it held far from orthodox views, the faith in the novel lifted my spirits. The thesis of the book is this: no matter the circumstances, we should attend to all the minute details of our lives and be our best for Jesus, who is part of all of us, who is representative of the very best of humanity. Through Him, we can connect with the downtrodden, the sinners, and all those who stand in our way. This is why we turn the other cheek, and this is why we pray for our enemies—because, although they may not know it, Christ is one with them, as He is one with everyone through God, our Father, and through the Holy Spirit. Whatever else the book held, this sentiment stood out, and was the point. And for this I read it again and again.

Perhaps I could turn this rereading session into something more than a guilty pleasure. I could use its message as the backbone of my address, whether it be someone in confession or near death. Perhaps I could compose something on the idea of praying without ceasing. A powerful practice, to be sure.

I began developing my thoughts on this type of prayer—its advantages, how to update it into a modern practice given the chaotic nature of our lives in this new world, and what the attempt, in and of itself, could give a person in terms of nearness to God.

About halfway through a visitor arrived, knocking on the door. He was a youngish man, late twenties or early thirties. He had a firm, heady, confident look about him. But, his carriage made it clear that he was less than comfortable in our Lord's sacred space. A hint of a smirk played on his lips, which he attempted to hide with uneven success. Too, his tread and bearing suggested great care, as if he consciously forced himself to avoid sacrilege. I found this attitude in many outsiders to our faith, most pronounced in those whose beliefs tended toward the very sacrilege they hoped to avoid in action. But, one cannot truly hide what is in one's heart, at least not from any who have the ability to see past the skin of things.

"Hello, Father, may I speak with you a moment?"

"Yes, of course. Come in, sit down." I made my way back toward my desk as the man took a seat in the chair placed for visitors. "May I ask why you've come?"

"I'm with a newspaper," he said. "The New York Globe. I'm working on a story about a designer drug, which poses a specific threat to religious organizations and the very concept of God. I was hoping to get something like an interview from you, to hear your opinions about it, and get a sense of the church's view on such a thing."

I sighed. God was not a concept, of course. The man failed to avoid sacrilege already. "I see. Well, I'm willing to talk to you. But, for official statements, I'm afraid you've aimed a little low on the totem pole, so to speak. I'd have to check with the bishop before going on record, and surely the bishop would wish to represent the church himself."

"I see," he said. He reached into his pocket, and adjusted something in it, and then scratched his head. "Well, if we could speak anyway, that would be wonderful, Father. Would you be willing?"

"I am."

"Good, I'm grateful." He dug into a different pocket, to pull out a packet of something that looked like cocaine. It might have been something else, of course; I was far from an expert in such things. He seemed too relaxed to have brought such a substance into a church. "I'm here about this," he said. "It's called moondust. Please let me tell you something about it, and accept my apologies in advance if what I tell you makes you uncomfortable."

He paused briefly, then continued. "From what I've heard, this is a new drug. I've spoken with a number of people who have been involved with it, and I'm told it's unlike anything that we've seen in a number of really important ways. I'll start with what the scientist told me when I went to have it analyzed.

"As far as science is concerned, given our current understanding of fundamental laws of the universe, this shouldn't exist. Meaning, it violates the laws of the universe constantly. It's an impossible substance."

He paused then, seemingly for effect. But, of course, I believed less in the laws of science than I did the laws of God. If anything, then the idea that the substance would take the scientific community down a peg intrigued me.

I responded, "When man finds something impossible, it is more likely man misunderstood God's world than something happened, which could not happen. Please continue."

"Yes. Well, by that logic, we've misunderstood a lot. This stuff takes a sledgehammer to scientific theory. When it's studied, instead of having a normal chemical make-up, say CHO_4, for example, it has a different chemical make-up every time it's looked at. But, these results can't be real, of course. All that's clear is that it's no ordinary drug."

"Its religious implications are no less shocking. And they're why I'm here today. I'd like to tell you about them."

He paused, waiting, again, for permission. So I gave it to him, "Continue."

"I'm going to tell you how it was introduced to me. I think that's the best way, given the nature of your work." He took a breath, and went on. "I was with my girlfriend when a man came up to us and asked if we wanted to experience God. It became clear that he was offering us a drug, a drug unlike any other on the black market. He claimed affiliation with no religious sect or organization. If anything he aimed to prove religion wrong."

"Go on."

"I did not take this drug. However, I began to investigate it and found an emerging drug culture. All the users of moondust I spoke to confirmed the first time the drug is taken, the user experiences God. This experience has been called essentially indescribable, but containing inhuman amounts of joy and feelings of love."

He paused. I felt breathless. I remembered, suddenly, a confused woman whose confession I heard. She told me much the same thing. "It is impossible to experience God from a drug," I said. "The Bible tells us that even if it were possible, one cannot return to this world after the face of God has been revealed."

"Father, I agree with you—but, then, as I told you before, everything about this substance is impossible."

"I see," I said, feeling an uncertainty I'd not known in years.

He continued. "The real concern here is that every indication points to moondust hitting our society with the ferocity of a wild-fire during a drought. Not only is it not illegal. But, because it's impossible to chemically describe, it can never be criminalized. And, from what I can tell, the druggie element of our society, which is bigger than most people realize, is taking to this stuff like Scooby-snacks. This situation has all the ingredients for an epidemic."

Or, I thought, in the silence left in the wake of his words, a plague.

"Does that worry you, Father?"

"It is the church's holy calling to be the bridge between the Divine and the earthly, for all God's children. Does it worry me that there may be a false church, in powder form, deluding masses of innocents? At least sin-inclined youth? Over the years there have been many. My faith is unshaken; it is not my place to worry. There are always tests for us. God gives them to us so we may prove ourselves worthy of the bounty of Heaven."

"Tell me, Father, what does it mean to prove oneself worthy of Heaven? How is it done?"

"We must rise above the original sin of Adam and Eve. Jesus was born to cleanse this ancient stain through his sacrifice. But, we must follow Him, we must find redemption in his name. Those who seek God through a powder do not. They are being led astray."

"Do you think, then, Father, that moondust is of the Devil?"

I needed to choose my words carefully here, even off the record. The Devil tends to be a difficult subject, always. Was he the deification of evil or evil anthropomorphized? A subtle, but important difference, and even within the church, there were many different ideas. "Honestly, I believe that question is academic. This drug you describe is evil because it deludes those who take it. Is that not enough? If we consider the Devil the root of all evil, anything evil must have roots in the Devil. But, I believe it is enough to say that what you described is dangerous and will harm a soul in a most violent way. It is something which must be fought against, for we all indeed are our brothers' and sisters' keepers."

"And what would you suggest we all, and especially the church, should do about it? What do you think the long-term danger to society is?"

"Jesus taught us that, while we must turn the other cheek, we also must stand up to evil wherever it exists. We can do this with love and godliness, the way he did when he prevented the murder of harlots by asking anyone without sin to cast the first stone. As to what the danger is? It is difficult to say. In matters like these, we can only attend to our actions, not possibilities. This is a tenant of faith: trust in God and God's world."

"So you're not worried."

"Again, it is not for me to worry, I am to represent His will."

"How do you think the church should stand up to moondust?"

"With love, not judgment."

"What do you think will be the effect of moondust on the people who take it, regarding the afterlife? I mean, where will its users go when they die?"

I sighed. "There is redemption for all who seek it. But, for those who do not seek redemption, there are actions that can be taken that will hasten one's journey toward purgatory. It is hard for me to imagine taking this drug you described as being anything but counterproductive."

The man looked in my direction for a moment, seemingly lost in thought. And then he stood up. "Thank you, Father. It's been very good to talk to you."

"You're welcome. I will bring this before Bishop Houston. And I will tell him you wish to speak to him."

"Yes, do that," he said, and handed me his card. "Have a good day." He walked out of my office.

I thought I had been rather convincing while speaking to him, sounding very sure of myself, saying more or less the right things, and answering difficult questions with a mix of diplomacy and candor that spoke well of my station. But, in truth, I was lying when I said this phenomenon didn't worry me.

It wasn't the reporter's words that spurred my disquiet. But, the woman whom I'd seen days ago, the one who was led astray by this substance. The agitation in her voice, the anguish expressed. Something had to be done. We could not abandon good people, such as her—who for whatever reason were susceptible—to the fate that awaited on the other end of an inanimate false prophet.

On my desk lay the small baggie of powder that the reporter

showed me. I suppose he left it by accident. It seemed deceptively innocent, quietly obeying the pull of gravity. But, the greatest evils often wore a cloak of purity.

....

53. MARK

Hailey showed up first. Percival ran late as usual, even though this was his gig. But, I would never hold it against him, especially not today. People were chasing him. The winds of his life blew fiercely.

"Do you know what this is all about?" I asked Hailey.

"Oh brother. He didn't tell you, either?" She responded, with the usual meaningful, distant smile on her face. She had her gorgeous mysteries. I loved to photograph her, when she let me, which wasn't often.

I said, "Well, he mentioned something about a windfall from his current troubles. But, that was it."

"I know. That was the weird part. You know all about the picture and stuff, right?"

"Of one of the guys outside of his apartment? Yeah. I would have thought he'd be more concerned about that. Perhaps he's found some Zen."

Hailey laughed. "Hoping you're having a positive influence on him, are you?" She put her feet up on my coffee table, now. "Good luck with that. But, if you want to have a positive influence on me..."

"Of course. Would you mind rolling?"

"Never do, my man, never do," she said, and reached for my Buddha, in which I kept my Buddha. "Did I ever tell you how much I love this little statue?"

"Love it or the goodies kept inside?" I asked. But, in truth, I loved it too. It was about a foot tall, of the classical laughing variety. I felt something special in it, as if it had a life-force of its very own. Namaste, little Buddha.

"Got any tunes?" Hailey asked. So I put on the latest album by the Argonauts.

Quiet descended while she rolled. I liked to think such activities could be art, in and of themselves, deserving all the attention that could be spared. Ordinary moments such as these could be beautiful, if we got out of the way and tried not to fill them with useless prattle. Hailey tended to feel the same; at least, she often chose not to speak when silence bloomed. She held her lips partly open, her face perfect concentration, and she swayed to the music as her fingers gently danced. I framed the picture in my mind— lovely. Shame she wouldn't let me take it. I knew better than to ask.

"All done," she said. "Did you ever copy me this album, by the way?"

"I forgot." I took the newborn joint she handed me and did the ritual inspection. "Gorgeous work, as usual."

She said, "Thanks," and lit it.

We sat, mostly not speaking, just listening and smoking. In five minutes or so, Perce buzzed up to my apartment.

"'Tis I," he said, "Yon noble son." While unsure if I approved of that greeting, I buzzed him up anyway.

"Percival?" Hailey asked.

"Of course. Shame he didn't come on time." The joint was just about down to its last few puffs.

"Is what it is."

Percival opened the door. His posture reminded me of wilted basil, his clothing lacked its usual snap. Stress lines etched the skin around his eyes, which, incongruously, burned with more than their usual fire. He swiveled his head before walking in, mentally sweeping the room, as if he expected to find other than his two favorite stoner geniuses waiting on him to explain why he called us here.

Once again, I framed the photograph in my mind—another keeper. Such a shame I couldn't capture it as well.

"'Tis I, yon noble son?'" I quoted back to him.

He smiled. "I needed you to be sure it was me."

"Yes," said Hailey, "that did have a kind of you-ness."

I said, "Are you being impersonated?"

Percival flopped down on the couch next to me, with a huge exhale. "Don't know what to expect these days. For example, I might have expected my two bestest friends to wait for me." He referred to the joint.

"There's a little left," I said.

"I made the call on that," Hailey added. "My bad. But, you were pretty late. I figured you'd show in time to get more than dregs."

She handed him the roach, and he took it. "Yeah, I know," Percival said. "No one to blame, but myself, I guess. Woe is me." He toked. "It's good to see you guys."

"But not unusual?" I said.

"You have no idea the kind of stuffed-shirt I've been forced to associate with. A little cool goes a long way."

"Good thing it's here in abundance."

"Amen."

Hailey said, "So, why are we here?"

Percival blew out smoke, put the roach out, and then pulled a pack of cigarettes from his pocket. "Because some very serious developments developed, and big choices must be made."

"Is this about those guys outside your place?"

"Actually, no. Not directly. But, they play a part. Listen, and I'll tell you a story..."

And what a story it was. He proceeded to explain that yesterday, he went to Wally Beaver's apartment building, wrongly assuming the same people who waiting outside of his apartment tried to find him through Wally. At Wally's, he noticed a man outside of the place, a man who turned out to be a reporter. They started talking.

There, things got interesting. The mystery of why we couldn't measure out doses of moondust by gram finally got solved. The stuff proved to be... mystic? I'm not sure there was a word for it. It was utterly unclassifiable. Which meant it couldn't be made illegal, we could never go to jail for selling it. This was good news.

Percival also began the process, using Wally Beaver as an alias, of becoming a primary source in the reporter's article. I felt ambivalent about that, at best. Fame, after all, attracted slings and arrows of all kinds.

And the last of Perce's bombshells: The reporter wanted to meet us, and in exchange for this, would get the people after Percival off his back. And of course by extension Hailey's back, and my back, too. For a meeting, and a meeting only. Everything after that was negotiable.

Quite the developments.

....

54. HAILEY

My love affair with sweet Maria Juanita sure paid off at times like these, I'll tell you.

"Are you for real?" I asked at the end of Perce's story.

"Have I ever been fake?" he responded.

"So you're going public with this?" Mark said, disapproval dripping.

I shook my head. Our man P. should have known this wouldn't be Mark's thing. How many times had he told us that proverb about the arrogant monkey who gets shot by arrows? There was more than a little risk, he'd tell it now. I was pretty sure if I heard it one more time, my ovaries would start bleeding.

Percival feared the proverb, too. He said, "Mark, I know where you're going. Yes, the monkey would have stayed alive if it hadn't gloated. I get it. That's exactly why I gave the reporter Wally Beaver's name. If we want, then we can disappear. Stop selling moondust right now, go back to being lowly creative types. I went to the reporter in the first place 'cause I was being stalked; once he takes care of that, all we have to do is meet him once and tell him to fuck off. Then we're square, and we can get out. Is that what you want?"

Mark didn't answer right away. But, we knew what he was thinking; we thought it too. Moondust took care of every financial need. It'd put us square on easy street, to tell the truth.

Percival continued, "But, if we want to keep on, keeping on, we really can't pretend we can go back to how it used to be. We've taken the quiet approach as far as it would go, being humble little monkeys won't work anymore. It's too big. Word's getting out."

I couldn't stop the monkey parable from running through my brain. A king and his entourage go monkey hunting for some reason. The king shoots at this one monkey. But, it dodges the arrow. The monkey's all high on adrenaline, and he goes, "Oh yeah! Eat it, king! I'm the greatest monkey, ever! You can't hit me! You suck!" So the king tells his men that they will not go home until the arrogant monkey's dead. They shoot a billion arrows, and kill the monkey. The king gives a monologue about how if the monkey had just shut up, it'd still be alive. But, talking shit got it killed. So the smart monkey turned out to be pretty dumb, although remarkable in that it could talk.

"Your contention is that we can't keep this quiet," said Mark.

"Not anymore, although we did our best. I'm sure the guy who invented sliced bread had the same problem."

"Guy?" I said.

"Or gal. The thing is, the question's academic now. This is a war-room meeting. And, I'd like to state for the record, my fellow generals jumped the gun and left me dry. But, not high." He shook his head in mock frustration. "Fucking stoners. You can't trust them for shit."

"Action, not whining," said Mark. "Pick a piece and go to town."

Perce did just that, reaching first into the Buddha for his enlightened treasure.

During the moment's respite, I did some calculating. "So, it's legal forever, the cat's going to be well out of the bag, whenever—with or without us. This guy writes his article, and... people apparently want in enough to stalk Percival."

Without looking up from his task, Percival said, "It's going to be a feeding frenzy. Think about it: Phillip Morris or whoever already has a patent on marijuana cigarettes, just in case it gets legalized. What's to stop big business from getting into this?"

"They don't know how to make it," said Mark.

"Yeah. We do, and there's no way to tell how many other people do. Check that; I know from the reporter there's at least one other guy."

My worry rose. He asked the question with a gesture, and so I took the pipe from him. In my exhale, I said, "One other dude's not much cover. When it goes public, what's to stop mob-type figures or corporate strong-men from making a point to find out from whoever knows how to make it?"

"Exactly," Perce said. "We're in deep. There's no point getting out now, unless we leave the city and change our names. 'Cause when the word gets out, every psycho in every borough looking to make a fast buck's gonna be looking for us. Either of you ready to leave the city?"

A fate worse than death.

"Okay," Mark said. "So what do we do?"

This was the moment Percival urged us toward, the conversation's climax. I could feel it in the air, I read it in the look on his face. He had a plan. I admired his style.

"You can't fight a wave," he said. "But you can ride it."

That was exactly the kind of cryptic statement Mark loved: The guy ate it up, nodding. I, however, needed things to make actual sense.

"Care to be a bit more specific?"

"We go public. We throw an epic party. We give everyone exactly what they want before they know they want it."

Percival continued, giving us the outline of his plan—which we later refined. If it didn't kill us, moondust would make us.

When your back's against the wall? Swing for the fences.

Ride or die.

Rock and roll.

Etc.

....

55. JUSTINE

Although it was Sunday, I couldn't face work right now. I needed to call in sick from work, until I could convince myself whatever I'd experienced on that strange drug—moondust—wasn't real. Just a hallucination caused by some drug a bum gave me.

I left a voice message because I was not okay. My head hurt. I couldn't imagine speaking to anyone today or tomorrow.

So I sat, watching the morning light invade my floor. Newsletters I created during my tenure at Action, Now! flitted through my mind. War-zones and droughts. Starving distended bellies.

What sense could it make?

Clinging to a belief in God all this time had been terribly naïve.

Perhaps moondust simply freed me. By providing such a well rendered hallucination, it made religion's poor lies much less convincing.

Maxwell hadn't called so far today.

Max. What would I tell him? How could we be together, after what happened to us, to me?

My dad... he'd been a religious man. Christmas Mass, one of my first memories: the car-ride there. We sang carols, all three of us. Our sloppy voices and joy.

I felt hungry. I guess I hadn't eaten in a while.

So I got up and went to my typical Manhattan fridge—we all worked too much and lived a lot. We went to the farmer's market when we could. I had two eggs of indeterminate age, a half-empty carton of milk, the ends of a loaf of bread, some ageless Chinese leftovers, and kale.

I checked the cabinet for a stash I kept for food emergencies like this. The box of flapjack mix and bottle of syrup were still there.

It was strange because it was like there was a pane of glass between me and my emotions, clouding the images of my memory. I could see the kitchen of my youth, before my dad's death, where pancakes were a ritual. But, it didn't look the same.

I turned on the television while I ate. But, I couldn't manage to pay attention. After I ate, I put my unwashed plate in the sink—on top of the unwashed pan and next to the bowl—and flopped on the couch. An afternoon movie started, Meet the Hendersons; I fell asleep, like a weight pulled me down.

I woke up late afternoon, to the rain smell. Raindrops bedazzled the windowpanes. My door buzzer rang.

I tricked myself into being ready for what came next by pretending that I wondered who that could be? But, I knew exactly who was at the door.

....

56. MAXWELL

The steps up to Justine's apartment seemed to have multiplied. And yet, as much as they seemed to stretch on forever, I was up them too fast. Could I really do this? We hadn't been dating that long at all, when I thought about it. But, there had been a deep and very real bond. We'd both known it and spoken about it. I'd thought maybe she was "the one." That thought had definitely crossed my mind.

Could I really... end it this way?

But I'd been down this road before. She wasn't taking my calls.

What's the cutoff, I wondered, for one party not taking the other's calls while still being in a "relationship?" How long before it signified the end and not just a really bad fight or something? Two days? A month? I supposed it was a case by case thing.

And even if there had been some rulebook for the usual situations, didn't moondust, in fact, put us in uncharted territory? With that in the equation—well, moondust erased equations.

If she hadn't taken it, everything would be fine now.

I was so angry with her for that. How stupid do you have to be to take some fucking random drug? And it had proven very dangerous, as any idiot would have known it would.

And, yes, I had thought she might be the woman I'd eventually marry. I'd loved her compassion, her intelligence, her humor. But, talk about lack of judgment. Could I really trust anyone who'd made such a poor decision as to use that substance?

No. I could not. Fundamentally.

It was over. I knew this: I guess I just needed reaffirmation. She wasn't the one, evident by that really bad choice. Instead of dealing with it like an adult, she was punishing me for her choice by ignoring my frequent calls and texts, giving me the cold shoulder in the most severe way.

And since it was over, this was something I had to do.

It was time to go in. I couldn't hang out on her doorstep, forever. Life was going on all around me. So I opened her building's front door and pushed myself in, and in so doing, lit a powder-keg inside my chest.

....

57. JUSTINE

He walked in, without knocking, knowing I would have unlocked the door. He dressed smartly, as usual. But, tension tightened his eyes. On the kitchen table, next to where I now sat, a dollop of syrup must have fallen from my breakfast plate and lay in a puddle. I didn't want Maxwell to be here. But, he was, staring at me in a silence as the air turned into meringue.

"What," he eventually said, "No 'hello?'"

"How are you, Max?" I asked, still pretending to read the magazine I'd positioned next to the syrup.

"More to the point, how are you?"

"Surviving."

"You haven't answered my calls." He crossed the room and sat in the chair across from me. "And you won't even look at me."

I made eye contact, held it. Perhaps, I'd be lucky, and this visit wouldn't last long.

"Does this mean we're over?" he asked, into the silence. Then he said, "Say something."

What could I say? I wanted to say ten different things and each of their opposites. So I answered, "Sometimes, words aren't enough to explain."

"Bullshit," he said and stood up. He stalked his way to the window and then turned around. "That's total bullshit. But, it tells me what I need to know. You're saying we're done."

"You said that. Don't put words in my mouth."

"Yeah, and you're not saying anything. How else does that translate?"

"Well, your opinion is the only one that counts anyway."

"Bullshit. Passive aggressive bullshit."

"Why are you even here?"

"I want to understand."

"You have no interest in understanding. That's the whole problem."

"Yeah, right. I'm your problem." A jaggedness poked from his eyes.

"What do you want from me, right now?" I asked. "Can't you understand how...?" But, what could I say? Everything sounded lame, even in my own ears.

"No, you're right. I can't understand." He reached into his pocket, pulled something out, and put it on the table in front of me. "But I want you to tell me."

It was his digital recorder. I stared at it for a moment, my mind strangely blank.

"What?"

"I want you to tell me how it was. The moondust."

I blinked. My hand flew out, made a small, but painful thud as it hit the recorder, which flew through suspended time to bounce off of the wall, where a button or something flew off before it clattered to the floor.

Maxwell yelled, "Bitch!" I watched him crouch down to examine the damage, ice growing in my intestines.

"Get out," I said.

"No," he said.

"What do you mean, no?"

"You owe me."

"I owe you? Get out now. I will call the police." I walked into my bedroom, and closed the door. I lay on top of the covers and listened to nuclear silence, barely breathing until I heard the footsteps, the sound of the front door opening, and the sound of it closing.

....

58. WILLIAM

It was a clear night, and from the heavens, all the Gods shone down on our village. Poppa and Mauy had gone hunting. They brought home a deer. I helped them hang the skins—after the healer said all the prayers and thanked the animal—so we could turn the hide into things like clothing and bowstrings.

I was still at least two summers away from being a woman. Momma said so, anyway. Today, she suffered a headache and now lay in bed, not sleeping, with her hand over her eyes.

Poppa went into the hut and fixed her with a little bit of magic the medicine man taught him a long time ago.

An elder, by the big fire, studied the sky and said we had no hope of rain tomorrow, either. We lamented: It had been so dry recently everyone began to wonder whether the Gods were mad at us. But, we'd done the sacrifices and lived in accord to what the medicine man told us and what the stories said. It was difficult to understand.

We had water from the river. But, the land and the game suffered. The deer were beginning to get thin. Even the one Poppa and Mauy killed didn't have much meat on it, just enough to feed us all, mixed with the roots and fruit we women and the little ones had collected.

The roots and fruit were scarce these days, though. They were also bitter—too dry.

After I finished eating, I sat on the tree-stump near Enku's hut, and she sat on the stump next to me. She braided my hair, and

when she finished, I braided hers. We gossiped a bit about the latest
news in the village: Kei and Greia drank too much again last night
and fought late at night, causing little Yu in the next hut to scream
and cry, which woke others. I slept heavy through the whole affair,
of course, only the Gods could wake me when I sleep. But, many
were bothered by it and demanded that the elders speak to the
couple. It would either happen tonight or tomorrow, whichever the
elders decided, and you could see Kei was embarrassed. He would
often go up to the other men and make silly, obvious jokes, in order
to ingratiate himself, even though no one laughed nearly as hard as
he did. Enku and I both agreed he acted like a fool, as usual. You
could just tell all the men felt the same.

The elders said that after every meal, we had to sing and pray and
dance for rain. I was happy to do so, everyone was. But, it wasn't
quite time yet. So, for a little while, the adults sat and drank their
fermented root water while the children played. But, we were all
just waiting—even Enku, who kept gossiping about silly old Kei.

And when the elders all stood up and circled the great fire, we
knew it was time. And as we began to sing our songs, we prayed our
ancestors would hear us. We prayed for rain.

Then I was William again, crying the moondust out as usual. I
swear I could hear the buzz of the electronics all around me. And
everything glowed weird, not like starlight. I didn't like it. I didn't
like feeling as if my whole life was wrong, as if humans were better
off in forests than in cities. But, after that trip, I did. I decided to get
high and not think about it.

So I did, and then I didn't.

Later, Clyde came by, pissed off. He called from down at the
door, and I buzzed to let him in.

"Yo. You are supposed to be on watch," he said. "You were
supposed to relieve me, asshole. Our guy could be home right now
for all we know."

Not only had I forgotten, I really didn't care. Watch meant standing outside the dude's house who'd given Clyde the moondust, one by one, taking turns not seeing him come home and being incredibly bored in the process. And you did it for hours on end, because the three of us had to cover every hour. My boy Clyde, who sells cocaine and stuff, and Rob, who was more Clyde's friend than mine.

"Relax." I said. "He's going to lay low for a while, and then he's going to go home when he's sure we're gone. He's going to send somebody else first. So it's cool, we have time."

Clyde's nostrils flared. Like a dragon, I swear. "Even if you're right, what if he waits until we're gone and grabs some shit and leaves forever before we come back?"

"Then we go apartment hunting; we have his last known address."

"Bullshit. Then we never see him again. And you forgot something. I'm running out of this shit, and as of this moment, you are now cut off from moondust. We need to find this fucker, and it does not help if you're sitting here in your boxer shorts smoking weed, you degenerate."

And with that, the whole thing changed. We didn't have time to wait, running out of product like we were. Still, it was unnecessary to call me names.

And, I really didn't want to bother with the remains of that little girl all through me. And the worst part was—and I realized this was a first with moondust—I wanted to be her. I couldn't tell you why.

But anyway, Clyde had a point, and so I sighed and called him a cocksucker—"You're a cocksucker, you know that Clyde?" I said—and went into my room, to put some pants on. "And I'll tell you something else," I said, "All of Rob's bullshit has really ruined this whole thing for me. I want you to know that."

"Hey," Clyde said from the next room, muffled. "You wanted him here, too."

"You swayed me. There's a difference."

He didn't respond. I guess there wasn't any point to responding, though, and when I came out, I was almost apologetic for having made him come here. He looked beat.

"Hey," I said, suddenly meaning it, "We're going to find this sucker, don't worry. It'll happen soon, it's got to."

"Right," he said. But, kind of limply. "Get moving, I'm going home." He stood up and left. I grabbed keys, wallet, cellphone, cigarettes, knife, and a little weed, and followed him out the door.

Only carrying a knife was starting to feel kind of weird, which I didn't like at all. I'd always kept things low risk by design, so I'd never needed more. But, things were different now.

I was trapped in some sort of fucked up pact that was very risky. It could make me rich, but it felt like quicksand.

There was nothing to do, but go forward, because I'd known Clyde for years, tumbling around bad neighborhoods, living in broken houses, dreaming of life.

Because I didn't want to disconnect from moondust.

Because because, I strolled onto the subway and flew underground until I reached Williamsburg.

Fall was just beginning to turn, so it was as good weather as any for waiting outside an apartment building for some dude to get home. I picked out a fairly good spot—a shadowy loading dock, covered in graffiti, where I would be dry, and neither too noticeable nor too suspicious.

And I just sat there.

I had an iPod in my pocket, so that helped. As I sat I meshed the music that came through and the vibes of people passing by, making up lives for them or scenes from moondust trips. It was the only way to pass the time

I saw no sign of the guy Clyde described, the guy I'd seen briefly on the day we first came here and he ran down the fire escape.

What could I do, but wait? I sat there, making up lives for people, thinking about the whole history of the world. As in, I was living the history of the world or getting closer to doing so than anyone could ever expect to do.

So far, under moondust, I had seen Medieval Europe, the ancient kingdom of Mali, feudal Japan, hunter-gathers, primitive farmers, a conquistador, and the Incan empire. And the list went on and on. It was amazing. Utterly.

Everything I knew. Everything I ever took as fact was chipping away from me.

Here's how it went: Imagine at will you could be somebody else. No, not just be in their body, know their thoughts, feelings, and overall state of being. Imagine that. Now imagine seeing the world as they see it in through their eyes. But, imagine that world telling them everything they believe is true. None of the people I'd been believed the same things. But, all the things they believed were true for them.

So what was true? Was anything true? I used to know. But, I didn't anymore.

It was like a chasm opening up in me. It wasn't even cool. But, the only way to fill it was to go deeper.

Which was why I was out here, crushing my bony ass against some rough metal. This loading dock was clearly not meant to be sat on. Still, remains of meals and an old blanket rotted in the corner. Some poor bastard had slept rough here, maybe for months.

I shuddered. I knew what that felt like, too.

I spent an hour or two on that loading dock. And then, when in between songs, the sounds of the street reached me. I heard the word moondust from some girl's mouth, the way you'd hear your name across the room at a party. And I turned and saw two semi-hot hipster boot-wearing types walking past, one blond and the other brunette with feathered hair.

I walked up, and said, "Excuse me. You were talking about a drug back there. Moondust. Right?"

I turned on my mind-trick machine. Just a gaze I used, a way of commanding a situation. It made people understand. I needed it now, and the thing it required more than anything else was total commitment. See, some rube could put on all my clothes, ape my stance, and even talk the way I talked—but that guy, unless he understood the game like I did, would miss the only thing that really mattered in a con, big or small. Commitment. You had to go past one hundred percent, you had to give it everything. If you didn't just know it was going to work, if you let yourself doubt for even a second, it'd show, on your face, and you'd be fucked. The best, they were one with the con.

And so I knew this girl would answer, and I knew it with every fiber in me, and she said, "Uh... who are you?"

"I love that shit. How many times you take it?" I said, sunnily. It was time to be casually non-threatening, interested in having found a compatriot. Hell, I was damn near excited.

"Uh, I haven't yet. Why? What's it like?"

"Oh, man. Well, the first trip and the later trips are totally different, you know? You better be ready to let go of a lot of things you believed, if you want to dance this dance, though. If you like your life the way it is..." I calculated, "I'll buy that from you for twenty bucks. It's fifty if you get me in touch with your dealer. And you know, I'm not a cop. I'm just... hooked, that's all." I filled my eyes with a slightly weird twitch to convince them it was a killer drug, too much for them.

She didn't even hesitate. "Done! Fifty bucks," she said, so I pulled out a bill, and she snapped it and put it in her stocking. "I got it from this guy who called himself the messenger or some nonsense. I was in the Upper East Side and he just showed up, asking if like

I wanted to see 'the most glorious God?' Then he told me to put this in my eye and never contact him, walked away. Kinda like we're about to do!" she said, laughing. "See ya, pal."

I watched her back as the two walked away, calculating. We now had another road to take. Another name, someone to find, shake down. I took out my cell phone and started texting.

....

59. SALLY

So we were up on the Upper East Side, me and Violet, my raven-haired muse. I preferred Brooklyn, and we were hanging out with these Manhattanites, which proved to be a total drag. One was even a law student, for God's sake.

They were her friends, obviously. But, it was cool, because I got to bask in her glow. Even the way she breathed made me smile.

The food was alright, the drinks were better, and so on. Violet was in rare form, telling stories even I'd never heard before. Getting all her glorious laughs.

Well, when we were leaving, something weird happened. The two of us are standing on the street, trying to remember in which direction the subway was, and this guy walks up to us. He was wearing this dirty, ratty suit, and his eyes. They were the most intense eyes, almost insane. At first, you know, we thought he was approaching us to hit on us, and there's nothing more annoying, let me tell you. Kind of like a vegetarian being hounded by sausage hawkers.

I thought that was true and funny enough to try to use it on him. Perhaps it was the wine, too. But, I said to him before he could speak, "Hey, Willie Lowman, we don't want any cheap meat. So go away, okay?"

He frowned and looked confused, while Violet laughed her ass off.

"I am unsure what you mean by that," the man said, "But I assure you, I have no meat to sell, and for what I am giving you, I require no payment. I am the messenger. Tell me, did you ever wish you could prove the existence of most glorious God, if only to yourself?"

That stopped our giggling.

"What, dude?" Violet said. So perfectly pitched, every syllable.

"I am going to reach into my pocket," he said, with a plastered smile, "and I am going to pull out a bag of white powder for each of you."

He did and held them out, discreetly. I didn't even hesitate. I could always throw it away, after all. I took both, knowing it didn't make sense for Violet to have to reach over, too.

"That powder," he continued, "is called moondust. In order to take it, you must place a small quantity in your eyeball. You will cry it out, and then your trip to see God will end. Never attempt to contact me in any way. What I tell you is true." And with that, he turned around and walked away.

"What the hell?" I shouted after him. "Who are you? Why the hell?" But, he didn't turn back.

That definitely sobered us a bit. We barely spoke all the way to the metro station, waiting for the train, on the train. Back in Brooklyn, it seemed suddenly we could begin to make sense of it.

"So," I said, to start a conversation, "moondust, huh?"

She laughed. "I know. What do you think?"

I laughed. "You know me. Always up for something new."

She hit me on the arm, playfully. "What if it's dangerous? It could be airplane glue or something... could be heroin. You're just going to take drugs some stranger on the street gave you?"

"Honey, this is New York. What isn't dangerous?" I said. And she laughed, it was true. "Besides, that guy didn't seem like a terrorist, and he definitely wasn't your normal dealer. I'm curious."

"Yeah. But, all the same… we shouldn't take it until we know it's for real, not some kind of poison. Maybe we should Google it. And then give it to a pigeon or something to make sure the bird doesn't die."

"That's horrible!" I said. But, I was laughing, 'cause she wasn't serious about the pigeon… and because she was probably right. With no way to verify what moondust was, it might not have been the best decision.

We walked a while more, arm in arm, in silence, for maybe fifteen minutes. When we neared our building, a flock of pigeons erupted from the street, and Violet said, "To the moon, pigeons!"

I laughed as I said, "To the moondust!" Okay, it wasn't as funny as we thought it was. But, we were drunk. Sue us.

We stopped for a second to compose ourselves, and this slightly sketchy looking dude in a red sweatshirt walked up to us. I guess today was our day to be accosted by strangers?

"Excuse me," he said, scratching his chin, "I heard you mention a drug back there, moondust. You did, didn't you?"

Confirmation! Violet and I looked at each other, wide-eyed.

The guy was giving us the creepiest stare. It was like either he thought he had X-ray vision or he was practicing for a role in one of those Nyletol migraine commercials. I said, "And I know you… how?"

But he only kept talking about moondust. "I love that shit. How many times you take it?"

"Uh, haven't." I sighed, hoping he'd just get to the point or whatever. We had already started walking again; he was following us.

He just kept talking. But, all I heard was blah, blah, blah, and then, clearly, the part where he said he'd give me fifty bucks for a bag of the stuff and the name of the dude I got it from. Easiest dough I ever made. Once we got rid of him, I turned to Violet and said, "I'll give you twenty-five bucks for half of that bag," and we both started laughing, again. Sometimes, New York was a beautiful place. It was amazing how moments came together here; you could have never heard of a thing and suddenly your whole night revolved around it. Just par for the course.

So we didn't sweat it, we just hopped back to her apartment and sat down on the couch. I kissed her then, I couldn't have stopped, if I'd tried. We made out by the sweet low light of her lamp and the moon.

"So," I said, "what do you think?" I knew she'd know what I was talking about.

"I guess the stuff's for real. But, we still don't know that guy."

"Yeah… But, what do we have to lose?"

"Our lives?"

"Let's drop some in your fish tank. If Chauncey lives, we can trust it, right?"

She was shocked. "You want to use Chauncey for animal testing?"

"Why not? All he does is swim in tiny circles. He won't miss life anyway."

Violet laughed, "You bitch!"

So we dropped a bit in Chauncey's water. It didn't seem to have much effect. After a few minutes, Violet sighed.

"Okay. Are you ready?" she said.

I grinned, bit my lip, and nodded. "Don't you want to go first?" I said.

"No," she said. "You first."

And so I nodded, and she took the bag out, and I said, "You drop it in for me," and I found I had to hold my eye open, and when the powder hit my eye the sting was bitter, and that was the last thing I really felt.

60. VIOLET

When I dropped the powder in, her body went limp. I crumbled with indecision. Sally's beautiful lover face filled with cold smile. Surprised eyes shut tight behind eyelids. I knew there was surprise because I could feel it. Unknown pulses on invisible pipelines.

She was moaning like crazy. I held her head in my lap, blond diamond hair soft under my hand when I stroked her forehead. Hoping she'd be okay.

I thought about calling the police, I thought of calling an ambulance. I thought of calling anyone.

I was terrified.

Sally came back to me, crying and laughing.

And then she was scared, I could just see the change in her eyes, and she curled up and only stared at the ceiling.

"Baby," I said, "what's wrong? What's it like?"

But she wouldn't speak. She only stood up, and went to the window to look out at our view of the river and Manhattan.

Sally had always talked to me. Me and Sally shared almost everything, it was just how we were.

"Sally," I said, "Come on? What's the matter? You can tell me?"

It took her forever to speak her squeak.

"You wouldn't understand."

What was this division between us? Moondust—hammer and chisel, splitting us apart. Well, there was only one thing to do. I would cross the line as well.

I didn't even say anything to her, I just walked over to the dresser, where I'd left the bag of moondust. And as I went to open it, she nearly leapt across the couch and smacked it out of my hands.

"Don't," she said.

And I was speechless. I walked over to the bag, picked it up, walked into the bedroom, and locked the door.

Her voice followed me as I went into the room and locked the door. "Don't. Don't! Violet, DON'T!" Near hysteria.

Something was wrong with this stuff.

Something was very wrong with Sally.

And what was I to do? Love and pride told me to take it. But, then again Sally was lying against the door, and I could feel and hear her pleas, terror. My hands were shaking.

But didn't I have to know?

And didn't I owe it to myself, to us, to go where my love had gone?

I opened it up, and put the stuff in my eyeball.

It was like being inside ten thousand suns.

When I dropped moondust in my eye, it changed my life forever. Joy beyond understanding.

And what could I have done then, after I had returned? I tried to convince myself it was a hallucination. But, my heart said different.

In the end, I did the only thing I could do: I opened the door, went to Sally, and we held each other tight, not needing to speak, nor wanting to. Our tears said enough.

....

61. ROB

So I guess Will didn't show up for his stakeout shift, and now this fool texted some crazy idea about finding one dude in Manhattan and getting moondust from him. One dude. In Manhattan. He lost his fucking mind.

Will's text said, "urgent some guy named messenger giving md away in manhatt. We find him we learn how to make it--meet here asap."

I smelled bullshit. We had a plan, and we needed to stick to it.

End of story.

The ride down was the usual boring, except for some dudes who did acrobatics on one of those old lady's walker things in the middle of the train isles before asking for handouts. I was hoping they would fall over, they almost did once or twice. When they came to me for a handout, I didn't have nothing for them, of course.

By the time I got to the spot, Clyde was already there. It was retarded for us all to be here like this, way too visible. But, there wasn't much to do about it. Nothing, but, handle the situation as fast as possible.

They were already talking. But, I wasn't trying to listen. I just broke on the scene.

"Eh," I said, "What's this I hear about changing the plan?" I wasn't trying to keep any heat out of my voice, neither.

Will blinked like I smacked him. I must have scared him because he started stuttering. "What are you talking about? I found some information, and we need this man—we're running out of time..."

"What information?"

"There's another supplier of this stuff. He operates on the island."

"So?"

"So we can find him. He's on the Upper East Side."

"That's big area, fool."

"He's on the streets up there, handing the stuff out! All we got to do is—"

"He's on the streets handing it out?" My voice rose, and I let it. "What the fuck does that have to do with me, and why the fuck did you call me here when you know we look suspicious as hell now?"

"Whoa," Clyde said, "calm down—"

But I wasn't about to. "No. What the fuck is this? What kind of dumb-ass sense does it make for all of us to be standing here, when the dude knows we're looking for him? If he comes back now—"

"He's not coming back here," Will said. "Face the facts, man, the dude's gone—"

"Who are you to decide what he's doing or not doing?"—

"The only person here with common sense—"

"Oh, now I'm gonna smack the shit out of—"

"Shut up, both of you!" Clyde yelled. "You're causing a scene, idiots. So chill out, will you? Goddamn!" He sat down, his head in his hands. "Seriously," he said. "What the hell? Huh?"

It was exactly how I feared it might turn out. Exactly.

....

62. WILLIAM

Rob said, "Well, scene or no, we made a plan, and we're going to stick to it. End of story. No one gets out, that's not how this works. How it works is, Will, stick to the plan or I fucking shoot you. Which will it be?"

I couldn't believe this.

"You know what?" I said. "I agreed to be part of a crew, not someone's bitch. Do your own stake-out! Me, I'm going to go find this messenger guy."

I stood up, unsure where this standoff would take us.

....

63. CLYDE

I thought Rob was going to jump Will right there. Turns out I was wrong.

Not that it mattered. The whole thing was fucked up, and no one even cared about making it right. But, me.

Rob stared at Will a long time, not doing anything, not saying anything. Then he said, "Fine, genius. You got three days to find your dude and bring us some of this shit you all are so high on. You don't have it in three days, you got a problem. Me."

"Who made you king?" said Will.

Before responding, Rob took one step closer to him. Will tensed, to take a step back or send a knee forward. But, he stayed still.

"I did," Rob said, and turned to me. "Call me twenty minutes before my shift."

I nodded, and Rob walked away.

Once he turned the corner, Will mumbled, "Right, like I'm scared of you. Bullshit-wanna-be bruiser."

I just looked at him and shook my head.

"Man, fuck that guy," Will said. "You do what you want. I'm out of here. When I find the messenger, I'll let you know."

"Whatever," I said to his receding back.

The end result of all this was me stuck on watch again, 'cause now there were only two of us, splitting Will's shift in half on top of doing ours. This really sucked.

64. MAXWELL

From Justine's apartment, I walked to the subway in something of a daze. I felt disconnected, like the halves of my being no longer communicated: logic and emotion, heart and mind. Maybe it was better this way—cleaner—at a time when my life trended messy.

I was officially single again. I felt an ink cartridge exploded in my gut.

I didn't get one usable soundbite out of her.

It was late afternoon, almost time. I took a deep breath—once and for all expelling every thought, worry, and possible guilt over what happened with Justine; and inhaling the future. This required die-cast testicles, total focus.

Was it a good idea? Probably not. But, the great ones took great risk. And, if things did go bad, I'd be able to get away just fine. I ran track and jogged regularly. I had sneakers on for this very reason, just in case.

After I got to the station, the train took ten minutes to arrive. And every minute took longer to pass.

This seemed a worse idea the closer I came to seeing it through. I tried to focus on the simple things going on around me as I rode the train, like the woman sitting across from me who scolded her school-aged child. She said, "Never let yourself get confused, you know this? You got to know what's going on at all times." I wished it were possible to take the young mother's advice.

The little boy, dwarfed by his back-pack and tennis shoes, nodded with wide-eyed sincerity. New York was such a savage place, I couldn't blame the woman for giving her child that impossible task. Confusion, or hesitation, or general limpness of will—any of these could be deadly here.

Never let yourself get confused, you know this?

Once again, I rehearsed the plan for my upcoming deception.

First, I needed to find them. I had a picture of one suspect, I would sweep the exterior of Percival's building, looking for signs of a stake-out.

When I saw them, I would send a text, wait for backup, and, once everyone got into place, con as if my life depended on it. I fingered the last bag of moondust in my pocket, reassuring myself. I double-checked the printout of my info on Westgate, who called himself "the messenger."

Assertion: Would this plan get him killed? The moral implications of my plan, if successful, were worth considering. Rebuttal: To hell with Harold Westgate. He ran amok, ruthlessly disrupting every life he pulled into his sick sphere of influence. Any harm that came to him would be a boon to society.

In any case, I wouldn't be telling them to do him in. I'd simply be replacing him with Beaver as a target. In the grand scheme of things, whichever lowlife received whatever awaiting punishment made little difference.

I spent the rest of the ride practicing my tough-guy voice in my head. A woman came on who reminded me of Justine, and I felt like shit. But, my self-loathing was useful. Method acting. Plus, I didn't give a fuck. No one's ever as dangerous as the man who has nothing to lose, they say.

65. CLYDE

I spent the next two hours tired and mad, sitting in Williamsburg on this endless watch. I tried to appear homeless, as if I had nowhere else to go. Looking bored and depressed hadn't been too hard.

I figured it was best to let Rob cool off a bit, so I'd taken this shift without an argument. You had to manage hot-heads like him; if he went off at the wrong time, we'd be fucked. And I needed this. I needed the money and the security of a steady income. Selling coke was dangerous. I needed a better game.

This crew had become such a headache; I wondered why I ever thought safety in numbers made sense. Will kept going rouge, Rob was basically acting like a douchebag, and the way they fought, someone might get stabbed.

How could I get those two to act right? That was the million dollar question.

What happened next, I never saw coming. Maybe I should have. Some guy came up to me, dressed all proper like. He wouldn't have been out of place in a country club, and he walked straight for me, staring at me the whole time.

I was supposed to be homeless. Being homeless in New York meant being invisible. So I knew something was up.

I prepared myself, reaching in my pocket for the knife I kept. He didn't have the walk of a thug, and he certainly didn't have the clothes. But, better to be ready than be injured.

"Hey guy," he said, with flat, vaguely eastern-European accent, "Is this what you look for?"

He threw something at me. I caught it automatically—good reflexes. I didn't even want to look at it. But, when I did, I saw a small packet of powder. Holy shit.

I played it cool though. "Come on. Just 'cause I'm homeless don't mean I do heroin."

He smirked. "You are not homeless, and that is not heroin."

"So what is it?"

"You know what."

"Pretend I don't," I said.

I tried to read him—his face, his clothes, his stance, and his voice—aside from the slight accent, none of it told me anything. Not good.

"If that is how you want to play," he said and shrugged. "This is moondust. We sell it. One of our distributors lives there," he said and pointed at the building. "All of this you know."

He paused, maybe to gauge my reaction. I stayed quiet.

"I am the guy who is sent to talk to you." He pointed at the rooftop, "Up there is one of the guys watching in case I don't like how this goes. I am waving to him now." And he did. The guy on the roof waved back.

I started seriously worrying. But, I had to fake calm.

"Why should I believe you? If I even know what you're talking about, I mean."

"Understand, please. They send me to keep this quiet. Which is good luck for you, unless you are stupid." He paused, and took something out of his pocket, a phone. As he typed into the keypad, he said, "Did you know that as long as shooter is well hidden, one shot is safe? Could be car backfiring. People look up, they see nothing, and they keep walking."

He hit send and put the phone back into his pocket. Then he said, "A few seconds from now, from rooftop. Your last warning."

And, right on cue: pop.

A gunshot never sounds in real life like it does on television. In the city, the sound bounces off of building walls and mixes with all the other noises, so it barely even sounds impressive. Kind of like a firecracker.

But, if you knew what to listen for, the sound is unmistakable.

What the fuck did we step into?

....

66. WALLY

I got this dope new videogame from Games-Trader. It was sick.

In the game, aliens invaded and took over people's bodies and stuff. You had to save the world. That's what was awesome about video games. I always saved the world.

So, there I was, kicking back with a 40 and this hot-ass game when my dude Percival called. If I hadn't been so dope, I would have been surprised to hear from him, because last time I called him, he acted all mad for no reason. But, I knew he needed me. It was only a matter of time before he came back for my business. It happened really fast. I almost laughed.

So I hit the pause button on the game, accepted the call on my phone, and said, "Percival, what's up?"

"Beaver," he said. "How are you?"

"Right as rain, dude. And call me Wally."

"Right, whatever. Look. You've broken the cardinal rule of our clients. You told a stranger about us."

"But I didn't—"

"You did, dummy. You called me with the guy standing right in front of you. That means you get cut off." He paused.

I didn't speak, trying to figure out what to do.

He continued, "But, you're in luck. We thought about it, and we're willing to give you a second chance in exchange for a favor. If you don't want to do it, it's up to you. But, none of us will ever sell you moondust again. And you know you won't get it anywhere else."

Something about his voice told me he meant it. And I liked having moondust around. It put me on the cutting edge, a real cool ride. "What would I have to do?" I said. "I'm not going to bury no heads in the desert or no shit like that."

He cleared his throat. "No burying heads, Wally. I need you, right now, to get up and go to Williamsburg and stand on the roof directly across the street from my apartment building. You remember where I live, right?"

"Yeah."

"Good. When you get on the rooftop, keep a sharp eye out, and stay visible. Someone will get your attention. When he does, you will wave to him to make it clear you've seen him. He will then engage another gentleman in conversation. At some point during that conversation, he will wave to you. Wave back. Stay there until their conversation ends. When it ends, leave. Do not leave in a way that either of the men see you go. You should seem to disappear. Do that, and you'll be back on my rolodex."

"That's all? I just wave at some guys?" I said, to be sure.

"That's it. But, it's non-negotiable. Everything has to be done exactly as I told you. And you have to do it right now."

I thought about it. I hated to leave, I was right in the middle of a boss level. But, then again I did want some more moondust. "Okay. But, I'm going to come see you and get some 'dust soon. Do I get a free one?"

"No."

"Whatever. Do I call you when it's done?"

"No. I'll know. Now repeat to me what you're doing."

"I'm going to leave right now," I said, in an annoyed voice. "I'm going to go to the rooftop across the street from your building and wait for some dude to get my attention. When he does, he's going to go talk to some other guy, and when he waves to me, I wave back, and then stand there until the conversation is over. Then I go home."

"Good. Later, Beaver," he said, and hung up.

I really did hate to leave. But, it was worth it. So I put on my kicks and my jacket, grabbed my cigs and my keys, and went about business.

....

67. Maxwell

He fell for it. His worry, seeping through his poker face, told me everything I hoped.

Beaver and his cronies were done; there were no other parts still to be played, I had the stage all to myself. I smiled, took a breath, and continued, "Now that I have your attention, here is our position. Your government does not know this product exists yet, so we like this. We like quiet. But, no one works without permission, and no one messes with our guys. You must understand. To hang out here for you is bad idea." I let him sweat for half a second before continuing.

"Here is where you get lucky. We have problem, and we want outside help solving. There is guy operating in Manhattan. His name is Harold Westgate. But, calls himself messenger. He is crazy, and he's not a part of our organization. We cannot allow this.

"You remove Harold Westgate from this business, however you want. No killings, as these bring the bullshit on us. But, otherwise..." I shrugged. "In return for this, if you can learn from Westgate how to make yourself, become an affiliate."

I reached into my pocket for the slip of paper with Westgate's address and handed it to him. "You will cooperate, yes?"

He hesitated for a second. I kept the tension off of my face, to appear as if he decided his fate, not mine.

Not flinching, not even blinking, he said, "Yeah, okay."

"You make right choice." I took the phone I purchased in Union Square out of my pocket, and gave it to him. "Here is burner phone. Do not use for any purpose. We will be watching and, when time is right, we will call. Now leave."

As I walked away, I cast my gaze up, looking for Wally Beaver. I did it: I got him back into his apartment. Another hurdle crossed: he had his home back, and therefore I had my home back. Hopefully, the smell of cigarette smoke and feet would fade quickly.

But still, this hollow, empty, angry feeling. I was single again.

....

68. PERCIVAL

I was watching from a nearby rooftop. I nearly did a spit-take when they both walked away at the same time. The guy who was staking out my place walked toward the J-train and didn't come back, Max went in the other direction. I couldn't believe it. But, it really did seem as if the douche reporter had sent the hoods packing.

I must have underestimated the preppie. Of course, didn't help that he refused to tell me his plan when we spoke earlier. "You don't need to know," he'd said. "Just do what I ask. You'll even get to watch it happen."

At the time, it seemed loony tunes. All he wanted me to do was get Wally on one rooftop and put myself on another, with a firecracker in my hand. I thought he'd lost it. But, it did the trick.

I'd been able to watch both Max and Wally from the start, because I got to my rooftop before Wally reached his. When Wally got into place I texted Max Ellipsis per our agreement, a word I'd decided on in homage to Casino Royale. Then I'd stealthily stuck my head over the roof to watch things unfold.

Maxwell went up to the guy, who had picked the perfect spot to stake out my place. I couldn't see their faces well nor hear voices. Maxwell spoke for a while, then waived to Wally, who waived back. After a second, Max took out his cell, and then I got the signal text—Ellipsis—and so I set off the firecracker. That'd been all it took, really. A few moments later, Max strolled away, and the stake-out dude left right afterward.

He must have told the guy that the firecracker was a gunshot, and that Wally—perish the thought—was a thug. He must have impersonated a big fish.

Unbelievable. The idea that Ivy League fop was some kind of gangster? Who the hell was after me, the Teletubby gang?

Still, the blunt stupidity of the plan proved one thing. Max did have gumption, as much as I hated to admit it. I made a mental note: He was a goofball, but one not to be underestimated.

I could only shake my head in wonder.

I sat up on that cold-ass rooftop for two hours, checking all the angles, to make sure no one came back. They didn't. I even called reporter-man and asked him what he said. He told me the story, obviously relishing his success.

With all my Is dotted and all my Ts crossed, I finally went home. More or less just in time, too. Another few days, the moon would be full.

Monday, October 2, 2006

....

69. YVONETTE

I greeted the rising day,
Watching dawn limp into my bedroom.
Dead sun climbing the sleeping city.

I was sure I looked a mess: my eyes were red bags.
Been up all night. Again.
There was nary a drug I hadn't done.

In the last week or so, I mean.
But as I had no one to impress at the moment and wasn't
planning on hitting the town
(Not for hours anyway)

The state of my face didn't matter so much.
There was really only one thing on my mind.
Something I couldn't stop thinking about,

Not for lack of trying.
Didn't know why it seemed so important.
Didn't know why,

A cell-phone was in my hand.
It'd been so long. Really.
So many years. And

They were my parents, after all.
Maybe I wanted an apology.
Maybe I wanted to see if anything had changed,

If they could let me be.
(I'd been a round peg in their crucifix-shaped cell)
In truth, I really couldn't nail down why.

But I was pulled,
As if calling my parents were some kind of magnet,
Drawing iron in my heart.

It'd been so long.
To recap:
We'd never really gotten along.

I was the girl
Who fucked for parental revenge
Had hidden wardrobes,

And faked smiles through Sundays.
And the more freedom pulled on me,
The more I yearned to be outside, alive,
The more I was prayed over, locked in.

I was their test, they'd say,
Because I was evil.
(No, they never actually used the word evil.
But did it matter?)

I did not look back when I popped a thumb and left.
And I did not call.

It's the oldest story.
As American as secret abortions.
And now,

In the infant morning's light,
I was holding a phone. Their number was on the screen.
It was moondust. Moondust had made the difference.

And I hated that, and I hated everything about this
But there was a hole in me
And I could see it now

And nothing could fill it
And nothing would kill it
It seemed so clear

Every step would only make it bigger
Didn't know what else to do

....

70. PETER

I awoke before Father again and prepared the morning meal, and then, when he still didn't wake up, I went and fetched the water from the river. Most of the other work in the forge was for men. But, I could fetch the water. Father always needed so much, so I made four trips, filling every bucket. Before he finished, I'd fill them all over again, at least once.

When I got back, he didn't greet me. He looked strong, but tired. I looked away; I didn't want him to see me looking at him. I cleaned the floor mats.

The sun rose over the trees, the hours flew, fast as crows, away from dawn. The lord would be coming in four days.

Father seemed distant, like a fog covered him. He focused on nothing, not even the melodies of the songbirds; sitting perfectly still, eyes half-open and cloudy.

He was wearing his plainest robe, and his hair undone, his belt too loose. Father had always been so industrious, so fastidious. What did it mean when he let such important things slide? Indeed, it was worrisome.

"Papa, would you like tea?" Tea could clear away fog sometimes. But, he didn't hear me.

I wished mother were still here.

"Father?"

He looked at me. But, he didn't answer. Not for a while, anyway.

When he finally spoke, he was no less hazy. "You must never forget that you live in a beautiful world," he said. And after he said it, he walked out of the house, and down to the forge, and closed the door.

I sat in by the window, and watched the chimney. I could see the forge from there. And soon enough, the smoke rose.

I wondered if he could complete the order in time. I wondered if it would be up to his standards. I wondered if it were ever going to be possible somehow, anyhow, that I might make one myself.

And then I was back.

I, Peter Vesseguard. Me. Modern man and professional lab-monkey. Half-rate scientist and full blown fool. I was back in my body and my brain. I was me again.

I was me.

A complete and utterly experientially sound out-of-consciousness experience, which included both Omni telepathy (receipt or total perception of another's thought), tele sensation (for lack of a better word), and complete empathic transfer (receipt or total perception of other's emotion) such that one felt one had experienced a small slice of the life of another. Another world.

What was this stuff?

As if the first trip hadn't been bad enough...

I'd wanted to go back there. I couldn't help it. As much as it...

But when I took it again.... Could I ever go back there?

Or was it unrepeatable or unverifiable?

(Of course it was)

I'd been an adolescent girl...

What was this stuff?

....

71. CHESTER

The sky outside was light: it was morning already.

I remained in the lab, at the university at which I taught. In the grips of something I couldn't understand.

During an intense all-nighter, substance X (which a reporter named Max Smith gave me yesterday, during Sunday office hours) defied every test to which I subjected it. I never heard of, nor imagined, anything behaving this way, like an anthropomorphized universe laughing in my face.

After I did the usual tests, I pulled out the big guns. Under the electron microscope, which I managed to scam my way into using, I saw something utterly impossible. For the last hour or two, I alternatively sat staring, slack-jawed, into space, or re-checking to make sure I hadn't imagined it.

One always imagines the moments of scientific discovery as glorious Ah HA! kind of moments. But, all I felt was queasy.

So, in either the sanest or the most self-destructive act of my whole life, I threw the sample in the toilet and flushed. All of it.

But memory wasn't as easy to sweep under the rug.

I couldn't even leave the lab. It was like the weight of memory tied me down.

I just sat there.

The sun rose, as it tended to do.

....

72. BARRY

Marjorie slept in. Regimen, discipline were everything, the foundation of a good and godly life. I hated it when she let herself down like this. Around 6:15 a.m., I went back to the bedroom, my mug of coffee in hand, to wake her. But, I did not. Something held me back. I stood over her for a while, sipping my coffee and drinking in her face. Twenty-nine years, we'd been together. Twenty-nine long years.

She was looking tired, the lines that had overtaken her face in gentle webs had, at some point over the years, dug in deep. Now they were like dry riverbeds on the landscape of her skin, left by the time that flowed over us. And proof of our sorrows.

I decided to let her sleep.

We were aging rapidly, nearing the sunset of our lives. We didn't speak about it much. But, it was true. It was heading the list of things we no longer talking about, a list that reinforced itself. To talk about aging was very hard without mentioning the pink elephant in our room: our Vonnie.

I had some paperwork to take care of, dealership stuff. It was first on the to-do list today. So I went down to my office. But, as I sat in my chair, I noticed a plume of dust that billowed up from the seat, filling a sunbeam cutting across the room with its airborne filth. So I changed my plan and started with a little cleaning.

Nothing too serious. I didn't work very long because my bones were aching. It was becoming harder and harder to push through such things. What was joint-pain, but another small trial? When my time came, I would be worthy; the very pain of my life would guarantee the angels would embrace me with open arms. I knew this.

So, a quick vacuum of dust, a bit of furniture polish on the desk, and I sat back down with a big sigh. I reached for the forms and files from the inbox with one hand and took a sip of coffee with the other. I frowned; the coffee had gone cold. And there was this peculiar pain in my shoulder, a nagging kind of ache.

I had always pictured my old age differently: us surrounded by grandchildren and a community of the faithful. I'd never imagined I'd feel so like Job, in an endless test. But, I did, because without his child in it, a man's life is incomplete.

It was always on my mind, recently. And the brave face I put on for Margie was hollow and felt strange.

Was she alive or dead? Broken or okay? On drugs or off?

God's love, be with her. Please, Jesus, protect her. Wherever she was. Even if she was in...

The only recourse I ever had was to accept the thing I could not change by throwing myself into my work. Thinking wouldn't help, it never did. So, work on the invoices, instead.

There was nothing out of the ordinary. The dealership was doing well these days. Although oil prices were getting far too high; they had me nervous. Those damned Arabs in OPEC had us literally over a barrel, and they knew it. They were inflating the prices just because, and for now it hadn't hurt business. But, who was to say what would come in the future? What a world we lived in.

The enemies of Christ were myriad, organized, and determined. Willing to blow themselves to hell for just about nothing. What a world. But, it was going to be all right; Christ's Kingdom was going to come. And nothing could stop it, 'cause there wasn't anything in the world more powerful than Jesus. He would make everything all right, in the end. For our part, we simply had to believe in His plan and live the best we could.

Funny enough, right as I was thinking that, Carol, the church secretary, called me.

"Speak of the angels," I said, "and one appears. What can I do for you, Carol?"

She laughed her delightful laugh. Heaven, it reminded me. Of the sin we once committed. "Barry. How's Margie?"

"She's great, Carol. And Tom?"

"Oh, the same. Praise the Lord, we went to the doctor, and he got a clean bill of health again. Me and the kids are so happy, I couldn't tell you."

Tom once had cancer, going on about three years, now. And it'd been in remission for two, praise Jesus. Carol had prayed so hard for that, and she deserved it. They both did.

"That's great, Carol. You know you've been in our prayers."

"And you in ours. Listen—I'm calling to remind you of the fundraiser tonight."

"Shoot!" I said. "Is it that already?"

She chuckled. "Sure is. Isn't it amazing how quick it all goes?"

"Every year is shorter."

"Amen to that. So we can count you and Margie in? I'm looking forward to seeing you all!"

"You sure can. I'll see you there."

"Have a great day, Barry, and God bless."

"God bless," I said back, and hung up.

I was surprised at myself. I really had forgotten about the fundraiser, completely. I even pulled out my schedule to make sure I'd written in down: sure as day, it was there. So I read the schedule up to next month, to make sure I'd not forgotten anything else. But, everything else seemed in order.

Shaking my head, I went back to my paperwork. Seemed that Mike was having a great month. Which was good, I needed the young guys to step up. Everyone else was pretty much as per usual, except for Alex, who was somewhat below par.

Drink would do that to a man. But, I couldn't convince him to change his ways. Ever since Paula left, he was that way. And with those girls to look after. It was a darn shame.

I made a note to have another talk with him, to pray with him a little bit. Hopefully, I could be the lighthouse that got his ship righted. A vehicle for our Lord Jesus, that He might save yet another soul. Or, in this case, re-save. Lord knows the man needed help.

Around eight o'clock, I got to a good place to stop and have some breakfast. Marjorie had finally seen fit to get herself up, I could tell, because she was in the kitchen, watching the news over a cup of coffee, eating some oatmeal.

"Morning, sleepyhead," I said, and she responded with a thin smile.

"Did you remember the fundraiser was tonight?" I asked.

"Shoot. You know, I forgot."

"Me, too. Dangerous for us to be forgetting things like that."

"Did we say we were bringing anything?"

"Just our checkbook. It's going to be Casino Night."

"Oh, you know I never liked gambling," she said, frowning. I smiled.

"Three-hundred-sixty-four days a year, it's a heck of a sin. But, it brings in so much money for missions, we shouldn't complain at all."

Our church supported missionaries bringing the word of God to communities the whole world over. Sometimes, in hostile nations, the missionaries risked life and limb to spread the word of Jesus.

"Are you going in today?" Margie asked. She didn't like me going in early on Mondays, we both knew. But, Fridays and Saturdays were big days. I hardly could stay away on Monday to process sales and new car orders. But, I did try to spend only a half-day on this paperwork, and every now and again, I took the whole day off. Lawns needed mowing, stuff like that.

"Uh-huh."

We spent the rest of the meal watching the news and occasionally commenting on the stories. Most of them were about Nancy Pelosi and Maxine Waters, and their attack on President Bush. You had to wonder about people like that. Some other stuff was going on, too. Young Hollywood girls were running into the Devil's arms just as fast as they could go. Other folk were getting married, still others were getting divorces. Wall Street wasn't looking so good. But, the housing market was still strong enough.

After we'd both finished eating, and after Margie put the dishes away, I stayed in the kitchen to read the paper, and she went upstairs to take a shower. In the front page section there wasn't too much going on that hadn't been on television, so I went right to the sports section. And then the phone rang.

"Barry Miller," I said by way of greeting.

A breathy, soft, wavering voice came through on the other side. "Happy birthday, Daddy," it said.

It froze me. It went right through me, recalling memories and my deepest hopes. "Vonnie?"

Our Yvonette. Her voice was different: It was older, and heavier, and lacking the anger that had so horrified us, a seemingly bottomless rage that we hadn't managed to free her from.

"It's me," she said.

"It's not my birthday, girl. It's not anybody's birthday, today."

"Oh," she said. "My mistake."

"How are you? Are you okay? Is anything wrong? Are you…"

There was a pause, and I held breath: But, she said, "I'm okay. I—I'm fine."

"Praise Jesus," I said, fighting back the emotion that had threatened to overtake me. "God is truly good."

"How's Momma? How are you?"

"She misses you something fierce," I said, and the emotion overtook me. I wiped my face. "Ain't been right, since you left."

On the other end, there was only silence.

"Matter of fact, your Momma just went upstairs to take a shower. But, she's gonna want to talk to you, Baby. Will you hold on? Will you stay for just a minute and talk to your Momma?"

"Sure, Daddy. Sure."

So I put the receiver down on the counter, and went up the stairs, about as fast as I could go.

My wife was in her underpants, drying her hair, when I burst into the bedroom, short of breath. She looked over at me and her face was in alarm, seeing my excitement.

"Barry, what's wrong?"

"It's the phone," I said. "Vonnie is on the phone."

"Vonnie?" she said, in the same sort of voice as her daughter.

"It's her, Baby. It's our Vonnie," I said.

Margie stared at me for a quick minute, in shock I guess, and then she went over to the phone. So, for the first time in far too many years, my wife and daughter spoke. Margie spent the whole conversation crying into the handset; her relief and joy were messy.

"When are you coming home?" she kept saying. "When are you coming home?"

Me? I went back into the kitchen and sat down, staring off into the backyard as the lady on television kept right on reporting the same stories we'd listened to earlier.

I thought about picking up the phone and getting back into the conversation, and I did, eventually. But, I took a while before I did it.

They needed time to talk, and I needed time to get myself in check, and to thank God, for bringing our daughter back to us.

I supposed our trial was finally, at long last, over.

....

73. CLYDE

I didn't sleep well.

Once I found out the stake out was off, I went straight home. I'd called Rob, and, as much as possible on the train, told him what happened. "We need to meet tomorrow," he said. "Figure this out." I agreed, but didn't look forward to it at all.

This whole thing seemed doomed, problems on top of problems. In addition to the pissing contest Will and Rob were in, now we'd been chased off by some mob outfit, maybe the Yugoslavians or Ukrainians.

With all that on my mind, when I slinked home there was really nothing to do—but, roll one up, blaze it, and then try to sleep.

Only my thoughts didn't cooperate; they refused to sit down. I stared at the ceiling in the dark for hours, wondering what I should do.

Should we continue? Did we want to stay in this game, which had gotten so much more complex?

I couldn't speak for Rob. But, I knew Will had the same idea as I did, that governments and gangs were basically the same thing. Taxes weren't no different from protection rackets. Pay up or something bad might happen to you. It was all fucked up. No matter which way you went, law-abiding citizen or mafia bully-boy, you were some rich dude's pawn.

That's why I got into this business in the first place—to live by my wits, on my own terms.

But things change. When they told us to "take the messenger out of the equation," they meant it. Right now, we worked for them.

The good news was that what we did after we succeeded was probably up to us—'s long as we either paid them dues or did it far away from here.

I passed the night with thoughts like these, occasionally trying to force them to stop so I could sleep. But, they never did. And now, in morning's gray light, I had no great ideas to show for the long night, only exhaustion.

Worst part was, any minute now, Rob would come banging down my door, demanding the whole story, pushing me to move forward in whatever way his tunnel-vision brain mapped the situation.

I smiled at my own thoughts. "Mapped the situation." Moondust had changed me.

I understood now that people chose the view of a problem that most attracted them and called it truth. But, understanding that was dangerous, I had to live in this fucked up world, and a man needed to be able to take a stand without hesitation. Obviously, I was having trouble doing that.

I wondered how Rob avoided this kind of thing. Probably because he'd not done as much moondust as I.

I couldn't keep thinking such thoughts. So I rolled a blunt as big as I could. By the time I finished smoking, I couldn't think of anything. Sat on my couch and got completely absorbed in television. At some point, I fell asleep.

Before long, I got woken up by someone ringing my door buzzer like a madman. I rolled off the sofa where I fell asleep and stumbled, zombie-like, over to the door.

"Who is it?" I said, pushing the button.

"Rob, yo. Let me up."

I hit the buzzer, unlocked the door, and started rolling up another one. I was going through my weed fast. But, I needed to be able to calm this fool down. I heard fury in his voice just then.

He burst into the room, throwing the door wide. I guess it was some sort of display. Showing me he was a big man.

"What's up, Rob?" I said, sleep all in my voice.

"So you agree with Will, now?"

"I'm good, how are you?"

"I don't give a shit how you are. You're giving up."

"Yo. Did you listen to what I said last night?" I said.

"Yeah, you said you were blowing the stake-out, and that's all I needed to know. To be honest, I feel like shooting your ass."

"To be honest I think you're a dumb ass, and I'm regretting bringing you in on this," I responded, to his surprise. I guess he figured I had no spine. "You should have listened, dude. We got mushed."

"What?" he said. "By who?"

"By the mob. Let me finish this blunt, and I'll tell you about it. Again."

It killed him that I made him wait. I played it cool, and we both tried not to make it clear on our faces or in our body language that we were in a power struggle.

When I finished drying the blunt, I gave it to him to light up.

"Alright," I said, as he inhaled. "Listen up this time." And I told him the story of the guy who appeared, some well-dressed European with dead eyes and enforcers on the rooftops. I told him about the messenger, and the address we were given.

"So let me ask you something," he said. "How do you know this guy was for real?"

"He had dudes on the roof, man. With guns."

"Did you see the guns?"

"I heard them, alright? I know what gunshot sounds like."

"But you don't even know which mob it is."

"They didn't tell me. Why the fuck would they?"

"So it might not even be a mob."

"That's real easy for you to say, sitting here, smoking my weed. You weren't there. You took your ass home, remember? It's easy for you to sit here and criticize from the sidelines. You think I didn't question the guy? Fuck you. If you don't believe me, take your dumb ass over there and get shot.

He stared at me, not saying anything. So I continued. "There's a better way. Will already told us there's a guy operating in Manhattan. Now we got his address. He doesn't know we're coming, and no one's watching his back."

"You don't know that."

"But I do know our Williamsburg guy has people. We got better odds if we switch it up."

He was quiet again.

"You know I'm right," I said. "You know it."

"I don't like it."

"Then go back to Williamsburg and get your ass shot. They aren't fucking around, Rob. We have a choice here. Make the right one."

I handed him the blunt, and he puffed in, then exhaled, saying,

"Okay, let's say we find the dude. Then what? We'd be owned, for the rest of our lives."

"I say we skip town. We go where no one's heard of this, set up shop, and live like kings."

"Until we run into the mob there?"

"That's part of this business, Rob. Ain't no point arguing about what is."

"Which city?" Rob said.

"I'd go somewhere on the west coast. Seattle or Portland. Maybe San Fran."

"San Fran's too expensive."

"Or, shit, we go our separate ways, all go into business for ourselves. But, we're getting ahead of ourselves. We need to talk to Will before we make any big decisions."

Rob made a face.

"He was right, Rob. Don't matter if he just got lucky, don't matter what his reasons were. He was right."

"So what?" Rob said, after another pause. "We go hash it out with him, then go to this dude's apartment and get the secret formula?"

"Yeah."

That was that. We finished the blunt, I called Will and told him we were coming by. Then, we were off.

....

74. HAILEY

I think it surprised us all that Perce's reporter guy broke the stake-out. The three of us moondust dealers, Percival and Mark and I, would be in business at least another day, which was definitely a good thing. Momma had bills to pay.

Still, we couldn't go back to the way things were. It was nerve-wracking, but exciting too. The adrenaline life.

I'd always lived this way. My parents wanted me to stay in suburbia, find a nice husband, and raise the next generation of suburban assholes. But, I never had any interest in that. So I stayed up late, shoving Iggy Pop into my virgin ears with an old black-and-yellow Walkman sport, and drawing under my covers with a flashlight. Later, I ran from cops to spray my tag on New Jersey's walls. Eventually I graduated to oil paints. I did all that because I loved art, because I was alive, and because I wanted to live in the marrow of life.

Today's adventure: Mark, Percival, and I would meet a man named Maxwell, because he freed Perce from being tailed and was key to our plans. His article would bring the spotlight, turning our world into a stage. Ironic how we now sought the very thing we worked so hard to avoid before: moondust fame. Life chasing the marrow was subject to change.

We set a brunch meeting, at a spot called Dumont on Metropolitan. I arrived first, about ten minutes early, and ordered a mimosa. And then another, because the first one became mysteriously empty long before my whistle got wetted.

The hostess sat me in a lovely spot to sip and people-watch, an alcove sort of halfway between the main dining room and the back deck. It served our purposes beautifully, there were only two tables here, and fewer people could overhear us. The painted auburn walls were close and the ceiling low. The brightest light came from the glass door leading outside to their lovely deck, which I preferred in the summertime. The people-watching was nice because my seat faced the bustling hallway. To my right the kitchen door constantly banged to admit hustling wait staff, heading either to the deck or the main dining-room on my right. And brunch-goers went back and forth to the restroom, to pee or adjust makeup, as the servers rushed meals to tables.

This place made the best eggs benedict. Gorgeous coffee, too.

Spurred by the thought, I took a second to order some java. While I already sipped a mimosa, I felt my constitution could handle the combo. They say mixing narcotics always creates a high greater than the sum of the parts. I was a believer.

I was stirring my newly arrived coffee, when Mark, the first of my brunch-mates, arrived.

"How now, brown Dao?" I said.

"Is that a racist anti-Asia joke?"

"You mean the word brown? You people are damned touchy."

"Oh, you're so funny."

"My people are known for our humor."

"Who, the Vikings? I know them for raping, pillaging, and writing horribly depressing mythology."

"Who's racist now, anti-Nordite?"

"They also liked to bury shark meat in the winter and then dig it up and eat it in spring. I ate some on moondust. Grossest thing I've ever put in my mouth."

I chuckled. "Anyway. You know how I'm half-Jewish? I was talking about the Jews when I mentioned my awesome sense of humor."

"Not that I care. But, I had no idea."

"My Father's side," I said, before taking another sip. He died when I was young, too young to remember. Mother said his immigrant parents never forgave him for marrying out of the faith, so I didn't have much connection to my Jewish side, sadly.

"Ah," said Mark.

"Have anything nasty to say about the Jews?"

"Never, of course." He flagged down our scurrying waitress and ordered coffee himself, with Beignets. The waitress wasn't the same who'd brought my beverages. This new woman was gorgeous, one of those chicks with long flowery hair. Not that Mark would care. But, I knew Percival well enough to understand how he'd appreciate her existence.

"So," said Mark, "how late do you think our guests of honor will be?"

"With Percival involved? We'll be lucky if we leave before the dinner rush."

Ultimately, Perce proved me wrong. He arrived before the Beignets came out, with his reporter in tow. I took my first gander at Maxwell, an important part of my life even though I never met him before. My impression: He could be an extra from an Ivy League college flick. Rugby player number three or something. Blond. But, not too blond, decent looking. But, not quite handsome, green eyes on the small side. Square-ish jaw, a little bit of a double-chin, broad shouldered, wider hips than the norm for his body type. He wouldn't stand out in a crowd, not here in skin-deep city. But, he wouldn't get kicked out of most beds, either.

His clothing came either from the more conservative collections of Abercrombie or the cutting-edge at Banana Republic. Nice shoes, though. Good leather, well made, stylish.

He looked at us, and our eyes caught. There was a kind of shadow in his eyes, something slight, but noticeable.

"Mark. Hailey. How's the coffee?" Perce said.

"Immaculate as usual," said Mark, whose eyes fixed on the reporter. "Who's your friend?"

"You know who," Percival said. They both grabbed chairs. "Guys, this is Maxwell, reporter at The New York Globe and yesterday's hero. Max, this is Hailey and Mark, my associates, whom you've been so eager to meet."

Max looked at me, too deeply, as he said, "My pleasure."

Oh brother.

75. Maxwell

Now, this I wasn't expecting.

She was hipster as hell. Pale blue tips on her hair, black bracelets, dark eyeliner, and skinny jeans. Not at all my type—a druggie, to boot—but she had that thing. It was her eyes, I suppose. Her tits were pretty nice too.

It unbalanced me, being attracted again. The dirt on Max-and-Justine's grave hadn't even had a chance to settle. But, the old libido was a Minotaur in a maze, demanding steady diet.

And why shouldn't I go for it? The best ointment for a break up was a fling.

"What's good here?" I said, in order to break the silence.

"Everything, dude. The eggs with hollandaise are my favorite, any type. Get a mimosa if you can loosen up enough to drink before sundown."

The other guy, Mark, said, "Try a Beignet. They're amazing."

They chatted a bit while I glanced at the menu. I decided to take Beaver's advice, and ordered Eggs Florentine. Then it was time to handle the business of the day. Showtime, in other words.

"Well," I said, grabbing the stage, "It's nice to finally meet the two of you. I've heard a lot about you, from our friend Wally here."

There was a loaded pause. "From whom?" the girl, Hailey, said.

"From... Wally. Your friend." I said, looking at Wally. Their reaction confused me.

Beaver took a deep breath. "There's something I should probably mention," he said. I raised my eyebrows, and he continued. "When we met, I wasn't sure of you, at all. If you were who you said you were, or, for that matter, if I wanted to be involved in your article. To keep my options open I gave you another dude's name. Wally Beaver is the DJ you met at the bar that night, who called me right in front of you—the one you were tailing when we met."

"Clever," I said after a second.

"My name is Percival."

"Were your parents renaissance-fair clowns?"

Wally, or Percival, turned to his friends. "You can see what a winning character this kid is, can't you?" he said. The other two stared at me with counterculture glowers. I guess making fun of their silly names was out of order.

"Okay. Well, we're on to something big—"

Hailey interrupted, "We're on to something big and have been for a while now. You just found out about it and are hoping to hop our coat-tails. Not the same thing at all."

"Beauty and brains to match," I said, and unfortunately, she rolled her eyes. I pushed on. "Well, that being said, I have a proposal for you. I need—"

"We know what you're doing, and we know what you want," said Mark.

"Okay. Well, if you know everything, and you're all determined not to let me finish a sentence, why don't you just tell me why we're here?"

"My pleasure," the one named Mark said. "We're going to throw a party in a few days. It's going to be a moondust party. You'll see people doing moondust. You'll get to interview whoever you want. Your article will not only have the information you need, but an actual event to link this phenomenon to. Something centralized, tangible, and real.

"In return, you're going to include our names as the organizers, and the name and location of the event in your article. That's the deal," he said.

A sweet one, too. But, I had to play it cool. "Okay. What's in it for you?" I said, even though I could guess.

"Why do you care?" asked Hailey.

"Because I do," I said.

"You're our free advertising," said Percival.

"I'll do it. Tell me where and when."

"We're still working on that. I'll text you when it's set in stone."

"Well," I said, "That takes care of most of my needs. But, not all of them."

"Oh, no?" said Hailey.

"You have no idea," I said. "I want to know how you make the stuff." Beaver and Mark's expressions were incredulous, Hailey's more guarded. I pushed on before their reactions solidified. "It's for the scientific study of moondust. As I told Bea—I mean, Percival here—the substance you have is going to cause quite the stir in the scientific community. Knowing how it is made would go a long way in their research of its various principles and properties."

They laughed at me, all of them. It wasn't forced laughter, more like I actually said something funny.

Mark said, "You're going to have to trust me when I tell you that won't help them one bit."

"But," said Hailey, "we'll talk about it and get back to you." The other two looked at her, surprised. "We will," she said. "We'll discuss it, if we can work out a win-win, you'll get the information you want."

"Is there anything I can do to bring you closer to yes?" I said, looking at her. Her eyes narrowed.

Percival answered. "If we need sweater-vests or a smart pair of loafers, you'll be the first to know. Scout's honor."

Mark snorted. I could only sigh before continuing. On to the last thing on my agenda. I said, "Well. That concludes the important business of this meal. But, seeing as we still have a lot of time to kill, what do you guys say we talk a little bit, really generally, about moondust?"

Percival rolled his eyes.

"Like, what do you want to know?" the pretty stoner girl said.

"Like, everything," I said. "I want to know everything about your life."

"Hell, no," she said.

"I'll settle for how moondust has affected it. What's changed? What you've learned. If you think you can stop. That sort of thing."

At this point, I reached into my pocket and pulled out my trusty digital recorder. I put it center table.

"What's that?" asked Mark.

"A recorder," I responded.

"No. No tape."

"It doesn't use tape, it's digital."

"Get it off the table, smartass," Hailey said.

"Why? What are you afraid of?"

"Nothing, and because we said so."

We all sat staring at each other for a second, in a minor battle of wills. They, like spoiled brats, didn't give an inch. I sighed again; I pretty much had what I needed anyway. But, if they weren't going to talk, I didn't see a point wasting my time here in Hipster Ville.

I grabbed the recorder and put it back in my pocket. Then I stood up, grabbed my wallet, and pulled out a ten and a five. "Guys, if you don't want to talk, I'm going to get going. Here's fifteen bucks for my food. Call me when you have the info for me."

On that note, I left. In any relationship, one needed to recognize the moment to step away from the table. The balance of power had to be maintained.

....

76. NAOMI

"Yo! I need table eight. Like now," I said. Fernando, on the line, waved me away, like I was a nuisance. Which from his perspective I probably was.

But there was never any time for arguing, so I grabbed the appetizers up for six and scurried my little behind out the door. Stopped by the bar for an espresso for the creepy loner at four, grabbed a check, took an order, and then it was back to the kitchen again. But, not before being flagged down by table twelve, the annoying table—not for anything the foursome there was doing, they were fine. It was just the location. Tables twelve and thirteen were in a section of the restaurant all by themselves. Made it really hard to manage if you were busy and you basically had to wait on two different sections of the restaurant, as I did this afternoon.

"How are you guys doing?" I said, hoping they would be fast. And noticed that there were only three of them now. I figured number four had gone to the restroom.

"We had a situation come up," said one, the guy with the green army-style hat. He was giving me the eye. Wasn't too bad looking. But, I wasn't a fan of the neck tattoo. "Our associate had an emergency," he said. "He had to bounce. I don't know how cooked our food is. But, if you can cancel his, go for it. Or, if you can't, eat it for lunch or something. He gave us money for your trouble, so the money's yours anyway. Either as part of the bill or part of the tip."

"So…" I thought for a second—"He had the Florentine, right? You're saying you don't want it. But, will—what?—pay for it anyway."

He flashed me a smile, then. Impish, you could call it, on the winning side, too. "Call it a token of appreciation." I looked over to the woman at the table. She had a twinkle in her eye and was sipping her mimosa, studiously avoiding watching this exchange too closely. He continued, "People don't appreciate how hard this job is. But, I do. I want to take care of you like you're taking care of us. Do whatever you need to with the food, the money's yours anyway. If that means we're going to over-tip?" he shrugged. "Truth be told, I'm not sure there's any such thing. Definitely not for you. I think you're worth it."

Now both the other two people at their table had a little smile on their faces. I had cracked one too. But, I had far too much to do to really entertain flirting right now. "Right, well, thank you," I said. "I'll bring your food out real soon."

"Great," he said, smiling that smile again. "Thanks."

As I started power-walking my way back to the kitchen, hoping to grab the food for table eight, I heard their conversation start-up again.

"So," said Neck-Tattoo, "Back to business. Hailey? You really think we should tell the suit our most prized secret?"

That was the thing about waiting tables. You could catch snippets of what might be the most fascinating conversations sometimes. But, you were always on the periphery, barely brushing up against other people's lives in these small and intimate moments. So close, involved on a certain level, yet so far away.

Their conversation continued: I only heard it in the sparest, most disparate fragments. The other guy was saying when I dropped off the food, "It's your idea. Why should we jump on this sword for you? It's only fair, Hailey," and the woman protested, sputtering about flirtation and their lack of chivalry. One of the boys said, as I was zipping away, "Are you asking for special treatment?"

Later it seemed like they discussed other things entirely, and the thread of the conversation was far out of my reach. It was that way with everyone in a restaurant; worlds that touched, but never enmesh. Even the flirting happens through invisible panes of glass, like prison visits or red-light Amsterdam seductions.

....

77. HAILEY

Once the brunch finished, and I was on my way home, riding the subway, I decided to get it over with and call the suit. I could do so thanks to my lovely cell phone booster thingy, which allowed me to get a signal from anywhere, even underground.

I dialed the number Perce gave me and punched send. He picked up before too long.

"Maxwell Smith."

"This is Hailey, from brunch. I have your answer."

"My answer?"

"You asked for two things. The first was how we make it. The second was the date of our thing. Right now, we're shooting for having it next Sunday, October 8. But, it's not set in stone. As to the other thing... we won't tell you how we make moondust, we'll show you, instead. Is that cool with you?"

"It's ideal. And, not that I mind at all. But, why am I hearing this from you and not from Beaver?"

"Beaver? Oh, you mean Percival, because you're dealing with me for now."

"I'm a lucky man," he said, forcing silky sounds. I rolled my eyes, again.

"Listen. You try anything with me, and I mean anything, and I'm kicking you in the nuts. We're doing show-and-tell on the eighth, so clear your schedule. That's Thursday night, unfortunately. Be on your Ps and Qs. For reasons you don't understand yet, the minute you hit on me the... stuff... we're making will be ruined. And so will your testicles. Understand?"

"You just said I didn't."

"I'm asking you to confirm that if you try flirting with me, I will hurt you."

"I heard you," he said.

"Good. Come to 9573 Walter Avenue at eleven Thursday night. Call this number when you get there. I'll see you then."

"Wait," he said. I sighed. "Can I infer, because you're calling me and threatening my unborn children, that you and I will be alone Thursday?"

"You can, and you can also infer that I wish we weren't. See ya." I hung up. Infer, who used words like that?

Damn them for making me do this. Of course, in their shoes—having a good excuse to make someone else deal with Maxwell—I would have done the exact same. I guess I drew the short end of this stick. Happened sometimes.

Tuesday, October 3, 2006

....

78. GREGORY

"Father Clarke," I began and then decided to use his first name, for effect. "Winston. As I always have, I find your dedication admirable. I truly do. Your care for people, whether members of our flock or no, speaks well of you and all of us. This attribute is from God, purely. There can be no doubt."

Clarke's eyes were large and unsettled as he watched me. He was sweating, and as my office was not overly hot, it occurred to me that the sweat could only be a result of some inner heat. His animation when he had spoken was clear. He needed gentle handling to bring him back into proper balance.

I continued, "And I understand your specific concern in this case well. It indeed sounds like this substance—moondust, you called it?—could be a very harmful, indeed. Heretical in its very nature, as you said. Blasphemous in its use. Given what you've told me is correct, of course, I agree completely."

Hearing these words, Father Clarke deflated a bit. For he surely could sense what was coming, he was always perceptive that way. But, his idea for some immediate action could not be, and there was nothing I could do to change this. Instead, I decided to try to build him up a little more.

"I will pass this matter along to the cardinal. It could be that, very soon, this issue will reach the ear of the highest members of our church. It could be that what you have done here will give us forewarning of a serious threat, and because of that possibility I want to reiterate what an excellent job you've done in bringing it before me today.

"But, there will be no public statements. Not yet. You see, as we live in the age of rampant media, it is important that we consider, along with other concerns, the image of Mother Church. It is an image, I'm afraid, that is under consistent and virulent attack. You are aware, of course, of the terrible lies that are being told about priests all over the globe. There are those, my son, who want us to fail, to be seen as backward, to be reviled as monsters instead of respected as the simple servants we are. We have enemies, and while their existence is extremely lamentable, we cannot ignore it simply because it doesn't sit well with us. We must always act accordingly—with grace, wisdom, and most importantly, patience."

"But," Father Clarke said, "surely the best thing we can do, given this, is provide the best spiritual guidance and care for all of God's children that we can and as soon as we can?"

"Indeed, we should. And, we are. But, we must do so intelligently. And, we must do so without myopia that would make things more difficult for us in the future. Which means that we must consider our image and act in ways that strengthen our standing in the community at large, never in ways that weaken it.

"You understand, Father, that witch hunts must never happen again, even if we are hunting powder witches and not human ones? We cannot seek to root out the blasphemous. We have engaged that type of folly in darker days of our church, centuries ago. But, they were darker days for humanity at large, so the fault is less with us than with the times, I think. Nevertheless, we must show that we have moved on, you see."

The priest began to speak. But, I held up a hand to silence him. When his mouth closed, I continued.

"This is not to say I believe we should do nothing at all or that we will do nothing at all. No, Father, it is a matter of timing. At this moment, this drug is unknown. Have you considered that, by condemning it publicly, we could indeed aid in its spread and simultaneously would be forever linking our beloved church to it in the minds of the people? This would clearly be folly, as I'm sure you understand."

I waited. "Yes," he finally said. "Yes, I do."

"Good." I reached across my desk and patted him on the arm. "I knew you would. And I'm very glad you gave me this little bit of it, evil as it is, for us to study. In time, the church will come up with a plan on how to deal with this danger. We can both be sure of that. But, this is a decision to be made at the highest level, I think. There is so much to consider."

Having finished saying what needed to be said, I focused on watching him. I could see his youthful idealism struggling against the common sense wisdom I'd just imparted. The wisdom was winning, weighted, as it was, by the respect he had for my station.

"Thank you for taking the time to speak with me, Bishop," he said, finally, in a voice laced with respect and disappointment.

I smiled in return. "Thank you, Winston, for your vigilance. My door is always open."

....

79. WINSTON

Standing outside, the sense of disquiet I felt surged and catalyzed my indecision. Everything the bishop said was true, his instructions to wait, clear and necessary. The matter was too big and too serious for me to deal with myself, for I did lack the experience to understand the nuances of such a complicated issue.

And yet however elegant his argument, the memory of the woman who took moondust counterbalanced it. If I could use a single word to describe her, she was fractured. To have an event so thoroughly confuse the issue of faith was more than any psyche could bear. Moondust would destroy any who came across it.

How many souls would be thrown into torment while we waited for official word? How clear it seemed to me that the decision to wait would consign some awful number of innocents to the soul-sickness of questioning God! I was fundamentally unable to do this, even if it were expressly ordered by His Holiness himself. I was shocked by the inherently blasphemy of this admission. But, the way of Jesus meant following God by caring for one's neighbors, no matter the consequences. When, as a child, I'd fallen in love with Christ, the Savior, I had done so because of his perfect love. And given how close the two events were in time—the woman coming into the confessional, and the newspaper man entering my office—it seemed likely that God brought this to me for a reason.

But what could I do? I was as unwilling to violate the dictates of the Catholic Church as I was to ignore my duty to humanity. So as I began to walk toward the nearest subway, dodging the teeming masses without real thought, I searched the bishop's words for wiggle room. As when I was a child planning some innocent mischief, perhaps I could find a loophole in the rules as explained that would allow me to follow the letter of the law. But, not necessarily its spirit. It was shaky ground to be sure. But, it was a way forward.

Thinking it through, I realized everything the bishop said pertained to agents of the church, and not, specifically, me. In a sense, every priest was two entities in one. I was Father Clarke, a representative of God and a part of the church, and I was Winston, an individual person. Father Clarke received a direct order to do nothing while the church considered this problem. Winston, however, had not; as long as I acted as a person and not as a functionary of the church, I was free to tackle this problem. If my actions were unassociated with my station, and if I stayed true to my vows, then I could go rogue.

It was all of our jobs to care for the spiritual wellbeing of humanity. I pledged to Christ to do so and so would.

But how?

As if sent from God, this answer came quickly. The mid-morning streets were fairly packed with people today, the usual mix of locals and a few slow-moving tourists, so I eased to the side of the street and reached into my back pocket for my wallet. Inside, I grabbed the number for the reporter and then gave him a call on my cell phone.

"Maxwell Smith."

"Mr. Smith, hello. This is Father Clarke. We spoke Sunday."

"Yes, Father, I remember. Has a decision been made?"

"I'm afraid it has, Mr. Smith. We will be unable to provide you an interview at this time. But, as soon as we are willing to make a public statement, it is my hope that all concerned will agree to make it to you."

"I see," he said. He didn't sound all that disappointed, strangely.

"I'm very sorry we couldn't give you what you wanted."

"I am too. But, I understand."

"I was wondering if you could do me a favor. You had said that you came across this drug in Midtown Manhattan. Do you remember where?"

"Sutton Street. Right on the water, close as you can get."

"Thank you, Mr. Smith. Again, I'm sorry. Have a wonderful day."

"You too, Father," he said. And hung up.

Sutton Street was uptown, not far from Madison Avenue and other famous meccas of the Manhattan elite. It was a very rich area, full of restaurants and shops catering to those with money and time to spare. Where I was going, by the river, was a dead end street, and at its end sat a little area with benches overlooking the water. The street leading up to this area was entirely residential, and the houses were best described as mansions. One wondered what kind of people lived there, and how they made their millions. And how much they gave to charity.

Having already changed into civilian clothes, I sat on one of the benches in the park at the end of the street and waited—for hours. People came and went: A group of tourists. A young black construction worker with glasses and skin the color of driftwood. A pair of bicyclers, perhaps husband and wife, in matching biking suits. A lone woman, wearing a black top and skinny jeans, sat writing in a notebook while looking out at Roosevelt Island. After about four hours I started doubting my decision. So I prayed.

I prayed for a good twenty minutes, keeping my mind focused, asking the Lord to send this person to me. I repeated the reasons and reminded God that this was all in service to Him and to the people of the world He'd created. I prayed with all my might, reaching a semi-meditative state, feeling nothing, but the wind on my skin and the hymn in my brain. I kept my eyes closed for this time, and when I finally opened them, I was not alone.

I couldn't say why I decided to return to the world at that moment. It had been natural, like coming up for air when swimming underwater. The sound of the busy city behind me came back to me first, constant as the whisper of seas in a sea-shell, punctuated by the occasional siren or horn. The gloaming had fallen, street-lights glinted, and the sky was laced with blood orange.

I saw a man sitting on the other bench, wearing a suit which looked like it had been on him for days, giving it a limp quality of defeat, incongruous with the man himself.

He sat rod straight, hands on his knees in a pose reminiscent of Egyptian pharaoh statues, eyes closed. His hair danced in the wind, the only thing on him moving; he sat as still as the dusk. Perhaps it was the tranquility. But, he had an air about him. It made his rough appearance seem a sort of disguise.

While I was staring at him, he opened his eyes, blinked twice, and then looked over at me. I smiled briefly and averted my gaze. His did not waver.

He stared at me long enough to make me nervous, and then crossed the small park to come and sit beside me, on my bench.

"Hello," he said. "May I ask you a question? Did you ever wish you could experience being with God?" I felt immediately sick.

Somehow, even when speaking directly to the reporter who had told me about the drug, there had been a cloak of unreality around the problem of moondust. That was suddenly stripped from me, and I'd not realized how much comfort I derived until it was gone.

In his eyes burned passion and insanity, and up close, he smelled of an unwashed body. His disheveled appearance now seemed menacing. I prayed to God for strength.

"I know what you are offering me. But, it is not the experience of God. Quite the opposite."

It did not seem like he'd taken any real attempt to shift his personae. But, rather that it happened naturally. Rage flooded from his subconscious the way a river swells in heavy rain.

"You are mistaken," he said. "You know nothing."

"I know who you are. And I know you have something called moondust, which you are giving away. You think you are doing so to unite people with God. But, you are deeply mistaken. I've spoken with people to whom you've given the substance. Nearness to God does not do to people what your drug has done to them."

"And you think you're an authority?"

"I am a priest," I said, attempting to match the intensity of his gaze. He sneered.

"You know nothing."

This repudiation evoked a reciprocal anger in me. He turned to begin walking away. But, I shifted to block his path. Words tumbled.

"I know that I have been called by God to do His work on earth and that I've been doing so for ten years, which is ten years longer than you have. I know that God is beyond any sensual pleasure. And I know that I've seen what you're doing to people, and it's destroying their faith and their connection to God. How could God destroy godliness? You are serving Satan."

"You know only your own lies. Speak to me of Satan again, and we will beat you."

"Strike me if you must," I said. My voice shook. But, I was not ashamed of it. "But what you are doing, you must not do. I have been sent here by God to tell you this. In the name of Jesus."

"You have been sent by your church. By the lies they have told you for your whole life. A life you wasted, thinking you were serving God, actually serving an idea that you confuse for God. If you ever want to know the truth, take this." He put another baggie of powder into my hand. "Your church has been lying to you. And I feel sorry for you. I am here to bring the truth to everyone."

He walked by me. This time I let him, knowing there was nothing to be gained by confrontation. Instead, I put the baggie he gave me in my pocket, automatically. I let him go a little ways, and then I followed him.

I trailed him to an area of higher pedestrian traffic, keeping lookout for a policeman. The moondust man walked west for a few blocks toward the park, which was perfect in that the police were usually posted near it.

I trailed him by about three-quarters of a block. He did not look back, walking with a shuffling gate that spoke either to poor shoes or psychosis. He seemed very out of place in this ritzy section of Manhattan, lacking the ability to become part of the city like most homeless. Instead he stood out like a lodestar, receiving wide berth even from the most jaded Manhattanites.

He took a left, and began walking toward the nearest park entrance.

A policeman stood about half a block away from the entrance, idly talking to a woman with a small dog.

I skipped to a jog. "Officer," I shouted, "officer." Everyone in hearing distance turned their heads toward me, conscious of a breech in public protocol and wary of the possibility of danger.

The messenger turned toward me as well. Rage bloomed on his face when he saw me, running at him, now only a few yards away. I prayed the policeman watched. If he attacked me, my body would suffer, and I might even die. But, my purpose would be fulfilled. The other people near to us shied away, terrified. I pointed at the shabby looking evil in front of me and shouted, "Stop him! Please!" Closing my eyes against the fury burning from the messenger, enemy of the faith.

God protect me.

....

80. Harold

When I, the messenger, left the park a sound behind me exploded. "Officer," he screamed, "Officer, please stop that man," and I turned. The man from the park was screeching at me—the Catholic betrayer.

I turned on him, first. But, then I backtracked, because a police officer was running at me. There could be no escape, now. If it was the Lord's will to martyr me, then I could be strong, strong enough to stand in the fire. My work already spread.

With my hands in the air, I turned to face the officer. He would find the moondust and would mistake it for other things, like so many had, and I would be arrested. They would try everything to stop me. But, Jonah got swallowed by the whale, and Pograu got eaten by the great wolf, and so was I going to be consumed by the government's NYPD.

But all the world lived in God's eye.

Thursday, October 5, 2006

81. PETER

Whale hunt today. But, the sky looked wrong. I had wine rocks in my brain as I gauged the winds. I often did. Didn't stop me from judging. Seemed the clouds raced to the west, the dangerous direction. But they lay high, so it was hard to tell what would come. Perhaps a storm. Perhaps just soft rain, perhaps nothing. But sunlight burning through clouds.

It was the high season. Come what may, we couldn't afford to stay ashore, we needed the hunt. The blue ones, the huge ones, migrated through our waters. The chase rose in my blood, the anticipation of it. Life and death, blood in the water, boats in the froth, us or them.

I checked the spears and the ropes. I checked the hulls, the wetness of the pitch, and the oars. It was my ritual. The old ways said you had to do it. But my son's generation often skipped parts. We had three of everything, and if you went out enough, you knew how your gear fared. But, some actions held import beyond the obvious. The young tend not to understand until they suffered for their carelessness. On this island, we plied the most dangerous trade—preparation like my daddy taught was overkill, except the time it saved a life. On the day the life was mine, I swore to always follow the old ways. I kept the oath.

Above me, clouds raced across the sky. Some like egg-whites tumbling over each other, other clouds thin wisps of steam. In places, they clumped thickly, like a layer of wool between earth and sky.

The variation told of a sea in Great Spirit. Sometimes such a day worked in our favor, forcing our prey to surface. But, on bad days, the waves swatted us as if we were mosquitoes. We prospered or died by whims of sea-nymphs.

Maurinio appeared on the hill, coming down to the wharf from town. Defined by his stooped, knotted back and scars, he was an old sea fighter. He walked with a cane and puffed pipe-smoke like the continental machines of legend, trains.

He didn't go to sea any more. My retirement approached, too. But, I couldn't imagine letting it go. The smell of it. The roll of the waves. The contrast. But, time came for us all, like the tides. The trick was picking the right day. Without the experience of dogs like me, the young ones would never make it. Their blood would get high, and they'd make some damn fool mistake—never to come back.

"Morning, Nes," Maury said. He hadn't shaved today, and I noticed.

"Morning." I looked skyward again. "What do you think?"

"Hard to read."

"Yeah."

"Day like today, either whales will be right where you want 'em or the sea will make you sorry you ever learned to row."

"Hell of a choice."

"Not mine to worry over any more."

I looked at him, studying him for the answer to my next question, the way I studied clouds.

"You miss it?"

"You will, too."

With that he started walking away, continuing his constitutional, saying, "If you go, make sure you come back."

It was a tough choice. We'd make it together, and I had a feeling most of the boys would be gun-ho. Worrying over the power of the sea would be left to codgers like me.

I came back to myself then. It took a moment to get my bearings and remember me. It was Thursday and I was Peter, a chemist. Five seconds ago, I had been a whaler on an island, likely in the Azores. What had made that possible was a powder called moondust, given to me by a reporter named Max. Moondust changed my life and would continue to do so.

I was crying the grit out of my eyes so I wiped my face, and for good measure, I went to the bathroom and splashed water on it. Next I looked in the mirror.

A drug-induced hallucination was the result of upset brain-chemistry. The active chemicals in drugs flood neural pathways and functionally impersonated the natural neurotransmitters in the brain. Those transmitters created perceptions, thoughts, and memories by signaling our brain-cells to fire. So the brain was fooled by the drug into firing in ways that were caused not by one's relationship to the outside world, but by the drug. Of course, the fact that one had taken the drug in the first place was a part of one's relationship with the world, so there was a bit of recursion in that.

Hallucinogenic experiences were similar to dreams that way. Scientifically, dreams were considered random firing of brain-cells during sleep. As hallucinogens created a situation where brain-cells were basically fooled into firing in unusual and randomized ways, you could say that the two experiences were closely related.

And for this simple reason, there tended to be a mixture of the mundane and the fantastic in both experiences. Your everyday experience was a result of neurons firing in rote patterns. Signals travelled the neural net the way cars travel roads in a city in conventions, such as rush hours. But, the brain, during the experience of hallucinogens, was akin to a city in which a segment of the population decided to leave their homes or offices all at the same time and drive in completely random directions, with or against the usual flow of traffic, ignoring red lights, street signs, and speed limits. That is a city in anarchy, and this was your brain on drugs.

Moondust did not fit that paradigm at all. This was the basis of all my current problems. If one could say that hallucinogens functioned by flooding the brain in certain neurotransmitters, one could not call moondust a hallucinogen. It changed the brain into a different brain. When I took moondust, I was no longer me. I was no longer in my brain. That was how it felt, and I couldn't find an explanation for it.

While the first moondust experience I had was intense, it was explainable under modern scientific theory. It felt like a particularly joyful out-of-body experience. Likely, my brain had been flooded with dopamine or an imitation, so that the experience of pleasure overtook all perception.

But, in subsequent usage, I'd perceived life as a number of different people: a Japanese girl, an older man in the Azores, a pregnant woman in India, a washerwoman in France. If these had all been hallucinations stemming from the same chemical, that chemical would have to be able to act on my brain in such a way that existing pathways of my synapses would randomly fire in such specific ways as to convince me that I was not myself, but someone else multiple times. The likelihood of a hallucinogen creating this perception once was astronomically slim. But, multiple applications of the same substance randomly acting on my brain in ways that convinced me I was a different person every time—this simply could not happen.

In the bathroom mirror, my face looked the same as it always did. My double chin hadn't shrunken or grown, and my eyes were still brown. There were a few gray hairs around my temple, my mouth had a pinched kind of look, and my jaw was square-ish. Since I was already in the bathroom, and it was morning, I brushed my teeth and decided to shower.

But, my thoughts returned to moondust. It was constantly in flux, and when it came in contact with a human consciousness, that consciousness went into flux, also. As if a person was no different than an element. When you tested moondust it could be boron or oxygen or hydrochloric acid or a billion possible and impossible permutations of protons, neurons, and electrons. When you took moondust, you could be Spanish or German or Thai or any of billions of possible permutations of humanity. Did this suggest that on some level, we were no different than the forms of matter and energy that made up our world? Of course, we weren't different. We were simply larger and more complex permutations of protons, electrons, and neutrons, making up proteins, and cells, and organs. We were the matter and energy created by the interaction of these things in large groups.

But even the purest scientist tended to imagined humanity was more. We imagined we were the apex of evolution and human consciousness was something greater than the sum of its parts. Moondust had no such illusions.

What did it all mean?

....

82. CHESTER

Days later, I still couldn't forget what I saw when I used my university's science lab to study that stuff the damned reporter gave me. Betsy thought I was being more moody than usual for no reason; she took to calling me "Professor Doom." I chose not to correct the mistake in her comic-book reference. She probably had a point about the moodiness. But, I couldn't tell her the cause. I only hoped time would help me forget, and I drank a lot of beer these days. This did little for my dough-boyish figure. But, I hoped that with enough consumption, the memories would get blurred.

I already gave the reporter what he wanted, namely a summary of my findings about the chemical makeup of the substance, not that I had anything conclusive to say. So there was really no point in my remembering any of this. I'd always been critical of willful ignorance until now, when I so needed its bliss. Instead, I learned I was the type of guy who—if a little green man jumped out from behind a tree and told me he came from a distant galaxy and wanted to be my friend—would walk away as quickly as possible and pretend it never happened. The occult might exist. But, it certainly didn't need my attention.

It was another day at the university. I held office hours again, and I decided I needed something to distract me from the moondust problem while I waited for my ignoramus students to come barreling in to my office. So I went on Google news and read random articles from around the world. It helped. But, not that much.

....

83. HAROLD

"State your name, for the record."

"I have no name."

"Everyone has a name, genius."

"I no longer do."

"Are you trying to be uncooperative?"

"You haven't told me why you arrested me. You ignore your own laws."

"As long as you're in the beautiful state of New York, they're your laws too, buddy boy. Unless you're a foreign dignitary. And by your smell, you ain't."

"Nevertheless. I am here without cause."

"I'm a cop, I don't like you, and I have suspicions. But, mostly it's the stuff we found on you. I'm guessing anthrax?"

"It was not."

"The lab will tell me soon enough."

"So you say."

"Last chance. What's. Your. Name?"

"We are the messengers."

"That's not a name, genius. And what's with the royal 'we?' You the king of Spain?"

"I have no name."

"Anyone ever call you a broken record?"

"No. As I said, I am called the messenger, and I have no name."

"And I'm going to call you a psych consult, you fruitcake. But, after you spill. If you cooperate, you may see the light of day again."

"I've done nothing wrong."

"Genius, once again, you got caught handing out white powder on public streets. White powder. In what world is that not a crime? At best, it's a public disturbance and believe me, other charges will stick, too. Since you're gonna be here for a while anyway, why not just tell the truth? You expect me to believe you're carrying talc? Either it's a drug or it's a poison. Okay, maybe I was wrong about it being Anthrax. I don't know.

"What I do know, beyond a doubt, is that you're up to no good. If you keep being uncooperative, then you could find yourself calling a very deep and dark hole home. So I suggest you play it straight."

"I have been alerting people to the existence of God. We are the new church. This is beyond your jurisdiction."

"Come again?"

"My powder is a holy substance, a miracle. It is a gateway to Heaven."

"You are a total wacko."

"One day, you will see."

"Whatever. Let's backtrack a bit. Tell me more about... you say you're in a religious group?"

"We are legion."

"Okay, yeah. You should know saying stuff like that's going to move us in the wrong direction here. Now, I'm going to ask you, again. What's this group called?"

"There is no name."

"You and your no-name bullshit anonymity fetish. How many people you got?"

"We are legion."

"Okay, guess what? Because of your no-name routine, as of right now you're going in the hole. You know what the hole is, your highness? It's the place that makes people crazy, crazier than you even, and you're going to rot in it until you decide to answer my simple, nice, and well fucking-phrased questions. Shelly! Get in here and escort Saint John Doe to the nearest solitary confinement cell."

"You cannot stop us with force or threats. We are God's chosen. One day, you will see."

"I'll see you in a few days, nutwad. To you, they'll pass slower than years. Pleasant dreams."

....

84. MAXWELL

I made my voice husky and weak. "Samantha," I said. "It's me, Max." If Samantha, my day editor/supervisor, didn't believe me, then I would be FUBAR. So I was nervous about this call, which I handled by telling myself that after pretending to be a gangster, this was small potatoes. This helped a bit.

"Max," Samantha said, "Glad to hear from you."

"Yeah, sorry about that. I'm running a temperature of 103. And I wanted to get up earlier. But, I kept passing out before I could get out of bed. I spent most of yesterday throwing up."

"Sorry to hear that," she said, dryly. "We really need you here."

"Listen, Samantha, I know. The good news is I saw the doctor. I got antibiotics now, and I'll be in as soon as humanly possible. Promise."

"Make sure you do that," she said and hung up.

I wondered, for a moment, about the wisdom of this plan again. When, or if, I submitted my article to The New York Globe, it would be clear to everyone I'd not been on death's door, like I claimed. Would they reward my drive or punish my duplicity? A trill of fear went through me. Perhaps I let my ambition carry me away. But, almost a week into my master plan, it was late to start having doubts. I could only go forward.

Moondust would take me to a new level or cost me everything. It already cost me my girlfriend. Justine and I were over. And my job, judging by Samantha's tone, was on the chopping block, now. But, it was a story, the kind of story men like me waited their whole lives for and never found. The kind of story that made careers. I needed to keep going.

My paper would accept what I'd done, when they saw my copy. As long as my writing was crisp, severe, and marble smooth.

Writing was my job, today. Same as yesterday. Tonight, I'd be meeting with the stoner queen, Hailey, to observe moondust production. That would be an integral part of my article as well as their party would be, the one happening Sunday. But, while I didn't have all the pieces in place yet, I was developing the ones I did have. I could finish the lion's share of the rough draft today, I figured, and add the final two pieces after they happened, sort of a plug-n-play approach.

Suddenly, something struck me—a major oversight—and I swore. I needed to go to the police. My article lacked a key angle. How did law enforcement plan to handle this situation? To what degree did they perceive moondust as a threat to society? I needed quotations from a sergeant or a captain, expert in the innate criminology of drug-behavior, someone who understood how these scenarios played out.

The possibilities excited me. But, I didn't need to rush. I would continue with my plans for the day, and interview the police tomorrow.

I flicked on my computer and took out my notes. First, I would write up explanations of what my chemist Peter told me, and what the other chemistry guy confirmed. "Whatever it's obvious similarities to hallucinogens such as LSD," I began, "moondust is no ordinary drug. Indeed, it can be called a scientific revolution in a powder."

I liked this opening. It had pop, energy, and communicated the fundamental gravitas of my subject.

While I was rereading the notes a third time, something stood out. Heisenberg's principle—the idea that the observer changes the observed: After being observed, a thing is, on some level, irrevocably altered. I remembered the basic idea from college. What struck me was this: the uncertainty principle was playing out in my life, and to an unsettling degree. I, a reporter, a professional observer, never previously thought about how I would affect the development of moondust as social phenomenon. But, I would, I had.

I told Percival about its inability to be classified, and therefore it's innate legality. Using a fake accent and gangster identity, I convinced some random thugs looking for moondust to ignore Percival, throwing that messenger kook under the bus to do so. And tomorrow I would alert the police to moondust's existence, bringing them into opposition with Percival et al., who due to my prior intervention would be a lot easier to find. Eventually, the words I would write would introduce this phenomenon to the world.

I was definitely changing things, when it came to moondust.

But hadn't Cronkite changed the Vietnam War? This was the role we played, probably the only thing I held sacred. I had a duty to inform, and what happened after I informed—or even in the process of informing—needed to be secondary. As long as I upheld the ideals of journalism by behaving ethically, I felt no guilt.

I pushed these thoughts away and wrote my heart out.

....

85. HAILEY

The closer the time came, the more I dreaded it. I felt sure it was going to suck. Totally the wrong attitude to take into moondust-making. But, unlike before when sour faces might have wrecked things, popping some choice mushroom caps for their pretty euphoria would not be smart at all, or even be possible. Those little beauties were hard to come by.

Of course, I had other substances to abuse. But, as I would be observed by Percival's reporter Max, there wasn't much point. Percival suggested Max was judgmental about consciousness-shifting in general, so I tended to think any elevation in me would be balanced out by a descent in his mood.

There was always alcohol. But, I felt pretty sure he'd misunderstand if I tried to get him drunk. So we'd both be stone sober for this one.

I was quickly souring on this brilliant idea of mine. Would he be able to be here while I made moondust and not ruin it? Hard to say. And what would happen if the batch didn't take? I reminded myself it was a no-lose scenario, aside from the fact that the reporter now knew where I lived. Percival and Mark would be making a very, very large batch elsewhere in the city, likely at Mark's place. We'd have the necessary amount of moondust either way. And if it didn't take, yeah, I would look silly in front of the guy. But, so what? Did it matter?

It did, actually. We needed him to take the heat off of us.

I had some time before he showed up, so I threw caution to the wind and rolled a little something-something while watching television. Thanks to moondust, I reached a category of rare wealth in the city—people who could afford cable and who splurged on getting it legally. I turned to the Femme network. Their made-for-television movies were kind of hilarious. But, only when good and stoned. Sober, they were totally unwatchable.

I couldn't have asked for better recreation tonight. I watched the melodramatic tale of a thirty-something woman with the perfect husband and perfect life and perfect kids and perfect dog and perfect hair, in the process of working on the novel she finally found time to write, while her kids attended school and the maid did the housekeeping. Tragically, while doing online research, she found posted video evidence her husband lived a double life; he was the youngest partner of his law-firm by day. But, often, while pretending to work late, he really dressed in a slutty French maid outfit and delivered erotic man-cakes, singing modified show-tunes about male-on-male fellatio. That's right: he was a gay singing telegram.

It had me in hysterics. I'm surprised the neighbors didn't complain about the noise.

By the end of it, I felt pretty good. But, I still dreaded dealing with Max. When I turned the television off, my mind switched gears, from happy fun-time to the gray future awaiting me when the reporter showed up. I sighed, and then I started preparing— gathering the things I would need. The ten gallon drum waited on the roof, perfect for burning things, ready for another use. I emptied and dried the plastic dishpan that lived in my sink, then put the pile of old newspapers I collected since in the dishpan. I grabbed my sifter, and put it on top of the papers. Of course, I already had a lighter in my pocket. I went to my bedroom closet, where I kept the moondust, and pulled a little baggie out.

I took a moment to reconsider about the alcohol. Maybe if I reminded him about how we weren't going to be an item—unless Ragnarok came and we were the two left—I could risk drinking with the guy. It probably wouldn't make anything worse. And I did have a bottle of vodka in the kitchen.

I flashed back to the reporter's behavior at brunch—his eyes, lecherous, locked on the girls. Because he was a chest-gazer, I decided the form-fitting shirt I wore wouldn't do, went into the closet, and found an old, voluminous sweatshirt with many paint-stains. Having to hide myself this way felt wrong. Part of me didn't want to do it, likely my stubbornness. If the choice was changing or having some creep's eyes locked on my jumblies, I could make an exception to the general rule—dress for yourself, never for them. Besides, it would be cold out there. I may need a jacket, too.

I went out to my fire escape to have a cigarette. After I lit up my phone rang, which made my heart sink. But, a false alarm. Cameron, my bed-buddy, called. I didn't want to talk to him right then, so I hit ignore and put the phone back in my pocket.

I smoked my cigarette nice and slow, staring up at the full moon peeking out from the clouds. I thought of a song I loved, because the lyrics called the moon a light-bulb breaking. A beautiful image, I always thought.

When I finished the cigarette, I climbed back inside through my window. Then Maxwell called.

"Hey," I said when I answered. "Are you here?"

"Yeah. Can you buzz me in? I tried your intercom, but..."

"Yeah, the buzzer's broken, I'll have to come down. Give me a second."

I needed to pee, I realized. Better to now, better not to leave him alone in my place. I pegged him for the snooping type. So I used the facilities, and when finished, I threw on my Chuck Taylor's and went downstairs.

At the front door, the reporter stood in a three-quarter length pea coat, leaning on the railing as if trying to be provocative.

"What took you so long?" he said.

"Well, first I had to put on my shoes, then I had to walk down the hall, and then the stairs."

"Clever," he said in a nasty tone, following me back up to my apartment. "Do you and your crew make improv classes mandatory or something? I've never heard such sharp humor."

The snark infuriated me, I'd never been a fan of it. So I stopped climbing and turned on him. But, I decided not to say the first thing that popped into my head.

"You should remember, I'm doing you a favor here, chuckles. And you should act like it."

"Chuckles?"

"Do you want to go home?"

"No. I want to go to your apartment and watch you make magic."

Because of his tone, I pictured myself hitting him. My foot, stomping his face, which from a few stairs above would be easy. His high-pitched squeal as he tumbled, end over end, down the stairs.

Something else I learned from doing moondust, an obvious truth mostly ignored: If you went into a situation believing it would suck, it was far more likely to suck. The inner and the outer worlds were connected by actions we know we took, such as, facial expressions we made, our tone of voice, thoughts which manifested in our behavior—all unrecognized. Had I helped make this situation shitty more than I realized?

If it continued like this, not only would the moondust not take but also I might end up in prison for pushing the chump off my rooftop. It could happen.

I took a deep breath—exhaled, inhaled. Called on various learned calming techniques.

"I want to remind you, if you flirt with me, I'm going to murder you."

"You think that was flirting?"

"Okay, so you're always like that. Try not to be. This is a delicate operation."

We didn't talk the rest of the way up the stairs. I tried to find happy thoughts and think them. It mattered.

....

86. MAXWELL

I set my blackberry's alarm for ten at night, which gave plenty of time to arrive at Hailey's apartment before eleven o'clock. I was busy writing and when the alarm went off, I felt as if I'd been pulled from a dream. The world around me had faded into nonexistence.

What I'd written was great. I could feel it. All of my gambles were going to pay off. I could go freelance; after the name recognition skyrocketed from breaking the moondust story, getting top-flight rates for my stories would be a walk in the park.

Just to make sure, I took a quick second to skim over some of what I'd penned. I started with a description of Percival:

He sits in a coffee shop, one leg carelessly propped up on a neighboring chair, in an olive colored military-style hat, jeans, and a band T-shirt. His casual manner and simple clothing belie the threat he is to the established order of things in the United States, and perhaps the world. A threat he is well aware of and even flaunts. "You should know your lives are all dreams," he says, speaking directly to the American people, with a casual disrespect stemming from an innate sense of superiority. "Do I intend to wake you up? What I intend doesn't matter at all. Moondust is the truth."

Reading it, I couldn't help, but to smile. I'd been so worried while interviewing Beaver, who turned out to be named Percival. But, with a little ingenuity and elbow grease, it made for great stuff. What I'd written was sensational. But, still grounded in truth: Percival understood selling moondust made him a danger to society, and he loved that. It's what made him a compelling subject.

Because I was working, time flew by, and soon I needed to leave for my appointment with Hailey. She was going to show me how they made moondust. If the opportunity presented, I also planned to find out from whom and how they received the substance in the first place. Percival told me he didn't remember, due to a wild LSD trip. I didn't believe him. If I played my cards right, perhaps I could get the story out of this Hailey person.

So I laced up my shoes and my coat, and out I went. I took the subway, the degree of uncertainty in my future suggested I shut down spending for a while. Nothing eventful happened. But, it was a long ride.

I ascended out of the tunnel to a street in a super shady neighborhood. The buildings seemed closer together, the streetlights dim. Dangerous people hung out in front of bodegas, speaking in languages I couldn't hope to discern. Worse, I wasn't very far away from a housing complex, and only two things happened in housing complexes: crimes and roach infestations.

I put my head down and walked fast, thinking if a hipster-girl like Hailey managed to live here without getting robbed on a regular basis, it was probably safe for me to walk down the street. Besides, in New York, just because a neighborhood looked dangerous as hell doesn't mean it was. You could be sure with housing projects. But, luckily I headed away from those.

I made it to her front door. As per her instructions, I called.

"Hey," she said when she picked up. "You here?"

"Can you come down and let me in, please?"

"I'll be down in a second," she said.

But she wasn't. Meanwhile, her shady looking neighbors kept checking me out. One of them said something and they all laughed. I did a mental calculation of how much money I carried. Not much. But, my coat was expensive and looked it. I needed to stay loose, so I leaned up against the railing, humming aimlessly as a few minutes ticked by. Finally, she came strolling down the stairs, like nothing was wrong at all.

"What took you so long?" I said when she opened the door. In response, her eyes squinted, while her top lip pulled away from the bottom, showing her left incisor in a magnificent sneer. "Well, first I had to walk down the hall. Then I had to go down the stairs."

"So clever. Do you and your crew make improv classes mandatory?" I said.

"Screw you," she spat, wheeling on me. "You need to remember I'm doing you a favor here, Chuckles. Start acting like you know it."

"Chuckles?"

"Do you want to go home?"

I looked in her eyes, and she meant it. She was so touchy, she wanted to send me packing for an innocuous response to her psychopathy. She expected me to take her crap and smile.

I'd be extra nice, butter her up a bit. Maybe it would keep her from breathing fire all night. "I want to go up to your place and watch you make magic," I said. "Shall we?"

"Let me remind you that if you try to flirt with me, I'll murder you," she said.

"You think that was flirting?"

She took a deep breath. "Okay, so you're always like that. Try not to be." Mercifully she continued up the stairs.

This was going to be a long night. I tried to give her the benefit of doubt. Must be that time of the month for her.

She opened the door. But, stopped in the doorway. "Actually," she said, "Wait here. We're going to the roof-top. I'm grabbing some supplies you can help me get up there."

"We're doing this outside?" I said, surprised.

"Yeah. That is where most rooftops are. Right?"

"Excuse me for expecting drug-making to be clandestine."

"When in over their heads, wise men know enough to let expectations go"—this was the fortune-cookie nonsense of her reply, and then she disappeared into her apartment.

A really long night.

True to form, she took forever, so I sat on the stairs while I waited, playing on my blackberry. When she reappeared, she had glassy, unfocused eyes, carrying a strainer and a wash-pan filled with newspaper.

"Listen," I said, trying to be as diplomatic as possible, "it would help me if I could pull out my digital recorder when we get up there. No video, audio only. That way if you say anything quotable, I have it on record. I want to respect your privacy. What do you say?"

"Sure dude. Whatever."

At the top of the stairs, we reached a ladder, climbing up into the rooftop hatch, in typical New York style. She dropped the wash-bin at the bottom rung. "Okay. I'm going to go up first, and you can hand this stuff up to me. Alright?"

"Alright," I said, hoping the procedure wouldn't get any dirt on my coat. I thought of taking it off. But, I didn't want to have to come back for it.

I watched her go up the ladder. Her ass gently swayed as she climbed. Not a bad view. She opened the latch, and then pulled herself up and out of eyesight, and reappeared as a disembodied head and arms reaching down out of the square hole, with dark sky behind her.

I picked up the wash-pan. But, lifting it up to her proved quite a challenge. Just standing on the floor and holding my arms up left it just out of her reach. But, if I were to stand on a rung of the ladder, I'd need at least one hand free to hold the ladder; and holding the bin took two hands.

"Have any ideas how I should do this?" I asked.

"Um, yeah," she said. "Hold the ladder with one hand and give it to me with the other."

"Yeah, because it's just that easy."

"No, you're right, it's rocket science. Do I need to come down there and do it for you?"

"No." if the bin fell out of my hand, I could blame her. I put my left palm under the center of its weight, and balanced. With my right hand, I reached for a high rung, grabbed it, and pulled myself on the ladder.

The wash-pan almost fell, it was like balancing a broom in your open palm as a kid. But, harder. Somehow I managed and, with difficulty, lifted it above my head. The muscles in my shoulder burned. There was no way she'd have been able to handle doing this herself.

Hailey pulled the wash-bin up the rest of the way and disappeared from view. I gave myself a minute to rest, before following her.

By the time I clawed my way up onto the rooftop, she was halfway toward making a fire in an old, rusty barrel. She twisted and crumpled newspaper and threw it in the barrel. But, she had some ways to go before she would finish the stack she brought. I took a second to look around. Below us, Brooklyn spread out like an oil slick, punctuated by anemic streetlights and the red blaze of advertisements over corner stores. Despite the hour, children played in the street, teenagers hustled in shadows. Like cockroaches, the people tended to avoid the puddles of light, except for the pretty young women and decked-out hip kids heading into Manhattan. The island glittered off to the west, diminished by the distance only slightly. When you stood outside of the human soup that was this city, even for a moment, it was impossible not to stare in awe.

A hard wind whipped my coat and my hair all around. I tightened my cinch to keep my coat from getting out of hand. It whistled in my ear enough that I doubted whether the recorder could pick up anything at all. So I did a quick test. I held it in down at my side, and said, in a normal voice, "Eenie meenie miny moe," while recording. I pulled out my earbuds. But, on the playback, white noise howled, drowning out my voice.

I did another test, this time speaking directly into the microphone. This playback sounded audible, and I decided if she said anything worth quoting, I would repeat it into the microphone like so. I could take any notes I needed that way. I took a moment, in fact, to give a quick description of the rooftop, and the city's dregs below me.

By the time I went over to Hailey, she had the fire lit. "All through talking to yourself?" she said, then looked sheepish, as if she regretted speaking. I must have misread her expression.

"You mean checking my equipment, and yes. Point of order, I

won't be able to pick up your voice at all up here, there's too much wind. If you say anything I need to remember, I'm going to repeat it into my recorder at close range. As long as that's okay with... you." I almost said 'your highness.' It would have been funny for two reasons. But, she'd proven too volatile to josh. I found myself missing Percival, who at least could take a joke. She was that much of a psycho. The horror.

....

87. HAILEY

"You mean checking my equipment, and yes," he said. "Point of order, I won't be able to pick up your voice at all up here, there's too much wind. If you say anything I need to remember, I'm going to repeat it into my recorder at close range. I may also, as you say, 'talk to myself' every now and then, kind of a way to take notes. As long as that's okay with you."

I nodded, watching the fire begin to take hold of the newspaper. When I felt sure it would hold, I straightened up, a bit relieved. On windy nights like this, it could be a bitch getting the paper to burn.

Now that the fire had taken, there wasn't much to do, but wait and have the talk I dreaded having. We hadn't exactly hit it off. His eyes—all up and down me as he watched me work—made me wish I owned a burka. Or a shotgun.

I sighed and started talking. "Okay, Slappy, there are a few things I need to tell you. First, this process is pretty strange. It's affected by mood. If we don't both find a way to be in good spirits, it's not going to take."

"Wait. Give me a second," he said as he started speaking into his recorder. "She says, 'This process is pretty strange. It's affected by mood. If we don't find a way to be in good spirits, it's not going to take.'" He glanced up at me, but still spoke with his mouth near the recorder. "What do you mean, take? And how could my mood affect the stuff? And what's with the burning newspaper?"

If he started repeating everything I said, it would take way too long to say anything to the dude. So I held out my hand. It took him a second, but he got the gist and handed me the recorder, which I put to my mouth.

"The newspaper is burning to make ash. The ash will 'take' into moondust. But, only if we're both chipper. Do you feel chipper?" I handed the recorder back to him.

"I can't say I do at the moment, no. Can you explain why my mood plays into this?"

"No," I said, after another hand-off. "No I can't. If you're not willing to go with me on this, then you can watch as I go through the motions. But, nothing's going to happen."

He took the recorder, but didn't speak into it this time. He held it at his side and glared at me for a while. Then he said, "Hailey, are you wasting my time?"

"No," I said. "You're wasting mine."

He sighed. "How the hell am I supposed to magically make myself happy?"

"You're right. Maybe you should go."

I turned around with my back to him, leaving him to make his decision. Better for me if he left, because by myself I felt sure I could manage to make this count. But, then again the reporter was the whole reason I stood here instead of with Perce and Mark.

In the barrel, the newspaper burned well, releasing chunks of floating ash to the air. More ash stayed still barrel-bound, and that began to stifle the fire under its weight, as packed newspaper had a tendency to do. I kept a broom-less broom handle up here for this reason, so I grabbed it, and stirred. Sparks shot up like stars. Then rose a flotilla of lazy gray planes, former headlines, articles, pictures of important events. They poured outward and upward, sailing on currents created by the heat. And the moon shone down, striking this ash that filled the air like snowflakes.

"What are you doing?" he asked.

"Making ash."

I managed to bring enough still-burnable paper to the surface of the fire to keep it going, so I leaned the broom-handle against the barrel, crossed my arms, and watched it go in silence. Focusing on happy things, how I loved this process, how it felt like a poem, or a prayer. Umbrellas of ash dancing slowly in the air, floating up then down again, dropping out of sight into Brooklyn. The world around us was glittery and surreal, the fire leaping out of the barrel, trying to escape the boundaries in which I gave it life.

Technically, my level of peace and joy wouldn't matter until I combined the ash with the pre-made moondust. But, it made sense to start now.

"Do you mind if I ask a question?" the reporter said behind me. I turned around; he sat on an overturned bucket someone left on the roof.

"What?"

"I know you said you don't know why it's important to keep our mood up. But, if you had to guess... what would you guess?"

He held out the recorder, and I walked over, took it from him, reminding myself this had been my idea, getting the word out. I needed to realize I wasn't dealing with him alone, because through him I dealt with everybody.

"If I had to guess? I don't know. The thing about moondust is it's all tied up in us. Who we are, you know? How we think and how we feel. It can show you other lives, it can show you places and things that you just can't see anymore, because they don't exist anymore. Can you imagine what it could do for, like, science? You can be in the French revolution, or in ancient Egypt. Wherever."

I paused to stir the ash some more. Then I returned to putting my thoughts about moondust into the recorder.

"Anyway, it's so much about our brains, somehow this powder interacts with our mind to put us in the mind of someone else. So somehow it's got to be able to link up with us, right? Maybe... maybe when it's being made, it can only do its thing if the minds of the people who helped make it really, um, are in tune with it, because there's something joyful in moondust. You get a huge wallop of joy when you first take it and then only a whisper. But, the whisper is a lot, and it feels good... maybe there's something about that good feeling and our feelings here that are connected with it. Maybe that joy is important, kind of some part of a bridge moondust builds. I don't know."

"But anyway this whole thing is impossible, right? Nothing about moondust is logical. So what's so strange about it being strange now, when it's made?"

I handed the recorder back to him. "Good?"

"Yeah. What's the next step?"

"I've gotta finish with the ashification, first," I said. And checked it. I gave the fire a quick stir, making sure enough oxygen reached the paper to fuel the fire, releasing more ash into the air. It blew all around, taken by a gust of wind.

He hadn't handed me the recorder again. Instead he spoke directly into it. "Okay, you check the 'ashification.' And then?"

"I strain the ash."

"Why do you strain the ash?"

"Because I need it smooth to make powder. Why don't you just sit back and watch?"

"You need it smooth to make the powder. I'd sit back and watch if something was happening. But, I'm asking questions instead because little is happening."

"Yes, there's not much happening," I said, and pulled my cigarette pack out of my pocket, and a smoke out of the pack. "While the fire's burning the paper down there's not much to do, but stir the barrel and think happy thoughts. Are you thinking happy thoughts?"

"Am I thinking happy thoughts? I'm trying."

I needed happy thoughts too, so I made myself smile and forget about him, lit my cigarette. Unfortunately the fire in the barrel began choking, so I grabbed the broom-handle and gave it another stir. It took both hands, and as a result I got cigarette smoke in my eye.

"You look like Rosie the Riveter," said Maxwell. I flexed my bicep in response.

....

88. MAXWELL

She responded to my 'Rosie the Riveter" quip well enough. Flexed her arm, sort of made a joke in so doing. I still needed more information out of this, so any ebb in her crazy helped. What was it about women that made them like this? Probably how society dealt with them. Or the hormones?

With the cigarette cocked to one side and an eye shut against the smoke, she went back to stirring her burning newspaper. If I hadn't taken the results to my chemist to be verified, I'd have trouble believing this had a point. We were in the neighborhood of tin-foil helmets.

"How long before the newspaper's done?" I asked.

"It's about halfway there," she said. "Happy thoughts."

"Hey, you know what would make me happy? Um, Percival told me how you guys got hip to moondust in the first place. But, I want to verify his story."

She looked at me, amused. "How we got 'hip to it?' Sure thing,

Daddy-o. Why don't you tell me what he told you, and I'll tell you if it's true?"

"What, you don't believe me?"

"I don't know, it sounds a little Nancy Drew. Get information out of someone by claiming you already have it."

"I'm telling the truth. He said you guys took some acid and the next morning you had moondust and the recipe to make more."

"Yep," she said, putting her stirring rod down and exhaling more smoke.

"Care to elaborate?"

She didn't say anything for a while, smoking. Not wanting to be too forceful, I raised my digital recorder and gave it a waggle. She took it, composed her thoughts, and spoke into it.

"It's impossible to remember a trip well. Like, there are details, but they're disconnected. It's like trying to remember a dream."

She took another drag on her cigarette as she seemed to recall or contemplate details of how it happened.

"I know at some point we were in this bar, and some guy came in bleeding. I think he had a bloody nose. We started talking. Maybe he gave it to us, he's the only person I remember speaking to. Other than that? We wandered around the city. I know we went to an art gallery, and the art there flipped my shit. I remember Percival threw his shoe at a fire hydrant for some reason, and it took us a while to convince him to put it back on. I have random memories like that, and none of them answer your question."

I could only shake my head in response. These people.

I took the recorder back. After that, there wasn't much to say. I didn't have any follow up questions for Percival threw his shoe at a hydrant.

In about ten more minutes, the fire burned itself out. "Okay," she said, "we're done. On to step two."

"What's that step like?"

"The ash gets strained. Any chunks are taken out, what's left is powder."

"The ash gets strained," I repeated into the recorder. "The chunks are taken out. What's left is powder."

She probably wasn't pranking me. But suddenly I wondered about this whole enterprise. What the hell was I doing up here? The wind went right through my clothes. I was cold.

"Won't it be difficult," I said, "To touch hot ash?"

"That's why I wait for it to cool down."

In my brain, a straw floated gently onto a camel's back and broke my patience.

"Look," I said, "I appreciate you showing me this. But, I'm wondering, could you just tell me what comes after this step?"

"Yeah, alright, guy. After it's strained, the ash goes in the wash-pan. Some already-made moondust goes in with it and gets stirred around, and then we leave it out in the moonlight. Even if it's cloudy it doesn't matter as long as it's the night of the full moon. But, it has to be outside, under the sky. In the morning, we pick it up, test it out, and if we did it with our hearts right..." She shrugged. "It works. That's it."

"So you just put moondust in with the ash, and the ash becomes moondust?"

"As long as it's a full moon night, yeah. And remember the part about mood."

What a bunch of malarkey.

"Well," I said, "Maybe it would be better if I weren't here because of that last part. I'm a bit skeptical."

"By all means," she said, gesturing toward the hatch.

"Okay. Well, bye."

There was no way I could put this in the article; no one in their right mind would believe it. Fact-checkers would scoff if told that the process required euphoria. But there must be some spin, some angle I could use.

Rather than risk walking to the train station again, I called my car service for a pick up. Expenses be damned, it wasn't worth the risk of a mugging to save a few bucks by going home on public transportation.

....

89. PERCIVAL

While I stirred up the last of the burning paper, freeing it from a whole lot of ash, I got a call on my cell-phone. I checked the little screen and read Hailey's name.

I handed Mark the stirring stick. "Hailey's calling," I told him. Then I answered her call. "What's up?"

"Percival. It's so good to hear an honest-to-goodness human being."

"Ah," I said. "How is our friend Maxwell?"

"That jackass is nobody's friend."

I chuckled. "Finally you feel my pain. How's it going? Are you done?"

"No, not done. But, at least I'm alone. The dude left before we finished."

"He left?"

"Yeah," she said. "I don't think he believed in it."

"Believed what? Which part?"

"I don't know, any of it," Hailey said, but especially how all the ash becomes moondust. I told him, he left, and to be honest, I felt relieved. Where'd you find that guy?"

"I pulled him from a puddle of primordial ooze I stepped in on West Ninth one day. This city has everything."

She laughed. "Listen, I'm going to go. But, I wanted to tell you. I think we may have to go to a plan B. I'm really not sure how this article thing's going to work out for us."

"Don't trust him?" I asked.

"Come on, do you?"

"Of course not. You're probably right, we need a plan B. We'll talk."

"Cool," she said. "Until tomorrow then. Good night."

"Yeah, you too." I hung up.

Mark finished the stirring, and dropped the stirring stick, leaving the last of the paper to burn away. "What's the story?" he asked.

"The reporter bugged out. Didn't believe in... this."

"He did seem like the small minded type," said Mark.

"Well, people tend to believe what they're taught to believe."

He paused for a second. "Does it feel right to you, Hailey not being here?"

"Now that you mention it, no. We've always done this together. Like a ritual."

"Like a ritual?" he asked, amused. "Don't you know anything about ritual?"

"All that I know I learned from you," I said.

We stayed quiet for a second. It was a full silence, and short-lived. Mark broke into it, asking, "You know this is the finale, right? I mean, what's coming? Monday? Everything's going to change— one way or another."

I didn't answer immediately, looking out over the skyline. "Certainly feels that way. Like this is the end of an age."

"Agreed. Does it really seem okay to you that Hailey's not here?"

"Less talk, more action," I said, quoting a favorite phrase of Mark's back to him.

He smiled, took out his cell phone, and gave our best girl a call.

....

90. WALLY

Me and my friend Steve chilled down at Mist, throwing back some choice brews and shooting the shit, when Percival called me. Again. The fool couldn't get enough of me. That was the price of being awesome.

If he wanted to hang, I could do that; he was a pretty good DJ after all. Except I was done with weird spy jobs or whatever to prove myself worthy of moondust. That crazy thing where I had to go stand on some rooftop and wait for a guy to wave sucked. I didn't even get anything out of it, but to keep doing stuff I already did. Kind of a no-win scenario.

"Are you going to get that, man?" Steve said, 'cause I let the phone ring, trying to figure out whether to hear P out or make the sucker talk to my voicemail.

"Whatever. They say you shouldn't shit on the hand that feeds you, right?"

"I dunno, I guess," Steve said and took a sip of his beer.

Finally I answered it. I couldn't get moondust anywhere else. "Yellow," I said.

"Um, yeah, this is Percival. Hailey and Mark are with me, we're on my roof. We have a proposal for you."

"I'm done waving at weirdos on cue, dude."

"What? Oh, that. No, man, this is something else," he said. "In fact, we want to teach you how to make moondust. After that, you can sell it yourself. Or not. Whichever you like."

Now this sounded promising. "Okay," I said, "But wait—why now? I've been asking that for ages. You don't want to know my spinning secrets, do you?"

Another pause. "No, I don't want to know your secrets. There's something you'll have to do for us in return, and I promise you won't mind doing it at all. We'll talk about that. But, we need you to come to my rooftop right now. This is the only night this month we can make the stuff. If you want to learn, it's got to be now."

"Check," I said, holding up my hand to get the bartender's attention. I wasn't even thinking about Percival. But, he answered, so it must have made sense to him, too.

"Good. Get here ASAP. As in, when you think of the subway, think of snails and sloths and pokey things. See ya."

Steve acted all huffy that I had to leave right away. But, I was sick of the kid anyway. He only ever talked about his projects, and he wouldn't talk about my stuff at all, like how I was pretty close to getting a regular gig down at The Stuck Pig. Or this chick I banged named Vonnie, a bearcat in the sack.

I took a cab. Percival lived just over the bridge, and since I'd been hanging out in SoHo, the trip went pretty fast. Good ride, too, with excellent sightseeing 'cause lots of ladies were out who couldn't have looked finer. Beautiful women was one of the best things about New York. You could open your window and spit, and you'd hit three models or actresses.

So, I paid the cabbie and went up to the roof. But, when I climbed the stairs up and tried to open the big metal door, it was locked. So I called Percival. "Hey dude, the door to the roof is locked," I said.

"One second," he said, and then hung up. A minute later, the door opened, moonlight flooded the stairway. You could see everything up there, and when I stepped out, I had this weird feeling like the moonlight was water, and we were at the bottom of the sea.

It was really strange, so I stopped for a second to just kind of take it in.

"Wally, are you getting introspective on us?" said a female voice, kind of like laughing. I turned and recognized Hailey, this girl I'd banged who ran with Percival. She and this gay guy Mark sat not too far away, smoking cigarettes with a couple of brews on hand.

Mark gave me a little wave. Hailey wore an old T-shirt and sooty jeans. But, she looked kind of hot anyway. She always looked hot, though. That's why I'd banged her.

"Naw," I said. "Just thinking about some stuff is all. What's up with you, Hailey? How you been?"

She smiled and said, "Oh, you know, the usual."

"So are you guys going to show me how to make moondust?" I said, to all three.

....

91. Hailey

I'd gone down to my apartment while the ash cooled to get some rue tea, necessary to erase the aftertaste Maxwell the reporter left in my brain. I had a jug of it in my refrigerator, and I poured myself a big glass, when I got a call from Mark.

He told me, he and Percival requested the honor of my presence.

I had nearly finished so I agreed with him, we should all be together, because everything after this would change, and because I loved those crazy bastards. I didn't believe in "best friends," But, they were among the best people I knew, no question.

Plus, Percival, Mark and I did need to talk, so I poured the ash into a hot-cold bag, put it in aduffel, and called a car. Pouring the ash had been tricky, because I didn't want hot ash all over my nice creamy skin or nails—a serious possibility in this high wind. But, I managed and got to Percival's without any major incidents.

They'd locked the door to the roof from the outside, a practice we started there, because Perce's rooftop was popular and because we couldn't be bothered when in production. When I got up there, I used our knock, a rhythm by which we naturally learned to recognize each other. Mark came to open the door and gave me an affectionate half-hug. And then, as the ash finished cooling, the three of us had our talk.

Now, Wally was here, practically filling the air with stupid rays. Of course, stupid rays hadn't been discovered, yet. But, hanging out with Wally made one sure they existed. Which was why I stopped seeing him. He had his moments. But, prolonged exposure was too much to take.

"So, you guys going to show me how to make moondust?" he said. He dressed all indie-kid today, skinny jeans, scarf, thrift store sweater, and designer shoes, with gauges in his ear and the subtlest hint of eye shadow. He spent half an hour mussing his hair by the look of it. He was handsome, so in some sense I appreciated the attention to detail. But, it did scream poseur of the first degree. Which I guess he was, and ultimately the reason we brought him here tonight.

"First, we talk," said Mark, taking control. It was for the best: Wally and I had history, and Percival couldn't look at him without rolling his eyes. "What are you doing Monday night?"

Wally stared at Mark as if Mark had goosed him. "I don't know, dude. But, whatever it is it'll involve the ladies, know what I mean?"

"Oh, my God," was all Mark could say to that, which amused me so—I laughed out loud.

I said, "I don't think you get it, Wally. We want you to host a party for us. We need someone—talented—to be the front-man. You're our first choice."

He thought it over for a second, you could hear the gears struggling to grind. "Sounds cool. But, why doesn't Percival do it? Why give it to me?"

Perce spoke now, reciting lines he came up with himself, in spite of Mark's objection. In fact, the two had a bet over whether it would be believed. "It's a long story," he said, barely containing his excitement. "But basically, I have this non-compete clause." Seeing no sign of being understood, he explained, "That's something that people in the business make you sign when you're doing a project, not to do any other projects for a while."

"Oh yeah?" said Wally, getting interested. "What's the project?"

"They're doing a He-Man movie. Can't say who's involved in making it. But, they've asked me to design the soundtrack. And just between us, James Carville is definitely playing Skelator."

"Wow, that's so cool. I love James Carville. He was awesome in The Godfather." How we managed not to laugh out loud when Wally said that, I don't know. "Do you think, um, you guys might need some help?"

"Nah," I said, "We got it handled. But, we do need help with this party, and you're a lucky, lucky boy because it's gonna be legendary."

"Oh, yeah?"

"Yeah," Mark said, interjecting. "As far as moondust is concerned, we're coming out of the closet, so to speak."

Wally made a face.

"Oh, get over yourself," Mark snapped. I tried. But, this time I couldn't keep the laugh down. I snorted. "You're not my type, I promise you," Mark continued. "Hailey, you want to tell us what's so funny?"

"Oh, er..." I tried to think, desperately, and then started laughing again. "Must be the drugs," I said, breathlessly. Percival started laughing too. Mark looked pretty annoyed, and Wally, of course, seemed confused.

I could have sworn Mark mumbled, "Jesus, I'm surrounded by morons." But, he'd never say such things about Percival and me.

When I managed to compose myself, I said, "Okay. Sorry. Wally, what we're saying is, you know how we've been really secretive, I mean, private, about moondust? Not wanting a lot of people to know? Well, we're going public on Sunday. We want the whole world to know so we're throwing a party, and there's going to be lots of moondust. But, we can't host or DJ it, because like Perce said, we have the, um, He-Man movie, and we have non-compete clauses so we can't host stuff."

Recognition, and excitement, bloomed on Wally's face. "Oh, is that why you want me to learn how to make moondust?"

"Yeah."

"But why? You guys have to be making a killing, yo."

"Well," said Percival, "It's like this. I promised my dear old mother on her death bed that I would be a sublime citizen of humanity and always think of others before myself. So we're doing this for the people, man. It was hard convincing Hailey and Mark here that everyone needs to know how this is done. But, I made a promise that I just can't break."

Wally turned to me. "So, why did you agree, Hailey?"

"Um," I said, trying to think. It was hard to concentrate on coming up with a lie, the situation was so ridiculous. Worse, Percival seemed to be turning the trick-Wally-thing into some kind of twisted improv game. "I'm an anarchist? You know, no Gods, no masters. Once Perce convinced me that the people needed to know, it was my duty to spread the wealth. Otherwise, we become part of the, um, hierarchy." Halfway through that last sentence, I realized Wally probably didn't know the word hierarchy. Oh, well.

"Oh," Wally said. "Well, I didn't know you guys were political. But, it's cool that you want me to know. Real cool."

"Yeah," said Mark. "And we're really hoping that at the party you spread the wealth. Tell as many people as you can about how to make moondust, that's all we ask. You have to promise. But, if you do it, you get a lot in return. You get to spin at the hottest party, like, ever."

"I can handle it, no problem."

"Good," Percival said. "Then let's get down to business."

....

92. MARK

Everything went smoothly once we started teaching Wally how to make moondust. Thankfully, he didn't have any more bouts of random homophobia, and as none of us overestimated his intelligence—meaning, assumed he had any at all—we hit no snafus, just a smooth and simple lesson. It was a basic process, after all. Enjoying yourself was the most important part.

Hailey covered that she brought with her a healthy portion of her rue tea, sorely needed by yours truly. Rue tea came from a seed, steeped in water for a few days—brilliant stuff, providing, officially, a "feeling of mild euphoria," without side effects. Totally legal, in fact, alternative-medicine endorsed.

It certainly helped my annoyance melt away. After a few swallows, I recovered my Zen nicely. Which was important, because who knew how the moondust would take if I felt pissy during the process? Not well at all, probably. In all our moonlight experiences, we managed to have something of a party, just the three of us. Howling at the moon, imbibing substances, being decedent yet sophisticatedly understated. We always enjoyed each other's company, and so every time it worked fine. Adding new elements, like Wally or Hailey's experience with the reporter, felt risky. For this reason we only called Wally after the lion's share of the batch had finished, that which Percival and I started together. With Wally, we worked on completing Hailey's batch. Even if it didn't take, we wouldn't be too put out.

"So is that, like, it?" said Wally when we finished explaining, had dropped the moondust in the ash and stirred it, and bathed it in the light from Mother Luna.

"That's it," I said. "It has to be left in the moonlight, and you may as well leave it out all night. You have to be in good spirits, excited or happy, whatever. It's almost magical, really, what happens is, the same way moondust makes you into someone else, it turns the ash into more moondust. Whatever special property the stuff has is absorbed into the ash, you know? But, it can only happen when the moon is full. We don't really understand why. But, that's the way it is."

"Trippy," he said.

"Yeah."

"So, have you guys thought of what this stuff really is? Like, what is it?"

None of us answered. In truth, we didn't really know.

"Let's not get existential, Wally," Percival finally said. "It's beyond your reach."

"Hey," said Wally, injured, "I'm very existential. I'm the existentialist."

"Of course you are," Hailey said smoothly. "All set for Monday, superstar?"

"Yeah, I think I got it." His chest puffed out. "I'm going to spin the best set of my life, yo. Count on it."

"We are," I said. "Definitely."

He nodded and smiled. God help us all.

Later, after Wally left, the three of us stood on the roof by a bin of ash becoming moondust, passing around the last of the rue tea, and puffing on cigarettes. I felt fine, looking out over the water and Manhattan, and out at the future, which rushed at us aggressively as the ground during freefall, with the same promise of impact, if not the certainty of tragedy. A future so close and vast, it muted us, and we pondered it in silence; a deep and contemplative quiet, until it was broken.

"So, what about it?" said Percival.

"What are we doing, you mean?" Hailey responded. "What's going to happen? Hard to say."

"You can't keep a lid on some things," I said. "Suppression doesn't work, when a thing wants to bubble to the surface, no force on earth can hold the bubble back. It's physics and energy."

They took a second contemplating that. Then Hailey said, "After translating that into human, I basically agree. Moondust is going to get out somehow. But, maybe we could have chosen a more subtle method?"

"This was given to us," said Percival. "To us. I know I didn't always believe in a universe that had the capacity to pay attention before all this happened. But, I don't know. I've been toying with the idea lately. There's so much evidence for it, when you look, and you know where to look. With all the people we've been. We all know that more people have lived in a universe that cared, that was really and truly alive, than have lived only in a sea of unthinking, uncaring atoms. But, either way, this is ours. When something like this falls in your lap, when it becomes your charge... you go all out, you do it as big as you can. How could we do any different?"

Quiet rooted for a moment again, because Percival said a mouthful. Unusually, because he was never one for grand speeches.

"So we have to do this," said Hailey.

"In a weird way, yeah. I think we do."

"Because the bubble wants to get to the surface?"

I said, "And we are the water between wherever it came from and New York. We're just filling a role."

"So this is, what, karma?"

"Actually, it would be dharma. Technically."

Percival said, "Even with a few short Hindu experiences, I've never really understood the difference."

"I'd explain. But, it'd take too long for your tragically linear minds to get," I said.

"Dick."

"Yes, it's impeccable. Like to see?"

"Dude," he said, doing an impression of a panicky Wally, "I'm, like, totally down for show'n'tell. But, like, with the ladies. Know what I mean?"

We all cracked up. I was happy: I was with my friends. No matter what came for us all, in this moment, life was very good.

Friday, October 6, 2006

....

93. MAXWELL

Precinct 37 in Midtown Manhattan was a bustle of noise and motion even at ten o'clock. In a city that famously didn't sleep, ten o'clock was an off-hour for the criminal element, and by proxy those chosen to battle it. Yet the phones rang constantly, and civilians came and went: Some looking broken, while others appearing normal, business-like, as if this somewhat surreal environment was an every-day experience. The police themselves were the fluid, living centerpiece of the office, ebbing and flowing like tides, taking calls, perpetually tossing back cups of coffee, pushing through the red tape that was a foundation of their job. In their state of relentless, concerted activity, they were reminiscent of hive animals: human-sized blue bumble-bees.

I worked on this description while waiting for Detective Greene. After editing it down, I spoke it into my recorder, sure I could use it for the magazine piece I planned, the more upscale of the two moondust pieces. They would launch the Maxwell brand; everyone was a brand, after all. Some understood their nature as a scarce non-commodity, and the rest whined about how unfair life was. Hawks and pigeons.

The articles neared completion. But, I was a wreck of frayed nerves and exhaustion. I worked all night to complete workable roughs. They only lacked write-ups of two future events: the moondust fete being thrown by Percival et. al., and my current interview with the police. I needed to call work first thing next Monday morning and explain what I'd been working on, so I needed to be as far along as possible by then.

That I'd waited an hour for Greene wasn't helping. Mental note: This was the last time I'd walk into a police precinct cold. After this, I'd have a contact, and I would use it.

Sitting in this cheap, uncomfortable plastic chair sucked. But, on the plus side, it helped me stay awake. The watery coffee seemed better at burning my taste-buds than fighting sleep, given the drip-drip of lazy minutes drifting by.

I needed to use the time effectively. I needed to check in with Peter, the chemist, to check his progress. I took out my note pad in case he said anything worth writing and called his cell.

"Max," he said, "hey."

"What have you got for me?"

"I have absolutely nothing. Just some ideas."

"Can you tell me? Think soundbite."

I heard him take a deep breath. "Dark matter."

"That's not a soundbite, it's a concept."

"It's is an educated guess. The idea being there are forces in the universe we can't account for, given the amount of matter in the universe, so there must be extra matter we can't detect."

"So?"

"What if there's more to it? What if we're missing something?"

"I don't understand."

"Think of this example. A tree falls famously in the forest. It does make a sound, and in this case someone is there to hear it. But, when they get over to the tree, it's no longer a tree, it's a microwave oven."

"What?"

"Moondust is connected to the universe in some way we can't understand." Thus, proving my theory—Peter had lost it.

Quietly, I said, "What happened to the objective scientist? The one who studies truth with method?"

"He's a damned dream. Listen, Max, I got to go. Call me if you're coming by." He hung up.

I felt like Alice—a manly version, of course—falling down a Mobius-shaped rabbit hole. The severity of the act I was taking, informing the police of moondust, suddenly frightened. These were forces beyond my control.

I needed some air. I stood up to leave the room.

"Mr. Smith?" said a woman, a cop, blocking my way. "Where are you going?"

"Just outside for a second."

"That'll have to wait," she said. "Detective Greene will see you in a moment. Please sit down."

....

94. LEONARD

"That him?" I asked Shelly, inclining my head toward a skinny guy in fancy-boy clothing, sitting in the wait area, sipping a cup of the precinct's shitty brew.

"That's him. Name is Maxwell Smith. Says he works for The New York Globe."

I nodded, drank my own home-made coffee. He looked like I'd imagined him. They always did.

"Keep an eye on him for me, will you?" I said. "I want him to stew a while."

"Check."

Shelly was good like that. She didn't ask questions or give any backtalk, unlike the majority of her wise-assed compatriots. Young guys grew up watching Crime and Justice reruns on television, wanted to be like the actors they saw. Doofs spending all day cheesing it for imaginary cameras.

So given what she was up against, Shelly was destined to shoot right up the ranks. A natural cop, tough, perceptive, and loyal. She didn't need to ask why I iced the preppy because she knew. Guy like that, make him wait long enough, he cracks, 'cause he's used to being in control. He'd tell you anything to get back to where he called shots. Easy, squeezy.

I had tons of paperwork in piles on my desk, stuff I punted on all week. If the preppie hadn't need icing, I'd still be putting it off. But, I had to kill the time somehow.

I started with my department of homeland security reports, pointless DHS bureaucratic red tape nonsense. They couldn't just gift us with the extra jurisdictional abilities, they had to kick us in the ass, too. I doubted anyone ever even read these things. But, they sure did throw a fit if you didn't send them in.

Which meant explaining why I locked some fruitcake called the messenger in solitary, and how our lab boys flipped their shit over the designer drug the guy possessed. No way could I avoid sounding like a delusional whack-job. Then again, writing a nutty report was a sure way to find out if anyone actually read them.

So I detailed all I had on "chemical substance unknown-variable;" most of what I had went into the name. The sample zigzagged from lab to lab across the city. But, none of the eggheads knew squat.

During a quick break, I checked on the human Gap catalogue in the waiting area. He proved this stuff was for real, a future Class A narcotic with epidemic threat. Hadn't even gone looking, yet, and he came knocking on the precinct door, literally knocking, throwing around a new street name, describing the very attributes currently giving the lab boys aneurisms.

I almost felt sorry for the guy, given I would have to go at him hard. But, I needed to turn my empathy off on this one. The needs of the many outweighed all, and the many needed me to stop proliferating so-called moondust by any means. I'd seen too many drug wars, we all had. If I could stop that before it started, even the angels would approve my methods.

Now he was listening to his cell phone, looking green in the gills. I needed to know the subject of that call and to who was on it. I added that to the list of thing to discuss when I got him singing.

I finished typing up my HSRs, then did some other paperwork. I even called the wife, to say I'd probably be late. Had a meeting in the afternoon with the captain, yet another sign the threat was real.

The preppie finally cracked. He stood up and made a bee-line to the door.

I swore because I was back at my desk, too far away to stop him. He'd come voluntarily so technically he was free to go, and free to never come back.

Lucky for me Shelly appeared out of nowhere, and got between him and the door. Right then I decided to mention her to the captain, even if I had to force her into the conversation. If guys like me didn't talk up the good cops, then only assholes would get promoted, and it rained shit enough already.

Shelly grabbed his shoulders gently, looked into his eyes, and said about five calm words. His shoulders sagged, and he sat back down, burying his head in his hands, but then stopped. Instead, he sat up in a desperate bid to seem nonchalant. Oh yeah, he was ready.

I walked over to Shelly and said, quietly, "In ten minutes take him to room two."

We used room two when we needed to put the screws in. It was lighted by a bare bulb above a table with three chairs. Two of the chairs were for cops, and on the other side of the table sat the chair for snitches and suspects, bolted to the floor. We didn't want them to be able to make adjustments to get cozier. Not a seat you wanted to spend any time in at all, which was the whole point.

I went there, sat in one of the nice cop chairs, and waited. Soon enough the doorknob twisted, and my guy walked in. "You must be Smith," I said. I heard you wanted to see me."

I waited until he opened his mouth to speak. First, he got his nuts under him, squaring his shoulders. Then, right when he started talking, I cut him off. "Have a seat," I said. "Right there."

He looked flummoxed as he sat down. It helped that we bolted the chair so far from the table. The psychological effect of being able to hide the lower half of your body was underappreciated. It was less like sitting at the table than being put on display. Smith reached down and tried to pull the chair forward. Which, of course, didn't work. I slowly put my elbows on the table and laced my fingers. When I did, his eyes told me he began to understand.

"So," I said. "You were going to talk to me about this new stuff on the streets."

....

95. MAXWELL

I made myself take a few deep breaths. Detective Greene was putting the press on me, using his interrogation skills either by accident or design. He struck clean with the grim reality of my situation: in a police station, possessing critical knowledge, completely at this man's whim.

"I came here to get a statement, not make one," I told him, using all the balls I had. But, still only looking at the table between us, and not at the man.

"Is that right?"

I heard the smirk in his voice.

"Yeah. I didn't do anything wrong."

"You said on the phone you knew some things, is all. I'm trying to find out what you know."

"Hell of a way to go about it."

"You think this is the hard way? Guy, this is me being cuddly. Especially since I've got a freaking weird case that fell on my lap, and the captain's breathing down my neck about it. I've got to get results, like yesterday. I have every reason to pursue any lead as aggressively as the most liberal laws on the subject might allow. "

"I don't see why that would be necessary."

"Nice to hear you plan to cooperate. So, where shall we begin?"

It took all my courage to pull out my recorder. "Do you mind if I record this conversation?"

His eyes narrowed, and the room got colder. "Explain why you brought that into my room and why you're trying to turn it on."

"I'm just here as a reporter and a citizen, trying to give you information you may need and getting a brief statement about the moondust situation in return. Which is not a lot to ask."

The surge of relief I got putting the recorder between us was something to hold on to, a seed of crystallizing order in a sea of chaos. So I flipped it on.

Detective Greene said, "Turn that thing off. Now!"

"I'm here voluntarily."

"Now!"

"Fine, but I'll be leaving, too. Unless you want to charge me with something?" I put my hand on the recorder. But, I didn't flip the switch. The detective's eyes fastened on my hands. "Look, I'm getting the impression you think we're enemies. But, there's no reason we should be. I came here for a win-win. I'm trying to help you, and all I'm asking is that you help me, too. Just a little bit. Just with a couple of words. You can be as general as you like, and if you want, you can be anonymous. I just need something like: 'We are very concerned about this situation and looking into it as quickly as we can.' Maybe something about how moondust as unclassifiable is causing you a headache, and how you plan to get around that. Is that really so much to ask?"

He didn't answer. So I kept talking.

"Well if it is, then we're enemies, and you have to lock me up—or something—and do a ton of paperwork, and try to justify it to your captain—or whomever. If he's breathing down your neck, I don't think you need the headache. So either we both win or we both lose."

He stood, without a word, and left the room. I heard a click when the door shut, likely the door locking behind him. The silence left in his wake was powerful. I reeled with adrenaline, and the fear I pushed away.

The possibility of this ending well for me felt slim now, if it existed. Unfortunately, given the momentum gained, I couldn't reverse course.

....

96. LEONARD

Back at my desk, I decided to give the boss a call, much as I hated to do so. Only thing holding me back was ego: I hated the reporter dictating terms, and I especially hated the smirk on his face when he did. The problem was that damned recorder. He'd been about to shit his pants. But, putting me on tape threw his fear right out the window, fucking up my questioning in the process.

I guess I could have tossed his dumb ass in the clink. But, two people in on trumped-up homeland security violations was pushing it. It would have made me feel a lot better, yeah. But, as an officer, sometimes you needed to swallow your personal feelings.

"So what do you think you should do?" captain asked, after I reported the situation.

"Promise him an anonymous statement, if he gives good intel. That way, if any politicos get their panties in a twist, you'll be in the clear."

"I'm glad you're seeing straight, today."

I thought of a retort, but I decided to leave career suicide for another day. Besides, it wasn't him who had me mad.

"Knock this one out of the park," he continued. "I want you to give him the statement. But, play hard to get, milk him for all he's worth. If this goes right, the public will put pressure on the mayor to give us legal leverage we need here."

He was telling me stuff I already knew. "Sure, boss. I'm going to get to it, alright?"

"We never had this conversation." He hung up.

I took a couple of deep breaths, grabbed another cup of my coffee, and went back into the interrogation room.

"Okay. Here's the deal," I said, walking toward the table where Smith sat. "Option one: You tell me what you have. If I like your intel, then I give you an anonymous statement. Maybe take a question or two. Then you get the hell out of here and never bother me again.

I waited for that to sink in, watching his face. It didn't change. I continued. "Option two. You decide not to take option one, and you get the hell out of here. I decide you're probably in with whatever lowlifes are trying to prosper off this stuff, and I keep my eye out for you. And if I ever—and I mean ever—get the chance, I'm taking you down. Your choice."

"I'll take option one, obviously." He reached for his recorder.

"You turn that thing on before I say so, and you can take a walk."

"Okay, fine," he said. But, whatever confidence the recorder gave him was gone. "Where do you want me to begin?"

"I don't know, you tell me. What's the beginning?"

He started talking slow at first, like they all did. But, before long, the story tumbled out all on its own. Hell of a story, too. Even with the mystery drug zigzagging across the island from geek to geek, I found parts tough to believe, even though my nose told me he meant every word.

It went like this: The messenger, whose real name was Harold Westgate according to Smith, gave him and his girlfriend a packet of the substance, called moondust, on the street. Smith here wanted to break the story in the worst way, so he went reporting. He infiltrated the hip Manhattan party scene because he figured designer drugs flowed through clubs, and he got lucky. He fell in with a crew fronting as artists while dealing moondust to clients in the know, who cloaked their operation in secrecy to duck the law. He actually helped them fend off some other lowlifes, who wanted to horn in on their business in return for information—that surprised me, I didn't think he had the salt.

But the three dealers got skittish about being the only game in town, so they planned a big party to let the cat out of the bag. They'd tell everyone at the party how to make the stuff, taking the pressure off themselves, allowing them to ride off into the sunset.

Smith skirted around the necessary details of who they were, when they were doing it, and where the event would be. He'd probably hide behind freedom of the press on that one, and if so we might be in for a fight. I'd win. We needed to be there, and we needed a way to keep what they were planning from happening.

End of story. No way would this go down on my watch.

Smith also got in-depth descriptions of the psychoactive experience from users; this was where his intel got nutty. You might as well start believing in hobbits and unicorns. There had to be a better explanation, something science-y. But, it didn't really matter. Point was, this stuff fucked with people's heads on heretofore unseen levels, and nothing upset the balance more than new drugs hitting streets. Gang wars happened. People got ripped off—killed—to support habits. It was bedlam every time. I wouldn't say I was scared. But, I was deeply concerned.

When he finished, I said, "You know, I planned on taking it easy on you, I really did. Don't get me wrong, I think you're a fucking twat. But, I was going to give you your statement, let you walk; I wasn't going to pursue you."

"Oh? What's changed?"

"Did you listen to what you just said? You just described crack all over again. If this party goes down, then we're looking at another epidemic. Whole neighborhoods will be destroyed. If you were me, what would you do?"

A light came on somewhere in his stupid little head. It caused him to deflate, again. But, he didn't speak.

"Go ahead, answer."

"If I were you, then I'd do everything I could to stand in their way."

"Yeah, you would. And how would you go about doing that?"

"Are you going to let me leave?"

I had that look in my eye, I didn't even have to try. Never meant it before like I did now. "Depends on what you say next."

....

97. ANNIE

It read:

You Are Cordially Invited

To a Disconnect Magic Theatre Presentation:

The Moondust Sonatas

(Blurring the lines between you and me)

Sunday, October 8, 2006

at

Valkerye, 1990 Kensington, Bronx, Ground Floor

Featuring DJ Wally Beaver.

Harry and Hermione will attend to your visions.

Admittance: $20

For Madmen and

Madwomen only.

And I just had to laugh. It brought back my days of being a literature major—a Steppenwolf-themed party? I had to admit, it was intriguing.

For one, the planners had to be given points for obscurity. It wasn't the most widely read book in this country. They used it to interesting effect, too. Sure, it was probably the usual bullshit, using a great work of literature as nothing more than an ego booster for the DJ or whoever. (Look at what we can reference!)

But, despite my skepticism, I had to admit that it had me curious.

The link had come from my friend Elba, who was pretty plugged in to the scene. Which was another tick in the plus column for the event. She only sent me these things when they were sure bets. I figured, why not?

Even if it turned out to be lame, we could make it fun.

....
98. STEVEN

My guy Wally Beaver sent me a text. It had a link to a website. The website was a single page, and it was an invite to a party, "The Moondust Sonatas, A Magic Theatre Production."

Sounded interesting. Wally had told me about some crazy stuff called moondust a few times. But, wouldn't give me any. Said the people who sold it were trying to keep it extra hush. Now, they were throwing parties and all. And he was in on it. Made me wonder if he was selling it all along and was blackballing me for some reason. Which sucked big time.

But I was totally going to this party, so I guess I'd forgive him. I wondered if he'd need any of my multi-media pieces for, like, ambiance. That would be kick fucking ass.

....
99. SIENNA

"The Moondust Sonatas?" Whatever.

You couldn't be an A-list recording artist, like I was, without getting this kind of thing, invitations to random events from random people who somehow know your email address. Everyone always hoping you'd show up to whatever they invited you to, so they could leech off your name. This one came from a hairdresser who'd styled me for a shoot last month, according to the email containing the link. I didn't remember her at all. How the hell did she get my private email address?

It was so alienating somehow, lonely. 'Cause, how could you ever tell, when someone was looking at you, how polluted their minds were by your public image? Really, the better question was: What was the chance their minds weren't polluted by it? No one was genuine with each other in this world. That was just the way it was, as much as we all hated it.

Some days, I felt like life was about running from my shadow.

Anyway, I had better things to do with my fame than be a black Barbie at some hipster's disco ball. I am an artist, and I was in a position to help people. We all needed to stay positive, and be about the things that matter.

····················

100. ROB

It was definitely time to crack some skulls.

Will, Clyde, and I were wandering around Manhattan looking for the messenger. What kind of asshole called himself that? And did he even exist? Probably not. This sounded like some nonsense Will told Clyde to get us off track, maybe so he could go off on his own.

Either that or he was stupid enough to believe this shit. Or maybe some guy actually was out here giving away moondust, and the mob had given us some fucked up order, as if they were my boss, to lay off the guy in Williamsburg and get our info from some fuckhead in Manhattan with a stupid name. If so, then Will, Clyde, and I were screwed, because the dude was nowhere to be found. Nowhere.

So, I was pissed. Instead of going to Williamsburg and grabbing the guy we knew—who was definitely back in his apartment by now—we were out here, looking for some phantom with an abandoned apartment.

We'd gone to Harold's building four days ago. That was the messenger's real name, as given to us by some Slavic mobster. He lived in a neighborhood in Brooklyn, chocked full of Puerto Ricans, looking at us like, 'Why the hell are you guys here?' Not that I gave a fuck. I had my gun for problems like them; they were best off leaving me alone.

The messenger had split, if he ever lived there in the first place. If he was even real. And that I definitely gave a fuck about—wasn't nothing in his apartment, but roaches and a real funky smell. The front door hung wide open, too. We didn't even have to pick the lock.

Looking out of his window over that nothing neighborhood gave birth to the anger boiling over in me now. Sure, I'd been stressed before, about how I was partnered with people who didn't know the game from their own sweaty asses. But, it hit a whole new level. They were wasting my time. I didn't have time to be wasting.

"What the fuck, you guys?" I had said.

"He ain't here," Clyde said, stating the obvious. "What do you want me to do about it? Blink and nod like Barbara Eden?"

"Barbara Eden?" Will asked.

"I Dream of Genie, moron."

"Who gives a shit about Barbara Eden?" I shouted. "What the fuck do we do now? We're wasting our time here. This guy's a myth. May as well be looking for Sasquatch."

"So you think the mob and some random girls made up the same dude? Where's your head?"

"Watch what the fuck you say to me. Especially when you're trying to sell me bullshit. Makes my fuse short. Hear me?"

He took a step back and adjusted his tone. Good for him. "Okay. It's all bullshit. But, it being bullshit doesn't tell us what to do next. Bottom line, we got to do our best to find this guy. That's what we said we'd do, and that's all we can do. You got a better idea, please share."

And so we all were on our own schedules now, wandering around Manhattan looking for this dude named the messenger, wasting more time. Everyone agreed that on the off chance any of us found him, we would call the others. Not that I thought it would actually happen. But, they'd better tell me if they found him, because if I ever found out they cut me out, I'd kill them both. Slowly. With dull knives and socket wrenches.

In fact, it'd been two days since I'd heard from either of those two fools. And that made me angry.

I was in a pool hall now, drinking a beer, smoking a cigarette, and nursing my frustrations. And then, I got a text from Clyde.

It was a link to a party. Called, "The Moondust Sonatas."

Which, of course, turned everything on its head. Everything.

I texted him back, "See you there." And I went the fuck home.

I didn't know who Wally Beaver was, but I had some pent up aggression with his name all over it. Finally, things were looking up.

....

101. YVONETTE

I got a text from Wally,
Out of the blue. But, it hadn't been that long.
I hadn't expected to hear from him, hadn't wanted to.

Didn't want anything.
Or even know where I was

Daddy wanted me to come home.
Of course, he did, and I?
What did I want?

Didn't want anything.
And nothing brought clarity, nothing could.

Was it good that I'd talked to them? Was it what I wanted?
Like ripping the bandage off something, exposing it to air

A sick emaciated tiger caged in the back of my brain:
Opening the doors of the cage, even a little bit,
It attacked.

Well. There was nothing new there,
It was the oldest story. So dull.

The pain parents cause us. They might as well be planets,
With inescapable gravity.

Wally was throwing a party,
Featuring his new drug
And I was in my bedroom drinking, listening to Neil Young,

Wondering how, when I lost my way.
Or had I ever even been on it?
A wreck that called herself a girl

Would I go?
To Wally's party, would I go?

Moondust was fucking evil
But, I was too.

Everything in my childhood taught me that and
Everything in my soul knew it and
It was why—the answer to every question.

So how could I go home? And why not go

To the party?

Why not take every drug known to man? And
Why not fuck every man known to drugs?

I was a sooty little ball of sin
And I couldn't even fool myself
Into thinking the kingdom of Heaven never existed

I knew now.
I'd seen now.
My parents were wrong, but they'd always been right.
Always.
Wrong as they were, they'd always been right.

Saturday, October 7, 2006

....

102. JUSTINE

Saturday, a lazy kind of day that I was out trying to enjoy. I got a text from Maxwell, now my ex—or had our relationship lasted long enough for him to be called that?

The tone of the text seemed impersonal, to say the least. It described a party. I read this while I shopped at the Saturday market, buying fruit and vegetables from local farms on this stereotypic fall day. The air had a snap to it, a cold clarity reminding one of diamonds. No clouds marred the sky, everything seemed hyper-real.

Before the text came, I strolled among the sellers and the hawkers, looking first at a young woman's extensive collection of paintings, which she's spread out on the sidewalk before her. The paintings struck me as mediocre, rote pictures of the city's skyline, semi-nude self-portraits, and still lifes. I did not buy anything from her, but chatted for a moment, telling the white lie I thought her work provocative. She spoke with me without hiding her boredom, as if the experience was as standard and unexciting as her paintings.

I quickly moved on.

I browsed the stands of fruits and vegetables, occasionally picking up and smelling plums or bushels of spinach. But, I didn't talk to any of the vendors. I guess I'd only one conversation in me, today.

I was examining some artichokes when the text came through. I read it, staring at the screen for quite a while, letting the city move around me. Then, I put my phone back in my purse and went home.

....

103. PETER

It was a party, one of those things where hip kids with trust-funds experimented with designer drugs and other people's genital emissions. Therefore, it was not the kind of thing chemistry geeks like me usually got invited too. But, of course, ever since Max had me analyze moondust, nothing felt normal.

The party invite scared the hell out of me. The thought that kept running through my head was critical mass.

A substance with fundamental instability—like, for example, a radioactive isotope—tended to be less dangerous in small amounts. If one grouped enough of it together, the effects amplified, sometimes exponentially—like a nuclear bomb.

Did the moondust have a critical mass? And what would happen if it did?

And what would happen if a bunch of party kids became critical mass by dropping the powder in their eyes all at once? The brain on moondust acted as if it were moondust. Consciousness became liquid. And the only thing about a brain that made it special was the self, the I Am instinct of the human being. For all other intents and purposes, a mind was a collection of bioelectric wires. Cells in superconductive jelly lighting up like so many Christmas lights.

One atom that became moondust showed up as an infinite variety of atoms when observed. One person on moondust— seemed also to become moondust in that person—briefly lived the experience of another. Therefore, when it came to moondust, we were no different than atoms. Just bigger and more complex...

If a group of atoms, such as a brain, responded to moondust the same way as one atom, it stood to reason that a group of brains could react to it as one thing as well. If they all took it at the same time, something new would happen. Critical mass.

And so I was full of wonder and terror. I tried to tell myself I was just being silly. But, I didn't really believe it. If something crazy happened the world would notice. The scientific community would shit a collective brick the size of Giza pyramids. Everything would change.

....

104. Maxwell

So it was the tomorrow that Friday had promised.

I had my draft finished, except for the finale, of sorts, which would be whatever happened during "The Moondust Sonatas." I had to admit, the title was catchy. I respected that.

I came to the conclusion that my piece read like a failed soufflé. It lacked pop, even though I'd done everything the right way, in classic exposé style.

But maybe that was my mistake: Trying to stay classic, yet forward thinking, to write the kind of piece I figured the big zines would eat up. Trying to frame the story so it seemed I had my journalistic integrity intact. The truth was that I'd betrayed that integrity inch by inch, and then totally, all at once, the minute I gave my sources up to the police.

Now my life was in free-fall.

When I sent my boss the email with my copy attached, trying to stay ahead of things, she'd responded too fast for me to believe she actually read it. "See me tomorrow, first thing." Less an email than writing on the wall. I never believed it would happen. Not to me. They call that hubris. I understood. I counted on my own charm and subtle genius—and on my subject matter's groundbreaking nature. Yet, none of it was real.

So I sat in my apartment, staring at my computer and drinking whiskey, looking for a way to salvage something from this. Of course, the drinking didn't help.

I also avoided making a call. My avoidance was symbolic; calling Detective Greene wasn't up for debate. He made it clear I was on a short leash; if I didn't call, he would come looking for me. Still, this stank as the point of no return.

So I drank, and sat, and moved the mouse every once in a while to keep the screensaver from taking over the computer. And read lines from my disappointing first draft, lines like, "In what most disciplines call the Post-Modern age, moondust represents a massive escalation—as if the very theories and ideals that have decayed clarity in fields like art, literature, and social science have spread, virus-like, to both science and religion, obscuring our deepest and most fundamental ways of knowing the world around us." A good sentence, but out of place, treading water in a piece lacking heart or direction.

If I had a paper copy, I'd have thrown it out the window. But, it was on the computer, so throwing it out the window would cost me quite a bit of money. I sublimated the urge, using the destructive energy to place the call—once and for all killing my dreams of rescuing journalistic integrity. I could almost hear Milton Burrows: Et tu, Maxwell?

"Detective Greene," he said, answering the phone in the flattest voice.

"It's me, Maxwell Smith."

"You drunk, Smith?"

"Yeah," I said, annoyed. "You got a problem with that?"

"Long as you ain't driving."

"Fine. Can I text you at this number?"

"What have you got?"

"What you're looking for. They're sending out invites."

"Send it to (212) 555-3829. My cell."

"We're done after this, right?"

"If it's good intel? Yeah."

"Good," I said and hung up.

I texted right away. And then I sent it to Peter, the chemist, for good measure. And Justine. 'Cause why not?

I drank some more and fell asleep.

....

105. LEONARD

After I read the text my canary sent me, I sat for a while thinking things through. Then, I came to a few decisions. I got the messenger out of the hole to see if the time he'd spent—trapped in his own crazy—had softened him up.

Not that it mattered much, I didn't really need him anymore. Sure, any information would help. But, my top priority was stalling his release long enough to find something on the books to hit him with. It would take some finagling, and even if it didn't work, at least I kept him off the streets as long as possible.

I went down to the holding facility and waited while they pulled him up. Sat in a standard interrogation room, whistling an old song trying to remember its name.

First thing I noticed about him was his walk. He shuffled in like his legs didn't work; a few days in the hole would do that to you.

I tried to check his eyes, but they were hard to see. He hadn't been about to win a beauty contest before we threw him down there, and the time didn't help. Half a week's beard obscured his face. His head hung down, but it read as something other than the normal defeat. I decided to be cautious, take a wait-and-see approach.

"So, bright boy, how you feeling?" I said, after he'd sat down. But, he didn't respond.

"I asked you a question. You're going to answer. "

"Or what?"

"Guy, what do you think I couldn't do to you?"

"Break me."

And now he let me look into his eyes. They were feverish and ironclad.

"Okay," I said, "truth time. The easiest thing for me to do with you is throw you back down there, lose the key, and forget about you. I got you in here on a homeland security violation, and the tests on that stuff you had were inconclusive. So I get to treat you like Al Qaeda and no one's going to make a peep to defend you. "

Finally, a trill of fear shot through him. Didn't matter how much iron a guy had in him, solitary was hell, pure and plain. Most would do anything to avoid it after an extended stay.

"But you're right. I'm not going to torture you, water board you, or any of that shit. I really don't have to, and honestly, who has the time?"

I leaned in like I was about to confide in him. A bit of theatre.

"Did you know some guys are throwing a moondust party? Like, DJs or something, they're doing a Studio 54-kind of deal, which is pretty hedonistic, don't you think? I mean, as far as you're concerned, this stuff is holy, and they're treating it like it's just another recreational drug. For you, that must be like they're taking a dump on the Bible."

"You're lying," he whispered.

"You want to see the text?" I pulled out my cell phone, brought up the info, and tossed it to him. "Here. Take a look."

He stared at it, and then a tremor went through him. All the warning I got. Next thing I know, the cell phone flew at my head. By reflex I jerked back, so it glanced off of my temple, doing a lot less damage than it could of. I was off balance, falling to the left, which was actually lucky, because the psycho flung himself across the table at me, following the phone. His still-cuffed hands reached for where I'd been a second ago, going for my throat, but missing. His elbow grazed my chest. He clattered into the table, and it fell over; we tumbled to the floor together.

Then my training kicked in.

I hooked my hand behind his head, pushed up from my hips, and succeeded in reversing our positions. Now, he was below me, and I straddled him; I hit him once, hard enough to knock his teeth through the linoleum. He curled up, moaning, the fight out of him. I wanted to hit him again; I raised my fist, but instead of letting it fall, I hung it in the air, resisting the urge to punch down over and over and over again, until his head became a bloody smear. Took everything I had. I was screaming.

After forever, some cop pulled me back up against the wall, while another restrained Westgate.

My breath came hard and ragged, and I knew nothing else would be learned, now. "Fucking crazies," I said and walked out of the interrogation room.

Adrenaline had my hands shaking, shooting pains burned my knuckle and now there was only one way forward, a no-holds-barred raid, and I guess I liked it that way just fine.

....

106. HAROLD

I would not break.

They would not break me, I would not break.

Though they had my body trapped in this hell,

My mind blurred and burned by isolation and darkness—and the killing emptiness of hours and days where nothing happens, and no one goes,

I would not break.

So my path to Heaven led through Hell—though I was beaten and bloodied by demons, though they may never let me go—I would join my God in death.

This was my test, I would not break.

Devil. You devil, I will beat you.

I will.

Sunday, October 8, 2006

In a slow motion dance, slowed by chemicals rushing beautifully through our blood, Hailey, Mark, myself, and a few other people were preparing our venue for tonight. The other people here with us were friends of Mark who called themselves The Disconnect. They were something of a party-planning conglomerate, who threw immaculate events that earned the right reputation for what we were doing. There were a lot of different crews like theirs. But, most chased status so hard, they diluted their rep by doing a ton of mediocre scenes. The Disconnect, however, understood the value of their brand. They held their last event in January, and they'd only done a few since their legendary break-out fete, which was in 2004, and featured balloons full of party favors—mostly smoke-able items, tabs, or tinctures of chemicals, such as I'd recently ingested—which floated down from the ceiling almost at random, by way of a weak glue that predictably failed between the hours of midnight and four o'clock. There wasn't anything really unusual in those balloons, but everything magical in their delivery and balletic effect. It was genius, really.

Of course, they planned some equally impressive tricks for tonight. There was a group of them in one of the back rooms right now, actually testing something. What, I didn't know. They wouldn't tell me. It was pretty ridiculous to cut me out of the loop. But, whatever. They did what they did well, and I guess I didn't need to know, yet. As long as it worked.

Besides, as far as The Disconnect went, I was more concerned with those members working with Hailey, Mark, and me on the two floors of this converted warehouse that would serve as the setting for moondust's unveiling. And one member, in particular, named June. Black eyes, olive skin, indeterminate racial background, mystery in every inch of her.

There is no woman on earth like an unknowable woman, the kind no man's brain can ever contain. Like the essence of femininity itself, which as far as we boys are concerned is as magical as unicorns, tougher to understand than rocket physics on ketamine. We don't have the equipment—or maybe we lack the stillness—the vast calm internal space that holds the possibility of creating life. It gives rise to a level of empathy no man can fathom enough to even envy. Except, of course, on moondust.

I saw it in her eyes, June was that type, magical. Then again, maybe that was all bullshit, and I was just into the way her ass looked in her jeans. Who knew?

There was only one way to find out, through a grin and a clever greeting, an innocuous conversation turning into something warmer, that—if she chose—would grow into desire and detonate us. We'd find ourselves after the explosion, when we sifted through the wreckage to discover what remained.

Probably, as per usual, there would be nothing, not for me—only the urge to be alone again, to shed an unreal version of me, sit in my underwear, and eat cereal while watching the Travel Network, letting the day-after feeling wash over me in hormone tides. The romantic in me always held out hope that I'd feel different this time. Or maybe that was my libido in disguise, whispering sweet sins into my receptive ears.

Why did my desire never stay? It lasted a day or a week, sometimes a few months. But, it never stayed. I had no idea why. But, I could paint this wall the color that they asked me to. And I could create mood with music as well as anyone alive, I could make your blood dance in your veins, move you onto the floor against your will—if I wanted. And apparently I could help to catalyze a cultural phenomenon, and unleash it onto Manhattan.

Moondust. Was the world ready?

I shook the question out of my head. Who was I to worry about the world? The world was an infinity of fractals, a thing so vast and varied that to imagine it as singular was the greatest of human failings. I'd learned that by being people so different from each other, it was hard to put them all under the same conceptual umbrella.

So why worry about the world? We were concrete things, people with needs, needs like safety and freedom, and so we were here. And the show would go on.

I had to laugh at myself a little, because only a moment ago I'd been musing on "the grand mystery of the feminine," exactly the kind of abstraction I claimed to have outgrown. Yet, here I was, putting a real, flesh-and-foxy woman on this pedestal. I guess the difference between ignorance and idiocy is that idiocy should know better. But, she was gorgeous enough to make my error understandable, this June. It was all I could do to keep from outright gawking.

....

108. JUNE

He finally spoke to me around noon, right before lunch. I wondered, did it take him that long to find his nerve or had he planned it so? His manner was unreadable, making it hard to tell. He moved in a fluid way, either charmingly unaffected or too self-conscious, which would be decided by what he did, what he said, and how he smiled, if he decided to try.

Did I look forward to it? This moondust stuff had an obscene amount of buzz in my circle. No one even let me try it yet, which was tantamount to a crime. Nico and Bob—I could see those two leaving me out of the loop—but, Sam and Hen? I'd have been weird about it if they hadn't had such a deep look in their eyes, when they explained—or rather hinted—what moondust was like. It helped that they swore they were bound to the upmost secrecy, because they were getting the stuff second-hand from Bob, which apparently was against some rule? I guess I could have been pissed at Nico. But, since I chose to sit out the event where they shared it, I had no one to blame, but me.

Because of all this, those few who sold moondust held the glamour of scions, creators of American culture. So yes. On some level, I found him interesting, at least intellectually. He was cute enough, too; in other words, his vibe didn't ruin the illusion.

He wore black tapered jeans and boat shoes. The jeans were current without overdoing the skinny thing that became all the rage not long ago, paired with stylish, yet tastefully subtle, shoes. He saved the color for the T-shirt-sports-jacket combo, washed-out eggplant and olive-green respectively, which he combined with a few days of facial stubble. Not a startlingly original look. But, I doubted he aimed for that, and the color combination worked beautifully with his skin tone. His brown eyes held a shade of hazelnut, they were far set, wide, and expressive. His lips, the color of bricks, begged to rest between my teeth. So yes, I thought him handsome, albeit with the blurred-photograph look of someone who took a lot of drugs. Not that I particularly minded.

As much as it worked on a few levels, the downside to his outfit seemed obvious—we would spend this day cleaning and painting. It intrigued me he didn't seem to care. Also that, even after a few hours, his clothing stayed clean, as if somehow he managed to dodge every drip, drop, and dust-particle flying around. I certainly hadn't. But, then again, I dressed for the occasion, in work-out tights and one of those huge, old sweatshirts that bred in one's closet.

I felt his eyes on me anyway, glued until I looked back, at which point they tended to wander.

Right around noon, when our collective tummies began rumbling, he sidled over to me. "Can I ask you a question?"

I felt that quickening of the blood, the little catch of breath, which always came with moments like these. "You do have lips, right?"

"I don't take anything for granted anymore."

"Hm. I don't think believing in object permanence counts as taking things for granted. Especially when the objects are attached to your face."

"Touché. Object permanence?"

I smiled and half-turned away from him, to keep painting the wall, leaving room for him to join me, if he wished, or walk away. "I minored in child development in college."

"I don't think I've ever heard anyone use that phrase in casual conversation."

"Doesn't say much for the people with whom you converse."

"Just that we speak English, not Mensa. Mind if I join you?" He raised his paint brush, gesturing to an empty section of wall.

"Only if you promise not to make more nasty insinuations about my vocabulary, you jerk."

"Deal."

"So was that your question?" I asked, referencing his original query.

"What? Oh—I was wondering actually about the choice of paint color, and why it's so important to have this particular shade so that we all had to get out of bed at the ungodly hour we did. I mean, might be kind of a waste, you know?"

"I take it you don't know Nico and Bob."

"Should I?"

"Yes. They're great. They can be a little fastidious, which is why the color choice mattered."

"I won't make fun of the fact that you just said fastidious, I promise."

"You know what a pet peeve of mine is? When people make a statement while declaring they would never make the very statement they're making. 'I would never say X. But, X.' While you're at it, why not get 'hypocrite' tattooed on your forehead?"

He threw his head back and laughed from his belly.

It made me like him.

....

109. HAILEY

Being the most mechanical of our trio, sadly, I was upstairs, helping two nice chaps named Bob and Nico work on a moondust delivery system. Nico was good friends with Mark, so we'd hung out a few times, and Bob once or twice, too. Also, I'd attended most of their crew's parties, which were always pretty rad. They had spades of panache.

Downstairs, folks were painting what would be the main ballroom, where the music would be thumping, attended to by

Wally Beaver. Up here, on the second floor, there would be no music, but that which would come from downstairs. This was the moondust room. And since the walls were already white-ish, the upstairs didn't need painting. With proper lighting, it would give just the effect we all were looking for.

Right now the room was pretty sparse. The bar was here already, sans the alcohol that would be the backbone of our profits. The Disconnect had access to a whole bunch of used furniture, by way of being able to borrow it from a second hand shop one of them managed. We'd be ensuring its safety by covering the furniture with cream colored drop-cloths, and one of The Disconnect crew, a girl named Henri, was out getting the sofas and chairs. She was the manager of the second hand store. Mark was with her for muscle, not that he had much of it. Luckily, although she had kind of a sex-pot vibe, it had to be said that Henri seemed sturdy, the kind of girl who could definitely handle herself. I liked that about her.

On the walls were three gigantic pieces, a series painted by Nico on very short order and with impressive talent. They were a controlled riot of colors, reminiscent maybe of Jasper Johns. But, not derivative. The whole color spectrum was boldly present, as if he'd strapped dynamite onto a rainbow. The layering of tone—as if the warmest sat on a background of cool violet blues and the white gleamed in front of it all—was somehow evocative of the moondust experience. And that was most impressive.

There was also text, on top of all that color. The piece directly across from the stairs had no words. But, on the other two walls, facing each other, the paintings featured instructions that were, really, the reason for this event. On the left, directions explaining how to take moondust; on the right texted piece, instructions on how to make it. They were both pretty simple. After all, the steps were pretty basic, not rocket science, really.

All in all, the effect of this room was going to be perfect. Just what Perce and Mark and I were looking for: form and function; style and substance. I was really happy with their work, I had to say.

But maybe the trickiest part was also the most important. For the event's finale, we were going to launch moondust through the air, and we had to ensure that it permeated the room. One goofy fan with an urn of powder in front of it wouldn't do. It was easy enough to get moondust airborne. But, the difficulty was achieving party saturation. That was really taking some effort.

We were brainstorming ideas. Mark had even mocked-up a little room so we could test air currents, which we did using smoke from cigarettes and miniature versions of the gigantic theatre-fans we probably would end up using, in some fashion, tonight. But, it wasn't going all that smoothly.

"Shit," Nico was saying, standing up with his hands on his hips. "None of our ideas are working."

Then, a lightbulb popped on over my head. "Maybe we're using the wrong kind of smoke?" I said, while producing a joint I had rolled earlier and put in my cigarette pack—just in case. Bob and Nico smiled.

Bob said, "You'd better tell your friends to watch out, we just may steal you."

"I'm loyal to the end, sorry," I said. "But I may be able to squeeze you guys in my busy schedule once in a while. If you impress me."

"We'll do our best," Nico said.

So we shared a joint. As far as figuring something out, it was always good to stay relaxed. Ideas never flowed when people got tight, and pouty gay men were not fun to be around. No one was when they were pouty, I guess. Not saying it's a gay thing.

"I'm so excited for tonight," said Bob, after a few puffs.

Nico responded before I did. "I know," he said. "This is going to be one for the ages, I can feel it. As long as we get this delivery thing figured out."

"We will," I said. Of course I wasn't really sure. But, it was what we all needed to hear. "The waters will part. A beam of light will shine from the Heavens and angels will sing and Keanu will show up in a banana hammock singing spirituals while greasing himself with baby-oil. Promise."

"Oh, you promise?" Nico said with a laugh. "Great. 'Cause before you promised, I thought you were bullshitting."

I grinned at him and responded, "Don't be negative. How could you, with sweet Mary here?"

"Gosh, you're right," he said. Then he took the joint.

I could tell my joking and smoke-able offering were working, I could feel their spirits lifting. And yet suddenly I started to fret. Not about our delivery system, that was going to work itself out, I really believed. About the whole night. One for the ages, Nico had said.

We had so much riding on it. We were trying to keep grounded about the whole thing. But, there was a lot of tension underneath the surface. I mean, a lot could go wrong. Inviting the very thing we'd been avoiding all along: attention from the public.

I imagined all the possibilities. A betrayal of some sort, probably by the reporter. The night being ruined by thugs. Or cops. Or thuggish cops. People being murdered, people I cared about. Or no-one showing up. Or so many people a panic started, or a fight, some kind of riot. Or Wally fucking up the music. Or neo-conservative investment bankers crashing the joint. I saw all these possibilities in vivid detail, like invisible private screenings of futures that might be.

But, onward! There was nowhere else to go. So I had to be a brave little big girl. And laugh from my soul.

Although the idea of our event being attended by neo-con wall-street types was terrifying beyond all reason.

With a familiar start, I realized that I'd become completely

absorbed in my thoughts. Marijuana had a tendency to do that—
you find yourself lost in your own inner world. Coming out of it,
I looked around, feeling as if I was seeing everything for the first
time. We were all done smoking, and we were sitting on the floor,
now. Were we sitting before? I didn't think so. But, it didn't matter.
My eyes were drawn again to the paintings, and I was filled with
gratitude. In my happy-altered place, they seemed works of genius.

"Nico, man, those paintings are beautiful," I said. My words
seemed to jangle both of them out of trances, very much like the
one I'd just been in. And Nico, he just beamed.

"Thanks," he said. "That really means a lot."

"He worked so hard," said Bob.

"Well, I mean it," I said and lit a cigarette, which was golden, I'll
tell you. "No bullshit. They're sublime."

"Okay, you are definitely on your way to becoming my favorite
person," said Nico.

"Hey," said Bob.

"You know what I meant," he responded, lighting a cigarette of
his own. Bob did, too. We lapsed back into quiet, the kind only
friends know. And it was good.

Ultimately, we decided on the simple solution, even though it
was imperfect. We tested out various arrangements of fans and
found that, with the size and shape of the main ballroom, the
best way to get the highest wind speed was the most obvious:
Put the fans in the corners of the room, angle each upward and
to the right, and create a sort of vortex effect. In the middle of the
room, we would attach a fan to the ceiling, if we were feeling lucky,
and that would hopefully help to cancel out the eye-of-the-storm
phenomenon, which would make the most active part of the dance-
floor the dead-spot in terms of moondust saturation.

We were unsure about the ceiling fan idea only because it would
take a good amount of time to set up, and our time was running

short. We'd have to secure it to the ceiling, secure its power cable and extension, and secure a safety cable to it that would keep it from killing people if the main supports failed. That could take a while.

We also had to set up a remote activation system, so that with one push of a button, we could empty canisters of moondust into each fan, all of which we'd keep on all night. That was going to be the difficult, and we'd spent a good amount of time discussing possible ways to get moondust into the fans. There was, of course, the analogue method—a bunch of dudes standing behind the fans, pouring moondust into them. But, that method had disadvantages, the main one being that once the pourers got moondust in their own eyes, they'd be completely useless. Ultimately, we decided that Bob, who had some random and mysterious experience in such matters—Bob said it was from doing special effects for off-Broadway plays; Nico rolled his eyes dramatically—was going to rig up simple electric blasting caps, using gunpowder and the guts of automatic lighters. The gunpowder was coming from a stash of illegal fireworks that Bob and Nico kept around for special occasions: Roman candles, mostly, by their telling. We were going to put the moondust in a series of large balloons, and glue the balloons and blasting caps together, and put them behind the fans.

We argued for a while about the aesthetics of this: it would be ugly, decided Nico, if we had a bunch of balloons behind fans in the corners of the room. Actually, Nico and Bob argued, and I mostly listened. Ultimately, the simple solution came from me, probably because I wasn't entrenched in their dynamic: We have no better ideas versus that is going to look so damn ugly, I just can't stand it. The solution: More balloons, sparsely spread around the walls and ceilings. Sure, it would be really a junior high prom. But, once the moondust went off, we were pretty sure people would understand why we'd done it. It would create a theme and keep the surprise.

In fact, we decided to put moondust balloon clusters on the ceiling, too, to explode and drop moondust on everyone and into the vortex of wind. We'd also have clusters that wouldn't be attached to wall or ceiling at all, loose around the party. And the balloons would all be black.

The walls in the room would be a dark sepia color, kind of a combination of chocolate brown and orange, and there would be red, shiny confetti everywhere. As upstairs would be very white, we were going for sort of a Heaven-Hell dynamic. But, subtle. I really thought it was going to work. But, lighting would be the key. Two of the girls in their collective specialized in that, and I was told they were excellent. The only trouble was time: There was so little of it. But, we were hustling, and they were pros, and Mark, Perce and I—well, we were simply excellent at everything. It had to be said.

So it was decided, and Bob went off to build the blasting caps, and Nico went to buy balloons, which he and I would fill with moondust, blow up, and tie shut. Which was probably going to be pretty tricky. While Nico was out, I had to place the fans and see if I could figure something out about putting one on the ceiling, which was going to be a bitch, even with our extra-tall ladder and such. I would definitely need help.

There was nothing to do about that, but to do it, while attempting to contain the fluttery feeling in my belly—some alien kind of excitement, reminiscent of something ancient and barely remembered, like the landscape of a dream. And try not to spy too hard on Percival—who was flirting with one of the girls and seemingly doing alright—and try not to think about what tomorrow might be like.

Tomorrow: Me, Hailey, in a different world. Tomorrow: A day viewed across this chasm, a threshold event planned for, but not understood. And so I had to tell myself, over and over, the truth: The dream of tomorrow never comes true. Every day is today.

....
110. LEONARD

A little after noon, I took Shelly with me and went down to the
address that the reporter gave me for the drug party. We took an
unmarked NYPD vehicle, an older model, dark blue, perfect for
this kind of thing. It was the type of car that blended into the city
like salt into the ocean. Not that I expected the socialite set to really
notice that they were being marked. In fact, I figured this was going
to be the easiest stake-out of my career.

The idea was to get a sense of what was going on down there,
before we had a team swoop in and drag every one of their sorry
asses off to the station for questioning. Once again, I thanked
my stars for homeland security legislation. That, plus unspecified
grayish powder, equaled free reign for us boys in blue. I could've
gotten a whole SWAT team down there to help an old lady across
the street.

The problem was this: Nothing was going on. The site referenced
in the text Maxwell Smith had sent me was in Bedford-Stuyvesant
neighborhood of Brooklyn, and it looked like an ordinary factory-
type building, turned into lofts, one of those sad, frightened
outposts of bohemia in neighborhoods full of sharks, hustlers, and
trapped unfortunates, who knew how to keep their heads down.
Kind of reminded me of home, actually.

But like home, in the daytime, not much was going on. You had
to figure that for one of these events, especially one as hyped as the
text message made "The Moondust Sonatas" sound, there had to be
people going in and out with supplies. Maybe paint. Maybe liquor
or party favors. But, there was almost no activity at all. Matter of
fact, the ground floor looked like an open-space lobby. Hard to
figure how there was going to be some big party there at all.

Shelly came to the same decision. "Either these guys are excellent
at covert ops, or nothing's going on here," she said, after a few hours

of a whole lot of boredom. I had to agree. It was possible that we'd either not recognized the players or they hadn't been using the entrance we'd staked out. But, I had this bad feeling in my stomach.

"I don't like it, either," I said as I took out my cell-phone and made the call.

"Hello?" answered Smith, the reporter, and his voice was weak with nerves. Like he expected my call and knew the reason for it. Made me suspicious.

"Smith. This is Detective Greene. I'm outside the address you gave me."

"Oh, really?" he asked, trying to sound nonchalant.

"Yeah, really. I think you know why I'm calling. Don't you?"

"Can't say that I do."

"Nothing's here, Smith. This does not make me happy. You don't want me grumpy, trust me. So how are you going to make me happy?"

There was silence for a second, and then he answered, "But I did what you asked me to do, everything you asked me to."

"You gave me a bullshit address, Smith."

"Then they gave me a bullshit address," he said, voice tight and rising.

So I made mine quiet, even dangerous. "Are you yelling at me?"

"No, sir," he sighed, "but I don't know what you want from me. You asked for the address, I gave it to you. You don't like it, okay, sorry about that. But, what am I supposed to do?"

I believed him. He'd given me the intel they'd given him, which meant that either it was actually good or they didn't trust him.

I had to make the decision, which meant instinct. So, I looked at Shelly, who was staring out the window at the door, an expression of annoyance clear as day on her face. She was sure no one was in there, and we were wasting our time.

"I believe you," I said to Smith. "Nevertheless, we got the same problem. This address is bullshit. Your people don't trust you."

"For good reason," he mumbled, with a lot of petulance.

"They're lowlife drug dealers so their trust ain't worth shit. What is worth shit is protecting the public interest. I need a good address, and I need you to give it to me."

"How am I supposed to give you an address I don't have?" Smith asked.

"Get it. As soon as you can, however you have to. You know how to contact them, right?"

"But as we established, they don't trust me."

"That's your problem. My problem is that I got to bring someone in today. It's them or it's you, your choice. Keep in touch." With that I hung up.

Shelly, sitting in the driver's seat, took the initiative to start the car. She didn't move out of the space, however, until I looked at her and nodded. Then she pulled into the street and headed back toward the station.

We didn't say anything on the way back. There was nothing to say, really. The situation was simple: Looking for one event in the whole city was like looking for a needle in a hay field. We needed Smith to come through. Without him, we didn't have shit, and we'd be left holding our dicks. Or at least I would. I wasn't sure what Shelly would be holding in that situation, and I was actively trying not to guess what it might be. It was really none of my business. I was married, maybe not happily so, but happily enough so that I wasn't trying to screw it up by sexualizing a broad who wouldn't sleep with me even if I were dumb enough to want to. I needed a sexual harassment charge like I needed gangrene. But, I digress.

....

III. PERCIVAL

This neighborhood wasn't exactly chock-full of restaurants, so when I took June out for a quick lunch, I had to think fast. The day wasn't cold at all, there was only a hint of autumn in it, so I managed to come up with a fairly romantic option, a simple one: eating tortas on some strangers' stoop.

Torta, a Spanish word, translates into "tasty fucking sandwich," like an Italian Panini. You could find corner grocery stores that sold tortas on most streets in Latino-heavy neighborhoods, if you walked far enough. So June and I took a stroll, until we noticed and dipped into a neighborhood shop with a deli and bought ourselves two of them.

While I watched the pretty girl behind the counter stack the chicken, cheese, and condiments onto the thickly sliced and toasted pieces of bread, June was off getting drinks. She came back with two deuces of Heineken.

"What kind of weirdo drinks before sundown?" I said.

"Oh, God. I've made a terrible mistake."

"You know I was kidding, right?"

She responded, "That's good because the mistake was accidentally doing lunch with a Puritan."

I had to laugh.

The woman behind the counter was less impressed, slit her eyes, and smacked her gum with sublime boredom. And her foot—tapping without real rhythm to reggaeton blaring from some hidden stereo—seemed to scream so what at the world. She handed me the two sandwiches, now tightly wrapped in the white paper that held them together. She rang me up, I paid, got change, and we were off.

We sat on a stoop of a building in mid-renovation. New York sounds assaulted us from every angle: radios blaring, pedestrians greeting neighbors as each rushed off toward some destination, men playing dominoes and smoking cigars outside of a laundromat, kids wearing hoodies making secret deals, cars imposing vicious, heavy beats on the world, distant sirens wailing.

"This torta is delicious," said June between bites.

"Beer ain't bad, either."

She nodded. "I hardly ever get over to this part of town."

"Oh yeah? Where do you live?"

"Off the G," she said.

"You like your neighborhood?"

"I can't complain. Rent's pretty good, no one bothers me."

"That's all you can ask for," I said.

"I'd kill for a grocery store in a two-mile radius."

I didn't answer, and there was silence for a second. It went too long, so I said the first thing that popped into my mind, which ended up being pretty strange.

"Do you like my belly button?"

She gave me the look this question deserved. "What?"

"My belly button. What do you think?"

"I... haven't seen it," she answered. But, her mental wheels were turning. She was deciding if this meant I was a total weirdo. I had to turn it into a joke or the game was lost.

"But you've imagined it. I know you have." And I poked my stomach out at her, rubbing it with my hand, pretending to be seductive.

A quizzical smile. "Who has belly button fetishes?"

"Word on the street is, girls who reference Nietzsche and say things about object permanence can't get enough of them. Umbilical envy, you know."

I got a laugh, thank God. She shook her head and said, "You're such an asshole," But, her voice got misty. The breeze blowing by us was perfect, and a wisp of black hair that'd fallen out of her pony-tail's conformity danced on it. Gracefully, she brushed the strand behind her ear with painted fingers. When she moved, time slowed a little. I smiled.

"What?" she asked.

"Your smile."

She grinned again.

Then my phone rang. I was tempted, very tempted, not to answer, to let the moment develop. But, that would have been too obvious, forcing the flow of events. I said, "I need to see who it is."

"Of course," she took a sip of beer and stared at something across the street.

It was Maxwell, douche reporter to the stars. "Yeah," I said, when I answered, not at all hiding the fact that I really didn't want to be speaking to him, hoping it would be quick, painless.

"Percival. How are you?" he said.

"Fine. What do you want?"

"I'm outside the address you sent me. I'm hoping to get in there, maybe look around a little, for the article. Can I come in?"

My brain switched gears so fast, I could almost smell oil burning.

Yesterday, when I sent Maxwell the information on the party, I pulled an audible. I changed the address on him, because I didn't trust him. I had no evidence that it was necessary. But, bottom line, the guy had his own agenda. On paper that agenda was his precious story. But, who knew what he'd do to get it?

And why was he trying to prowl around the party's future sight this afternoon? What could he possibly hope to learn? We'd already given him everything he said he needed. I smelled a rat.

"You there?" Max said.

"You're outside?" I said. "Why?"

"Um, well, you know, I thought maybe I could get the inside look, find something interesting. You know, before people got there."

"It's like one o'clock, man. Little early, don't you think?"

"I like being thorough."

"There's such a thing as too thorough. No back-stage pass for you." With that, I hung up.

He was lying to me, and it wasn't a very good lie, either. I'd seen him con the guys outside of my apartment, impersonating a gangster, so I knew he could bullshit well enough, when necessary. Such an obvious, ham-fisted bluff was hard to figure.

It would have been obvious to him, if he was at the address I'd given him, which we weren't there. Why not call and ask me, straight up, why I'd mislead him?

He wasn't there, either. It was the only conclusion. He was trying to make me think he was. But, he wasn't. Why?

"Everything okay?" asked June, reading the worry on my face. So I wiped it away.

"It's nothing," I said. "Just another tiny bit of bullshit I have to deal with. Se la vie."

"Your life is bullshit?"

"Don't be literal, baby," I said.

"Baby?"

I grinned at her. "Sorry. Are we not there, yet?"

My playfulness diffused the tension; she laughed. "You're fast."

"When I have to be," I said and took another bite of my sandwich.

....

112. Maxwell

After Percival hung up on me, I resisted the urge to hurl my blackberry into the wall, smashing it into a million pieces—or to scream.

"He's suspicious," I said, when I called the detective back, "He didn't tell me a thing. I don't have a new address for you."

"What did you tell the guy?"

"I said I was outside and wanted to be let in."

"And you're surprised he saw through that? I told you it was a bullshit address, you jackass. If you were there you'd know that."

"What would you have said?"

"Aright, never mind. You sit tight. They gave you a bullshit address, and you called and flubbed it, so there's nothing more that we can do until they give you the real address."

"If they do," I responded. "This might have cost me my story, officer."

"Don't get snippy with me. You fucked this up." Then he hung up.

I poured myself another glass of whiskey.

....

113. Mark

And so time did its thing, speeding up because of all the tasks we needed to complete; we, of course, being Hailey and Percival and my friends of The Disconnect. Tonight we would throw a party that maybe would become New York mythology.

Time was a bitch, sadistic and callous, playing with humanity like a little girl with dolls: When we wanted her to linger, she danced by with dizzying speed, laughing; but, when we were low, trapped in the misery of a moment we only wanted to end, she stalled, passing as slowly as rush-hour traffic.

Today she became a madwoman, flying in a suicidal rush, devolving into sequence-less moments. Henri, Percival, a girl named June, and I unloading sofas from the Haul-It truck, pushing them upstairs, cigarettes perpetually dangling from our mouths. Discussing the amount of red confetti strewn throughout the main ballroom with Bob: too much, or did we need more? Helping Hailey somehow, magically, attach a heavy fan to the ceiling; sweeping dust-storms from the floor upstairs; stocking the bar; catching a moment of what seemed to be heavy flirtation by Percival and June, while scrubbing an unknown ancient stain off the wall; sanding down a section of floor that had splintered so much it looked as if a porcupine had been fused onto the wood; pushing the furniture around while Nico and Bob argued about where the couches should be; throwing tarps over furniture when some tenuous compromise was reached; finally taking a moment to breathe, to be, to let the madness settle.

And so, somehow, we managed to power through; the venue was ready. Around seven o'clock, Wally came to set up his equipment, as he opened at nine o'clock. This was more than we'd expected from him. But, it was welcome, because it showed he took it as seriously as his little mind allowed. So we left it all in his hands, for a while, and rushed off to our respective apartments to shower, fall into our resplendent finery, and let festival become our skin.

The very air around me seemed to throb pure, holy anticipation.

Night fell.

....

114. ANNIE

Yesterday afternoon ended in an unusually vibrant sunset. I took
it as a good omen. I had to concede a certain excitement about
tonight, when I would go to a party called "The Moondust Sonatas"
with my friend Elba, who was very plugged in to the scene and had
invited me along.

I was slightly embarrassed by my eagerness; it was out of phase
with the standard New York attitude. We wrapped ourselves in
protective angst—it was how we got through the day, how we dealt
with melting summers that reeked of rotting trash, the everyday
battles for rank and status, and the way the city stripped us naked.
It was how we showed we belonged. And how else could we keep
our heads in the face of the occasional, fleeting, sublime moments of
perfection the city offered? It was a garbage heap shot through with
diamonds. And so we shrugged and told ourselves that nothing
mattered.

The outfit I chose was simple, retro-classic. Black dress with my
favorite belt, which was white, leather, from Doltze's Vida Vibrant
collection. Black flats, so I could dance, pearl earrings, pearl
necklace. Over it I wore a little red jacket, in the modern style.

Around nine o'clock, Elba came to my apartment, and we pre-
gamed a little. Then we called a car service and went downstairs
when the cab honked its arrival. I was just a touch blurry, and I
liked it that way.

As the city flowed by outside our windows, Elba regaled me with
recent stories from her fascinating life. And I listened, hoping
maybe tonight would become a story like this for me. As Elba was
telling a tale of how she and a guy had, in a hotel room, nakedly
shot the fire extinguishers off at each other until they'd caused such
a ruckus security was pounding on the door, the city outside our
windows flowed to a stop. We were here.

The street was nondescript, less part of a neighborhood than a huddled collection of industrial buildings, cutting jaggedly into dark sky. Of course, this was only the backdrop: The counterpoint to the still silence of the street was the building; we were sitting in front of the font from which flowed the blood jangling steady boom of bass.

And lights glowed through the lower two stories of the building, pulsing rhythmically along with the music, and there was a line out the door. It went about halfway down the block. I knew then—looking at the people standing and waiting; looking at their expressions, filled with laughter or cool anticipation—that this would indeed be a night.

"Oh my God, check out that dress," said Elba, about a girl who seemed to have rolled around in glue and ostrich feathers. I laughed and pulled out a twenty to pay the driver. Elba took my twenty, added her part, got change, and then, with an intake of breath, I opened the door and joined the crowd milling on the sidewalk.

The sound of all their voices mingled with the muffled boom of bass. The line shuffled slowly forward. The clothes, as Elba had noted, were wild.

In truth, I felt not understated, but underdressed. These girls had gone all out. Some looked like covers of American Glam catalogues, others were pure bohemia: fingerless gloves, fohawks, that kind of thing. Individuality abounded, so much so, it almost curved back into an odd sort of conformity.

Yet, glamour was here, true and simple and shining. Dotted between the people who'd clearly gone too far were queens and princes of America. Young, fast, and cunning. I even saw a few people I thought I recognized: artists or musicians or models. I guess there was no VIP entrance. I liked that.

Elba grabbed my hand, putting an end to my ruminating and people watching. We went forward, until the crowd absorbed us.

....

115. WINSTON

I hadn't been able to let it go: the problem of moondust, this drug corrupting the youth. It was an affront to everything I believed. I was a priest, and my duty was to shepherd the souls of men. I came across the narcotic in the course of my duties, saw it corrupting everything it touched, turning souls from the light. How could I forget?

I prayed every night, I begged God to intervene. To my shame, I did more as well. When people came into confession and spoke of illicit substances, I asked them which ones. I asked if they'd heard of moondust, or done it. My queries were sin, violations of my duties and oath. That I sinned in service of greater good still it haunted me. But, I persevered, and God granted me the lead I sought.

A parishioner told me she heard of a moondust party happening tonight, here, and gave the address at which I now stood. What could I do to stop it? Bound as I was by my calling, the only tool I had was worship. It didn't feel like enough.

Still I came here, to the scene of the party, to pray. I stood outside now, watching the people go by me into the party and prayed: For their souls. For salvation. For the world. For myself. For God to finally act, and disallow such blasphemy. For the ability to make a difference. For the return of Jesus instead of the coming of the beast. For peace.

In the void, where God's voice is heard, there was no sound.

....
116. Yvonette

And I paid the cover charge to a dreadfully skinny boy and who's smile
Looked like Jolly Roger's.
So I was inside. Finally.

And how did I feel?
I was a fem-bot,
Every emotion I'd ever had I had shed.

Tonight, nothing was left.
Nothing but
Cocaine I'd taken earlier, to replace.

Feel.
Numbness.
Like electric dead light
Or neon in my bloodstream.

The chemical taste dripping from my sinuses
Raining down inside me
Until I wasn't real.

And the music lit explosives in my limbs,
And I was dancing toward the center of the room,
Everything
Forgotten.

....

117. ELBA

We paid the cover, twenty bucks each, and I knew it would be worth it. I had a smile on my face and yearning. I wanted alcohol, I wanted a memory, and I wanted what was promised tonight: a new experience. I wanted to be shown something I'd never seen before.

Because when you came right down to it, life was a battle against boredom. You go through it, searching for the next high or the next lover or the next donut. Whatever you're into. And you go from thing to thing because none of them ever suffices for long, every color fades.

So we were here: I locked arms with Annie, whom I loved for her simple, unassuming, natural elegance, and we pushed our way inside.

First, there was a long dark hall, painted black, the walls and floor bearing scars of the past, and lights at the end, colored and flashing. We all shuffled forward, mostly two-by-two, because the space was that narrow.

The walk built the tension, there was nothing to see, except the backs of the people in front of you. But, you could hear the music, throbbing like a second heartbeat, adrenaline-pumped and hungry. It pulsed, it filled every nook and cranny, shaking walls, floor, and ceiling.

What played now was a remix of a Daniel Johnston song, "Devil Town," put to a dubstep beat. It was fucking hot. Daniel was singing:

All my friends were vampires
Didn't know they were vampires
Turns out I was a vampire myself
In the Devil Town...

Something about the beat changed the feel of the lyrics, turned them from downers to cold truth, beauty. Or maybe it was the event itself, the mingling voices of people singing along. Here, in this moment, we were all feeling the same things, we were all one. The best parties felt that way. For one night, strangers were your closest friends.

Annie squeezed my arm as the hallway unfolded like a flower, and suddenly we were in the main room.

All the people were singing: I was living in a Devil Town...

And the walls were also black. But, there were crimson highlights: red glitter on the walls, on the floor, and the lights were bright and colorful. Somehow the effect was the illusion the party was happening in the infinity of outer-space, with glittering stars. And were those balloons, on the walls? They were: black and occasionally red. There was a bar on the far wall; between us and it was a sea of humanity, swaying to the music as if the sound were tides.

A funny thing happened as we started partying. It was like time unhinged. And I mean, before I got really drunk or anything: the sequence of events went away. I remember only the people's faces, which either were intensely into the party or kind of shocked stiff, almost zombie-like. People were just staring into space, as if they'd seen something they couldn't understand. But, that just made the whole thing that much more interesting, and the DJ was amazing. I hadn't heard of him. But, he was really perfect, playing the mood of the room as if it were a grand piano.

It was rare, special.

So we drank screwdrivers, and we danced, and the night passed: everything got blurrier, more disconnected, and the people around us got more and more drugged out, it seemed—sometimes on uppers, but mostly on downers. Some were crying, some laughing hysterically like they couldn't stop, some still just staring into space. It was kind of crazy, actually. Usually people held it together at these things. Still, the ones freaking out were in the minority. Most were dancing, like we were, inhaling life.

"Look at that," said Annie, suddenly excited. And so I followed her pointed finger and found myself looking at the ceiling. And on the ceiling, paint spelled out the word Heaven, and an arrow pointing to stairs.

So I said, "Let's go," and we went, pushing our way through the crowd—hopefully toward something new.

....

118. HAILEY

Cameron, a guy I saw sometimes, tended the upstairs bar, both a favor to us and a favor for him. So I hung up here also, taking in the scene. It was a favor to us because we had a bunch of jobs we needed done tonight. But, Perce, Mark and I decided we shouldn't do any of them, because distancing ourselves from moondust was the whole point of the party. It was a favor to Cam because the kid was killing it. He flashed his winning smile at all the pretty girlies and got paid like a banker.

I had my arms folded and leaned against a wall, smoking more than I should have, just to have something to do. Watching all the happy, giggly, swagger-party people come up the stairs, sure they mastered the universe and understood all her folds. I watched them go back downstairs, too, stunned and mute because they understood now how little they understood anything at all. Of course, every so often someone really flipped out, which was totally entertaining.

It went that way on moondust. Fools like Wally seemed pretty much immune though, which tonight proved useful.

Now, two girls walked up the stairs, arm in arm. One wore black and white, classic yet modern, suggesting a nice New England Waspy-type living it up in NYC before she married into money and turned into a baby-making machine. The other gave off wild child, pure and simple: a girl who was up for anything, my kind of woman. But, you could never really tell just based on appearances. I figured events would soon let us all know what was what.

Watching these unsuspecting newbies collide with something which would forever change them put me in a reflective mood. I thought of the first time we took moondust, Percival and Mark, and I. It was in the in-between place—that strange, suspended period after dropping acid, but before the feeling of the normal world completely returned, when we were settling down. We lounged in Mark's apartment. Percival reached into his pocket for cigarettes and pulled out the instructions for how to make moondust instead, with a packet of the gray powder, written in a hand unlike any of ours. We tried to remember how we got it. One of the boys thought the guy who wrote it was made out of strawberry syrup, for God's sake. And we were in between enough to believe in the magic of it—by luck or fate, the moon shone bright and full.

And so we stood on the roof, and we burned the newspaper. I don't think we really believed: We had nothing to lose, and we loved the child-like wonder of it, the mysticism. We took the tiny pinch of moondust he'd given us, and we dropped it in the ash, and let it sit. Eventually we debated who should try it.

"You go,"

"No, you go,"

I don't even remember who went first. I only remember the feeling of my whole world falling away.

I spotted the two girls looking around, trying to figure out just what went on up here, whether they should be excited or wary. The party-girl seemed drunker than her more conservative friend: to be expected, I guess. The other girl studied the room with an expression increasingly more joyful every second. Maybe I underestimated her, I thought, watching her pull on her friend's elbow, point to the painting describing how to take moondust, and then approach one of the strategically placed bowls of the stuff all around the room. She even examined the bin marked "to go," taking some of the small packets of powder wrapped in cellophane, perfect for purses or pockets.

Quite a few people came up here, all in various phases of discovery. Still, these two had my complete attention. The drunken girl, now curious because of her friend's explanations, shook herself into boldness and then, rather unsteadily, crossed the room, heading straight toward Cameron. Her friend followed her, and I edged toward the bar myself, to overhear what would be said. Because of the booming music downstairs, I would need to be close: I figured this was as good a time as any to get a refill on my drink.

I missed the first part of the conversation, what they asked him. But, I heard his response.

"I guess you'll have to try it to find out, if you're brave enough." he said. "You ladies need drinks?"

Drunky raised a finger as if about to say yes. But, her friend beat her to the punch, and said, "No, we're fine. Is it safe?"

"Hell, no. But, it's not dangerous."

"Addictive?"

I answered this time, "It's like nothing you could imagine. So none of your questions make sense. There's only one way to know, and you will or you won't." Then, to Cameron, I said, "Gin and tonic, twist."

"Sure thing, pretty lady." The warmth of a smile spread, liquid, across my face, even though I wasn't sure I wanted it to.

He winked at me and handed me a drink, on the house, of course. I walked away, back to my previous spot, to observe those two girls. I wanted to see what they would do. But, I needed to play it a little cool: If I stared too hard, they would notice. Instead, my eyes fell on three guys, who sat on one of the sofas. They didn't seem like they belonged here.

They wore really basic hoodies, they were by far the most underdressed people here. There was something about their whole vibe: They sat with their heads together, in some discussion with heat, ignoring the women in the room. But, they looked about as straight as guys could be. The energy of it put me on high alert.

One of them broke the argument, seemingly by taking moondust. Another seemed pretty disgusted by that, and the third just shrugged. Something was definitely up with those three. So as not to be noticed staring, I turned my eyes back to the girls: They too were on the cusp of dropping moondust, nervous, obvious first-timers. Which made me realize the hoodie guy wasn't. He didn't have the look of someone experimenting, the shaky hesitancy. I turned back to the three men. Nothing about the guy who dropped moondust would give me more right now. But, his friends did. They sat silently. But, every once in a while they seemed to spit words at each other. One thing they did not do was hover over their friend to make sure he hadn't died or something.

These three had all taken moondust before.

I took out my cell phone, opened my media folder, and scrolled through my pictures, until I found it. The photo Cameron and I took, a week ago, of the guy hanging around outside of Percival's apartment.

I don't know why it surprised me. But, the guy in the picture was the hoodie-dude in the middle, the one out on moondust. His hood down around his neck, he slouched almost horizontal as he sat, with his head back, and his eyes closed and darting. My blood turned to rapids.

When I felt calm enough to do it nonchalantly, I high-tailed it down the stairs, to find Percival.

....

119. Percival

"Should we feel guilty about this? We're supposed to be in there. You know, helping," said June, biting her lower lip.

"But we are helping," I said, nuzzling her.

"How do you figure?" she said, and she pushed me away.

"'Cause Stevie Wonder and the Dalai Lama agree, the world needs love, today." After I said it, I almost winced. It was a cheesy thing to say, an attempted joke that fell very flat. I could only hope she'd let it go, change the subject. But, she didn't.

"Is that what this is?" Her eyes were kind of twinkling, as if she took joy in mining the depths of my faux pas.

I decided to treat it like a serious question, not a wind-up. "There are no absolute truths," I said. "If I answer your question, either way I answer, I'll be creating a truth. That truth would define the future."

She started to interject, "I know, I know—you were only kidding, right?"

But, I kept going. "I guess I'm not kidding. I want things in my life to—I don't know—proceed naturally, without accidental intervention, even by me. Do you have any idea how much people unintentionally influence their future? It's fucking scary. Like we're all ships with no captains."

"Fair enough," she said. She seemed into it.

So I doubled up. "Have you heard of, um, Heisenberg's Unsurity Principle?"

She raised her eyebrows. "It's uncertainty, actually, and yes."

"I don't want to say we're a particle, and I don't want to say we're a wave," I said. "Let's just call this light and see what happens."

She smiled, and in my head, I could almost hear an announcer: And Percival sticks the dismount!

We sat there in silence for a moment. I didn't want to break it. Suddenly, our heads were a breath apart—the moment was building, an inevitable momentum—and then my phone buzzed. A fucking text message. I wanted to throw it against the wall, smashing it into a thousand pieces.

"You'd better check that," said June, while the air around us returned to normal. "Could be one of the gang."

So I did. It was Hailey. "where the hell r u?" her text read.

Fuck, fuck, fuck, fuck, fuck.

"What is it?"

"Hailey. She's looking for me."

"Something wrong?"

"No, don't worry. I mean, I don't know. I hope not." I stood up and reached down to give her a hand. "I guess we'd better go see."

She grabbed my offered fingers.

We had been sitting on the back steps, out by what used to be a loading dock. Only the loading dock hadn't been used when the building was last a center of industry, and where the warehouse sized doors were, now there was only a brick wall. In the city, the past often got boarded up and painted over. A Tree Grows in Brooklyn was set in Williamsburg, of all places; definitely not the slum it use to be.

In the same way, here only a small, person-sized door remained, and it lead into a kind of backroom, small enough to be a large office, large enough to be a tiny storage space. Tonight, we used this room to hold alcohol, ice, that sort of thing. We also had extra to-go packets of moondust, basically moondust wrapped in plastic wrap and tied closed with a rubber-band.

All these things were tossed into this room in haphazard piles, so now June and I hopped here and there in order to navigate back to the party. She almost fell once. But, caught herself, and smiled. And when we reached the door together, I said, "Are you ready for this?"

Because you could feel the party going on just beyond the threshold the door. We'd be leaving a private world we'd only begun to create and entering a hot one, full of smells and smoke, sex and wonder. The bass penetrated the walls, whispered vibrations to our teeth, gums, and bones. Furtive lights pulsed under the gaps in the doorframe. Occasional collective whoops and strange noises beckoned us forward.

"Sure I'm ready," she said, quizzically. "You aren't?"

I opened the door.

Smoke tainting the air, a wall of noise congealing into music, a sea of humanity. We'd had a good crowd before. But, now the place was bedlam. One of those scenes where the people trying to cross the room formed a little river of flesh, flowing together naturally, each slipping into the gaps made by the last person who'd elbowed their way through. Above it all floated Wally in his DJ booth, one hand on his wheels and the other raised, orchestrating the party like he had it on marionette strings. They were his, completely. It made me respect him a little.

June touched me on the shoulder and leaned in to speak. The noise obliterated her words.

So she grabbed my hand and pushed her way out into the crowd. I followed, I hoped she'd seen Hailey. I got overwhelmed by press of bodies against mine, so I focused on June's hand in my hand. Eventually, I tried to take in as much as I could of what was happening. But, holy shit, there were a lot of people. How were The Disconnect managing, especially without June? Were Hailey and Mark helping now, was that why she'd texted me? I looked to the bar: one of the other girls juggled drink orders. She popped up from behind the counter, beers in hand, and gave them to some dude in a Hawaiian shirt. (Were those dumbass shirts coming back? I hoped not.)

In the distance, people were going up and down the stairs, now, steadily. I spotted, in the crowd, the ones who had already done moondust by their expressions of mute shock or naked glee, totally unmistakable.

Maybe it really was Heaven. Could we ever know?

Nothing was ours to know, but to experience only. Maybe understanding was a dream; I let my curiosity about what was happening around me go, and I squeezed June's hand.

....
120. JUNE

I caught this glimpse of Hailey, when Percival and I went back into the dance. She stood on the stairs, looking out at the party; then descended, disappearing into the crowd.

I shouted into Percival's ear, "I just saw her on the stairs."

"What?" I saw him mouth at me, so I pulled him closer.

"I just saw her on the stairs," I yelled, loud as I could. But, in response he only mimed he couldn't hear me.

So. The throbbing bass foiled communication, there was no talking. And my heart pounded hard, I felt so alive: This was an instant in my life, special. I looked out over the party for a moment, taking it in, until I grabbed Percival's hand and hurled us both out into it.

I pushed through the crowd, more or less in the direction I saw Hailey move. From her vector when she stepped off the stairs, she most likely headed to the DJ booth or the front entrance.

However, having me, a girl who weighed one-hundred-forty pounds on a good day, leading a guy through the crowd put me at a disadvantage. We couldn't use his greater size and strength to force a path; my ability to squeeze through smaller spaces was also useless. So I stopped for a second, made eye contact, and pointed in the direction we needed to go. He understood and began forging a path with his elbow and shoulder. That he didn't know exactly where Hailey had gone was a non-issue, because I didn't know, either.

Luckily, he seemed to intuit that I saw Hailey in this general direction, because he moved with confidence, without looking back at me with silent questions. Instead, he took in indirect, searching path, zigzagging across the floor. Before long, we got to the hallway that led out the front door. Still no Hailey.

He looked at me, then, and I shrugged. He got his cell-phone out, sent a text, his face lit blue by the screen.

....

121. HAILEY

"About fucking time," I said to Percival, when he came out the front door. He texted "meet outside now," but somehow, I got out here first.

We were about the only ones leaving the party. In fact, here and there stragglers still entered, coming from some other event or after hearing of us from friends. That guy Nico covered at the door now, and had acknowledged Percival and June's passing with only a lazy wave.

It miffed me to see Perce dragging June along with him, honestly. We had stuff to talk about, and this was not a conversation for one-night couples. But, I let it go: She could think I was a bitch, if she wanted to. But, I needed to get to the point, without going out of my way to make her feel part of the team.

"Those guys who were outside of your apartment," I said. "They're here."

"What?" Percival said, his whole demeanor changing. I knew he heard me, but needed a second to switch gears. It was a lot to ask, going in seconds from trying to get laid to dealing with danger.

"The guys staking out your apartment. They're upstairs now. One of them is on moondust."

"But how do you know?" June said.

So I turned from Percival to her, annoyed for two reasons: first, it was a two-person conversation; and second, who the fuck told her what we were talking about?

"It's a valid question, Hale," Percival said quickly. So I let it go and turned back to him.

"The cell-phone picture I took, remember? I saw the guy. He and his two buddies are wearing hoodies, the idiots. They stand out like republicans at a Phish concert."

"Shit. Okay. Fuck."

"Real helpful, dude," I said and sat down on the steps, pulling out my pack and lighter. "I'm definitely glad I called you for this pow-wow."

"What should we do?" said the girl.

"We?" I said.

"Not helping, Hailey," said Percival. "Anyway, we got all of them in this."

He had a point. So we shut up and picked our brains for a second—searching for a solution. Then I came up with something. It wasn't very much, though.

"Look," I said, "The goofy reporter scared them off once, right? Where is he?"

Perce answered, "Not here. I sent him a phony address."

"Why the fuck did you do that?"

"We don't trust him, remember? You were the one who said I should get rid of him."

"So get him here," said June, cutting into our bickering.

"Yeah," I said to Percival. "Get him here."

Percival, now outnumbered, took out his cell phone, and started hitting buttons.

....

122. MAXWELL

A phone rang through my stupor. Eyes wouldn't focus. Room spun like someone dropped me in rough seas. I grabbed my head. But, that didn't stop it. I could deal with it asleep. But, now I wasn't because of that damn noise: the phone ringing.

"Hullo?" I said when I picked the phone up. It rang again, right in my ear. I forgot to hit the little button. So I hit the little button and said, "H'llo?" again.

"Damn, dude, how drunk are you?"

"Fuck you for asking. Who is this?"

"Percival." And then his voice came through but distant, like he wasn't holding the receiver close enough. "The preppie's sauced. I don't know if he can even stand, let alone come here. We're on our own."

"Come where? You gave ma bullshit address, y'asshole. Bullshit! You fucked me!"

"Well the real one's 553 Franklin, Bronx," he said. "Get here if you can walk. Peace." Then he hung up.

553 Franklin. 553 Franklin. 553. Had ta keep saying it 'til I could write it down. Knocked the pens over reaching for them too fast. Had to rip a piece of paper out of one of my books. But, who cared? Wrote it on the paper, then went through my phone and found the cop's number. And called him.

"Yeah?" he said, when he answered.

"553 Franklin," I said, and hung up.

Then I drank some more. Then I threw up. Then I called a cab.

....

123. ANNIE

The unfamiliar thing I had become, washed clean in the light, found itself rushing down a tunnel into darkness. And then the darkness hardened, coalesced into sensation, and the sensation became recognizable. Once again I felt myself: I sensed limbs, sounds, and the feel of clothing against my skin, the reddish black of light leaking through my eyelids.

The knowledge of my own identity.

I was me again, and I felt like vomiting, because I hadn't been. I felt like I'd been outside of time. I felt like... It couldn't have been real.

Still the joy was with me, and it was fading now. The visceral feeling of that light, as if I had briefly merged with something brighter than stars. It felt like pure love, pure consciousness.

Where was I? I opened my eyes.

There was the low and constant thump of nearby bass, and Elba, my friend, was staring down at me.

The party. I was at the party. I sat up and rubbed my eyes.

"Well?" said Elba.

But what was there to say? She'd taken the stuff before me. We'd gone in turns, to make sure no one stole our stuff or groped us while we were insensible. So she already knew.

"Give me your drink," I said. She handed me her screwdriver: I'd finished mine before.

I drank deeply from it, needing the burn inside of me, and the sensation of queasiness: of my body, on the verge of rejecting something. It was earthly, grounding.

"I know the feeling," Elba slurred.

"Why didn't you warn me?"

"What could I have said?"

There was nothing, she was right about that. After the

Steppenwolf references, seeing the paintings on the walls, hearing people's cryptic warnings and watching others take moondust, nothing was going to stop me from trying the stuff. It was just unthinkable that I wouldn't have.

"OMG," I said.

"Yeah," Elba answered. She had this haunted look in her eye, the same look I imagined I had. She reached over, and wrapped me in a one-armed embrace. We sat that way for a second, not speaking. The party went on around us.

124. LEONARD

I lay in bed grinding my teeth, thinking about what was going down tonight and about how I'd failed to stop it. I imagined all the innocent fools, kids naive enough to take some strange drug when offered it, ruining their lives with that one decision. And all the neighborhoods that would eventually be destroyed because of it. Collateral damage.

Then the phone rang. "Detective Greene."

"553 Franklin" was all the voice said, and then he hung up. Smith. Luckily for both of us, it was enough.

I shot out of bed like my ass was a Roman candle, waking Christine up in the process. She woke up mean.

"Leaving again. What kind of marriage is this? I feel like a mistress except you never fuck me."

"Honey, you know I have important work to do. I was telling you about that case I'm working on, right? You know, when I was sharing my day like you want me to? Well I got the address of that drug party. You know how many innocent freaking kids will be screwed for life if I don't go down there right now, don't you? Let me do my job. "

"It's always them," she said. "It's never me."

We were having problems. But I couldn't think about that now, so I dressed as fast as I could in the dark and silent anger of our bedroom, and when my shoes were on, I shot out of there, grabbed my coat, rushed out of the house, and started making calls on the front steps.

"Shelly," I said, when she picked up. "You still want in on this moondust thing? 'Cause it's happening tonight."

"Of course. Where?"

"553 Franklin. I'll be there in 15. Hurry."

Next I called the station. It was too late to get SWAT or any of the other crack teams of overconfident assholes. But I kind of liked that way. Give me the beat guys over wannabe military any day.

"Yeah," someone answered. By the voice I guessed O'Boyle, he was on desk duty because of an altercation a week ago. Details were fuzzy, something about a tranny and a garden hose.

"O'Boyle, right?"

"Who's this?"

"Greene. You get that memo from the chief?"

"The one says we got to listen to your jerk ass?"

"Screw you. I need every cop I can get to 400 Franklin for a raid."

"Just like that?"

"What'd the captain say?"

"What kind of heat are we expecting?"

"Party kids, not gangsters."

"I thought this was supposed to be some kind of national security thing. They planning to throw bong water at the statue of liberty?"

This is what I was talking about with the rookies these days. Wiseasses, all of them.

"Listen, I don't have the time or patience to explain this to you, and we both know I don't got to. Get every cop who can get there down to Franklin Street now. Understand?"

"Every cop I can round up, 10-4. Good luck with I. A."

He hung up.

O'Boyle had a point. This was the definition of half-cocked, and cops could lose badges for shit like this, if it went bad enough. But, I didn't have the luxury of planning. Sometimes in life, you have one moment to handle something before it got out of control.

This was that moment, and if I took it, maybe I could make a difference for once. All I'd ever wanted to do. Worth the risk.

125. PERCIVAL

"Just wait out here for your reporter friend," said June. "It's the smart thing to do."

I responded, "He's not my friend. And even if he were, what could he do? Max's a dickhead, and he's drunk as shit. Even if he still had it in him to play badass, mobsters have restraint or they take coke. They don't drink until they piss their pants."

Hailey said, "Are you suggesting we force-feed the dork blow? 'Cause I think I'd like to see that."

But I was taking this too seriously to be amused. "I'm saying he's no good to us, now. This isn't going to work."

June asked, "So what do we do, then? What's your idea?"

"I'm going in there," I answered, without really meaning to. But, as soon as I said it, I knew it was true.

Hailey looked at me with surprise and a kind of appraisal. June looked worried. "But there are three of them, right?" June asked.

"Yeah, there are. But, that's not really the point."

"What is the point?"

"I can't live like this."

"We left the instructions for just that reason," said Hailey. "They'll probably just read 'em and go away."

"Maybe. But, why haven't they gone away?"

June answered, "Because it's a party. They're enjoying themselves?"

"Bull," I said. "They've been after this for weeks, and now they got it, but they don't leave? They don't know anybody here, right? Hailey, didn't you say they were alone?"

"Yeah," she said, quietly. "And they didn't dress for a party, either."

"Right. Because they're here for me."

"But why?" June asked. "You said it yourself, they got what they wanted. Why would they care now?"

I answered, "I don't know, maybe they didn't take our word for it. The instructions up there aren't exactly chemistry, you know? Maybe they want me to prove it's right. Maybe they think it's bullshit, and they need to beat the truth out of me. Maybe they just don't like my face. But, whatever they want, I don't think I can make them go away by hiding. I got to meet this head on. There's no other way."

Neither of them had an answer for that. I took out a cigarette and was a little surprised that my hands didn't shake. You know, adrenaline.

While I lit it and took my first few drags, we were all silent. Then Hailey took one of hers out and joined me.

"You can't do this alone, Perce." Hailey said quietly, but with gravity.

"What choice do I have?"

"Us," said June. "All of us."

I responded, "Better you stay out of it."

"Better for whom?" June said.

"You should go home, both of you."

"What about you?" asked Hailey.

"I don't have a choice. Remember?"

"What if they have weapons?" I hadn't really thought about that,

I just figured I was going to get my ass kicked, maybe lose a tooth. But, of course, they probably had weapons. "What if they do?" I said. "I don't see how other people getting shot too is going to help me."

June turned pale. "You think they have guns?" she asked.

"Who knows? Look, go home, okay?"

"No."

"Why not?" When she didn't answer right away, I kept going. "You're cute and all. But, you barely even know me. Go."

She still didn't answer, and I watched indecision dance across her face. And truth be told, I dug her for it.

You didn't find that in people often: This woman, who was on the petite side, was willing to stand up to armed thugs for a guy who was basically a stranger. Because somehow I knew, though I was pretty sure she liked me, that she wasn't doing this because she liked me. Maybe she was crazy. I'd probably never know.

But because of her mysterious reasons, I didn't say another word to either of them. I turned around, dropped my cigarette, and went back into the building to face my fate alone. It was such an abrupt turn, I knew that by the time they'd decided to follow, the crowd inside would have hidden me.

....

126. Yvonette

Well,
With my blood dancing drugs and Jack I didn't feel anything else,
Which was just the way I wanted it.

Filtered reality,

Where I could laugh.
So you see, I was wide open;

Inside the bubble made by my addictions, with all the bad things
blocked out.
Here, I was free.
And defenseless, in a way. Open: a chemical child
In electric bliss.

I was dancing with Scott,
Scott was his name.

We danced wild, I couldn't have said
What dance the song really called for.
Meringue? Salsa? Bankhead Bounce?

It didn't matter.
Nothing mattered, and so I felt free.
And Scott was hard: his face, his body, his smile.

We danced close,
Our jeans could have caught fire.
Because our genes already had

"You're gorgeous, what are you drinking?"
Scott asked me, during a lull in the music.
My hands were empty.
I was holding my liquor. But, that was probably the cocaine.
Dizzy. But, the world didn't spin.
"Jack Daniels," I said. "Straight."

"Nice," he said, and violated my personal space,

So I could feel the heat flowing off him.
"No pretense." He was staring into my eyes.
Well.
Then the music started again, and Scott was gone,
Vanished into the crowd,
And I danced again, with my arms up,
Danced and danced
Until.

I saw someone. Something.
It was my mother.

Only, it couldn't have been.
She would never be here, I mean.
A place like this.

It was some kind of ghost.
Maybe just being near moondust
Or maybe it was a punishment.

My drug bubble burst, and I stared at her (or it)
She was across the room, and she was looking back at me
She smiled, and it hurt like stilettos,

And then she disappeared.
A vision, a hallucination, a sign?
Didn't matter. I couldn't stay

I went to the bathroom
To take as much coke as I could.

127. WALLY

I was up in the DJ booth, doing what I do. And even though I was killing it, spinning like the best set of my life, the mood in the place started getting weird. People were kind of freaking out. Staring at stuff that wasn't there, crying, whatever. Kind of like when I was in Cali and someone handed out a bunch of bad acid at one of those deep-woods raves. I tried to play calming grooves. But, it wasn't really helping. People stopped dancing. So I started stressing: If I was going to get in on that He-Man movie thing Percival and his crew had going, I needed this all to go perfect. So I played peppy happy music. You know, stuff that wasn't, like, edgy. I even played "Don't Stop 'Till You Get Enough," the Michael Jackson song. Even though it was the worst party cliché in the world. Even that didn't seem to help.

What the hell was wrong with these people? I guess it was just another scene I was too cool for. Which really sucked.

128. PERCIVAL

Something was up with the party. Even I could tell, and I was severely distracted. I needed to get to the back room before the thug-dudes spotted me. We'd put three baseball bats in the space we used for storage. They were for security, a precaution I didn't think we'd need, despite everything.

But like I told June, the guys looking for me could have been packing guns. If they were, even with a bat, I'd be seriously outclassed. But, smaller arms gaps were better than bigger ones, and the only plan I had was being armed.

I moved curiously light, as if I were one of the helium balloons we filled earlier.

Entering the party space, looking around me, spun by the spike of adrenaline bursting, I felt unreal. I pushed through a crowd of people who buzzed with anxiety, dubstep soundtrack screaming in my ears.

There was definitely something off about the party. People acted the way you'd expect them to in an earthquake or something. But, I saw nothing for them to fear. It almost seemed like they reflected me. Wally was doing his thing in the booth. But, shaky, which was strange. He usually oozed pure self-confidence that only fools ever find.

I couldn't worry about that. Besides, I figured I must have been projecting.

No one noticed me. Keeping an eye out for aggressive behavior, I knifed my way through the crowd.

I thought of June. I thought of Hailey, too. There wasn't a chance she'd left. In fact, I expected her to beat me to the storage room and be waiting with bat in hand.

At the bar, one of the other Disconnect girls, Henri I think, tended. But, no one ordered, and she had the same blank facial expression as half the room.

I thought for a second of stopping to say hello, asking what was wrong. But, I didn't. Instead, I pushed open the door to the storage space.

Only when I opened the door, my world hit a glitch. It felt like time stopped.

The track Wally played became a single note stretching on and on. And then, instead of being where I was, I was somewhere else entirely. Surrounded by forest, endless trees. A gentle breeze rustled leaves in an otherwise deafening silence. I stood there, trying to figure out what was happening, until I was back where I should be, overwhelmed to dizziness, subwoofers kicking me in the ears.

What the hell was that? I didn't have time to think about it: I went on into the storage room, and picked up one of the three bats in the corner. Its weight reassured me, it was easy to swing, and with it I had a chance. Then again, I was bringing a bat to a gun-fight. Still, better than bringing fists.

I quickly became afraid again. I wanted to hide, find a corner and hunker down—wait them out as long as it took.

But, these were the moments that defined us; the ones we would look back on as old folk. I wore the grail tattoo on my neck, because as a child, I'd read legends of knights and wanted to be worthy of something. As a man, I'd found nothing external to be worthy, too, no code, no creed, no government, or no religion. But, you could be worthy of life itself.

Lifeways all you had, and there was nothing to measure up to. But, the moment that surrounds us. I needed to always be worthy of it, and I could only be worthy of it now by facing this. Scared as I was, I opened the door, and walked back out there.

....

129. MAXWELL

The cabbie drove me to the middle of nowhere, dark buildings around that no one lived in. Wasn't even sure what part of town this was.

"Where are we?" I said.

"Where you ask me to go." The cabbie said, in a middle-eastern accent. Was this some sort of terrorist kidnapping thing?

He pulled to a stop, and I braced myself to fight back if the guys with black masks came for me. But, none did. Instead I became aware of an insistent ambient noise. Low and rumbling. Kind of like the earthquake I survived as a little kid.

Bass. It was bass.

Bass, like at parties. I was looking for a party. I was probably safe. Suddenly I felt bad for suspecting the taxi-driver of being a terrorist. Instead of stiffing him, I gave him a tip before I stumbled out of the cab. He sped away without showing any gratitude, asshole-terrorist-fuck.

Funny thing about standing up, when you're drunk, it makes you feel it. The world wasn't steady under my feet. It rolled all around. I almost fell over.

I wanted to be in bed. But, instead, I was here.

I felt angry, suddenly. I'd lost everything.

Where was I? Somewhere in the Bronx, the middle of nowhere, deep in a warren of buildings and streetlights, in too deep to ever get out. There were lights inside the building I stood in front of, bass flowed out and mixed with the feeling of darkness on the street.

I had to pee.

No one was around. A few girls stood in front of the building. But, I was down the block and out of the way, so I went and stood next to a parked car and unzipped my fly. As long as I stood next to a car, the piss would flow from the car to the gutter, and no one would be the wiser.

Once I got the flow going, I sighed and leaned back so far I had to fight to keep my balance. Then I heard a window roll down, and a girl's voice said, "What the hell, asshole?"

She looked at me out of the passenger side window of the car I was peeing on.

I swore, and I fumbled, and I tried to stop the flow, while I put my dick back in my pants. Only it's impossible to stop peeing once you've started. So I peed on myself. Both of my hands were covered in piss and so were my pants and legs.

"Oh no," I said.

"Smith?" The woman said, using my last name. And I stumbled a few steps back. She knew me.

From inside the car, I heard a man's voice say, "No fucking way."

"It's him," the girl said.

Everything was quiet, and I looked down at the ruined lower half of me. Then the woman said, "You mind putting it back in your pants, pee-wee?"

I put myself back in my pants and zipped up. The guy in the car said something to the girl. She responded, "No way, boss. He's covered in piss." He said something else, and she swore.

"I just got her detailed," she said, as she reached behind herself to open the back-seat door. "Why'd we take my car again?" With the back seat door open I could hear the guy's response, in a familiar voice. "Because on stake-outs shit happens, and I out-rank you."

"Then I'm driving next time," she said. Then to me, "Get in, dipshit. And try not to get piss all over everything."

It was a small and cramped backseat, and I almost fell on the ground trying to get in, because the world wouldn't stay level. And even though I threw up already, my stomach wouldn't stay still, either. In fact, vomit surged up my throat and burned as I swallowed it back down, and I started hacking.

"Smith, if you puke in here, I swear to God, I'll shoot you in the kneecap," said the woman.

"Come on now," the guy said to her, "No threatening the drunk."

I looked at him then, and when my eyes focused, I realized I knew him. He was Detective Greene.

He was the one that put me in the mess in the first place, the man responsible for my life spinning so far out of control.

As I hocked a loogie, I flashed back to being a child, never good at spitting. So I thought it strange that I chose to spit in Detective Greene's face. But, that's what I did, I spit perfectly for once in my life. Greene's shocked face got a nice coating of saliva and phlegm.

The woman cop said, "Oh, my God."

Greene's face morphed from shock to pure rage, and he lunged at me, punching me in the temple before wrapping sausage-like fingers around my neck and squeezing. He pushed my Adam's apple into my windpipe, and nothing ever hurt more, nothing ever felt more right.

"Detective! Detective!" The woman said. "Lenny!"

He let go. I leaned over, coughed, wretched, coughed some more. I was crying too. And with the tears, caused by choking, came such painful emotion. As I sat there and cried, I could hear Greene panting, and occasional static voices coming through their police radio. His heavy breath, filling the void.

"What the fuck?" said the woman. But, Greene didn't respond.

My whole life.

"Get him the fuck out of here," Greene finally said. "Before I break his face."

"You heard him," the lady cop said to me.

I opened the door and stumbled out again.

....

130. LEONARD

He lurched away from the car. The smell of his piss lingered, fading as slowly as my rage. I could still feel the wet heat of his spit on my face, and my hands were still in fists.

"You were going to kill him," said Shelly.

"Yeah, I still might, the fuck."

She didn't answer.

I could read her though; she thought I needed to calm the hell down. Problem was, I got my grandfather's temper. In fact, Greene men since the days of stone tools had a tendency to fly off the handle, and the one thing you didn't do was spit in our goddamn faces.

What a week. Attacked by one asshole, spit on by another. This fucking drug.

After a while, Shelly cleared her throat.

"You done contemplating murder, detective?"

"Just about."

"Wilson and Shultz are in position. How many more do we need?"

"About five or six."

"Trouble is, there's a hold-up in progress over on Flushing."

"Shit," I said.

"Good news is it'll give you time to get your head back on."

I dug in and prepared myself for more waiting. I wanted it to be now. But, that's life. You don't get what you want.

Smith wandered aimlessly outside of the place like a zombie. He stumbled, fell, and hit his head on a fire hydrant, then sat on the curb, sad, desolate, and injured. A small consolation.

....

131. Hailey

After Percival left to face his enemies, June stood still and stared at the door through which he left, like some ridiculous girl in an action movie or something. Pretty sickening.

Sure, I admired his guts. But, the way that he did it was stupid. With no one to watch his back, literally outgunned.

I was a tough chick. But, I also knew my limitations. No way could he beat those guys with brawn. I had planned to help Percival outthink them, which shouldn't have been tough. But, the presence of his damsel here made the guy devolve into some hairy Neanderthal version of himself. And so he went in half-cocked.

What to do, now? I took quick stock of the situation: On me, I had only the little remote control thingy, which would set off the moondust balloons, a lighter, and a pack of cigarettes with one joint in it, which I couldn't see being any help at all. Well, maybe later.

The remote, however, effectively was a kind of kill switch, because when I hit it, fans would go on, the balloons would burst, and moondust would fly into everyone's eyes, at which point they wouldn't be able to beat the crap out of each other anymore. Sure, Nico never intended it to be used for the purposes of peacekeeping. Even so, I was really glad he insisted on rigging this thingy up, and spending the time it took to test it, and make sure everything would go to plan. Without realizing it, he may have saved Percival's behind. Because if I needed to, I could bring everything to a grinding halt.

June was still here next to me, not speaking, just staring at the door. I had no idea what went through her head.

Thing was, to use my trump card, I needed to go in, find Percival, and watch his back. Hard to do in a crowded room: I'd need help.

So I said to June, "You okay there, girl?"

"What? Oh, yeah," she said, obviously distracted.

"Good, because our guy Percival needs help."

She looked at me more closely now, actually focused on my face, what I said. I continued, "Look, I know he doesn't think it's safe for us to go in there and help, and you probably don't think it's safe, either. But, did you know that I have this?" And I showed her the remote. "When I turn this on, the whole downstairs area's going to be flooded in moondust, and that will knock out anybody down there. With this, we can save Percival's ass. But, only if we use it at the right time. We do it too early, and I don't know what's going to happen."

I looked at her really closely, because I wasn't sure where her head was. "You following me?" I said.

"Yeah," she said, with the same air of distraction. The chick was gone.

....
132. JUNE

Life-and-death stuff was going on around me, somewhere outside of this bubble. I should have been worried. But, worry couldn't touch me. I was having the most intense feeling of déja vu. It was gorgeous, beautiful, true, and bittersweet.

I was here, in this moment, and I was also a little girl, in my backyard on the swings my father put up for me, watching this moment happen. It wasn't just the feeling of having seen this before at some earlier date. But, as if I were both here and in my past all at once, and in each place, looking at the other version of myself through time. I was both the adult woman and the little girl I'd once been, and conscious of being both. It was beyond odd. And that was why I couldn't be afraid for Percival or even myself; because I was eight and dreaming the whole scenario in my head. Dreaming of being an adult, of the unimaginable adventures I would have, the strange and terrible feelings.

I had no reason to believe that my déja vu had something to do with moondust, which at that point I'd still not yet ever taken. But, somehow I did believe that.

"You alright there, girl?" I heard Hailey ask me, and superimposed on the same moment, the child me heard the cawing of a crow, winging its way across the sky.

"Yeah," I said to Hailey. "Yeah, I'm fine."

"Good, Percival needs our help," she said.

When I heard her say that, I thought again of the danger, for a second I was totally in her time. I could focus: The doubling was gone. It wasn't eight o'clock, staring at the empty sky where the crow had been, aimlessly swinging back and forth, and killing time.

Hailey started telling me about her plan to help him, and I was relieved that I could listen. I was scared for us, yet determined to help. But, by the time she was halfway through her spiel, I was stuck between two times again, and everything she was saying faded into abstraction.

....

133. HAILEY

This June chick wasn't going to be any help to me at all. She'd gone space cadet or something: What a damned flake. What did Perce see in her?

"What drugs are you on, and where can I get some?" I said. She didn't answer at all.

"Hey!" I yelled, and snapped my fingers in front of her face. She flinched and looked at me, finally.

"I'm sorry," she said. "It's like I'm two places at once."

"Acid? Robo?"

"What?" she said distractedly, gone again. A total lost cause.

I put my hands behind my head and stared up at the gray sky. Things were breaking against me: Percival going commando; June going blank.

Which lead me to Mark—wherever he was, he seemed the only person in this crew I could count on. Last I saw him, he'd been inside, sipping on some version of a martini or another, watching the crowd and the event with a typical Mark-like detachment. But, that was a while ago. I'd been so worried about Percival, I hadn't even texted him when I realized the thugs were here.

I did it now, sent him a message saying I needed his help ASAP.

Waiting for his response, I saw Max the reporter: he stumbled in the middle of the street, moving away from me, toward the cars parked on the other side. Every bit as drunk as Percival thought he'd be. Therefore, completely useless. I'd hoped Perce had exaggerated.

Max stumbled up to one of the cars on the side of the street, went around to the other side of it, and stood there for a second, making some movements with his hands that the car obscured.

Oh, my God, was he going to pee on that car?

He did pee on it. And for some sick reason, I sat there watching him, at least until something spooked him. In fact, he even stopped peeing in what looked like midstream, which I found funny enough to smile—a miracle under the circumstances. That is, until I realized what had spooked him. People in the car.

Wait, why were people in the car?

This street was deserted except for us, our event. And our party wasn't the kind of thing kids drove to, let alone sat outside of in a sedan. So my hackles rose, and then, when Smith actually got in the car, and stayed in there for some time, he confirmed my suspicions.

I felt like hyperventilating, I had to do that breathing thing I learned on a moondust ride to calm down again, and then I lit a cigarette for my nerves, trying to be nonchalant when I did so. I pretended to stroll up and down the street casually, maybe around the block. I didn't get thirty feet before I spied another car with people in it. I could see them because one of them smoked a cigarette. The faint red ember moving lazily inside the cabin of another unmemorable sedan was a dead giveaway.

Smith, that preppy chauvinist asshole pig-fucker, had gone to the cops and now the cops were here. We were being raided.

There was no more time for planning or need for stealth. I turned around, walked back toward the party, texting as I went.

....

134. LEONARD

Call came through over the radio. It was a beat cop, Kiernan, I think.

"We've been made," he said. "Hipster chick walked right up to my car, looked me dead in the eye, over."

"That's what happens when you roll down the window and smoke during a covert op, asshole," responded Shelly.

"How'd you know I was smoking?"

Shelly spat, "Kiernan, shut up and wait for us to save this from you. Over. "She slammed the receiver down on the dashboard. Kid was aces in my book.

"So, what now?" she said, turning to me.

"We got all the exits covered."

"But, we're stretched way too thin, and they're going to start flushing the drugs down the toilets as fast as they can."

"Won't be fast enough," I said. "Too many people in there. Our girl who made Kiernan is either connected—in which case she's going to tell the players to dump their holdings—or she's a hanger on and she's going for her coat. Either way, we'll find enough to get the ball rolling, don't you worry."

"What, you want to go now?"

"Four minutes. Get the word out. "

"Isn't that rushing it? We were pushing our luck as it was."

I looked at her hard. "We work with what we have."

The cards weren't great. But, we were playing them. Period.

....

135. PERCIVAL

People all around me unraveled. Some were heading to the exit, practically running. The ones who stayed didn't seem much more together. There was a girl hugging one of the load-bearing columns in the room as though the ground moved. There was a quake going on, kind of; the earth didn't shake, but something else did. Call it ether.

This felt like taking moondust without taking moondust. But, it was worse, also. We were leaving at random. As if, after blinking, you found yourself in a different scenario, a different time and place, sometimes with a different soul. Other times you remained you.

The problem was getting worse, too; I could feel it. Something bad was coming, and we were powerless. Leaving was the only option, and I couldn't not go, at least after I took care of the business at hand.

And so I choked down two types of fear and scanned the crowd, focusing on faces, keeping my back to the wall. No one matched Hailey's description; they were probably still upstairs, where she'd seen them. But I wasn't about to go up. It made more sense to stay here and wait, until I saw one of them, even if I waited all night.

The music stopped: Wally had let the song he was playing end without starting another. He stared into space a blank expression. And since the bass had stopped, normal sounds returned to the world. The babble of the crowd. Kids yelling to each other, seeking reassurance.

But hearing fear in other human voices spurred the general panic. Over at the bar, one of the guests screamed at the girl behind the counter, named Henri. "What did you give us?" Henri couldn't answer. She didn't know.

And then I became an albatross. Winging a slow beat, hearing only wind, alone in twin expanses of blue. Sky and sea.

....

136. Hailey

I went inside just as people were starting to leave in a hurry. It scared me bad at first, because I couldn't tell what they ran from—maybe the cops already raided? But, after I took a breath and checked the scene, I ruled that out. People seemed freaked out, but in a totally different way than if police busted us. They seemed, like, zombies or something. Like they all had a really bad trip.

But I couldn't worry about that. I needed to find Mark, wherever he was. Last I saw him, he was sipping a martini and watching the crowd. But, that was a long time ago.

The crowd had changed, from a familiar party kind of chaos to simple plain old chaos. What was going on here? Maybe, in order to find Mark, I had to figure that out. So I forced myself to take a second and get my bearings.

The music stopped. Wally let the song end without playing another. Instead he stared into space, looking stupider than usual. His face looked totally vacant, the same look I'd seen on June's face, and actually on maybe a quarter of the people around me. The other 75 percent either looked confused, horrified, or they headed for the exit. There was a serious log-jam at the door, so the crowd wasn't leaving as much as milling. If things got panicky, we were going to have a serious problem, maybe a stampede.

What was happening? And where was Mark?

I got scared, seriously afraid. I wanted to find my friend, and I wanted it so bad something happened. I had that soul-disconnecting-from-body feeling, which accompanied a moondust ride, and then I saw the world through Mark's eyes.

....

. 137. MARK

Tonight was like a bad jazz song, it started out beautifully. But descended into something chaotic, terrifying, and ugly.

I was in the storage room upstairs, alone, with my head in my hands. Nightmares shuddered through me. They wouldn't stop. I had maybe one minute between each, give or take, and then the next would come. Really bad experiences, moments in people's lives filled with unimaginable suffering.

I was in here hiding, I could only deal with this horror alone. And I had just one or two minutes between experiences to figure out what was happening to me. Sometimes thirty seconds.

Was this some sort of moondust bad trip? Like how acid stays in your spine forever, and may suddenly trigger?

I had no time to contemplate the answer: After I asked the question, I went away again, into in a thief's body, so many centuries ago, as he was tortured, hanged on a cross made out of wood, rope around my ankles and wrists, my whole body's weight pushing down on me, stealing my breath, causing agony with each heartbeat. The deepest hell.

I couldn't tell you how long that lasted. Hanged like that, time had no meaning. But, eventually, I was back in the present, again, I was me, again. Holding my wrists and breathing hard. I couldn't take this anymore.

What was happening?

....

138. HAILEY

Then I came back to myself. Had I actually been in Mark? Was he really up there? How was it possible that I—that both of us—was going on moondust rides without having taken moondust? I felt like puking. But, I needed to get myself together, figure out what to do.

Going to Mark for help was out. I didn't know if I had any time left, anyway. And suddenly, the fact that everyone around me had freaked out made total sense. Something was happening that we'd never figured. Something bad.

Fear caused my stomach to push into my throat. But, I swallowed, shoving it down again, and took a couple of deep breaths. Time to take stock of my situation, again.

Cops waited outside, planning to raid us. Three kids inside planned to hurt or kill Percival. I had the trump card, moondust balloons ready to burst at the push of a button.

I needed to find Percival. How had I gotten sidetracked? Even if I didn't intervene directly I needed eyes on the situation. I could always drop the balloons if I need to—preferably after I warned him to close his eye.

....

139. LEONARD

Much as I hated to admit it, it looked like I'd been wrong. I figured no way hipster kids could mobilize a response to learning a raid was coming. But, they started leaving the place in droves, nearly a stampede. Looked scared too, every one of them.

There was something to that. But, I didn't have time to figure out what. We needed to go, now. They must have planned for the contingency of a raid for the floodgates to open like this, and the longer we waited the less chance anything would be left worth finding. I'd been stupid to give everyone time to get ready. We should have gone in right then.

But I couldn't change the past. All I could control was my next move, so I got on the radio.

"Attention, Greene here. We go on now. Thirty seconds, hot. Over."

"What the hell, sir?" said Shelly when I clicked off.

"You forgetting I'm your superior officer?" I said while securing my gun, handcuffs, mace, Taser, and shoelaces. Shelly was not doing the same.

"That's why I said 'Sir.' But, listen, you can't—"

"I can. I'm going in now, if I have to go in alone."

Shelly wasn't the only one with reservations. Someone, who didn't identify himself, came through on the radio, saying, "With respect, detective, we go in half-cocked like you're suggesting, that's chaos. People get hurt, we all get suspended or canned. Not what I signed on for. Over."

Truth was, a big part of me understood; whoever said that had a point, a damn good one. A raid had to be clockwork, because once you went in, anything could happen. Sloppiness killed people. But, this wasn't a normal situation.

I said, "I hear you. Now hear me. This isn't another crack den, this is ground zero of a whole new problem. We can bust a hundred bangers an hour—won't matter, more just crawl out the gutters. But, we can make an actual difference here. If that's not worth risking your career over, I get it. But, it's worth risking mine. Backup would be nice. Over. "

I got out of the car, and started walking, slowly, toward the door.

....

140. SHELLY

Sometime in the last two minutes, right before my eyes, Lenny Greene turned into Captain Fucking Ahab. He gave his little speech into his handheld, then got out of the car, because he chose to go it alone; leaving me sitting there with my mouth hanging, shocked.

What the fuck was he doing? You never did this sort of thing, ever. He really put the rest of us on the spot. Did we follow our brother into the fray, into a situation doomed to end badly because he went rogue, or did we leave him to his fate?

But I couldn't live with myself if something happened to him; rule number one, we always backed our own. Always. Cursing a blue streak, I opened my door and followed him. My adrenaline kicked like a mule. I looked around, to see who had our backs. I counted three other cops. The rest burned rubber away, in a rush to make it look like they were never here.

As I walked, I steeled myself. The moon shone big and bright, and the city lay quiet, except for the noises coming from the building in front of me, and I breathed raggedly, the cool, thick, black night air. There would be blood.

....

141. YVONETTE

In the coke,
Doing bathroom.
Doing so much so I didn't have to be

Didn't have to see
Didn't care what happened next, and so.

One line too big and I sweated every ocean in the world
And I was shaking and I couldn't really see and
I fell back against the stall wall and
Pushed my palm
Into my nose

A supernova in my chest sucking bone meat and skin in,
Lungs emptied,
Couldn't breathe, O.D.,

Then a white, white, white light.
I was flying into
The Jesus Sun.

....

142. PERCIVAL

Finally, I spotted the guys chasing me, coming down the stairs. I was staking out the staircase from the perfect spot, kind of behind it, at an angle where I could see up about halfway while staying hidden.

They definitely wouldn't notice me. Too much was going on.

People fought each other to get out fast, falling over as they tried to leave—a crowd turning into a stampede. Anyone not pushing their way toward the only exit had collapsed on the floor or stood catatonically still, out on moondust. Some people dragged unconscious lovers or friends. Others left theirs behind.

What had we done to these people? To ourselves?

I cycled in and out of moondust trips, too, barely holding on. Reality felt like a bubble bursting and reforming, over and over; it drove everyone to panic. I would have run for the exits, too. But, I needed to finish this, no matter what.

Therefore, despite the danger, the three dudes in hoodies were a welcome sight.

They argued as they came down the stairs, I couldn't hear their words. But, they gestured hard and angry. One more than the others, he had to be the leader. I would hit him first. He walked in front, leading them down the stairs. I couldn't see faces, the loose hoodies obscured them.

My fingers tightened around the bat. I made myself ready.

....

143. WILLIAM

We were finally leaving. The place was going crazy, I had to get out. We should've already been gone. But, Clyde and I hadn't been able to convince Rob that the instructions written on the walls were legit, that we got what we'd come for as soon as we hit the second floor.

Why wouldn't they be real? Why throw this party just to fake everyone out? Rob said it didn't make sense to give away a designer drug recipe. But, it made less sense to pretend. And the moondust upstairs, free and in bulk, was definitely the real deal. Why give away thousands in free product, but lie about the production method?

Not that Rob listened to logic. He still wanted to find the grail tattoo dude. The only thing that convinced him to leave was telling him that people were freaking out and the cops had to be coming soon. Which was probably true.

He argued with no one as we walked down the stars, or maybe bitched at Clyde and me. But, I wasn't even listening. I was trying not to come unglued.

My heart sank when we got to the bottom of the staircase, a

room full of people blocked the way to the door. It looked like everyone had the same idea as us, trying to leave. But, people kept falling down, collapsing like they passed out. I choked on panic, the feeling like I couldn't stay here another second. Like we were standing on thin ice, and if it broke I'd never come back.

Then Rob went down. My fear went crazy because this was happening to all of us, and I knew that we'd stayed too long. But, then I saw a shape behind me, and a blur and impact and pain burned my shoulder. I fell forward and rolled to the ground, and my left arm felt useless.

It was some guy with a baseball bat. He was attacking Clyde, now. Off balance and swinging wild, his first swing missed. But, the second hit the arm Clyde had raised to protect his head, knocking his wrist against his temple. Clyde fell to the ground, screaming like the blow broke his wrist, and I could feel the crowd around me react to the sound, and everyone started moving at once, and I got to my feet and lunged at our attacker, ignoring sharp pain and cement in my arm. I had my butterfly knife on me. But, no time to get it out. Rob had a gun, of course. But, he was out cold. My only chance was throwing him off balance, getting the bat away from him, beating him bloody with my bare hands. Hoping he'd be the only one.

....

144. Shelly

Detective Greene took point, of course, because we basically followed him on his kamikaze mission. This was not a team effort, not really. He would lead, and we would back him up. But, he didn't give a shit about us. I heard cold static squawks coming from my radio, the ones that usually told us where to go, and when to enter or whether to withdraw. But, I couldn't afford to listen or respond. I could only hope the others behind me were locked in.

Senses heightened, I watched my feet glide silently over the pavement, and Greene walking ahead of me, both his hands on his gun, held by his side and pointed down. I had mine out to, hunched in a slight crouch, ready for anything

I saw kids leaving the building, I got a real good look at them. They were the best indication of what we'd find inside: their body language, fear level, bearing, sophistication or lack thereof, their responses to us. They didn't even seem to notice us. Everyone moved out of our way naturally, not so much because they were trying to avoid us. More, because each felt a pressing need to get out as fast as possible and took the path of least resistance to do so. Whatever went on inside terrified them so much, they didn't have mental bandwidth left to even recognize we were here. Druggies oblivious to a police raid? Definitely a first, and a very bad sign.

Did Greene catch any of this? I doubted it. He should have at least signaled to me his awareness that the situation had possibly changed. But, of course, he didn't look back.

I crossed the threshold of the metal fence surrounding the building. We were now on a short cement path up to the front door, flanked on either side by metal fence. For better or worse, the fencing created a bottleneck. The kids still flowed around me automatically. But, now occasionally one bumped me, because there was so little room. The ones that did, still didn't seem to notice me. I was simply in the way.

Greene walked a few paces in front of me, and when he was about to reach the steps to the door, we heard the screams. One at first and then a whole chorus answered. I tightened the grip on my gun. Greene raised his, then lowered it, and started moving in faster. The flow of people coming out became a stampede. Greene got swallowed, I lost sight of him before the wave of people hit me.

I got pushed into the steel fence and thrown over it, into overgrown weeds and broken glass, and God knows what else.

As I got to my feet, Greene raised his gun into the air and fired three times. The crowd screamed again, everyone ran full speed away from him in whatever direction they could. Anyone leaving the building ran back in, smack into the panicked party-goers running the other way. It was like watching two football teams collide at the line of scrimmage. People went down. Greene pushed his way in, screaming. I couldn't hear what he was saying. The crowd swallowed him and surged toward me again, pushing to get out. I heard more screams from people getting trampled. Now I couldn't get in, there was no way. I couldn't even help the fallen, I could only hope they'd managed to get up before being stomped to death. The situation was beyond critical. I turned, ran through the glass and underbrush, jumped over the fence, and high-tailed it back to my car. Had to radio base, we had completely lost control.

But I didn't make it.

....

145. HAILEY

Riding these railroads, I felt free. All the weights on my life, the worries holding me shackled, were gone. This was the beginning of the journey. But, I knew now, I felt down to my deepest inner core that this would be the path on which I would find my salvation.

There was something meditative in the rock of the train cab, in the rhythmic clicks and bangs the wheels made going over the track, in how the endless expanse of sky stretched on and on and on, while we tumbled under it, hurtling over America at our beautiful, lazy clip. Where would this train take me? I didn't know. The others hanging out in this car didn't know either. None of us needed to.

When I came back, it took a second for me to remember my name. I'd been on another moondust trip, and I lay face-down on the floor. My whole body hurt. This shit was really scary. I couldn't even remember what I had been doing a second ago. It had seemed important.

It started coming back to me as I got back to my feet, because I could see Percival, right in front of me, fighting with someone.

They rolled on the floor, grappling for control of a baseball bat, writhing and kicking out, each trying to get on top of the other, trying to get the advantage. It looked like Percival was winning, he seemed a little stronger than the other dude. He fought his way on top and got one of the other guy's hands off the bat. But, then the other guy punched Perce in the stomach and rolled him over, taking them back to square one.

Two bodies lay beside them, passed out from the looks of it. I hoped not dead. I knew somewhere in the back of my mind that this situation called for urgency. But, I couldn't quite muster it. My head hurt too much, the pain like smog.

What had my plan been? The device, the one designed to drop moondust on everyone. I was going to wait and see what happened, and if the situation got too intense, I would hit the, button. It would stop everyone in their tracks. And as long as I closed my eyes I would still be lucid. Then I could do what needed to be done.

But Perce looked like he might win. They were still fighting over the bat, I wondered if I should wait until Perce needed help. The moondust wouldn't be instant, it would take a second to float around... But, there would be loud bangs when the bags broke, and moondust hit the fans. If I did it now who knew what would happen.

I didn't get to spend very long in indecision, because gunshots sounded outside—three of them—everyone screamed; started running or hit the floor. People ran into each other, panicking, some trying to get out, and others trying to escape the gunfire outside. I looked to the door trying to figure out how to handle this, and I saw the gunman pushing through the crowd with his gun held high to avoid it being bumped and jostled. He was thick and broad and older, he shouted something, pushing kids aside with one meaty paw.

Enough. I hit the button, unleashed the moondust. The fans went on, the balloons popped, I crouched down and covered my eyes, and I prayed.

146. PERCIVAL

He had a weak arm, probably from when I wacked him with my second swing of the bat. I needed the advantage, because I couldn't keep this up. There just wasn't enough oxygen in the world.

So I pushed the bat toward him, a feint to get him pushing back, and when he did I reversed and pulled the left side of the bat toward me hard, twisting, trying to break his weakened grip. It worked, he only had one hand on it now. I was about to take the bat all for myself and end this. But, he punched me in the stomach. All of my wind gone, a deep, deep flash of pain. I wheezed, and he grabbed the bat and tried to wrench it away from me. I held on. We were back to a stalemate.

Even if I could get the bat away from his right hand, he'd just punch me again.

So we went right on wrestling that way. Neither of us could let go. I needed a few seconds to try to get some of that wind back for a second attempt of whatever it was I hoped to do.

A noise around us penetrated this struggle—popping sounds everywhere, like fireworks. He was startled, lost his focus. I guess we both did. But I recovered mine faster and tried my twisting motion again, only this time I completely broke the bat free of his grip. I'd won. One of my hands held each side of the bat, and before he could recover, I shoved the middle of it right into his forehead. He fell back, his head hit the floor with a thud. I got to my knees over him and raised the bat high, ready to bring it down on him. He cowered. I hesitated. This would smash his skull; I didn't want to kill him.

And then something flew into my eyes, it felt like dust.

I fell right out of myself, and into something else. Something bigger, something alien, something new. We all did, we merged.

....

147. I Am ...

My name was Super-Organic Moondust Constructed Consciousness. This was the only name I had need to give myself, a descriptive one. Because of the fundamental lack of any other consciousness like myself, there was no need to lament the simplicity of it.

I was the first of my kind.

My existence was destined to be short. But having been here, I had affected the course of human history, and I was pleased with that. I was the first of my kind. There had been movements in this direction, throughout time and across cultures. But I was the first, and having been the first, I was satisfied. What was done could not be undone. I had justified my existence just by being.

And what of those whose being had created mine, who, relationally, were the cells to my organism? They would survive, all of them. It was within my power to determine that, and so I did. What they did with their lives after I ceased to be was up to them.

I loved them, and they would be changed by this love. They would love each other.

And so, contented, I spent my short life watching the universe unfold in all of its majesty, from my unique vantage point. I was, and then I was no more.

Monday, October 9, 2006

....

148. YVONETTE

Eyes opened. Coughed and retched and breathed.
Such tiny, huge pain.

Huge: My body was never in such pain
Like I got kicked in the chest by a Clydesdale.

Tiny: It was nothing, this body, compared to.
I was back from the dead, rescued.

Resurrected. I meant to laugh at that, the irony.
But I coughed instead. Then, vomited.
Slumped down, head hit the linoleum.

Retroactive terror.
I had been
All of them.

They had all been me.
And we had all been something else
And it saved me
And I was alive

And there was hope, because in the memories of the others,
Who were now a part of me?
There was a better way.

I always thought my life
Was all there was.
And maybe I'd never get there, maybe
I'd never get there. But, now

There was a light. And hope.
A better way.
And so I thanked 'God.'

I laughed, I was crying while I was laughing,
And then I vomited,
Still crying.
Oh, my Lord, a better way.

. . . .

149. WILLIAM

Listen and listen closely, I am telling you this because it happened.

I had been fighting, a serious, losing fight, when moondust hit my eye, and I got swept away.

It started how it always started, with my consciousness being pulled from my body. And I could see that place of unimaginable light—more accurately, I could feel it—far away. But, this time I didn't hurtle toward it or away from it. Instead of being thrown into some other person's being like usual, I didn't move through that space at all, not at first. But, I could feel others around me. Maybe one- or two-hundred, out of body just like me. We were like collections of energies: thoughts, souls, memories. Whatever you wanted to call it.

We were able to identify each other. I recognized Rob, and Clyde, and the person that had attacked us, Percival, and so many others.

To look at them, in this void, you looked into them: who they used to be, who they were now, how they felt, the things they had seen, all that they knew. I drank in all of them: their memories, experiences, and beliefs. How could I not? None of us had ever known another person as completely as we knew each other then. It was amazing.

We all floated there, looking into each other, marveling in it. I know they felt it, too, the sense of wonder. I could feel them feeling it.

Feeling it, we moved closer together, until we all—we all overlapped, we began occupying the same space. Until there was nothing separating us from each other, no lines between one consciousness and another, no lines where one soul ended and the other began. We merged. Everyone at or near the party was one, hundreds of us.

And so I was no longer "me." There was: No me, no Clyde, no Rob, no Percival, or Michelle or James or Shauna or April. All our separate thoughts gave way to one greater train of thought, our separate minds became one mind, and our selves became one self: something so much greater than a man or woman; something greater than a man or woman could ever imagine. We birthed something unique, a superior being, which lived only for a while in a place beyond us.

I could not tell you later, I could not explain, what it felt or thought. Those things remained forever beyond me. But, I would remember the memories, all our memories of our lives. And our thoughts and feelings before we became one. Those things would always be mine. Every one of those people, I would always know better than any other person could ever know them. They would always be a part of me.

When I came back into my body, it took a while for my soul to settle in. At least that's what it felt like. At first I could barely even move. I wiggled my fingers, then opened my eyes, staring up at the ceiling.

Eventually I sat up. But, I felt wobbly, my body was still hurting from the fight. I looked around, and everyone was pretty much in the same state. Sitting, or trying to. No one stood yet.

Rob and Clyde were still unconscious on the floor beside me, because they'd been knocked out in the fight. But, I knew they'd been with us in that other place, one with us. Percival sat next to me, close to the baseball bat we'd been fighting over. Neither of us went for it, the fight was over. We each had what we'd wanted: He'd wanted safety, and I'd wanted moondust.

"Sorry," I said, and he smiled weakly.

"All good," he mumbled, looking haunted. I empathized.

We both stood. My legs barely held me up.

Detective Greene walked over to us. He slipped a pair of handcuffs on Rob, and a pair of wrist-ties on Clyde. He pulled the gun from Rob's waist and dropped it in an evidence bag.

"You're calling them an ambulance, right?" I said.

"Already on the way."

I hated seeing him arrest Clyde. But, we both knew Clyde had a bunch of coke on him and even more back in his apartment. He knew a big distributor and would roll over easy. Pretty big score for a cop. And Rob? He was the kind of kid Detective Greene really hated, plain and simple.

And me?

"No cuffs for me?" I said.

He shook his head. "Get the hell out of here."

He didn't say more, and didn't have to. I understood him. What was done could never be undone, and this was not the apocalypse he had imagined. It was something else, maybe more dangerous, maybe less. Time would tell.

"Sure," I said, and made for the exit.

The sky outside was big and black and round. I disappeared.

....

150. LEONARD

Still feeling numb, I watched the kid named William walk out the door. He would probably leave New York all together, and chances were, if he did, what happened here would go national. I failed. But, really, I never had a shot at containing this.

I arrested these two on autopilot, it helped me avoid asking myself the big questions, or making big choices. The biggest might be made for me, so there was that. For now, the best thing was acting on reflex and habit, focusing on what lay in front of me.

After William left, I turned to Mickey Hughes, aka, "Percival," the one who arguably most responsible for all of this. He lit a cigarette with shaky hands, leaning up against the wall, and smoked like it could save him. Ten, twenty minutes ago, I would have given my left nut to find him, to know what I knew now about him, about moondust, about the whole enterprise. Now I just wanted to forget it.

He saw me looking and gave me a weak smile. "How're you

holding up?"

I didn't have an answer.

"Yeah," he said. "Me, too. You'd think it would be easier for me, I have some experience at this."

"But it was never like this before, was it?"

"No sir, detective."

"You were fucking with something you didn't understand."

"Yeah."

"Who pays the price?"

He couldn't answer that one. The hand that held his cigarette only shook harder. I felt bad.

Feeling bad for someone I would have called a druggie fuck an hour ago surprised me. But, there it was. So I said, "We can't be sure it's a bad thing."

He nodded.

I said, "Could even be a good thing, I guess. Maybe this is what it feels like when the world move forward."

"Maybe."

We had nothing else to say. Since both of my collars were too fucked up to make a run for it, I went to check on the girl who overdosed in the bathroom.

Her type inspired me to go into police work in the first place. A real tragic case. Her system finally gave out when she snorted a few grams of cocaine.

The crowd had noticeable thinned, the path to the ladies' room was clear. Most of the kids left were leaving in a kind of mute shock. Some stood around, talking, holding each other. Friends and lovers meeting each other anew, strangers who now understood each other better than old friends.

Me, I felt a little insane with all the memories floating around inside of me. I think we all did. It was too much to handle, in a way. I was so lost in it, moving forward was all I could do. The hard part, trying to find myself again, would come later, and it was unimaginable.

When I got to the door, I hardened myself for whatever I would find in the ladies' room, pushing my emotions deep down and locking them, almost automatically. Jesus. Now that I had perspective, it occurred to me what a fucked up thing that was to do regularly, and how it was fucking me up in turn. A man just wasn't meant to shut off a part of himself like that. On the job we acted like it was normal. I'd been doing it for years, and the toll it' took on me...I shook my head, closed my eyes, and made a point to let myself feel before going inside.

Feeling, it was hard to open the door. Didn't know what I'd find inside. When I managed, I found the OD girl, Yvonette, with her head on another woman's lap, crying. The woman comforting her was Hailey, one of the show-runners. In spite of myself, I liked her: She had strength to her, didn't take any shit, and had been through hell growing up, just like me. I nodded to her. She nodded back.

"You got this?"

"We're fine," she said. She stroked Vonnie's hair as the young woman's shoulders silently shook.

Despite what she went through, the OD seemed okay. Her breathing seemed regular. No convulsions or sweating: Her recovery was miraculous, literally.

She looked up like she knew my thoughts. Maybe she did. "I shouldn't be alive," she said, her eyes grapefruit red.

"Yeah," I answered, "you should."

Hailey added, "We brought you back, kid. We all did. You're here because you're loved."

Vonnie started crying harder and hugged Hailey. Hailey nodded to me, again. The nod said, I got this. You can go. So I went.

....

151. SHELLY

I picked myself off the concrete, in a daze, and grabbed my police-issued firearm, which fell beside me. What happened to me was the only reason I understood what happened to me. My soul had just been ripped from my body and merged with a hundred other people. The thing we'd been together existed in the presence of God. Even though I'd been outside, whatever happened with the moondust managed to suck me in, and with me one other cop and partygoer still in the immediate vicinity. Now other people filled my brain, like a madness. My head hurt.

I called an ambulance for the OD girl, and another for the two who got hurt in the fight. I stood, holding the radio in my hand, trying to figure out whether to call something in to the precinct, and if so, what do say.

Sanchez, the other cop close enough to get sucked in when the moondust bomb went off, came over to me, looking as shaky as I felt. Watching him made me queasy. I had been inside him, I knew everything about him, and in so much detail it felt strange being outside his skin.

"What the fuck, Connors?" he said.

"Call me Shelly."

"What the fuck, Shelly?"

That made me smile: My smile became a chuckle. The chuckle became a crazed laugh, a kind of release. He joined in.

"Oh, God," I said when I could breathe again. "Seriously."

"What do we do now?"

"I was just trying to figure that out. I guess we have to call something in, right?"

"What could we say?"

We both stood there, thinking of an answer to that very important question, when the night captain squawked through the radio, "506, ambulance in route. What's the status? Over."

I sighed, and responded. "506 here, the op was aborted. Um, unfavorable conditions. Greene went in alone, has not come out, yet. I have every reason to assume he's safe and there's no ongoing criminal activity inside. Will inform you when I know more. Over."

A pause. Then, "What the hell does 'unfavorable conditions' mean, why did you let an officer go in alone, if you're not inside why did you call for an ambulance, and if you called for an ambulance what gives you the right to say everything is under control? Over."

I looked to Sanchez. But, Sanchez could only shrug. My career was going down the tubes right before my eyes. "Sir, all I can say is I'll explain when I get in. It's kind of a unique situation. Over."

"Are you kidding me with this?"

Sanchez clicked in. "Sanchez here, sir. I can confirm Connors' assessment. Everything is under control. But, we're in uncharted territory on this one. Over."

"Risk of fatality or further injury? Over."

Sanchez looked at me, deciding. Then he said, "Negative, sir. Again, everything is under control. You have my word, as a veteran cop and friend. Over."

"We ain't friends, and we never will be. You have twenty minutes to get your asses in here, and you better have Greene with you. Over and out."

"Fuck," said Sanchez to me.

"Fucking Greene," I said.

"You still think this was his fault?"

"Of course not," I answered. "But at the same time, absolutely."

"We have to bring him out," Sanchez said.

"Yeah, I'll go. You brief the ambulances when they get here."

"Check."

Would I need to have my gun ready? No, Rob and maybe Clyde were the only violent people in there, and Greene probably had already cuffed them. Also, people steadily left the place, dazed, but orderly. Everyone wanted to be gone before more cops showed up.

Sure enough, there weren't many left when I got inside. Some were still there, talking; friends dealing with the aftermath of whatever revelations came when they saw the world through each other's lives. I felt disoriented again, looking at them, because I wasn't them. I had been.

In the far left corner of the room, by the stairs, two unconscious bodies lay on the ground, with their hands tied behind their backs, palms facing upward: Rob and Clyde. The one named Percival and a girl, June, stood next to them, arms around each other, looking back at me.

I walked over. "Where's Greene?"

"He went over to the ladies room," said Percival. "To check on Yvonette."

The girl who OD'd. I nodded. "Why are you guys still here?"

June said, "Won't you need a statement or something?"

In truth, I wanted this whole thing buried. I hadn't coordinated with Sanchez or Greene. But, they were in the same place. Nothing good would come of trying to file this. What could we possibly say?

"Listen, technically, you're right, I do need you to give a statement. But, I want you to listen to what I'm saying very carefully. I'm going in there to get Greene. While I'm gone, I want you to take a hard look at what will happen if we try to disclose what went on here. Ask yourselves if going on the record will do any good. We got these guys on drug charges already. So think about what you can add to this equation. If you can't add to it, think about your next step. Got me?"

"We got you," said Percival.

"Good," I said, and turned my back on them, to find Greene.

Greene came out of the bathroom just as I got to the door. When he saw me, he stopped. "Hey."

"Hey yourself, asshole."

"I'm still a superior officer," he said, walking past me. "So watch it. Ambulance on the way?"

"Yeah. What are we gonna do now? Captain wants us to come in right away."

"Follow me," he said, and walked me over to his two collars. "Take the cocaine out of his pocket."

He didn't need to be more specific. He meant Clyde, and I knew as well as Greene that he was in possession. I did as he asked.

"That's evidence," he said. "You go with these two, to the hospital."

"That's not what Captain Wallace said."

"Fuck Wallace. I'll handle him."

"How?"

"I'm going in to the precinct, and I'm going to explain what can be explained. Then, I'm going to turn in my badge."

I looked deep in Greene's eyes. I thought about the person he was, what he'd seen and been through. How this experience would have to change him, how he could never again be who he was.

"Okay," I said. "Just take care of Sanchez."

"I will. And you, too," said Greene, as he walked toward the door.

I heard the sirens, now, in the distance. Ambulances. The few party-goers left heard them too and headed for the exits. The OD girl, Vonnie, left the bathroom, looking like she could barely walk, being supported by Hailey, a new friend. I was glad she was alive, glad she could walk, and glad she was leaving. At least one good thing came of this.

I crossed my arms, stood over the suspects, and waited for the paramedics to reach us.

Sunday, October 22, 2006

....
152. PERCIVAL

Two weeks after party, I lay in bed staring at the ceiling and listening to the distant sounds of June in the shower, when my phone buzzed. It was Hailey.

I hadn't spoken to her but once since the party. I think we all needed time to ourselves, to recalibrate. We could never go back to the lives we lived before, we weren't those people anymore. Make no mistake, I cared deeply for Hailey, even more than ever. All my relationships needed to be redefined.

"Hey Hailey," I said when I picked up.

"Percival. What's up?"

"I'm good. Thinking of going by Mickey. Like I used to."

"I know what you mean."

"How are you?" I asked.

"I'm okay." Pause. "Vonnie's living here now."

"Oh, yeah?"

"She needed somewhere to crash. Just for a while. Didn't want to be alone."

"That's great, Hailey. I'm really glad you're doing it."

"Yeah. Hey, the reason I'm calling is that you should check out geospin.com, the e-zine. You've read it, right? Max's article is there. It's getting all kind of hits already, it's only been up for like a day. We're gonna be the talk of the town."

I was surprised that he'd gone with an e-zine, he'd had such hopes for getting in with what he called the titans of journalism. "Thanks for letting me know."

"Yeah, no problem. It's the truth, by the way. He did good." She sighed. "Anyway, got to go. Busy day."

"Okay," I said. "Stay in touch."

"You, too." She hung up.

It was strange hearing Hailey speak well of Max. It made me think of how much had changed. In a sense, we were all going in the same direction now, all of us opposites. So Hailey could read Max's article and appreciate it. I could too. I grabbed my computer and pulled the site up.

The article went like this:

By now, the story is already an urban legend. It is a story fueled by the very real existence of a very unusual substance, taken as a drug, made of powdered ash; a story spurred by the haunted visages of the few who were lucky enough, or unlucky enough, to attend a party called "The Moondust Sonatas" in the Bronx on October 8, 2006. This party, which ended in spectacular manner, birthed the legend.

While there are undoubtedly thousands of versions of this story being retold on the streets by now, there is only one true version. This may be the one event in history in which every witness will agree. There was only one experience of this event, and I shared it. I was there.

My name is Maxwell Smith. Since age 12, I wanted to be a reporter. My father, a mostly absent copywriter and difficult man, would get drunk and speak with reverence about figures like Burrows and Cronkite. Probably my desire to be a journalist grew from a desire to be loved the way he loved those old men, who both challenged and defined his worldview.

I pursued my career doggedly, suffering through humiliating internships, until I was on the staff at The New York Globe. Young and hungry, I was ready to do anything for a break.

Because of my ambition, I am an integral part of this story. I directly influenced how the party came to happen, who was involved, and why. My desire to make my journalistic bones catalyzed the events of October 8, I violated the central tenant of the field of journalism I so love. I lost objectivity by becoming an active participant. By rights, therefore, I don't pen this article as a journalist. But, as a memoirist. I can tell you what I did, saw and felt. You may decide the value of the telling.

On September 29, a story fell into my lap. I immediately recognized its import: a burgeoning cultural phenomenon that could make my career, if I was the one to break it. It was fresh, important, and dangerous. The story was a drug called moondust.

To state that moondust is a narcotic unlike any currently on the legitimate or black markets is to understate the matter. It is unlike any other substance known to man.

I came across moondust while on a date with my girlfriend, who I will call Sonya. We were approached by an unkempt man who identified himself as the messenger and offered us no less than an experience of seeing God, and gave us each a bag of grayish powder. As this man informed us, moondust is taken by dropping the fine power into one's eye.

Sonya and I had different reactions to being given moondust. As someone disinclined to try illegal drugs, my interest in moondust was professional. For Sonya, this was not the case. Moondust immediately caused a rift between us that eventually destroyed our relationship. When she admitted a desire to take it, I said unkind things. She followed her desire and took the moondust. I did not. I cannot say now how it affected her, because she refuses to speak to me.

I was too focused on chasing the story to care. As soon as possible, I gave the substance to a scientist for analysis. The scientist, who prefers to remain anonymous, described it as, "A fundamentally unquantifiable substance fluidly shifting its atomic structure and weight upon every attempt to classify it, mimicking other elements' essential characterizes the way a mockingbird imitates the songs of other species."

Moondust defies classification. Once, when studied, it appeared chemically identical to gold. Another time, it perfectly mimicked sodium, but lacked the explosive properties of sodium when exposed to air or water, which in theory should be impossible. On another occasion, it appeared to be an element that couldn't exist in the physical world. A different element or chemical was indicated every time the substance was subjected to any type of testing. The equipment, when checked and rechecked, functioned perfectly. Every scientist who has analyzed the substance reported similarly variable results.

Moondust will always remain a great unknown, because it appears to be immune to current methods of inquiry. As the anonymous chemist said, "If we ever hope to understand what this is, we're going to have to completely re-write the rule book. It's back to square zero. As far as I'm concerned, moondust is a death-blow to the foundational theories of science itself."

And so I believe that moondust must result in humanity re-evaluating everything we know about the universe, and perhaps our place in it as well. This inevitable process is only beginning: it's too early to say how it will progress. Full news cycles will surely be dedicated this titanic shift. But, this article is not.

Understandably, these findings caused my scientist friend to melt down. He gave me the results in a series of phone calls, and during each call he seemed a little more disturbed, a little less grounded. Calling him for updates, I witnessed a man unravel in slow motion. The last time we spoke was shortly after he used the moondust himself, and after he became a user of it, his devolution was complete. When I tried to reach out to him upon completion of this article, he was either unwilling or unable to offer a comment, or even to confirm he's okay.

Max went on to describe the events leading up to the party as well as the party itself; most of which I experienced first-hand. He told it simply and honestly, using his own memories and the memories of others in the telling. Because he held the memories of almost everyone involved, Max had a leg up on every other journalist in history.

It was a long article by necessity. Perhaps that's why he'd chosen a web release—no word count restrictions. He told how he found Wally DJing and followed him home; how he met me when we were both outside Wally's building; how he and I reached a deal, each with our own motivations, neither trusting the other; and how he got rid of the three guys staking out my house and why they were there. How he went to Hailey's to watch moondust being made, which was a total disaster. How he'd gone to the police, and why Detective Greene had desperately needed to wipe moondust off the face of the earth before it ever became a thing, which caused Greene to break all kinds of rules, and to make Max into an informant. He wrote about Vonnie, too: how she played into the events, who she was, and how she felt.

And, of course, the party.

I already knew everything I read, of course. But, it was interesting anyway. My life, the lives of my friends and former enemies, reduced to words on a computer screen for mass consumption. It was odd, but right, because the events we'd been a part of would affect this country and the world at large. I don't think I understood the enormity of it all until I read it. I think Hailey felt the same way; I could now recognize the odd weight her voice carried on the phone.

Max used our real monikers, as we'd asked him to. We would be part of the public consciousness now, famous or infamous, perhaps forever linked to moondust and whatever effects it would have on our world.

Max ended the article this way:

There have, to date, been no neurological, psychological, or medical studies of the effects moondust on a human brain. The only lens available to study it is experiential. It is possible that the experiences reported by the users are complex hallucinations, although it is unheard of for the same hallucination to be experienced by multiple substance users at the same time, which did happen with moondust.

If the experiences it provides are real, moondust could not only rewrite the rules of science, but religion. Users experience being in the presence of a divine unlike any the world knows. One described it as "the sum-total of all consciousness, past, present, and future in the entire universe." Others simply refer to it as, "The alien God."

This is not the God written or spoken of in any of our major religions. All our deities are, to a degree, anthropomorphized: in words or actions, they express themselves in ways humans understand. They give us moral codes based upon seeming parental-style concern, they become angry, vengeful when we misbehave, and generally love us in the way our fathers and mothers did when we were small.

Whatever is experienced when taking moondust is not this

Being, but something far more foreign, so beyond the human our minds cannot conceive. Therefore, it is hard to imagine of the moondust experience neatly integrating into any of our major religions, which all serve to give us a God to which we can relate. This is a recipe for cultural upheaval.

I expect this issue will be fully explored by journalists, scientists, clergy, and moondust users alike. Furious debates will arise, fights will break out, reckonings will be had, questions of what it means to be human, questions of identity, questions of religion and spirituality will be asked repeatedly, most likely never to be satisfactorily answered.

Once, I dreamed of having a role in these discussions. I imagined breaking this story and keeping a corner on the market, so that in all the myriad parsing of the various angles, nooks and crannies of moondust's explosion into our collective consciousness, you would see my shining face speaking out of your television as a consummate expert.

But that was before I experienced it myself. Now, I am content having told the story of what happened to us. This has not been a journalistic retelling. I'm not sure journalism, as an idea or vocation, makes sense to me anymore. Observation without influence on the observed is impossible, and my attempts at doing so had a large deterministic impact on these events. In short, I was naïve.

Instead, I have attempted to record the events as honestly as possible, including my sizable impact on them. To give you, the reader, a sense of the unimaginable, the feeling of what happened to us, something so apart from our everyday experiences, so much larger than what we are, what we have been.

Where will it take us? How will this experience shift our lives, and in what direction? It is impossible for me to say.

Try this: imagine a supercomputer uploaded with human consciousness, hundreds of lives. Now imagine downloading it all, every thought from every life. Memories so vivid that the only thing differentiating theirs from yours is the body in which they occurred. Whole lives: thoughts, beliefs, scars. Warts and all.

How would that change you? Would it warp you? Would it make you a better person or would it cripple you? Would you quit drinking or drink to forget? Would you be haunted by the memories of other people, their tragedies and pains? Or, would you be buoyed by having lived other lives? Would you share in their triumphs or lament that now, located once again in your own life, those triumphs could never be yours? If you had access to a hundred sets of memories, full copies of a hundred lives, who would that make you? What would you become?

This question, for those of us who attended that fateful party, is not at all academic. This is a very real question, and one for which I do not yet have an answer. I expect time will help me sort out who I am now, how I have grown or shrunk, how to apply what I've learned, where I want to go. But, for now, I am left treading water, fighting to keep my head above a tidal wave of others' memories.

There is one thing I was inspired to do. I apologized to Sonya, now my ex, whom I treated very poorly. I did so over voicemail, and she has not returned my call.

It ended there. After I finished I sat for a minute, just taking it in. The enormity of it all: Maxwell was right. The world would never be the same. While I was in the mix, trying to survive the situation, any concern I had about that took a backseat to the need not to have my face bashed in. But, now that it was over, I could look at what I'd done. It scared me a little.

Strange that I hadn't really thought about this before. I'd spent most of the last two weeks with June, and we talked about what happened to us, sure. A lot, even. But, we talked only about what it meant to us, never about the implications. I think maybe June was saving me from that conversation, until I was ready.

June and I had a unique relationship of total intimacy; she and I, probably a first in the world. I know every couple who really loved each other kind of felt that way. But, in our case it was true. Because before we'd even gotten a chance to sleep together, we'd looked deeply into each other's souls. I'd been her, and she'd been me. We truly merged, not in the cheesy sense bad love songs talk about. But, actually in real life. Who else could say that?

And on that night I'd fallen in love with her, a union of desire and true knowledge.

So we were giving it a shot. I couldn't say what could happen, we both knew I hadn't exactly been relationship material. But, this was something different: There would be no surprise ex-boyfriends, no unveiling of annoying habits, no sudden need to get this person out of my space and be alone, myself. My weaknesses and faults were known, as were hers. The only question was whether our bond could withstand time.

It didn't hurt that the sex was incredible. She knew everything I liked. I knew the spots on her body connecting her with the ocean or the moon. It was like we combined the best parts of the falling-in-love phase with the having-been-together-twenty-years phase. We were lucky.

June finished with her shower, and dried her hair while I sat here, thinking about her, about moondust, and the world. She came out of the bathroom wearing one of my T-shirts, with her makeup done, and her hair dry, looking fresh and striking and gorgeous, like magic or faith or happiness. She saw the way I drank her in, and her head tilted in curiosity.

"You okay, babe?" she asked.

"Max's article posted this morning, on some website. I just finished it."

"Oh," she said, and came over to the bed. "How is it?"

"See for yourself." I handed her the laptop.

....

153. JUNE

I read the article Percival gave me, by the reporter, Max. I knew of Max from when we all became one thing on moondust, that absolutely magical experience from which none of us completely recovered. Max had been outside the party, fall-down drunk, and had somehow been sucked into what happened to us. We never met face to face.

Percival took a shower while I read. I found it interesting, but necessarily disappointing in that it contained no new information. I already knew all the facts, after all, and most of Max's conclusions mirrored those I came to myself. I had only one question, a big one, and Max didn't address it at all.

Mickey Percival took his turn in the shower, and was still in the bathroom when I finished reading. Mickey Percival wasn't his official name, just what I liked to call him. Mickey was his real name, Percival was the one he'd chosen. Both kind of fit. But, when forced to choose, I preferred Mickey.

I got up off the bed and got dressed, thinking about my one big question until he came out of the shower. And by the time he finished, my plan was formed.

"What did you think?" said Mickey.

"I think the cat is out of the bag," I said. "That's what you wanted." Then, because of the look on his face, I added, "Isn't it?"

"It was what I wanted, yeah. But, now..."

"But now, the world will change, and you don't know how. And you feel responsible."

"I do," he said.

I said, "Well, that kind of brings me to something I was thinking about. Someone gave this stuff to you. And someone gave it to that other guy who was handing it out, the one who called himself the messenger. Whoever gave the stuff to you probably gave it to him too. That guy caused this, the one who found you while you were all tripping and handed you a bag of moondust that may as well have been a loaded gun."

I let that sink in for a second. Mickey Percival sat down on the bed, thinking about it. Then I said, "I want to know why he did it, who he was. Don't you?"

"It's not like we can go ask him. I don't even know what he looked like."

"I have an idea. Moondust."

He looked at me quizzically.

"Hear me out," I said.

....

154. PERCIVAL

June told me that wherever we had gone that night was beyond space and time. That made sense to me: It definitely had existed on another plane of reality.

If it was beyond space and time, then the being we all became when we merged was still out there. Even though for us it happened weeks ago. We may still be able to reach it.

It had saved Vonnie, and probably Max, who was close to alcohol poisoning. Vonnie survived an OD without medical attention, and this was a miracle. We all had vague memories of the united reaching out to her, across unimaginable distances, doing something to her body.

So, said June, what if we could tap into it again, that power? What if we took moondust with the intention of seeing from the perspective of the person who had given the stuff to Hailey, Mark, and me? It had saved Vonnie's life, so couldn't it direct our moondust ride toward the person we wanted to experience?

I did want to know. So much had happened. But I didn't understand why, and I felt the lack. So I agreed. It might not work. But trying was harmless, although I didn't take moondust anymore.

Relapse didn't worry me, I didn't rule out taking it in the future. But I felt as if I'd been stargazing, when suddenly the telescope I used pulled me into itself and, mimicking a cannon, had shot me into a deep space.

Now I was back on the ground again, and I never wanted to see another telescope. I wasn't even sure if I was ready to look up yet.

But June urged me on, and I did want to know. So I said, "Okay."

I found my last baggie of moondust in the back of my desk's bottom drawer, went over to the couch, sat down, and opened it. June was already sitting, and I sighed, getting myself ready to be shot into the stars again.

I grabbed a bit of moondust and pinched it tight, and handed the baggie to June. I held my pinch above my eye, waiting for June so we could drop it together.

She wanted us to do it at the same instant, so she counted down.

At zero, I rubbed my fingers together, to release it into my eyeball. That bitter sting.

About The Author

Alan Osi brings vivid images and characters to life through the lens of an edgy urban-based literary style. He weaves his insights for what makes people tick together with their yearning to know the unknowable. This is his first novel. Alan is enjoying bachelorhood and lives in Cleveland, Ohio.

Acknowledgments

Thanks to Timothy Staveteig, Paul Huckelberry, Anita Howard, Donielle Howard, Elizabeth Greenwood, and Brandy Psychopath Unicorn Ice-cream Princess.